FIZE OF THE GABRIEL RATCHETS

"Let it be known to Corpus Privy," Fairy Peg was saying, "that Gerard Hopkins Manley, Federation Contract Diplomat, shall from day's end be known as Prince Consort to the throne of Ribble Galaxy."

The Corpus members gasped, as if they were one body.

"As custom requires, our Consort will be trained immediately. On the day of Conclusion, he will be presented to the Noble Assembly as Fize of the Gabriel Ratchets."

Gerard was stunned. It was one thing to be lover to the Ruler of the Seven Systems, quite another to be Supreme Commander of the Gabriel Ratchets.

"*If* the day of Conclusion comes," Duca Echi said with open contempt, "*then* shall we honor the Consort and Fize."

"Duca, you *will* honor him, as will this Corpus!" The coldness in Fairy Peg's voice sent a chill through Gerard. "Who does not honor him, does not honor *me*!"

"Warren Norwood has a fine, innovative touch, with plot intricacies that leave the reader breathless."
—Anne McCaffrey

THE WINDHOVER TAPES

FIZE OF THE GABRIEL RATCHETS

Warren Norwood

For Jared,

Best Wishes,

W. Norwood

5/14/83

BANTAM BOOKS
TORONTO · NEW YORK · LONDON · SYDNEY

THE WINDHOVER TAPES: FIZE OF THE GABRIEL RATCHETS

A Bantam Book / July 1983

ISBN 0-553-23351-3

Published simultaneously in the United States and Canada

PRINTED IN THE UNITED STATES OF AMERICA

O   0 9 8 7 6 5 4 3 2 1

*For Margaret Marie Norwood
and Karen V. Haas, with love
for totally different reasons.*

1

The crewmen stopped in front of Gerard's cabin to shift their grips on the corpse. "Not to get too close, sir," one of them said through his muffling filter-mask.

Gerard grunted in acknowledgement, but could not take his eyes off the body. It had a grey-blue cast and looked totally dehydrated. Like a parody of a death mask, the face was a hard bony shape covered by taut, oily skin. The lips had shriveled back to reveal an uneven row of wide, brown teeth. The eyelids had curled into dark, narrow twists of skin which emphasized the wrinkled, dry surface of lifeless yellow eyes. It had not been a peaceful death, Gerard knew, nor was the death mask a parody.

He stepped back into his cabin to allow the crewmen to pass. Two deaths in as many days with the same horrible, unexplained symptoms made Gerard nervous. He already had a string of reasons for regretting this trip with Peg On'Ell, but this mysterious disease which was slowly working its way through *Shivelight*'s passengers and crew was by far the most disturbing. For the umpteenth time he cursed Fed for sending him on this mission, and wondered why they insisted that he continue. He had accomplished so little in three years, he doubted whether he or Fed knew what they were doing.

The crewmen and their grisly load had disappeared around the curve of the corridor, and Gerard reluctantly shut his cabin door and sat heavily on his bunk. "I'm useless," he said into the stuffiness of his filter-mask. And bored, he thought.

He did not feel like sleeping, but the only reading tapes available to him were in Kulitti, and, despite his speaking

1

ability in that guttural language, reading it taxed him severely. To Gerard, Kulitti never looked like it sounded. Such a notion was irrational, he knew, but it was the only explanation he could offer for his reaction to the written words. Still, he was not the least bit sleepy, so he turned on his viewer, selected an index, and began searching for a text that might interest him enough to overcome his severe case of ennui.

Hours later, as he struggled through a surprisingly interesting account of the royal feuds, his attention was momentarily diverted by a slight tremor that passed up through the deck. At first he thought he had imagined it. Then he felt another tremor, weaker, but longer. Should have stayed on Kril instead of making this senseless trip to Leewh, he thought. With a sense of certainty that surprised him, Gerard suddenly knew the worst was yet to come.

Before he could reflect on that thought, his vidscreen made a brief beeping noise, and the page of royal history he had been reading was replaced by the gaunt face of Omna-Kye, Princess Peg's personal physmedicant. "Free are you, Diplomat Manley?" Omna-Kye asked curtly. Gerard's few previous encounters with Omna-Kye had led him to the firm belief that the old physmedicant kept himself alive by magic. Now, the face was gaunter, the eyes had a strange, distant look, and Omna-Kye's skin glistened with the oily symptoms of the sickness. The magic was about to run out.

"Free I am," Gerard answered formally.

"Report then to our princess in the control center."

Before Gerard could respond, Omna-Kye's face was replaced by the page of Kulitti script. It was certainly an unusual order, for Gerard had never before been allowed to enter the control center of a Ribble vessel. He wondered what was happening, but wasted no time speculating on why Princess Peg On'Ell, titular leader of the whole Ribble Galaxy, should require his presence in the control center of her royal cruiser.

With as much decorum as he could hastefully maintain, he responded to the summons. It wasn't until he reached the control center door that he realized he had only seen two other people in the corridors, both of them Gabriel Ratchets who had snapped to attention as he passed. A third Ratchet admitted Gerard to the control center after carefully checking him for weapons. The Gabriel Ratchets never allowed outsiders to carry weapons into the princess's presence.

The control center was smaller than he expected. Still, compared to his own cruiser, *Windhover,* it was quite large. There were six control couches, and an acc-web which could easily accommodate four other people. Only three of the couches were occupied, one by Princess Peg, one by Omna-Kye, and one by Zk Yerra, whom Gerard recognized as *Shivelight*'s Command Navpilot.

"Be seated, Diplomat Manley," Princess Peg said with a gesture to the vacant couch between herself and Zk Yerra. "There are questions we would ask you."

One look at Princess Peg's face told Gerard that she, too, had contracted the mysterious disease. She did not look as sick as Omna-Kye, but she was definitely ill. As he sat down he nodded politely to Zk Yerra, eyeing him carefully. "Commander," he said. Zk Yerra's strained smile at the undeserved title confirmed Gerard's mounting suspicion. They were all ill.

"Your mask may be removed," Princess Peg said firmly. It was an order Gerard reluctantly obeyed. He held his breath for a moment after removing the mask then breathed carefully. The air smelled clean, almost sharp, but... He caught his thought and stopped it. If he was going to catch the disease, he was going to catch it, and there was nothing he could do about that, mask or no.

Omna-Kye caught his reaction. "Breathe freely," he said. It was another command. "Our disease will not touch you."

After three years in Ribble Galaxy, Gerard had become accustomed to obeying commands. He breathed, and prayed Omna-Kye was right.

"Brief we will be," Princess Peg said in a tone that demanded his attention. "Can you pilot our ship?"

The question caught Gerard totally off guard. He started to speak, then shut his mouth. There he sat in the control center of an alien cruiser, surrounded by devices which were totally foreign to him, and the most powerful person in the galaxy was asking if he could pilot the ship. The question was ridiculous.

"Your tongue is caught?" Princess Peg asked with a hint of sarcasm.

"Badh," Gerard finally managed to stammer, using the

3

most formal form of address, "Badh, I am totally unprepared to pilot this vessel. I, I cannot even begin to comprehend the controls I see around me. Forgive my unworthiness, my ignorance, Badh, but I cannot."

Zk Yerra spat out a Kulitti word which Gerard was unfamiliar with, but the tone of it was pure disgust.

"Patience, Yerra." There was a cold calmness in Princess Peg's voice which carried the weight of a decision firmly made and totally unshakable. "You must pilot, Diplomat Manley. We will help for so long as we are able, but you must pilot. Yerra weakens even as we speak. His assistant, Isvoyo, already seeks the chasm of death. Our faces are open to you. You see our pain. Pilot you must."

For an instant Gerard felt as though he were being sucked into a swirling whirlpool. He clutched the arms of his couch to steady himself. It was impossible. There was no way they could teach him to pilot this ship. Not before they all died. He stared at Princess Peg and blinked rapidly, as though that involuntary action would make her and this whole bad dream disappear. She returned his stare with a steady gaze that gripped his heart like an icy-taloned claw. She meant for him to pilot her ship.

There was no place for him to run, no place he could hide, no way for him to escape what she had told him to do. Nothing in his Federation diplomatic training had prepared him for this. Cruisers the size and complexity of *Shivelight* were not simple skimmers that one could learn to fly with a couple hours of practice. One small, ignorant mistake at the controls could kill them all, or send them into regions of subspace from which they might never return. It was insane. Or desperate, he realized suddenly.

Princess Peg gave him a half-smile, as though sensing the sudden beginning of his understanding. "We start now," she said flatly.

Gerard listened, speechless, as Yerra began pointing out the various controls to him. He knew he should be concentrating on what Yerra was saying, but his mind was racing to an ultimate conclusion and would not focus on the instructions. These people were *dying*, all of them, from Princess Peg on down, and he was their only hope of getting back to Kril, alive or dead. That meant . . . *his* only chance, too. Suddenly Yerra's words seemed crisp and clear, and totally meaningless. "Begin again," he snapped. Yerra scowled at him with thin, drawn lips.

"Patience, Yerra," Princess Peg said quietly. "We think Diplomat Manley understands now our plight."

"I do, Princess, oh how I do. Forgive me, commander, for not understanding sooner. Please, for your sake and mine, begin again."

Gerard sent a wordless prayer to the goddess Fara as he tried to focus all his mental attention on Yerra's instructions. When Omna-Kye groaned loudly and was removed from the control center by the Gabriel Ratchets, Gerard scarcely noticed. Omna-Kye would die, but Gerard was determined to do everything possible to live. If that meant trying to pilot an alien ship with minimal instruction, he would do it. It was insane, but he would do it. It was hopeless, but he would do it. He would will himself to do it.

Yerra's instructions seemed like an unconnected jumble of procedures. Do this. Don't do this. Don't do that. If this, then that. But gradually, ever so gradually, Gerard began to see the pattern to it, began to see that the controls resembled *Windhover*'s in a form that was totally backward, but recognizable. Like the ghost of an image which grows on a vidscreen into definite shape with related parts, the functional arrangement of the control center began to make sense to him. These controls for navigation. These for subspace flight. These for normal space flight. Yerra wasted no words, and Gerard wasted no questions. Then, just as the hope of understanding began its way through Gerard's cold ground of desperation, Yerra gurgled heavily and coughed up blood in great hacking gobbets that splashed on the control panels and stained the front of his uniform.

"Quickly, Diplomat, help me," Princess Peg said as she rose from her couch.

Gerard blinked uncomprehendingly. Yerra couldn't die now. He wasn't finished with his explanation of the controls.

"Now, Diplomat."

Her tone snapped him awake. Together they lifted Zk Yerra and moved him to one of the vacant couches behind them. They strapped him in, and Princess Peg punched several controls on the armrest, which brought a flat metal box the size of an eating tray out of a hidden recess in the couch. The box positioned itself over Yerra's chest, then settled on it with a hum and a buzz and a flash of lights that startled Gerard.

"Battle medic," Princess Peg said simply. "It will ease his pain, but it will not keep him alive."

"But who, now, how?" Gerard stammered.

"Peace, Diplomat," she answered with a sad glance at Yerra. "I will show you. Return to your couch."

Gerard did as he was told, but as he sank into his couch he also sank into despair.

"Listen, Diplomat," Princess Peg said as she sat beside him, "There is still much to learn."

"Forgive me, Badh, but can we not send for help? Or turn back to Leewh? Or wait for rescue? Isn't there something else we can do? I can't fly this ship. I'm a diplomat. I don't know a damn thing about Ribble ships and Ribble engineering. This is stupid! It's crazy! Please, Badh..." Gerard heard the panic in his voice and felt it tearing through his mind in search of answers. The soul of a scream was clawing its way toward his throat.

"Gerard."

One word, his name, spoken with an assurance which startled him, pushed the panic down for a moment. It was the first time Princess Peg had ever addressed him as anything but Diplomat. Why her saying his name should give him a fragment of control, he did not know, but he grabbed that fragment and tried to steady himself with it. Despite his efforts, the panic started to rise again.

"Gerard," she repeated, "you must listen. There is much, still, you must be told. Listen, Gerard, listen."

There was no magic in Princess Peg's voice, no special control learned and cultivated that gripped his mind and helped him quell the panic. But there was something there, something regal and self-assured, something that demanded his attention. And by paying attention he forced his panic to subside. It was still there, still a real and frightening presence, but it no longer dominated his thinking.

Gerard listened. He listened and began to understand. The pattern he had started to see before Yerra collapsed re-emerged, stronger and more precise. The panic diminished, pushed aside by information and procedures, until he was barely aware of it wedged stubbornly in a dark corner of his consciousness. He began to see the controls as *Shivelight's* designers had meant them to be seen, a logical and precise arrangement of tools for piloting the ship. There were far more controls than he could hope to comprehend, but the basic ones, the ones necessary for his survival, began to stand out from the panels in a way that almost begged him to use them.

Gerard started asking questions, specific questions about the interrelationships of the controls. Only much later did he see the look of strain on Princess Peg's face. "Badh," he said hesitantly, "perhaps we should rest for a while. And eat. Fara only knows how long it's been since I ate."

Princess Peg straightened her shoulders as though she were about to reject his proposal. Then she leaned back tiredly in her couch. "Perhaps it is best. Will you eat survival rations?"

"Certainly, Badh. Where must I go for them?"

"Nowhere." Princess Peg turned to a section of the control panels she had not explained to him and quickly punched several buttons. Moments later a drawer opened in front of them. It contained three pairs of colored tubes. "Take the red one first, then the green one. The yellow tube contains a drink and should be taken last."

Gerard did as he was told, watching Princess Peg to see how the tubes were opened and manipulated. The red tube contained a grainy mush which had a surprisingly pleasing flavor. Gerard tried to chew it, but it slipped past his teeth and down his throat almost as fast as he could squeeze it in. The green tube contained a not-so-pleasant mush. It had a musty taste which climbed into the back of his nose and smelled distinctly like stale body oder. When the full effect of the smell hit him he nearly gagged, but forced himself to finish the contents in several quick gulps. With more than a little hesitation he followed Princess Peg's lead in opening the third tube and was grateful that the mind-flavored liquid immediately eliminated the previous taste and odor.

After replacing their empty tubes in the drawer, Princess Peg pushed another button and the drawer slid closed. "In a minute or two you should feel tingling in your fingers and toes," she said. "That is zindwar, the stimulant. The tingling will fade and you will feel better."

Gerard already felt it. A burning sensation ate at his fingers and toes as though they had been doused with acid. He clutched the arms of his couch and tried not to let his discomfort show, but Princess Peg spotted the tears rolling silently down his cheeks.

"It will pass, Gerard."

It did, but it took longer than she expected. When Gerard finally felt normal sensation returning, he also felt eager to resume his training. "What next, Badh?" The eagerness in his voice surprised him.

So did Princess Peg's low chuckle of amusement. "One moment more to rest."

Gerard leaned back and tried to relax. What he really wanted to do was jump up and down. To distract himself from the rush of energy, and to answer a question that had been hovering noisily in his mind, he turned to Princess Peg and asked, "Forgive me, Badh, but why is it you have not been stricken down like the others? You do have the sickness, don't you?"

Her expression was at once sad and stern. When she spoke, her voice was very formal. "Yes, Diplomat, I have the sickness. Dear Omna-Kye thought I might have some partial immunity and gave me a drug to enhance that. I fear he was wrong."

"Is there more of this drug, Badh?"

"No, Diplomat, there is no more. Why ask you?"

"So that you could take more, Badh." Gerard was struck by how beautiful she was. He had noted her beauty often before, but at this moment she seemed somehow more beautiful, as though the beginning symptoms of the disease were magnifying her best characteristics—the long, straight nose, the arched eyebrows, the high cheekbones, the slightly squared chin. For the first time since meeting her three years before, when he had presented his credentials, he felt attracted to her as a person. He wondered if she felt anything at all about him as an individual, then dismissed that question outright. Still, he wanted to do something for her, something more personal than pilot her ship back to Kril. He wanted to save her life. But how?

"Badh," he said suddenly, "I have a drug in my personal medkit that might help you. It probably won't have any effect on this disease, but it should stabilize you. I mean, well, what it's supposed to do is keep your system from deteriorating until you can receive further medical help."

Before Princess Peg could respond, the vidcom buzzed,

and a woman's haggard face appeared on the screen. "Pardon, Badh, pardon."

"Speak, Winsea."

"Pardon again, Badh. The consort, Inslowhe Ti'Griff, is dead."

Gerard watched Princess Peg's face twist from sorrow to anger and back to sorrow in one brief continuous motion.

"Without pain he died," Winsea said.

"Peace," Princess Peg said quietly. Then she rose and left the control center.

Suddenly Gerard felt very much alone. He stared at the control panels uncomprehendingly. His sense of understanding had slipped beyond his grasp like a handful of water slipping back into the sea. He was alone. The panic unwedged itself from its corner in his mind and started flexing its cold tendrils. Behind him Yerra groaned. Gerard almost jumped from his couch to Yerra's side. Standing there he could see that Zk Yerra was approaching the comatose stage of the disease, but that didn't matter.

"Yerra, can you hear me? Can you understand? I need your help. I don't know what to do."

Another groan. Yerra gave no sign of comprehension.

"Please, Yerra, if you can hear me, if you can understand, blink your eyes. Move your fingers. Something."

A croaking cough bubbled from Yerra's throat.

The panic was growing stronger, pushing aside his newly acquired knowledge and shoving his doubts and fears to the surface. Gerard fought it. He forced himself to return to his control couch and review all that he could of what Yerra and Princess Peg had tried to teach him. One panel at a time, one dial, one readout, he demanded answers from himself. Some things he could not remember. Some memories he doubted. When he got confused he started over. He cursed himself for not taking notes, but he refused to give in.

The swish of the door startled him. As he turned to see who it was, Princess Peg said, "You will do two things. You will go to your cabin and bring me this drug of yours. You will also pilot us safely back to Kril. Do you understand, Diplomat?" her voice was hard and remote.

"I understand, Badh." As quickly as he could, Gerard went to his cabin and retrieved his medkit. When he returned, Princess Peg was sitting stoically in her couch. Zk Yerra was gone. Or his body was. Gerard didn't ask.

As soon as he sat down Princess Peg started speaking in a steady, unanimated voice. "Listen carefully, Diplomat Gerard. I must return to Kril. Therefore, I will give you final instructions. Then you will give me this drug of yours. Recorded in my journal is a message saying I chose your drug. If I die, you will not be punished or blamed.

"Ahead, in less than ten hours, you will encounter the Concepcycline Cloud. You cannot warp through it. *Shivelight* is not equipped to pass through that distortion of space by itself. You must stay at the controls. Take as much zindwar as you can tolerate, then stay at the controls. Do you understand?"

Gerard wanted to run. He had a vision of the black whirlpool sucking him down again, a vision as clear as it was dark. Then it passed. "No, Badh, I don't understand. What is this cloud? How do I fight it?"

The hint of a smile almost curled the corners of her mouth. "As best you can, Diplomat Gerard, as best you can."

Five hours later, Princess Peg strapped herself into her couch and let Gerard give her the stabilizing drug. Before it took effect, she fingered her arm controls, and the battle medic slid into place over her chest. The last thing she said to him was "Peace." Then she closed her eyes and let the drug take its course.

Gerard ate again. He took a double dose of the zindwar and grunted loudly as the burning sensation tortured his limbs. Princess Peg had told him he should take it one more time before entering the Concepcycline Cloud, and Gerard wondered whether he could tolerate it. But the burning subsided, and he knew that he would have no choice. It must be done. She had said it would take at least thirty-one hours to pass through the cloud, and he would certainly need the zindwar to stay alert for thirty-one hours.

Four crewmen were dead, not counting Zk Yerra. Omna-Kye was dead. Inslowhe Ti'Griff, Princess Peg's consort, was dead. But Princess Peg was alive. So were eleven other people sick in their cabins. And so was he.

Yes, he thought, you're alive, Gerard Manley, but for

how long, and for what fate? I ask myself that, but Self doesn't answer. What's the matter, Self? Panic got your tongue?

Gerard smiled. Since being sent by the Federation to Ribble Galaxy "on a mission of indefinite duration designed to re-establish normal diplomatic relations between Ribble Galaxy and the Federation," he had found that he talked much more to his *Self* than he ever had before. He had made no real friends on Kril, none whom he could talk to with any degree of intimacy, so he talked to himself.

Why don't you review the controls one more time, Self suggested in an annoyed internal whisper.

"Thanks," Gerard said aloud. "I think I will."

From the moment *Shivelight* entered the Concepcycline Cloud Gerard had to fight the controls. *Shivelight* bucked and yawed, gently at first, but as the hours wore on, the aberrations in the ship's behavior became more violent and unpredictable. Gerard would fight the strange controls, lose the batttle, then suddenly discover they had resumed smooth flight. Just as suddenly, a new fluctuation in the fabric of space would grab *Shivelight* and shake it like a grisk shaking a lennit.

Gerard cursed the alien controls. he cursed himself for ever accepting this assignment from Fed. He cursed Princess Peg for putting him in this position. Then he cursed himself again. But mostly he cursed Fed, first for sending him to Ribble Galaxy, and second for not removing him when he had proved ineffectual. He cursed Fed in six languages, relishing each curse as he spoke it, and praying to Fara at the same time that he would live through this nightmare, just so he could one day curse his superiors in person.

Somehow the cursing helped him maintain control. The open anger gave him an edge. His confidence grew as he overcame each new problem, and slowly he began to believe that he could pull the *Shivelight* through whatever the Concepcycline Cloud had to throw against him.

Five hours into the Cloud, the first alarm went off. Within ten minutes warning indicators were flashing, buzzing, and honking at him from the control panels. Dials spun crazily, and indicators fluctuated like seesaws. Readouts gave him impossible numbers. Nothing he did with the controls had any noticeable effect. Desperate to find a

11

cause for the electrical insanity that had broken loose in the control center, Gerard turned on the external view screens. What he saw caused a voiceless scream to echo in his ears.

Ahead of *Shivelight*, space resembled nothing so much as a dark, swirling whirlpool into which they were plunging at tremendous speed. The darkness of Gerard's vision had become the darkness of reality. The tortured fabric of space was mirrored by the tortured fabric of his mind as panic churned him toward madness. Only Fara knows how long his screams echoed in the control center as *Shivelight* was flung in erratic spirals through the whirlpool, man and ship totally out of control.

*   *   *

Message to: Greaves Lingchow
FedDiploSvc

It would seem time to reconsider his presence and re-evaluate his effectiveness. As soon as he returns from Leewh with our Badh, I will attempt to get her opinion and advise you accordingly. A reasonable precaution would be for you to start preparing someone now to take his place, preferably someone less emotional.

—Glyph

*   *   *

2

"Gerard."

The voice was very familiar. Gerard knew he should recognize it, but he didn't. The voice, however, was insistent.

"Gerard."

It demanded that he come closer, that he pay attention,

that he do as he was told. The voice said, "Eat." He ate. The voice said, "Take the zindwar." He took the zindwar. The voice said, "Ignore the burning." He ignored the burning. The voice said, "Look ahead." He looked ahead, but not with his eyes, with his mind. He saw what was going to happen. He knew what twists the fabric of space was going to take. He saw how he was going to compensate for those twists. He saw himself piloting *Shivelight* out of the Concepcycline Cloud.

Then he recognized the voice. It was his own.

Gerard knew he was insane. Whatever grip he once had on reality had been ripped away from him. This was the end, madness in a swirling aberration of space.

The voice told him to shut up and calm down. He did, and as he did he put his hands on *Shivelight*'s controls and began making minor adjustments. The ship moved steadily through a minor buffeting. Gerard didn't notice. He was already beginning to compensate for what was coming next. Another minor buffeting. Another set of adjustments to the controls. He was anticipating the anomalies, *seeing* them before they were encountered, and seeing what he had to do to handle them. Hour after hour, he coped with the worst the Concepcycline Cloud had to offer and came out on top. It was impossible—he knew that—but he did it anyway.

When he finally considered the full impact of what he was doing, he was awestruck. Somehow the combination of the zindwar and the crazed electromagnetics of the cloud had opened a prescient window in his mind. Or maybe it was the zindwar alone. He didn't know, and he didn't care. Whatever had caused it, the effect was going to save his life. Maybe.

Gerard took advantage of a brief lull to check on Princess Peg. She appeared to be sleeping quietly in her couch, the battle medic humming softly over her chest. Nothing about the medic's readouts looked alarming from his ignorant point of view, but just to reassure himself he put his hand beside her neck and checked her pulse. Her cool, dry skin was soft and delicate under this touch, and he let his fingers linger over the strong, steady beat in her artery. Slowly, almost subconsciously, he sensed a connection with Princess Peg, a linkage which stretched out into the future. A warm, hazy, inexplicable vision began to form in his mind's eye. Focusing on it was difficult. The details refused to resolve themselves. The images would not hold shape long enough for him to identify them. Gerard thought he saw Princess Peg with her arms out to him, but before he could be sure the vision crackled with static and switched abruptly to a bright torus contorting against the stars.

Returning quickly to his couch, his brief respite ended by a new wave of prescience, Gerard resumed his duel with the fluctuations of the cloud. Hours passed like minutes. Minutes stretched into an infinity of seconds. Then the seconds dissolved into an unbroken continuum. His past swelled up behind him like a gigantic wave and swept him to its crest. There he rode, out on the frothing extreme of his personal history, cutting into the future with every sense, every instinct honed to a perfect edge. He was becoming something new, something greater than the sum of his past. With an exhilaration which sent brief spasms of pleasure coursing through his entire being, Gerard was totally aware, totally attuned with the cosmos which surrounded him, and totally alive.

As the feeling became stronger, so did he. He slipped easily into the stream of time, gauged where the current was strongest and moved with clean, simple determination toward his goal, carrying *Shivelight* and its dying complement with him. Seventy-three hours after entering the Concepcycline Cloud, Gerard piloted *Shivelight* into the untroubled currents of normal space.

There was no sense of triumph, no outburst of self-congratulation. There was only a small laugh in gentle acknowledgement of what he had done and how he had changed. That was all he allowed himself, because that was all he needed.

Carefully and deliberately, Gerard used the ship's instruments to check their position in space and set their course for Ell System. When he was certain that all was in order, he prepared the ship for a long warp, set the distress beacon to start transmitting as soon as they re-entered normal space, and turned command over to the navcomputers. Ten minutes later *Shivelight* started its first warp for home, but Gerard was already deep in the womb of dreamless sleep.

*　　*　　*

The main alarm klaxon woke him. Momentarily disoriented, he listened to the klaxon with fascination. Then he remembered where he was and what he had done, and calmly switched off the sound. Immediately a new sound demanded his attention. The vidcom was buzzing frantically. Gerard waited for a face to appear for a long moment before realizing that the receiver was turned off. As soon as he flipped the switch he was greeted by the ugly face of Targ Alpluakka, Commander of the Gabriel Ratchets. Targ started to speak, but when he saw Gerard he closed his mouth.

"Greetings, Commander," Gerard said, trying to keep his voice level against the waves of relief that were slapping against his tongue. "It pleasures me greatly to see you. We are in dire need of—"

"What?" Targ interrupted. "The Badh. Where is the Badh? Where is Zk Yerra? Why are you in the control center? How—"

"Patience, Commander, please. The Badh is alive, but very sick. Zk Yerra is dead. At least I think he is. So is Omna-Kye. They all contracted some terrible disease, and I don't know how many of them are still alive. Where are you? When can you get to us?"

Angry disbelief set itself in Targ's face, making the scar across the bridge of his nose stand out against the dark skin. "Impossible," Targ finally spat. "*Shivelight*'s exit from the Concepcycline Cloud was monitored by a patrol ship. I demand to speak with the Badh."

"You can't," Gerard said as calmly as he could against the irritation caused by Targ's response. "She is in a stabilized coma. I told you she was sick."

Targ cursed in Kulitti. "You lie, Fedscum."

"Go to Krick," Gerard responded. "I don't care if you believe me or not. All I care about is that you get to us as soon as possible with as many physmedicants as you can muster. And someone else to fly this damn ship. I flew her through the cloud, but I'm not sure I can get her back to Kril."

"Madness!" Targ screamed. "Lies! I demand to speak to the Badh!"

Without answering, Gerard directed the visual pickup

15

to the couch where Princess Peg was resting peacefully in her coma. "Speak to her, Commander," he said quietly, "but do not expect an answer. She lives, but she needs qualified physmedical help. I've done all I know how to do." Turning the pickup back on himself, he stared squarely into its glass eye. "Please, Commander, how soon can you get to us?"

Targ was giving orders over his shoulder in rapid-fire Kulitti, too fast for Gerard to understand most of what he was saying, but the words "security alert" and "Fedscum" aggravated Gerard's growing sense of discomfort.

When Targ turned back to his screen, his face was unreadable. "Soon, Diplomat. Three hours at the most. How came you through the cloud?"

The question implied something Gerard didn't understand, but he decided not to pursue it. "I don't know, Commander. I fought the controls for seventy-one hours almost as though I was in a trance. Then we were out of it."

"Incredible," Targ said coldly. He meant exactly that. He obviously did not believe a word Gerard had said.

"Perhaps, Commander, but here we are." Gerard sighed. Despite his long sleep, he felt tired and listless. If Targ Alpluakka didn't believe him, it was of no consequence. Or was it? "We will have to be quarantined, Commander. Omna-Kye didn't know what caused the disease, but he seemed very sure that it was—is, contagious."

"Assured you can be, Diplomat, that we will take all necessary precautions."

Targ's tone carried an implied threat under the assurance, but Gerard felt too drained to respond to it. "Good. Now, if you'll excuse me, I'm going to get something to eat."

"Eat well, Diplomat. Eat well."

"Thanks. Manley out."

Gerard returned from the galley almost immediately and punched the buttons for survival rations. There had been two dead crew members, a man and a woman, locked in a death embrace on the galley deck. He ate the survival rations without tasting them and took the zindwar the same way, all the time thinking about those bodies in the galley. The burning symptoms of the zindwar were a

16

welcome distraction, helping to raze the symbols of death from his thoughts.

As the burning subsided a new image crowded into his mind, an image of pain and torture with him at its center. It angered him. Or maybe, he thought, it just tips the scales, the last grain in a trickling pile of anger and frustration that started when I got to Ribble Galaxy. Targ wasn't very courteous or receptive then, either.

For the better part of two hours Gerard mulled over his growing sense of frustration. Maybe it would be a better idea to go straight to Kril and get help there, rather than wait in space for Fara only knew what kind of inadequate medical assistance. After all, Princess Peg had said she had to get home. But wasn't that taking an unnecessary chance with her life?

The buzz of the vidcom interrupted his thoughts. "Attention, *Shivelight*. You will slow to point-nine-nine-three immediately," a faceless voice said harshly. A second later the face appeared. It was just as harsh as the voice.

The strange face caught the angry results of Gerard's reflections. "Kravor in Krick! Doesn't anyone in this Fara-forsaken galaxy have any decency left? Just click on your vidcom, give your commands, and sheesie slime on who or why. Go to Krick. All of you. And tell Commander Alpluakka I'm going to warp this royal casket to Kril, and he can do as he damn well pleases. All defense systems activated!"

Gerard switched off the vidcom before the strange face could respond and, after several seconds of fiddling with the controls, found a way to cut the vidcom's buzzer down to a barely audible level. He had no idea whether the defense systems were activated or not. They had not been part of his crash piloting course. But he did know how to work up the new course for a short warp to Ell System. Without hesitation, he set up the new course and punched the warp button as soon as he got the proper readouts.

Damn Targ and his flunkies anyway. All Gerard wanted to do was bring this nightmare to an end.

Shivelight was challenged as soon as it exited warp. Gerard told the new nameless face to eat grisk droppings, and began setting up the deceleration procedures. He was sure he could bring the ship into braking orbit around

Kril, and just as sure that someone else would have to land her.

The second challenge that he acknowledged came from the sentry ship off Kril itself. He told the officer in command that he wanted one pilot sent across who could land *Shivelight*, and that if anyone tried to come with the pilot he would blast them to space dust. Then he turned off the vidcom until the third braking orbit, when the sentry ship pulled to within a thousand meters of *Shivelight* and, after receiving Gerard's permission, sent across a pilot on a one-man sled. They landed without incident.

Even before the pilot started shutting *Shivelight* down, the external port opened and a horde of suited figures flooded through the ship. Both Gerard and the pilot were anesthetized by dart guns seconds after the figures sprang into the control center.

Gerard sat frozen in his couch, seeing, but unable to focus, hearing, but unable to understand. Rough hands lifted him and carried him out of the ship. Loud voices assailed him as he was jostled and jerked, bounced and bruised through the heart of a grey mist into a world of sensory deprivation.

He knew he was conscious, that he wasn't dreaming, but he could not smell, nor hear, nor see a thing. He tried to pinch himself. Nothing happened. He was cut off from everything but his own mind. The cosmos shrank to the size of his thoughts.

Panic threatened him. It was rudely shoved aside by madness. Anger kicked madness into oblivion and was in turn washed away by waves of self-pity. Fires flickered on the fringes of his brain, casting an eerie glow over his thoughts. Chalk-white moons split on his horizons and sent fragments of ice hissing into the fire. Steam rose and threatened to smother his last breaths of sanity. Then the steam condensed high in the top of his skull and fell in a cool, soothing rain that finally tapered off to an occasional drip in a distant puddle. A voice spoke to him.

"Wake up. Diplomat Manley, wake up."

Gerard didn't know how to wake up.

"Can you hear me? Diplomat Manley, can you hear me? What drug did you give the Badh?"

Searching for his tongue Gerard thought, The Badh, The Badh, The Princess of Peg Oh Well took the drug and ran for Ell. The tip of his tongue fell out of hiding from the roof of his mouth. Cold water hurt his teeth.

"What drug did you give the Badh?"

Wetness touched his eyes, and they sprang open of their own accord. A face hovered before him.

"I am Omna—Seay, physmedicant to the Badh. What drug did you give her? We must know."

Gerard wrestled with his tongue and finally pushed out a word. "Medkit." Then another. "Stabilizer." And another. "Antidote." The face disappeared with a distant cursing sound. A needle bit into his neck and blackness overwhelmed him.

Standing before the long, curved table, with power-bonds on his wrists and ankles, Gerard felt groggy and ill. Squo Lyle and eight ducas of the Corpus Privy sat before him, looking stern and old. It was Squo Lyle who spoke. "Charged you are with many serious offenses. You took unauthorized control of Her Majesty's Ship *Shivelight*. You endangered the Badh's life, first by giving her a foreign drug, second by taking *Shivelight* through the Concepcycline Cloud, and third by refusing to allow other ships to come to your aid. For these crimes alone we could order you executed." Squo Lyle paused and stared at him.

Gerard wanted to speak, but he knew he must wait, for an invitation, or for an opportunity if the invitation didn't come.

"Charged you are also with twenty-seven other crimes against the Badh and the Free Rules of Ribble Galaxy. However, the time of your death has not yet come. A tape of questionable authenticity was found in the Badh's cabin which purports to exonerate you from some of the most serious crimes. If the Badh recovers from her illness, and if she validates the tape, Corpus Privy may see fit to spare your life and allow you to live out your natural days in the labor camps on Hinson Keep."

Holding his tongue was difficult, but Gerard sensed that Squo Lyle wasn't finished. However, it was Duca Cessaid from the Prindleswitch System who spoke next. Gerard had met him several times in the past.

"Be you aware of the gravity of your crimes, Diplomat Manley?"

This was the invitation he had hoped for. "No, Duca-sir, I committed no crime by intention. I—"

"No defense is allowed. Answer my question."

Gerard hesitated. If he said the wrong thing now, the whole session might come to an end. He had to tell them what happened without making it sound like a defense. "As the Badh ordered, Duca-sir, I am not aware of the gravity of my crimes."

Duca Cessaid smiled coldly, revealing his blackened teeth. "Admit you then to the crimes?"

"As the Badh ordered, I committed some of those mentioned, Duca-sir."

"No defense allowed," a voice cried from the other end of the table. It was neither a voice nor a duca Gerard recognized.

"Grant you my right to question the criminal, Duca Echi?" Cessaid asked.

"Most certainly, sir." Duca Echi's voice dripped with venom and sarcasm.

"Grant you my right to hear the criminal's answers?"

"No one seeks to hold your rights," Squo Lyle interjected, "but, as you are well aware, a criminal in these crimes has no right of defense."

"Ah," Duca Cessaid said, "but will our honorable Squo allow a duca's right to question until satisfied, regardless of the nature of the answers?"

Gerard recognized an ally when he saw one and prayed silently to Fara that the next answer would be positive.

"Such is your right," Squo Lyle answered solemnly.

The pressure on Gerard's chest eased as he slowly released his breath. Maybe he was going to get a chance after all.

There was no smile on Duca Cessaid's face when he turned back to Gerard. "When did you take control of *Shivelight*, Diplomat Manley?"

"When the Badh ordered me to, Duca-sir, before we reached the Concepcycline Cloud."

"Where then were Zk Yerra and his co-commander?"

"Zk Yerra was on the verge of death, Duca-sir. His co-commander had already died."

So the questions went, specific questions to which Gerard gave specific answers. Duca Cessaid knew what he was doing. He would ask a series of questions which led Gerard to describe a moment of tension, then backtrack to some seemingly trivial point, all the while letting his audience wonder about the resolution of the tension. By the time

Cessaid finished, Gerard felt that they had covered the story fairly well—except for his prescience in the Concepcycline Cloud. That he played down, and talked instead about flying by instinct hyped on zindwar. Several of the other ducas asked questions and also seemed favorably inclined toward Gerard, but they were obviously a minority.

"Are there any more questions?" Squo Lyle asked finally. "Very well, and so be it. The criminal is ordered to detainment on Hinson Keep pending further decisions of the Corpus."

"But Squo-sir—"

"The criminal will be silent. This order is not a judgment. The Free Rules apply. Diplomat Manley, you are remanded to the custody of the Gabriel Ratchets for transport to Hinson Keep."

Grinding anger broke from Gerard's throat in the shape of a hoarse roar. Arching his back and raising his bound hands high over his head, he vented such a terrible sound that even he was surprised by it. More than anger, more than frustration, it was the bitter complaint of a living pawn against those who controlled his destiny. On worlds populated by emotional sensitives, that sound would have caused mortal agony and death to those who heard it. In the Corpus Privy Chamber on Kril, throne planet of Ribble Galaxy, it caused surprise and a touch of consternation, but little more.

Only one person truly heard what the roar expressed. She was an old, gnarled duca, sitting at the far end of the curved table, who had asked him several questions. When the roar finally subsided, she rose and quietly addressed the echoing silence. "By the Free Rules of Ribble I rebuke the Corpus. Here stands a stranger who brought our Badh through great peril safely home to Kril, a diplomatic emissary who performed an extraordinary feat of courage and bravery and saved the life not only of the Badh, but also of several of those who served her. Yet we, Corpus Privy to the Throne of Ribble, in our arrogance, in our uncompromising allegiance to rules never meant to cope with such a situation, are going to punish him for what he did."

Gerard heard the old duca speaking, but the words were slow to form meaning in his brain. Her Kulitti was thickly accented and her diction clipped, but her voice was steady and pure. Gerard fought hard to quell the turmoil inside him as he tried to understand what she was saying.

"By the Free Rules of Ribble I rebuke the Corpus again for rushing to judgment and action. My son died on *Shivelight*. He, who should have been most able to save our Badh, failed. This outsider succeeded. For that success we condemn him to the hands of the torturers on Hinson Keep."

"Covesty lies!" Duca Echi shouted.

"Silence!" Squo Lyle's command was greeted by a snort of disgust from Echi, but he spoke no more. "Our esteemed Duca Kye speaks by the Right of Free Rules. By our duty we listen."

Omna-Kye's mother? Gerard examined her closely, noting most the bright eyes in her age-crumpled face, eyes that seemed to burn with a youth belied by her body. Was it possible?

"By the Right of Free Rules I rebuke the Corpus a third time. Gerard Manley is a diplomat—"

"A cheap hireling," Duca Echi interjected.

Duca Kye ignored him. "He is a diplomat representing the Federation, yet this Corpus has chosen to abridge his diplomatic rights and privileges. Of all our mistakes, this may prove to be the most costly."

Gerard watched Duca Kye as she looked around the table, letting her eyes rest momentarily on each member. Most of the ducas seemed to ignore her, looking elsewhere or staring past her. Finally she brought her eyes to rest on him.

"Diplomat Manley, I apologize for this Corpus and beg you to remember—"

"Begging a criminal?" Duca Echi asked.

"I beg you to remember that some of us did not approve of this action. As for my colleague, Duca Echi," she said shifting her gaze, "he was born where no decent soul would live and can be excused because of his origins."

Refusing to rise to her insult, Duca Echi merely nodded at her with a sneering smile. Gerard could have cared less. He knew for certain now that there would be no reprieve from the order sending him to Hinson Keep. He hated them. He hated all, even Duca Kye and Duca Cessaid, who had tried to help him. He hated Princess Peg for not being there to save him. In fact, he hated everything about Ribble Galaxy and would have given anything he possessed at that moment to be rid of it.

But he possessed nothing except his life. He wanted to scream again. Somehow, there was no energy for screaming. Swelling rapidly inside him was a total sense of hopelessness. Nourished by fatigue and seduced by circumstances, its name was Despair.

The remainder of the proceedings mattered little to Gerard. He listened from a distance that increased geometrically every few minutes until he found himself completely withdrawn into a dark pool of warm, quiet peace where he let himself slip below the surface. A monitor rose from the pool and took his place. It watched him collapse on the chamber floor, listened as they tried to revive him, and noted that he was carried gently and laid finally in a soft comfortable place. Then the monitor, too, slipped below the surface, and Gerard Manley, Universal Contract Diplomat, was disconnected from the cosmos.

*   *   *

Message to: Pelis Foffey Turingay-Gotz
           FedTreatySvc

New developments here threaten our joint enterprise. Key-One has caused a problem which he alone cannot resolve. We will try to assist him so that the solution places him under our influence and in our debt. Failing that, you will have to encourage your sister service to send a replacement. He is, after all, expendable.

—Toehold

*   *   *

3

His father smiled broadly into his sleepy eyes. "Time to arise, Gerry. Much is to be done this day if we are to be on time for your appointment at The Academy."

Gerry didn't want to go to The Academy. He wanted to stay at home with his father. If Mother were alive, she wouldn't make him go away. Why did he have to go? His father could teach him, like he had always done. Gerry shut his eyes and tried to make the world go away, but his father's hands shook him loose from the last ties to sleep.

"Be up with you, Gerry. 'Tis not a day to dream away the morning."

After rubbing his eyes until they hurt, Gerry opened them again. "I feel not so well, Father," he said with a whine he hoped didn't sound exaggerated.

" 'Twill feel better after you eat, Son."

"I feel not hungry."

" 'Twill eat anyway." His father gave him a stern look that Gerry knew was the first indicator of impatience.

"Tell me again, Father, why I must go to The Academy."

"As you rise and dress I will tell you what I have told you a hundred times already. There is no school on Commissigh that is acceptable to the service."

"But we could stay here. There's a school here," Gerry said as he rose from his bed.

His father sighed. "My son could stay here and attend the Perrish School, but his father could never come to visit. Want you that?" The hurt look in his eyes made Gerry turn his head.

As he pulled on his shirt, Gerry finally made the decision. If he had to go, he would go, but he would be bad and they would dismiss him and send him to be with his father on Commissigh. "It is best a son obey his father," he said, purposely misquoting the scripture.

"Remember that when you awake, son."

Gerry shook his head and started to ask what his father meant, but his father was gone, and his room was dark, and he was back in bed. What a silly dream, he thought as he drifted off to sleep again.

"Time to arise." The grinning face was wicked and cold, made ugly by a scar that ran across the bridge of the nose. It was not his father at all. Who was it? Gerry remembered the face and it frightened him. He pulled the covers over his head and plunged back into sleep.

The smell of frying crispins and freshly brewed hovery teased him awake. Today they would run the first test of the program he had designed, and Gerry felt good as he got up and wrapped the synsoft chimono around him. They had rooted out most of the glitches in the two weeks since he'd come home from the Academy, and now it was time to see if the program actually worked. Patting the computer cabinet affectionately as he stepped into the kitchen, he said to his father, "Hungry I am this morning."

His father turned with a grin that made the scar across the bridge of his nose look like a crack in his face. It wasn't his father at all. Gerry turned and fled.

A brief flutter in his stomach told him it was time to eat. He opened his eyes and blinked at the low grey ceiling over his head. Then he remembered. This was part of the survival test, six days of forced immobility without food. How many days had it been now? Gerard had no idea. But he knew that this wasn't the first time during the test that hunger had awakened him.

"Time to eat," a voice said from behind him. He tried to move and felt all the power restraints tighten. An upside-down face appeared over his. Scar-nose. He squeezed his eyes shut and let the fingers of his mind pull him down into darkness.

It was night. Through a high window he could see stars. Gerard tried to move, but his muscles felt leaded and stiff. Slowly, he wiggled his fingers and toes, increasing the circulation in his arms and legs. It hurt. Then, after a while, it felt better. Encouraged by that response, he flexed his hands and wrists until his arms began to feel normal. Muscle by muscle, he gently limbered his body until he could ease himself into a sitting position. Dizziness threatened to steal his strength, but he fought it off. Moving slowly and carefully, he swung first one leg then the other off the low bed and held onto its side until he was sitting up without dizziness.

Two thoughts struck him at once. He was terribly hungry. And he had no idea where he was. The last thing he remembered was what? Being in the Privy Chamber? No. Something after that. Being carried somewhere. He remembered some dreams, too, and Targ Alpluakka's ugly face coming toward him from somewhere. Have to keep still, he thought, as a brief wave of vertigo swayed him.

A small piece of memory fell from its niche in his mind

and clattered to the floor of his consciousness. Hinson Keep. They sentenced him to detention on Hinson Keep. Sitting up suddenly became too much work, so Gerard let himself fall heavily back into bed. He closed his eyes and tried to remember everything that had happened in the Privy Chamber. When he opened them again, light was streaming in the high window.

"Welcome to Hinson Keep," a voice said quietly. Pain shot through his neck as he twisted to see who was talking. He saw no one. "Are you hungry?" The voice, he realized, was coming from a small grille in the wall over his head. He was hungry. He was famished.

"Yes," he said in a croak that startled him.

"Good," the grille responded. "Someone will come to you."

Gerard forced his stiff body to sit up and looked around the room. It was small, perhaps three meters square, with a four-meter ceiling. The walls and ceiling were a dirty ochre color, smooth and glassy-looking. His narrow bed, two straight-backed chairs, and a small table all were made of stress-formed dark wood. The bed had a thin red mattress that was actually quite resilient. Looking at himself, he saw a pocketless jumpsuit the same color as the mattress. He feet were bare, and from the feel of his face he hadn't shaved in several weeks.

The someone who came was Targ Alpluakka. "You sleep heavily, Diplomat. That is not healthy." Targ stood just inside the narrow doorway. Behind him Gerard could see at least two Gabriel Ratchets. "Are you ready to eat?"

Gerard nodded. His throat was dry and scratchy.

"Good. Tell us how you poisoned the people aboard *Shivelight*."

"Poisoned?" Gerard rasped. "I poisoned no one."

"Diplomat, Diplomat," Targ said in a tone one would use with a child. "We know they were poisoned. We want to know how."

Games, Gerard thought. They're playing games with me. "No poison. Sick." His throat protested when he tried to swallow. "Everyone sick."

"But not you, Diplomat? Why were you not sick?"

"Don't know. Maybe immune." How incredibly stupid they must think I am. Why poison a shipload of people, then fight your way through Krick to get them home?

Targ stepped away from the door with a wave of his hand. The two Ratchets came quickly into the room and jerked Gerard from the bed. Then, following Targ, they dragged him out of the room, down a short, wide corridor, and into another room much larger than his and filled with strange shapes and appliances. It did not take Gerard long to realize he was going to be tortured. The hard metal chair they strapped him in was certainly not designed for comfort.

"Targ," he croaked. "Water. Speak."

At a signal from Targ one of the Ratchets stuck a small tube into his mouth and clipped it to his upper lip. The clip was surprisingly painful. Hesitantly, Gerard sipped on the tube. What he got was not water, but it did not taste bad and it soothed his throat as he swallowed. He sucked greedily until the Ratchets pinched the tube closed.

"Do you think you can speak now?" Targ asked.

Gerard swallowed and tried. "Yes. That's better. That's much better. May I speak freely, Commander?"

"As freely as you wish," a new voice said from the doorway. "Consider yourself at home on our humble planet." A slender, dark-skinned man with a strikingly handsome face stepped in front of Gerard. The familiarity of the face was confirmed when the man spoke again. "I am Markl Holsten, and you are my guest."

Holsten, Gerard thought, one of the Privy-Admiral's relatives. That's why the face looked familiar.

"My father, the governor, apologizes for not attending to you personally, but he had other obligations. Has Commander Alpluakka told you what we have planned for you?"

"I would not take your privilege, high-son," Targ said in a very formal tone. Gerard sensed that Targ and Markl were not on the best of terms.

"Thank you, Commander. First, Diplomat, let me assure you that what we do to you will cause you no permanent physical damage. We would not want any evidence of our methods visible for all the galaxy to see." As he spoke, Markl's face seemed to twist and grow heavier. "However, you will *think* every bone in your body has been broken and every nerve torn apart bit by bit before we are through. We are very thorough. When we

27

are finished with you, you will have told us everything we desire to know."

Markl licked his lips several times and Gerard noticed a small tick under his left eye. "You will confess to every sin you have ever committed and many that you have not. You will tell us shameful and vulgar things about your innermost desires that you would not even admit to yourself."

The intensity of Markl's voice had increased with each vivid phrase, but the volume had gotten lower and lower until he was almost whispering through hissing breaths. Then, suddenly, he squared his shoulders and resumed a normal tone. "Shall I explain our devices to you? No? Pity, for they are unique in the exquisite ranges of pain they can bring to our guests."

Gerard felt his heart sink. He closed his eyes, then opened them quickly, hoping he could prepare himself for what was to come.

"Shall we start with your fingers?" Markl asked quietly. "It is a simple procedure. We ask a question. You give us a false answer. We pull off one of your fingernails. That takes about five minutes. Then we ask another question and pull off another fingernail."

"Suppose I answer truthfully?" Gerard offered.

Markl smiled with obvious delight. "Ah, that brings us to the beauty of our method. You see, in the first stages, there are no true answers. Truth must be confirmed by pain. And reconfirmed. And reconfirmed, until there is absolutely no room for doubt. If the first answers are indeed true, we shall know somewhere, say, in the process of cracking the individual vertebrae in your back. Yes, I think they would be confirmed there."

A metallic shield dropped in front of Gerard's face and pressed his head back against the chair. The first question was "How did you poison everyone aboard *Shivelight*?" The pain started at the tip of his left thumb, but before it began to fall from its breathtaking peak it was piercing a hole in his brain.

The second question was "What poison did you use?" The pain from his left forefinger was twice as bad as his thumb, which throbbed in a dull, aching counterpoint to the sharp forefinger pain. His screaming was answered with laughter.

The third question was "Why did you poison them?"

The pain from his middle finger had barely begun when Gerard spotted the pool of darkness. With a violent kick and a roar of defiance, he threw himself off the edge of his thoughts and plunged into the placid safety of darkness. Angry voices called after him, but he shut them out and let himself dissolve into nothingness.

"Question still unanswered. You answer, Student Manley."

Gerard stared at the shifting opening in Senior Instructor Fssississfiss's body that spoke, and tried to look confident. "The answer is that only those who accept all the possibilities of the future can fully accept all the improbabilities from the past."

"Rough and crude your answer is, but closer to the truth you are. Truth you tell, however badly."

The break gong sent them on their way and Golifa slowed her stride to match Gerard's. Her iridescent eye and constantly wiggling mouth seemed to show amusement. "Student Manley tell truth," she said in a high-pitched imitation of Fssississfiss. Her laughter was a bubbling sound emitted from the top of her bare, twin-pointed head. "Rough and crude. Tell truth bad."

Gerard laughed with her.

"You cheated, Diplomat." Markl Holsten stood over his bed with a slight grin on his perfect lips. "You hid from me and ruined my game."

Gerard ignored him and looked at his left hand. Every finger was totally intact.

Markl laughed. "You expected blood? Come, my dear Diplomat, I told you we would leave no evidence. Will you come with me, or shall I have you dragged?"

Contemplating his uninjured hand, Gerard smiled. He didn't know exactly what had happened to him since he blacked out in the Concepcycline Cloud, but he knew that he had opened doors to talents he never would have guessed that he had. If he could keep those doors open, he was going to save himself a lot of pain. No sense in making them drag him. He might as well walk to Markl's little playroom and exercise his new talent. "Lead the way, high-son," Gerard said quietly.

Markl waited for Gerard to climb slowly out of bed, then led him down the corridor and strapped him once again in the cold metal chair. Gerard accepted the offered drinking tube and noted to himself that the clip didn't hurt as much this time. Instead of the shield in front of his face, Markl slipped a heavy helmet on Gerard's head and spent some time adjusting it. When he was finished, there was silence. Gerard took a sip from the drinking tube and was surprised to find the liquid heavy with the taste of zindwar. He took several long pulls on the tube and waited for the burning to begin.

Just as it did, Markl's voice spoke in his ear. "Are you ready?"

"Go to Krick," Gerard replied, concentrating on the burning of the zindwar. Markl asked another question, but Gerard shut it out. When the burning sensation reached its peak, Gerard looked for the dark pool. At first all he could see was a rippling grey fog. He concentrated. The fog thinned. As soon as he caught a glimpse of the black, shimmering surface, he plunged into it and disappeared.

Pale light was filtering through the high window when he awoke. His scalp itched. He smelled bad. He had no idea how much time had passed since being taken off of *Shivelight*. And he knew that if he was ever released from this place he would be sent back to Fed in disgrace. But he smiled anyway. Without cause, he felt good.

Markl came for him that day, and the next time Gerard woke up, and the next time, and the next. Sometimes Markl found ways to make Gerard feel more pain, or to hide the pool, or to slow his entrance into it. But always Gerard managed to fight off the questions, find the sheltering pool, and disappear. It became a contest, a personal struggle between Gerard and Markl, but as soon as he realized that Markl was operating under restrictions imposed on him from the outside, Gerard knew he would eventually win.

After the first session Gerard saw no more of Targ Alpluakka. There were times when he was sure that Targ was around, times, as he was seeking his solace in the tranquil pool, that he was sure he heard Targ's voice insistently trying to question him. But he never saw Targ, never heard him when things were "normal," and never had any indication from Markl that Targ was nearby. That puzzled Gerard. He didn't know why, but it did.

It was all part of a pattern of irrational understanding which he had discovered. Intuition was the only word he could dredge out of his memory from those many philosophy classes he had taken at The Academy and later at DiploSchool, that seemed to describe or suit the pattern. But then it was only the kind of intuition delineated by Bergsonhenri, the ancient Terran philosopher.

The only interruption in the contest with Markl came one day when Gerard returned from one of his escapes into the pool of darkness to find himself in a new room being examined by a physmedicant who seemed to be meticulously counting the hairs on Gerard's legs. His first reaction was to chuckle, and that immediately brought the physmedicant around to face him. It was Omna-Seay.

"Ah, Diplomat, I see you have awakened. You are well?"

"You're the physmedicant. Am I well?"

Omna-Seay seemed to study the question before he replied. "It would be said by others that you are more than well. Odd this seems in light of your, ah, current status. Indeed, your health was one of the reasons I was called."

Gerard found the detachment in Omna-Seay's voice annoying. Then he remembered Princess Peg. "Did the Badh send you?"

That obviously startled Omna-Seay. "No. No indeed. The Badh still suffers greatly from your drugs and is far too weak to be concerned with you."

"But the antidote—"

"Poison. She lives without your poison."

"Fool," Gerard spat.

"No, Diplomat," Omna-Seay said, the detachment returning to his voice, "you were the fool."

He slapped Gerard's arm with a flattened palm, and immediately a stinging itch developed in Gerard's shoulder and neck. Another drug, he thought, as he drifted off to sleep.

Fingers picked at his flesh. Something scraped his face with monotonous strokes. Cruel teeth raked his scalp. Then all was soothed as soft flesh rubbed pungent oils into his skin.

Sinsera came to him in his room, risking dismissal and disgrace, risking most of all a repetition of his rejection. She came to him naked and without pretense, the soft silver fur

31

of her body tipped with a natural musk that even he could recognize. Sinsera was in heat, consumed by a biological need which turned her normally sensuous being into an organism of total lust. She came in the night, whimpering, desperate, and Gerard could not turn her away.

It was an awkward, ragged coupling they finally achieved, with Sinsera twisted into a grotesque position, ankles locked behind her shoulders, claws digging into her own flesh, pulling herself open so that Gerard could enter her. Yet, once inside her, he found the oils of her estrus sensuous in a way that tingled and prolonged his efforts until he thought he would explode before he finally climaxed.

Later he thought of the detached ecstasy he had felt, of how he had observed himself being taken through a series of ever-stronger orgasms until Sinsera finally released him in total exhaustion. When he awoke the next morning she was gone, and two days later she left DiploSchool without ever seeing him again. In his registry box there was a brief note. "A friend thanks you."

This time Sinsera took him in the darkness, smothering his flesh with her soft fur, sliding hot oil over him in rhythmic strokes that demanded his response, yet forced him to suffer every second of sensation. At the ultimate moment he cried out in joy and surprise, knowing it was not Sinsera who milked the heat from his body, but too deep in the well of his pleasure to care who it was.

Click-click. Click-click. The sound aroused Gerard's curiosity enough to make him open his eyes from the languid peace of his sexual release. Click-click. Voices. "Your uncle is sending Caberon Onsie." Click-click. Click-click. "The pleasure technique is working no better than the pain." Click-click. ". . . will not be pleased." Click-click. Silence.

Gerard smiled as he drifed off to sleep. Markl had brought Sinsera back to him.

After stretching and yawning, Gerard reached to scratch his beard. It was gone. His face was smooth and soft, as though it had been treated after shaving. His hair was short and felt soft and clean. His jumpsuit was clean also. As Gerard took stock of this new treatment, he wondered if this was another of Markl's techniques. Or, if it signalled a change in his status?

Gerard did not have much time to reflect on it, because, shortly after he started wondering what was going on, the door to his room swung open and revealed a grinning Targ Alpluakka. "Good morning, Commander," he said with a smile that felt uncomfortable on his newly shaven face.

"To you the same, Diplomat Manley. How feel you?"

The question and Targ's tone disturbed Gerard as much as it puzzled him. Was Targ trying to be friendly? That didn't make any sense. "Well enough, Commander. What new tortures have you and Markl devised for me?"

"Tortures? Surely you jest, Diplomat. You have not been tortured, nor will you be."

"And I'm not on Hinson Keep. And the Badh never got sick. And you're not Commander Targ Alpluakka."

"Believe, Diplomat. There is no torture. It is forbidden for one in detention. Bid you come with me."

Targ's smile was as false as his denial of torture, but Gerard followed him out of the room and made an automatic right turn down the corridor toward the torture room. Targ had turned left. "Please, Diplomat, this way," Targ said with a softness that was totally out of character. "The ship awaits us for your return to Kril."

"Why?" Only when he asked the question did Gerard realize that he had slipped into a routine, a regular escape from reality. Targ threatened to change that routine and Gerard wasn't sure he liked the idea in the least. He'd become dependent on his ability to slip into himself and avoid the discomfort and pain of facing his oppressors. Well, if he could escape Markl with that technique, he could escape Targ the same way.

"The Badh has spoken. You are to return to Kril."

There was no emotion revealed by Targ's statement, nothing that Gerard could take as an indicator of what was to come, but he felt an irrational confidence in his ability to cope. He turned and followed Targ down the hall with easy strides, aware for the first time that he was wearing boots. Reality, or dream? He was no longer sure.

When they boarded Targ's ship, Gerard decided it must be reality. His dreams were never this detailed for so long. Or were they? No, this had to be real. He had to make himself believe that it was real so that he could deal with it in that way. Targ led him to a small cabin and told him to strap in, watching until Gerard did so. When Targ left, the closing of the door was followed by two distinct clicks, and Gerard was sure he had been locked in.

Hours later, when the all-clear signal came after launch, he unstrapped and was surprised to find that his door was not locked. He checked the bulkhead doors at both ends of the short companionway his cabin was located on and discovered that they too opened freely to his touch. Nonetheless, he was still a prisoner. He might have the freedom to roam the ship if he cared to, but there was no point in it. He was being carried as a prisoner.

The thought depressed him. Without exploring further than the companionway doors, he returned to his cabin with the feeling that he had been there before. It was too much like his cabin aboard *Shivelight* had been for him to escape the rush of memories from that eventful trip. That depressed him even further.

Sleep, sleep is the answer, Self whispered to him in a smiling voice. Gerard smiled back and made himself comfortable on his bunk. Maybe sleep was the answer.

They were in Golifa's room for an end-of-term party. Gerard couldn't quite put names with all the bodies present, but he knew them all to a greater or lesser degree. Somehow the subject had turned to dreams and their meanings and causes. A slender Sylvan woman with a mean slash for a mouth was spouting a line of mumbo-jumbo mysticism that Gerard found irritating. Finally when she said, "Dreams are Hnsa's way of communicating with the individual soul," he could take it no longer.

"Hnsa, schminsa," he said sneeringly, taking delight at the expression of shock on her face. "Dreams are nothing more than biochemical reactions aroused and directed by the subconscious. The supreme spirits, and that includes your Hnsa and my Fara, have nothing to do with dreams except as we direct."

Beside him, Golifa bubbled in laughter. "Are you so sure of your literal definition?" she asked teasingly. "Would you participate in an experiment designed to prove you wrong?"

Gerard was sure the potent cherry wine had not yet clouded his judgment. "Where and when?" he asked with a confident grin.

"Here. Tonight. I will write a dream for you to have and seal it in a pouch to be delivered to you in the morning.

No one will know the contents of the dream but me. Then anyone interested in our results will meet with us here tomorrow evening, and you will tell us what you dreamed—"

"If I dream."

"And reveal the contents of the pouch," Golifa finished.

An abnormally large grin crept over Gerard's face. "Shall we wager?"

"Of course. If you do not have a highly pleasurable dream, exactly like what I describe in the pouch, I will give you a cruzzean massage." A ripple of delight ran through the party. Golifa's cruzzean massages were rare gifts bestowed only upon a limited number of recipients. As the ripple died away Golifa fixed her exquisite eye directly on Gerard until he felt almost uncomfortable. "If you *do* have the dream I predict, you will write ThLina a poem and present it to her with a formal apology. Do you accept?"

"Certainly. I've always wanted one of your famous massages."

Dawn found Gerard sitting at his console humming to himself and putting the last touches on his poem.

WHEN GERARD MET THE PRINCESS OF GALAXY VI

She walked through his eyes
   to some untouched center of his soul,
And with fingers like a sun's corona
   reached out through the cold drift,
     across unknown distance,
      through the side door of time
   burned the print of her presence
    on his heart's eternity,
And the warp of his universe flexed
   into harmony and discord.

He knew nothing that he would not tell her,
And nothing that he could,
For he was potent and sterile,
Suspending in the duration of becoming,
Waiting for his space-time wave
   to break into the future
     onto the warm beaches of stars,
     or the cold sands of the void.

He could do nothing but wait
in the well of his gravity,
Troughing the wave with reason,
anticipation,
and wonder.

At the appointed hour he showed up at Golifa's room and immediately upon entering made a formal apology to ThLina, then recited the poem to her, as everyone stared at him in fascinated silence. Then he turned to Golifa and asked, "How?"

"If you are awake, I would like to talk to you."

"What?" Golifa's voice sounded strange and distant.

"If you are awake, I would like to talk to you," the distant voice repeated.

Gerard shook his head. "Yes. Yes, of course. Just give me a few minutes to freshen." He had no idea how long he had been asleep and didn't care. But it annoyed him tremendously that he had missed the end of his dream and the massage Golifa had given him as a kind of consolation gift. He washed his face and wondered what had triggered that dream memory.

Five minutes later Targ entered the cabin and explained to Gerard in a very solicitous way that he was to consider himself a guest aboard the ship. His meals would be brought to him. He was free to use the ship's limited exercise and recreation facilities. And, so that he was not bored, Targ himself had planned for long, informal chats with him on the flight to Kril.

Gerard was bored.

* * *

Message to: Greaves Lingchow
FedDiploSvc

Do not recall him. Repeat. Do not recall him. He will soon be of much use to us. Any attempt to change his status here will be resisted by several powerful forces.

As for your demands: If you walk naked into space for a thousand parsecs, you might have them met.

—Glyph

* * *

4

The audience room was spare and simple. More surprisingly, it was far smaller than Gerard had expected, especially when compared to the grand hall where he had first presented his credentials to Princess Peg four years before. Could it actually have been four years? It did not seem possible, but it was true. Six months of that time had been lost on Hinson Keep. Not lost, he corrected himself, invested. Hinson Keep had provided a training ground for his new talent, and, even though he didn't look forward to the idea of having to use it again, he was pleased that he had learned to use it so well.

Rocking heel and toe in a gentle rhythm as he remembered what had happened on Hinson Keep, Gerard almost lost his balance when a hand was laid gently on his arm. It was Fianne Tackona, Junior Archivist, and Gerard's constant companion for the two weeks since he had returned. "The Badh comes," Fianne said quietly.

When Gerard looked toward the door, he realized that four Gerard Ratchets had entered the audience room without making a sound. They stood in pairs on either side of the door, their stark grey uniforms fitting perfectly with the bareness of the room. Two of them were humanoids and carried the short quin cutlasses. The other two were ridlows, unarmed until one considered the bony ripping hooks that terminated their longer, lower set of arms at knee level, and the small, razor-sharp daggers they wore horizontally on their waistbands. Even the Gabriel Ratchets, Royal Guard of the Throne, were forbidden power weapons on Kril.

Moments later Princess Peg entered the room followed by a retinue of five or six people, the only one of whom

Gerard recognized was the physmedicant, Omna-Seay. Following Fianne Tackona's example and instruction, Gerard went quickly to one knee, did the neck-snapping nod of obeisance, and returned to his feet to find that Princess Peg had stopped within a meter of him.

"Good you are to come, Diplomat Manley," she said in a soft voice that sounded stronger than she looked.

"As the Badh commands," Gerard returned formally.

Her gentle laugh was accompanied by a small smile which seemed to have found a home on her face and refused to vacate it. "So it is. The Badh commands. The Diplomat appears. Let us talk." With a gracious sweep of her arm she motioned Gerard to a chair at the small table beside the throne. He waited for her to be seated, but, instead of taking the throne, she took the chair opposite him, arranging the wispy folds of her multi-layered dress as she sat with an accustomed regalness.

A saint she is, Gerard. His father's words, used to describe the woman he was going to marry, the woman who would be his mother but who would never be his mother, rang softly in his inner ear. The emotions those words carried were shaded by distance and time, but still startled him with their impact.

"Pardon, Diplomat, you look unwell."

"No, my pardon, Badh. I am well." Why had those words... what connection to Princess Peg... how...?

"Then you will join in refreshment?" There was a quizzical tone in Princess Peg's voice, but her smile remained unchanged.

"Most certainly I would be honored, Badh."

"You may call me Princess."

"An honor unworthy of me," he responded quickly. Her offer was a matter of form and he had remembered his part.

"Ah, but I insist, Diplomat. And I shall call you Star Pilot, so that all will remember how you served our throne."

"I am doubly honored, Badh."

"Princess."

"Triply honored, Princess."

"Enough of this, Star Pilot." She looked at her retinue as though expecting something. "Has EllKoep emptied its larder? Where are our refreshments?"

Almost immediately a servant appeared beside the table,

38

set a small tray in front of them, then withdrew as silently as he had appeared. A Ratchet, Gerard thought. No ridlow would ever consent to acting as a servant unless he were also a Ratchet.

Princess Peg poured the clear wine into small, dark cups. As he had been tutored by Fianne, Gerard tasted his first. The guest should always be poisoned before the Badh. The wine was dry, with a warm, nutty taste that pleased his palate and his throat. Following the form, he handed her the cup and took a taste from hers.

"You approve, Star Pilot?" she asked with a twinkle in her eyes.

"I recommend, Princess."

"Good. Now tell me about our journey."

"Pardon, Princess, but what would you know?"

"All my Star Pilot can remember," she said firmly. "You may begin at the moment you were called to our control center."

"As the Badh commands." Gerard tried to keep the story as straightforward as possible, giving her all the facts, deleting his emotional reactions to all that had happened. She let him talk without interruption until he came to the part where they left the Concepcycline Cloud.

"Tell me again, Star Pilot, what happened after you were rendered senseless by the sight of the cloud."

"Pardon, Princess, but I'm not sure I can describe what happened."

"It is very important to me that you try."

"My best is poor, but all I have to offer." He didn't remember where the quotation came from, but it seemed appropriate to her request. Princess Peg acknowledged it with a nod, so he tried to describe for her how he had sensed the fluctuations in the cloud and compensated for them as they occurred. He closed his eyes as he concentrated on that strange time, trying to draw as much from the memory as possible.

"How quaint. Marradon would love you."

He opened his eyes at the interruption and did a double take. The voice had not been Princess Peg's, but that of a lookalike standing beside her chair.

"Forgive my sister's rudeness," Princess Peg said with a hint of disapproval in her voice. "She often speaks prematurely."

Gerard rose and looked from sister to sister. The likeness was remarkable. Not knowing the form for this meeting, he chose to bow low and come back up with a smooth, unhurried motion.

"With quaint manners, too," the sister said. She was laughing at him.

"Inez Nare-Devy, Chattel-shi of Kril," Princess Peg said by way of formal introduction.

A chair was brought for Nare-Devy, and Gerard waited until she was seated beside Princess Peg before resuming his own chair. They were a striking pair, princess and sister, a double vision of beauty. Yet, despite the striking similarity of their appearance, Princess Peg seemed somehow more beautiful, her dark, curling hair softer and more lustrous, her deep brown eyes more tender and knowing.

"Continue your story, Star Pilot."

Unable to remember where he had left off, Gerard started over again, telling how he had opened the view ports, seen the swirling cloud spread out before him, and fallen unconscious. Again he closed his eyes and tried to concentrate on all that he could remember. Again he was interrupted when he told about exiting the cloud. And again Princess Peg asked him to repeat his story.

Before he could begin the repetition, a male voice said, "Badh, perhaps tomorrow." It was Omna-Seay, and the look on his face was one of obvious concern.

Turning back to Princess Peg, Gerard thought she looked suddenly tired and pale.

"Yes, perhaps tomorrow. We will send for you, Star Pilot." With that she rose on the steadying arm of Inez Nare-Devy and left the audience room with her retinue and the Gabriel Ratchets. Gerard stood by the table and stared after her as she left, intrigued by her in a way that tickled a nerve low under his heart. She was indeed beautiful.

"Shall we go?" Fianne Tackona waited for him by the door, amusement written all over his ageless face.

"Why do you smile, Fianne Tackona? Is not the Badh worthy of my admiration?"

"Most certainly. Most certainly. Though I suspect not so much as you give her."

Gerard noted Fianne's comment, but made no response to it. If he had learned nothing else about Fianne in their two weeks of almost constant companionship, he had learned that the archivist was given to comments from an odd perspective. Why the Badh might not be worthy of all his admiration was something Gerard didn't speculate upon. She was a powerful, intriguing, beautiful woman who held his fate in her fair hands with regal grace and style. Why should he not admire her?

That evening as they sat in Gerard's sumptuous quarters on one of the upper floors of EllKoep, sipping more of the nutty wine, which Fianne had procured for them, Fianne asked Gerard a surprising question. "Did you find Hinson Keep interesting?"

"As interesting as a torture chamber can be," Gerard replied without thinking. There was bitterness in his voice.

"Torture? Impossible!" The incredulity in Fianne's voice was as naked and honest as a stone in the sun.

Wondering if he should say more, Gerard looked at Fianne carefully. Perhaps he shouldn't have mentioned the torture, but Fianne Tackona had implied many times that he was one of Princess Peg's confidantes, and surely she knew about the torture.

"There was no torture ordered or approved," Fianne continued, "and Markl Holsten assured us that you were well cared for."

Fianne's voice told Gerard that he really didn't know about the torture. He smelled the stench of bad politics and wanted to avoid stirring up any more trouble than he already had. "Perhaps I dreamed it. As I told you before, I was delirious much of my time there."

"One does not speak so bitterly of dreams. The Badh will want to know more."

"Need you tell her? I returned well and unharmed. Let it rest there."

With a smile of compassion like one which might pass from an older brother to a younger one, Fianne said, "Do not worry yourself."

Long after Fianne left, Gerard sat sipping wine, thinking about all that had happened to him since his arrival in Ribble Galaxy and wondering if the random events of the universe had finally given him an edge in the odds. Perhaps now he could play a useful part in healing the wounds between the Federation and Ribble. Maybe this new situation would give him the advantage he needed to begin pressing for reconciliation. Fara knew that there was much bitterness and hatred on both sides that would probably never be overcome. But now, for the first time, he began to see that there was a path he could follow, an inside lane that just might lead to a resumption of normal relations between two old enemies. That thought cleared a quiet place in his mind where he fell asleep surrounded by the soft, warm fog of nut wine.

Gerard was called to wait upon Princess Peg the next day but never saw her. After hours of sitting in the antechamber with Fianne, they were finally dismissed and told that they would be called later. At Fianne's suggestion, they spent the rest of the day in the archives, where Fianne proudly gave Gerard a tour of the most extensive non-computerized library he had ever seen. Each scroll, and book, and microcard that Fianne brough forth for his examination only made Gerard want to see more. When Fianne finally suggested that they should have a late supper in the archives, Gerard was quite surprised that they had been there so long. He was even more surprised when he woke up in the archives the next morning to the sound of Fianne's cheerful singing.

"For someone your age, you have a terribly creaky voice," Gerard offered by way of greeting.

"We sang better last night, Diplomat."

"We sang?" Gerard only dimly remembered that. After dinner they had drunk much wine.

"We traded songs, and you, Diplomat, cheated me by falling asleep in the middle of your last song."

"My apologies, Fianne Tackona," Gerard said with a small bow that hurt his head. "The wine was more potent than I realized."

Fianne laughed. "Can you find your way to your apartments? The Badh has requested our presence in two hours."

"I can find my way."

"Good. I shall come for you shortly before we are due in her presence." He held a small packet out to Gerard. "Take this with a great quantity of water. It will soothe and clear your head."

Gerard went to his chambers, took the salty brown powder from the packet as he had been told, then spent almost an hour soaking in a huge tub of hot water. When Fianne arrived to take him to the Badh, Gerard felt much better.

Princess Peg was waiting for them in a small pavilion which sat in the middle of a large, formal garden laid out like a simple maze. Gerard noted at least twenty different kinds of flowers in bloom in a variety of colors. It was a place which showed immaculate care and attention. So did Princess Peg, who seemed dressed for some formal occasion in a low-cut gown of exquisitely embroidered cloth. "Princess," he said with the knee-down bow and head-jerk, "this wonderful garden pales before your beauty."

Fianne let out a little gasp of shock that told Gerard he had probably overstepped the bounds of propriety, but Princess Peg only laughed.

"Do you court favors with your flattery, Star Pilot?"

"The favor had been granted," he said with lowered eyes. Why was he edging toward flirtation? He certainly hadn't intended to. Still, it seemed to amuse Princess Peg, so perhaps there was no harm in it if he didn't press too far.

"No wonder you are a diplomat, Gerard Manley. You have a smooth tongue."

"Now it is the Badh who flatters," he said, glancing at her briefly and then back down again. "You are too kind."

"You may replay my kindness by walking with me."

Gerard stole a quick look at Fianne, who flapped his elbow in response. Taking that as a signal, Gerard offered Princess Peg his arm. She took it lightly, and they walked slowly down the steps of the pavilion and onto the first path they came to. Gerard was surprised when neither Fianne nor the Gabriel Ratchets who had been standing silently in the corners of the pavilion accompanied them. He looked back twice, almost as though he were wishing they would follow.

"What seek you, Star Pilot?"

"Nothing, Princess. I am merely surprised that we walk alone."

"You are nervous, also." Her eyes sparked with amusement as she looked straight into his, and for the first time he realized they were almost exactly the same height.

"It shames me, Princess, but indeed I am nervous."

"Why, Star Pilot?" Her eyes searched his with open curiosity. "Do I make you nervous?"

"The Badh toys with me," he said formally.

"Rebuke accepted," she laughed.

They strolled rather aimlessly, Princess Peg telling him about the various flowers and plants, and allowing him to pause momentarily to examine an occasional flower more closely. Only when they stopped at a small bower that shaded an ornately carved stone bench did they talk about anything more serious than the garden.

"It has been told to me that your stay on Hinson Keep was darkened by unpleasantness. This is true?"

Gerard stood before her and shifted his weight uncomfortably from foot to foot. She had not offered him the seat beside her, and he would have declined if she had. He wished Fianne had accompanied them. "It is true, Princess, but it was nothing of consequence."

"Torture is always of consequence," she said with a hard edge in her voice. "What was done to you?"

He didn't want to talk about it and hoped to put her questions off with his answer. "It is difficult to say, Princess. I was delirious much of the time. The memories are unclear."

"So." Her tone indicated an understanding, or a deduction of logic, as though he had given her some final clue. "Is that all you will say?"

"Pardon, Badh, it is all I can say."

"It is enough. Shall we continue our walk?"

They finished their tour of the gardens in silence. Princess Peg seemed distracted by her thoughts and offered no further commentary on the flowers. Gerard was reluctant to intrude on her privacy. When at last they returned to the pavilion, she bade him goodbye in an offhanded way.

As he returned to his chambers with Fianne, Gerard, too was distracted by his thoughts. Fianne recognized that and soon left him alone to wonder why Princess Peg had such an annoying effect on him. Whatever the reason, he knew he would have to overcome it and learn to be comfortable in her presence if he were to successfully complete his mission for Fed. She was the key to bringing about negotiations, and he could not let the fact that he found her personally distracting interfere with what he had to do.

The following day he was summoned again to the garden

for another walk, and again Princess Peg asked him about what had happened on Hinson Keep. He avoided the answer as he had before, and soon the conversation turned in other directions.

Slowly his days evolved into a pattern of morning walks with Princess Peg and afternoons in the archieves with Fianne Tackona. Despite her usual appearance of good health, Princess Peg sometimes exhibited signs of momentary weakness, residual effects of the disease she had contracted on Leewh. When those moments came she would often lean heavily against Gerard until her dizziness passed. No matter how many times it happened, Gerard always felt awkward and uncomfortable standing with his arm around her. He felt embarrassed for her, and protective of her, and annoyed with himself because of his discomfort in her presence.

One morning, as they walked along the Koep wall shortly after dawn, he felt her tremble and automatically drew her close to steady her. When her spell passed, she pulled slightly away, but held firmly onto his arm.

"My sickness is like the sickness in Ribble Galaxy," she said softly.

Gerard had to strain to hear her. Perhaps she was whispering because they were always accompanied by a Ratchet when they walked the Koep wall. The Ratchet was close enough for his shadow to mingle with theirs, and perhaps she did not want him to hear.

"None seem to know the true cure for the illness," she continued in her hushed voice, "and it lingers to sap our strength."

"Time and peace cure many things," he offered lamely.

Behind them the Ratchet cleared his throat. Gerard cast a glance over his shoulder and saw Targ Alpluakka striding toward them with an angry look on his face. Turning Princess Peg to receive Targ's bow he said, "Good morning, Commander." Targ ignored him.

"A thousand pardons, Badh. I request audience."

Princess Peg nodded. "It is yours, Commander."

Targ shot a look at Gerard that almost made him wince. "Now my pardon, Badh," Gerard said, releasing himself gently from her grip on his arm. With a simple bow he turned and walked quickly to the other side of the wall and out of hearing distance. When he looked back he saw that Targ was watching him, so he deliberately turned away again and tried to admire the grounds of EllKoep. When he heard Targ arguing loudly, he moved farther down the wall away from them. He had heard Targ say "that diplomat," and he wanted to hear no more. After what seemed like an interminable wait, a Ratchet came quietly up behind him and said, "The Badh requests your presence."

Targ was gone. Princess Peg sat on a small bench beside the wall, looking pale and drawn. He stopped a full meter in front of her, then on impulse did the knee-down, head-jerking bow.

"Unnecessary, Star Pilot. I would request something of you."

"I am yours to command." Gerard responded with a strong note of sincerity. He felt at that moment that he would do whatever she asked of him.

"No, this is no command. Take me inside, Star Pilot."

Without further conversation they left the Koep wall, and, holding Gerard's arm, Princess Peg directed him to a wing of EllKoep he had never entered before. Finally they came to a small, cozy room where Princess Peg seated herself heavily in one of the large, overstuffed chairs. The room looked well-used and had a comfortable kind of clutter about it. Before Gerard could take it all in, Princess Peg motioned him to sit in the chair across from her.

"My retreat," she said with a limp gesture. "Here and only here can I truly be alone. Pour us some wine, Star Pilot."

As he poured the wine, Gerard wondered what this was all about. Why had she brought him to this private room? Did her actions have anything to do with Targ's angry outburst? Fighting the urge to ask questions, he decided to let Princess Peg proceed at her own pace.

"I told you I have a request, but before you give an answer you must listen to all I say. There is much about us you do not know, and much about you that remains a mystery to us. Kril is rife with factions, each seeking power and influence in its own way. The Noble Assembly does its best to drain power from Corpus Privy and the throne. Corpus Privy does its best to check the throne and the Noble Assembly. The responsibililty for making it all work is mine. Understand you that?

"Of course you do," she said without waiting for his answer. "That is why I have chosen to ask you to do something that you need not do if you cannot, or will not. You are in a unique position, Star Pilot, an outsider looking in, with a light in your hand that may offer us a clearer view of the future.

"There is talk of rebellion on Evird. You have heard that? Rebellion! The mind twists at the thought. If this precious galaxy is to sustain itself and achieve its proper place in the universe, it cannot suffer from internal divisions. It must remain united. It must."

Had she brought him here for a lesson in politics? Gerard couldn't believe that.

"Look not so impatient with me, Star Pilot. With good counsel I believe you can help my galaxy, and, in doing so, help your beloved Federation as well. However, there is a test which must take place before we can explore those possibilities. It is a personal test, one that you need not assent to, but one which could do much to clear the way for you."

Gerard started to speak, to say that he would gladly submit to any test, but she raised a hand to silence him.

"Hear me out. One cannot fail the test I propose." She hesitated, then continued, "One can only reveal the truth, and the truth will determine the course for the future. Consent to this test, and you willingly reveal the true answer to any question put before you. Decline, and it will be understood and not be held against you.

"Serious this is, Star Pilot, more serious than you can guess or imagine, so serious that Commander Alpluakka threatened to resign if you submit to it." She smiled lightly. "He will not resign. He enjoys his power too much. But doubt you not that in the heat of his anger his threat was serious, as serious as the test itself. Think carefully. You need not respond now, but you must respond soon."

Despite wanting to say yes immediately, Gerard held himself in check. "Pardon, Princess, but may I enquire the nature of this test?"

"I have told you. It is a test of truth."

She seemed perfectly content to say no more, but the corners of her mouth flickered nervously. Gerard suspected she was holding something back, but wondered if there was anything he was unwilling for her to know. There were many things, of course, but they were from his past. There was nothing pertaining to the here and now that he felt should remain hidden from her knowledge. But who else would know? "And who will be present at this test?"

"Myself and one other. What comes of it will be known only to us."

Should he trust her? He already did. The long walks and conversations in the garden and high on the Koep wall had led him to trust her without openly acknowledging it to himself. So this was a test of his trust as much as anything else. "Then, with your assistance, I will submit to your test of truth."

Her smile seemed to brighten the room, but she slumped deeper in her chair as though some tension had been released in her. "That is half the test already," she said softly. "Leave me now, Star Pilot, for I must rest. Go to your ship and prepare it for a journey."

"My ship, Princess?" Gerard couldn't believe that they would be going on *Windhover*.

"Yes, Star Pilot. I must trust you as you trust me. Go now. Flight information will be sent to you."

Had she read his mind, Gerard wondered, as he tried to find his way back to his quarters? For her to go anywhere with him aboard *Windhover* was not only a sign of trust, but also of something else, something deeper than trust, something he couldn't name or put a label on. Whatever it was, it stirred an emotional reaction in him just as elusive of name and label. Somewhere along the line he had lost part of his objectivity about Princess Peg, and he would have to get it back prior to her test . . . if he could.

Fianne and Targ were both waiting for him in his quarters. Before he could greet either of them, Fianne said, "You must decline the test."

Targ stared at Gerard with a lazy sneer. "Too late it is, friend Fianne. He has already agreed."

Gerard felt immediately angry and defensive. "Yes, I agreed. Was I to say *no* to the Badh?"

"Yes. Yes," they both answered almost simultaneously.

"It is a mistake, Diplomat, a—"

"A stupid mistake. Worse yet—"

"Let me speak, friend Targ." With a node to Fianne, Targ turned his back on them. "Listen, Diplomat. You have no idea what this test will do to you. It has broken strong and forceful men, good men who knew what to expect. You must tell the Badh you have changed your mind."

"Why?" Gerard interrupted. "Why all of a sudden are you two so worried about my well-being? The Badh told me about the test and I agreed to take it. I—"

"Fool," Targ spat at him as he spun around with a flushed, angry glare. "Be you now aware of what Fianne said? The test *breaks* men."

Gerard stared back at him uncomprehendingly.

"Agchk! It is no use. Talk to him, Fianne." With that Targ left the apartment, slamming the door behind him.

Fianne looked at Gerard with keen eyes. "Determined you are to do this thing?"

"The Badh asked and I have answered," Gerard said firmly.

"Then be careful and beware, for the Truthsayer of Filif-cy-Nere wields strange and horrible magic. I will pray for you."

As Fianne headed for the door, Gerard asked, "Is that all you have to say to me?"

"There is nothing more to be said. Farewell, friend."

After Fianne left, Gerard gathered what few of his personal belongings he thought he would need and quickly left EllKoep. As a rented skimmer carried him out to the starport, he tried to push the scene in his quarters from his mind. He couldn't quite get rid of it, but he did find it a quiet corner where it was out of his way.

"Hi, Windy," he said as he stepped through the port. Her return greeting was a series of buzzes and flashing lights. If a ship could be glad to see its pilot, Windy was. She had a backlog of stored messages for him to deal with and more than a brief list of chores for him to accomplish. In short order she had him hard at work, and three days later, when Princess Peg boarded accompanied by Omna-Seay, four Gabriel Ratchets, and two personal attendants, Windy still was not totally satisfied that Gerard had accomplished all the tasks she had set out for him. But when she protested too much he shut off her buzzers and lights and told her to prepare to launch. She did.

*   *   *

Message to: Pelis Foffey Turingay-Gotz
            FedTreatySvc

All plans must be suspended for the moment. The current situation could work in our favor, or much against us. Regardless of the outcome, Key-One's position will have to be reevaluated. Trouble on Evird could also cause delays, but there, too, we must bide our time.

As for your demands, they are one step short of insanity. Here we kill people who ask for such things. When the time comes, we will assume command as planned. Foolish requests from you and your superiors will not advance the appointed day.

Beware.

—Toehold

*   *   *

5

The journey to Filif-cy-Nere was accomplished in nine short days and two easy warps. Gerard was tired when they finally landed, because he had given up his cabin to Princess Peg and slept in the pilot's couch. But, surprisingly, he and everyone except the Ratchets arrived in a good mood. The Ratchets did not seem to allow themselves noticeable moods of any kind.

Geowyatt Starport was an unimpressive sight at best. Gerard had never seen so many space junkers sitting on the ground in one place before. What startled him was that many of them were in active berths and apparently still capable of flying. Geowyatt itself was a city of contrasts. As the giant skimmer carried them on a twisting path through the crowded streets, Gerard saw squalor and luxury side by side along almost every kilometer of the trip. He wanted to ask dozens of questions, but Omna-Seay had been given the task of pointing out the sights and was doing so with relish, so Gerard let his questions go. They were not important anyway.

After what seemed like an endless ride, they finally left the sprawling city and entered a country of rough, terraced hills cultivated as far as the eye could see. They picked up speed there, and for an hour Gerard contented himself with watching the scenery. The hills slowly changed to rocky ridges, and the ridges to low mountains before they finally slowed to a halt in front of a low stone building at the foot of a cliff.

They entered the building at the invitation of a wizened old man who sat by its entrance. Inside, they were greeted by a little girl who curtsied several times to Princess Peg before saying a word. "Two thousand pardons, mighty one. Mistress mine begs you forgiveness for no meet you. Old she claims. Pardon, mighty one. Follow you will?"

Telling everyone else to remain, Princess Peg took Gerard's arm, and together they followed the girl through a door and down a long, sloping hallway.

"A cave," Gerard said, his voice echoing hollowly.

"Marradon's home," Princess Peg whispered. "Be quiet."

The hallway—it was more hallway than tunnel—turned, sloped more steeply past a series of dark, wooden doors, and turned again to open into a small, richly furnished room, lit indirectly, as the hallway had been. The girl motioned them to be seated, curtsied several times, and left through a narrow side door.

"It has not changed," Princess Peg said suddenly. "It has not changed at all."

Gerard sat quietly in a padded quiltwork chair and watched Princess Peg move slowly around the room, touching pieces of furniture, stroking tapestries on the wall. Physically he felt tired and relaxed, and her reminiscent motions soothed him. Emotionally he felt blank. He didn't know why there was no trepidation, or concern, or anxiety about his impending test, but there wasn't. He felt so blank that he didn't even worry about that, so blank that he started getting drowsy in the chair and had to shake his head to stay awake.

"Welcome, my children." The voice behind him creaked

in a rhythmic way, almost as though the sounds were practiced. He rose and turned to see Princess Peg on one knee before an old woman in a black hooded robe. Unsure of what to do, he remained motionless.

"Rise, Sister. You have no cause to kneel here."

Marradon, he thought, trying to return her open appraisal of him with an equally open look.

"This young man must be your diplomat. Welcome to my home, Gerard Manley. I am honored by your presence."

"It is I who am honored, Truthsayer." Gerard bowed deeply.

"You must call me Marradon," she said. "Titles are not used here. Shall we have refreshment first? Or," she asked, staring straight into the center of Gerard's eyes, "are you impatient to be tested?"

Whether he had been hiding his impatience, or whether Marradon had triggered it, Gerard didn't know. But her suggestion that the test could take place immediately appealed to him greatly. "The test first," he said with an assurance that surprised him.

Princess Peg gave him a strange look, then smiled approvingly. "Is he not a wonder?"

"We shall see, Sister. We shall see." Marradon led the way through a door hidden behind one of the tapestries, then down a short flight of curving steps into a huge natural cavern. From the size of the stalagmites and stalactites, many of which had met ages ago to form stout columns, Gerard guessed that the cavern could easily be several hundred thousand years old. It was damp, but not unpleasantly so, and the air carried the faint, fresh scent of flowers and grass. At the center of the cavern was a round table large enough to accommodate fifteen or twenty people. Here too the lighting was indirect, and, as he seated himself after Marradon and Princess Peg, Gerard wondered how it was accomplished.

From the folds of her robe Marradon brought forth a small silver-and-crystal bell, which tinkled as she set it on the table between him and Princess Peg. The bell immediately fascinated him. Its sound was like an iris which narrowed the range of his senses and drew his attention fully to the bell.

Princess Peg lifted it and rang it twice. Gerard's focus shifted from the bell to the brown liquid depths of her eyes and remained there as though commanded by some outside force. He wanted to look at the bell again, but he couldn't.

"This is the test," Princess Peg said quietly. "Will you answer my questions truthfully?"

"Yes," he replied without hesitation.

"What is your name?"

The question didn't even seem silly. "Gerard Hopkins Manley."

"Where were you born?"

"Highgate School, Posiman Township, Southern Sector, Barcley, on the planet Maytar in the Dangure System." Was that complete enough, he wondered?

Princess Peg continued with a series of mundane questions, his parents' names, the schools he attended, the names of his professors and instructors, then questions about the Federation and his mission to Ribble Galaxy. The answers spilled out of him effortlessly. He was surprised by how much he remembered and how much he told.

"Tell us how you flew through the Concepcycline Cloud."

"Prescience," he answered simply.

"Start from the moment you entered the control center of *Shivelight,* and tell the whole story. Leave out nothing."

With a speed and clarity Gerard would have thought impossible, he told the story. The only time he hesitated was when he mentioned checking Princess Peg's pulse and letting his hand rest on her neck longer than was necessary. He heard himself stammer as he said that, and felt a strange quickening of his pulse. He knew what it meant, but he refused to admit it to himself, and as gracefully as he could picked up the thread of his story again and hurried through it. As he told them finally about exiting the cloud, he felt the same rush of energy as he had then.

His eyes had never left Princess Peg's the whole time, but it was not like looking into eyes at all. It was like that view of normal space, clear, and bright, and full of stars. He was eager to answer another question.

The bell tinkled again. "Do you love me, Gerard Manley?"

Yes! Yes! A voice inside him shouted in joy. Was it true? Did he love her? "Yes," he said aloud after what seemed like a timeless hesitation. He wanted to say much more, to tell her that he hadn't meant to fall in love with her, that he intended no disrespect by it, that he was unworthy of even saying the words. But all he could do was repeat himself. "Yes, I love you."

The bell tinkled rapidly, and Gerard suddenly felt like he was sliding down a sharp, slick incline into blackness. He felt no fear, and when something, or someone, caught him and stopped his slide, he felt no surprise. He felt nothing but total exhaustion.

"He is without guile," Marradon's voice croaked from a distance. "When he recovers, you must return his trust."

Gerard listened carefully. They obviously weren't aware that he was awake.

"But if he asks—oh, Sister, help me." Princess Peg sounded closer to him.

"The rules must be obeyed. He awakens now. Explain what must be done."

Gerard opened his eyes when he felt Princess Peg sit beside him on the low couch where he was lying. "Hello, Princess," he said weakly.

"Brave you are, Star Pilot, and honest. The Truth Bell tested you well."

"And wore me out."

"It has killed lesser men."

Gerard laughed gently. He felt lightheaded and giddy.

"The bell does not kill. Lies kill," Marradon said as she sat on the other side of him. "Tell him the rules, my daughter."

Princess Peg took his right hand in both of hers and squeezed it gently as she looked at him with an expression he had never seen on her before. When she spoke, her voice was quiet and steady. "The rules state that you must be allowed to question me with the Truth Bell. You have passed the test. Now, so must I."

It didn't make sense. What was he supposed to ask her? "I don't know what, I mean, why? What would I ask?"

"Anything you wish."

Marradon took his other hand and her dry fingers checked his pulse. "First you must eat."

They helped him to a small table, and he realized they were in a new room. Marradon left, and returned moments later trailed by a different young girl, who carried a tray of assorted foods. Gerard was suddenly ravenous, and had to force himself to eat and drink slowly. They talked little, and only about the food. When they finished eating, and the girl had taken away the tray, Marradon asked him how he felt.

"Better. Much better. I'm ready to proceed by the rules."

Princess Peg looked at him sharply, and Gerard thought he saw a flash of fear in her eyes, but it disappeared as quickly as it had come. "Perhaps you should rest more," she offered.

"No. He has chosen. There can be no delay." The sternness in Marradon's voice was tempered with a hint of amusement. She led them silently back to the table in the cavern. As she withdrew the bell from her robe this second time, Gerard noticed on her right hand a heavy ring inlaid with a small burnished sunburst, the royal family seal. She set the bell between them and told Gerard to ring it twice while looking directly at Princess Peg, and then to ask any questions he wanted answers to.

The bell was cold under his hands, but somehow, it was also vibrant with life. He stared into Princess Peg's eyes and rang the bell twice. "Why did you bring me here?" he asked.

"To test your honesty."

Gerard saw a small glow appear in her eyes, like a dull light behind the pupils. Then it faded. "Was that the only reason you brought me here?"

"No."

Again the light glowed and faded. So, that's how I know if she's telling the truth, he thought. "What were the other reasons?"

Her face twitched before she answered. "I wanted to know if you were prescient in the cloud." True. "I wanted to know if your mission from the Federation was honorable." True. There seemed to be more, but she hesitated.

"Is there another reason?"

"Yes." The glow in her eyes flashed brightly.

"What was it?"

"I, I," her voice faltered, "I wanted to know if you had fallen in love with me."

Gerard hesitated, afraid to ask the next question. He glanced at Marradon, and she nodded approvingly, a smile

55

making the lines around her mouth dance. Suddenly the question came easily. "Do you love me?"

"Yes, Gerard Manley, I love you." Her voice was sure, and the glow in her eyes remained after she finished speaking.

Gerard didn't know what else to ask. It was as though he had asked the most important question in the whole universe and gotten the most perfect answer. Only then did he see the problem. He looked again at Marradon, but she offered him no assistance. As he searched for the right phrasing for the next question, everything he thought of sounded crude and indelicate. He loved this woman, had loved her for Fara only knew how long, and she loved him. But where did that leave them? "Will we, can we ever consummate our love?"

"Yes, there is a way, if you wish it."

"Do *you* wish it?"

"Yes." The sustained glow in her eyes was accompanied by enthusiasm in her voice.

It was enough. There was no need to ask her anything further. Remembering what had happened when she questioned him, he tinkled the bell rapidly and was not surprised when she slumped heavily onto the table.

"She will recover, as you did," Marradon said with a chuckle and a shake of her head. "Can you carry her?" He nodded. "Then let us take her to a place more comfortable."

As Gerard lifted Princess Peg, Marradon tucked the Truth Bell soundlessly into her robe. With some effort he carried Princess Peg back to the room where they had eaten. Her limp form was heavy, and by the time he laid her gently on the couch he was almost staggering. "So much for love lightening one's burdens," he said with a small gasp.

Marradon laughed. "Love is itself a burden, Gerard Manley. Pray that you learn to carry it easily."

"You pray, too," he said as he collapsed in a chair beside the couch. "I suspect we will need all the prayers we can muster."

"Do you *see* trouble?" she asked seriously.

He knew she meant the prescience. "No, Marradon, I see nothing in the future. The only time I've ever had that talent was when we were in the Concepcycline Cloud. I may never have it again."

"I suspect you will," Marradon said quietly as she placed a light blanket over Princess Peg.

Gerard wanted to change the subject. "By what magic does the Truth Bell work?" he asked.

"No magic. It was designed by an ancient neurophysicist, who carried the secret of its design with him over the chasm of death."

"Are there others like it?"

"None that are known. There were once many, but they were destroyed because they were seen as great weapons. Those sisters who went before me barely managed to save this bell, and for centuries kept it hidden it total secrecy, using it only under the strictest conditions at times of direst need. Even today there are those who would destroy it if they could."

Gerard thought of Targ and Fianne. Then he remembered Princess Peg saying the bell had killed lesser men. If a man died while being questioned, then the rule of reciprocal questioning could not be applied. A sudden chill passed through him, followed by a quick prayer of thanks to Fara. He had been lucky.

A small whimper from Princess Peg brought Gerard quickly to her side. He felt closer to her than he ever had to anyone else in his life, including his father. Yet he realized they were total strangers. He took her hand and gently kissed the tip of each of her fingers. When he reached her thumb, her eyes opened. "Hello, Princess."

She smiled at him lazily. "You have said that before."

"True. How do you feel?"

"Weak. Hungry. Displaced."

"I felt that way once myself." He turned to ask Marradon for food and saw that she had personally brought in a tray and was setting it on the table. After helping Princess Peg to her chair, Gerard was surprised when Marradon said, "There are sleeping quarters through that door to your left, and beyond them a small cleansing room. Peace be upon you both."

Before either Gerard or Princess Peg could recover enough to respond, Marradon left. Gerard looked at Princess Peg and suddenly felt awkward and shy. "Will you eat, Princess?"

"Will you join me, Pilot?" Her low voice suggested more than food.

They ate in intimate silence, toying with each other's free hand, caressing each other with their eyes. When they finished, Princess Peg emptied the contents of the small flagon of wine into their glasses. Handing him a glass, she said, "Come, Pilot," and led the way through the door Marradon had indicated.

The sleeping chamber was plain and small, dominated by a large, low bed. At the foot of the bed their space duffles rested side by side. Seeing them, Princess Peg laughed. "Ah, Marradon, you are indeed a witch."

Taking Gerard's glass, she set them both on the bedside table, then turned to face him. Instinctively, he reached for her, and she came softly and willingly into his arms, nestling her head into his neck. For a long moment they stood there, holding each other in unfamiliar closeness. "Shall we bathe first?" she asked quietly.

"Together?" Gerard was surprised by his suggestion.

"Mmmm. Yes, I would like that." There was a sultry hint of excitement in her voice.

The cleansing room contained a dark, polished stone tub that would barely accommodate the two of them. By the time Gerard entered the room Princess Peg had dimmed the lights and was sitting in the half full tub. The outline of her upper torso played shadowy tricks on the rippling water. He joined her tentatively, acutely aware of her limbs against his as they fitted themselves into the small space. Finally they adjusted themselves face to face, arms around each other's necks, his aroused genitals brushing lightly against her in the soft water. Slowly and gently they pulled themselves together, squeezing the water from between them until their flesh seemed bonded together. Only then did they kiss, awkwardly seeking the proper position of heads and noses.

The growing passion of their kisses was heavily counterpointed by cramped legs, and knees wedged hard against the sides of the tub. "This won't work," Gerard said finally.

With a sloshing effort he stood in the tub, then helped her to her feet. They scrubbed each other standing up, shyly and incompletely. Then they rinsed each other the same way, interrupting their clumsy bath with long, searching kisses.

Gerard felt chills inside and out. Stepping from the tub, he reached for the one towel he saw and handed it to

Princess Peg. She followed him out, dried herself quickly, then wrapped the towel around him and rubbed it slowly down his body. The coarse cloth stimulated every nerve ending into twitching sensitivity. When she reached his legs he could stand it no more and quickly bent over and pulled her up into his arms, kissing her with a hunger and desire that rumbled inside him like the beginnings of an avalanche.

He wanted it to last. He wanted to feel her pressing against him like this forever. Slowing the mad run of his hands over her soft flesh, he gently broke away. A large shadow of doubt passed through his mind. Was this really proper for him? For them? And what would it mean later?

"Pilot," she said softly, "I love you."

"And I love you. But I don't know why. And I don't understand it. I feel so unworthy of you, so—"

She silenced his protest with a lingering kiss. "Take me to bed, Pilot."

Their love-making was slow and awkward, tender and clumsy. His first orgasm came long before hers, and hers came long before his second one. They had no rhythm, found no concerted melody of flesh. Their bodies promised that would come later.

"Pilot," she said as they tight in each others arms, "I am happy. You pleasure me greatly."

"Hmmmm," Gerard sighed with contentment, "I've never been in love before, not like this. The closest I ever came was in a dream given me once by a friend."

"A dream?"

"Yes, a very real dream, about a princess, as a matter of fact. She wanted to prove to me that dreams can come from outside as well as inside. She did."

"Did you love her?"

Gerard laughed softly. "No, Princess. Not the way you mean. She was a Drai, a fellow student at DiploSchool. I'm not even sure she was actually a *female*."

"I am jealous."

"Don't be, Princess . . . Princess sounds so formal a name for the woman who's trying to arouse me again."

"Shall I tell you my secret name?" she asked as she rubbed herself against his thigh. "When I was young and innocent, I fell in love with a cousin. He called me *Fairy* Peg because he said he enchanted him."

"Then I shall call you Fairy Peg, for you certainly have enchanted me."

"Only in private," she cautioned, "only when we are alone." She raised one leg high over his body and opened her loins to engulf his thigh. "Please, Gerard?"

He didn't need coaxing. He moved against her and slid deeply into her arms and body. Again there was no magic, no simultaneous waves of ecstasy catapulting them into the heart of the cosmos. But they were linked in a way that transcended their bodies. For one peak moment Gerard felt as though he had made direct contact with Fairy Peg's mind. Then the contact faded and spread until he was enveloped in the warm presence of her that caressed him inside and out. Sleep came gently as the waves of sensation soaked through the sands of his body.

When he awoke, Gerard was first aware of Fairy Peg curled up against him with her back pressed against his side. Then he noticed the room seemed definitely brighter than it had before they went to sleep. He had no idea what time it was, or even what day. How long had they been there? It didn't matter to him. As far as he was concerned, they could stay forever.

At Marradon's insistence they stayed one more day, a day Gerard found remarkably comfortable and relaxing as he shared conversation with Marradon and Fairy Peg, "Princess" in Marradon's presence. Gerard asked occasional questions about the caverns, how the lighting worked, and other inconsequential things, but mostly he listened to the women reminiscing about the two years between twelve and fourteen Fairy Peg had lived with Marradon.

As the day moved leisurely on, the contrast between the two women became less and less noticeable. It did not matter that one was old and withered and the other in the full flush of womanhood. They thought alike, often completed sentences for each other, and even phrased things the same way. yet Gerard was constantly aware that Fairy Peg held Marradon in a position of respect. It was a fascinating relationship, one that went beyond teacher-student, or mother-daughter, or sister-sister. It was a complex of all those things, but greater than all of them put together. When Marradon announced it was time to sleep, Gerard was sorry he would see no more of it.

Fairy Peg excused herself as soon as Marradon made her announcement, and Gerard rose to follow her.

"Stay a moment, Gerard," Marradon said. It was a command as much as a request, and Gerard sat back down without thinking.

"It may never pass for us to meet again, Gerard Hopkins Manley, and there is that I would share with you."

He glanced away from her for an instant toward the door to the sleeping chamber.

Marradon laughed. "Fret not. I will not keep you long. In exchange for that favor, I require your total attention."

The creaks in her voice had grown less noticeable. Just now? Or have I gotten used to hearing her, Gerard wondered. Looking at her intently, he suddenly saw a woman much older, worn by time and trouble until she was barely more than an animated corpse with living eyes. He shuddered. As he did so, she seemed to become more vibrant again.

"You saw me as I will be," Marradon said steadily. "It is your talent. Even raw and untrained, it is a great gift that you must nurture if you can." Marradon sighed heavily.

"I am an old, old woman. The fires of love and lust which raged through me for almost a century are now no more than scorch marks on the walls of my heart. Even the dry ashes have long since blown away. But I do not envy you and my dear cousin. You will struggle fiercely to sustain your love, but in time it will bring you a pain that tears at the fabric of your soul. I do not see these things, I *know* them. You will know them too, and because of your talent, you may know them before they happen.

"You will become what the past dictates, no more or less."

Gerard wanted to argue with her. The last thing he believed in was a future determined by his past. He wanted to tell her she was wrong, that the future held infinite possibilities, but he knew it would be pointless. Her philosophy had long since hardened into rigid categories, and he would be infinitely wrong to try to break those categories open. She deserved far more respect than that, so he bit his tongue and listened.

"I sense some disagreement in you. That is good. You would be stupid to accept an old woman's words without an argument. But believe me, Gerard Manley, the day will come when you remember my words and wonder at the truth in them.

"Ah, but my prattling keeps you from where you would most want to be in the whole universe. Listen, then, to one more caution duty demands I give you, and I will let you go.

"Your talent has great potential to help or hurt. A time will come for you, when in choosing to help, you will know that you also choose to hurt. Weigh that time carefully and with great compassion, but once you choose your course, do not look back, or the past will haunt you forever.

"Go now. I am tired. The desire written on your face is a sad thing for an old woman to look upon. Go."

Gerard thanked her guiltily and backed out of the room with a low bow. His desire to join Fairy Peg had been subdued by Marradon's words, and for some illogical reason he didn't want to break the mood she had created in him. The sight of Fairy Peg waiting for him in the bed changed all that.

"Mmmmm," Fairy Peg said softly, "I thought she might keep you all night."

"So did I," Gerard said as he hurriedly undressed and climbed into the bed with her.

She was naked and came to him immediately. The fire in their loins preempted any gentle foreplay and they moved together in a furious slapping of flesh against flesh in cadence with the drumming lust in their blood. It was over quickly, and, burned clean by the fire, they slept.

Only twice on the return flight to Kril did Gerard have a chance to speak to Fairy Peg alone. The first time he asked her to come to the flight deck. When she did, he gave her his Manley signet ring.

She thanked him with a kiss. "I cannot wear this, Pilot, but I shall treasure it always." Then, with a strange look in her eyes, she left him.

The second time was in the galley. "Princess," he said quietly, fearing they might be overheard, "what role can I play in service to the throne?"

"You shall be consort," she whispered.

"Impossible! No one would stand for it. Corpus Privy and the Noble Assembly would tear—" He cut himself off as Omna-Seay joined them in the galley. The look on

Omna-Seay's face said he had heard at least part of Gerard's outburst. "A thousand pardons, Princess," Gerard said as contritely as he could. "You are worthy of higher counsel." With a bow to Fairy Peg and a courteous nod to Omna-Seay, he returned immediately to the flight deck.

Except for quick trips to get food and use the head, he spent the rest of the trip locked on the flight deck wondering what new twists the future had in store for him.

*　　*　　*

Message to: Greaves Lingchow
         FedDiploSvc

Be cautioned. Your impatience will ruin our enterprise. You and your superiors must learn to control it. The Badh moves in her own way and in her own time. Ribble Galaxy moves with her, not with you.

As to the eventual effectiveness of your diplomat, we can only speculate. His status at the moment is uncertain. It could quickly shift in either direction, and only time will tell us which why he will move in the spheres of influence. If you cannot be patient, find yourself a replacement who can be.

—Glyph

*　　*　　*

6

Standing next to Fairy Peg in the chamber where Corpus Privy had accused him and sent him to detention, Gerard felt like an alien in a world where the atmosphere was too thin. He was acutely aware of the Corpus members staring at him, and of Fairy Peg by his side, a powerful stranger whom he had made love to on a distant world. No, a powerful stranger whom he loved . . . and made love with.

"As is our custom, by our right as Badh, we come for declaration," Fairy Peg was saying, "of personal union."

The simultaneous sucking of breath by the Corpus members, as though they really were one body, focused Gerard's attention on Fairy Peg's words.

"Let it be known to Corpus Privy that Gerard Hopkins Manley, Universal Contract Diplomat, shall from day's end be known as Prince Consort to the throne of Ribble Galaxy."

Squo Lyle sputtered uncontrollably. Ducas Echi and Cessaid both sounded as though they were growling. Gerard had begged Fairy Peg not to do this thing, but her answer had remained constant. "Honor will be served, Pilot." Seeing the reaction of the Corpus, hearing their anger, he knew her decision had been wrong.

Sudden feminine laughter from the side of the chamber made him turn his head. Fairy Peg's sister, Inez Nare-Devy, was laughing in mysterious delight, oblivious to the stares of anger now directed at her. Her eyes looked directly at Gerard every time she opened them in her rocking indulgence.

Fairy Peg touched Gerard's elbow, but he was so confused and puzzled by Inez's outburst that she had to squeeze it to get his attention. Abruptly he went down on one knee beside her. Just as abruptly, Inez stopped laughing. Fairy Peg placed her hand lightly on Gerard's shoulder and gave him a brief smile before continuing her speech. He realized then that Inez's laughter had not been spontaneous.

"So I stand before councillors and *friends*, consort by my side," she said in her most royal tones. "Those who would deny my rights may speak."

Gerard glanced quickly around the table. The ducas were whispering among themselves, but no one seemed prepared to speak until Duca Kye rose slowly to her feet.

"Gracious Badh, you have stunned this Corpus," she said with a stern face that was contradicted by the twinkle in her eyes, "but I, for one, am delighted. We wronged your consort once. Now you have made it right more than we ever could. Blessings, Badh."

"And blessings again," said a surprising voice from the other end of the table. It was Duca Echi. "We who are your Corpus can do no more than bless and accept. When shall the consort join the Gabriel Ratchets?"

What? Gerard couldn't believe the question. Fairy Peg

had said nothing to him about joining the Gabriel Ratchets. The quiet sneer on Duca Echi's face reminded Gerard of a sadistic instructor who had punished him regularly at The Academy. He shuddered involuntarily. As soon as this ceremony was over, he was going to resign his consortship, or whatever it was called.

"As the custom requires, our consort will be trained immediately. On the Day of Conclusion, he will be presented to the Nobel Assembly as Fize of the Gabriel Ratchets."

Fize of the Gabriel Ratchets? Supreme commander? It was ridiculous, so ridiculous that Gerard suddenly felt calm. It was one thing to be lover to the Badh of the Seven Systems, and quite another to try to become Fize of the Gabriel Ratchets. Him? Gerard Manley? They'd kill him. Anger laced through his unnatural calm. Why was Fairy Peg doing this?

"If the Day of Conclusion comes," Duca Echi said with open contempt totally unconcealed by a brief bow, "so shall we honor the consort and Fize."

"Duca!"

Fairy Peg's word rang in Gerard's ear. Duca Echi snapped to attention as though yanked by a hidden wire. He glared at Fairy Peg.

"Duca, you *will* honor him . . . as will this Corpus." The coldness in her voice sent a chill through Gerard. "You will honor him now as Consort to the Throne. You will honor him on the Day of Conclusion as Fize and Consort. Who does not honor him, does not honor *me*."

For the first time Gerard understood that there was something going on far more fundamental than Fairy Peg taking him as consort. A message had been passed to Duca Echi and Corpus Privy, a message that would surely spread throughout the corridors of power as soon as this ceremony was over. It was a message from the high ground of power defying anyone to challenge the Badh's decisions.

With a brief bow of ostensible submission, Duca Echi sat down. Almost immediately Squo Lyle rose. "Indeed, Badh, we honor your choice, and on the Day of Conclusion we will honor him again." Whatever emotions Squo Lyle had felt, whatever had caused his sputtering before, was effectively hidden by his smooth tone and blank expression. "The Badh has spoken. May the consort be honored."

Fairy Peg moved her hand from Gerard's shoulder, and he rose to attention beside her. Without a word or a smile she turned and strode regally out of the chamber with Gerard at her side. Behind them echoed unenthusiastic repetitions of, "May the consort be honored."

With their escort of Gabriel Ratchets, Gerard and Fairy Peg walked swiftly and silently back to her chambers. As soon as the door closed behind them and they were alone, Gerard exploded.

"What in Krick was that all about? Why didn't you tell me I would have to become a Gabriel Ratchet? And what else was going on in there? Well? Well?" For some reason he didn't feel as angry as he tried to sound.

Fairy Peg smiled and held out her arms to him. "Come, my consort, and I will tell you."

"You can tell me just as well from across the room."

Her smile broadened. "Do you refuse your Badh?"

"I refuse nothing. And everything. I want no part of this Gabriel Ratchet business."

"But Pilot, you must." Her smile disappeared. "It is the custom and cannot be broken. Do you not wish to be my consort?"

"Not if it means being your dead consort."

"Speak you of death on such a joyous occasion?"

Gerard spun on his heels to see Inez standing behind him.

"Did you see their looks, Sister, when I started laughing? It was wonderful. Confused they were by that."

"Yes, Inez, you were indeed clever to think of such a trick to break the tension." Fairy Peg's tone was not as approving as her words.

Gerard's thoughts were twisted and confused. He wanted to be alone with Fairy Peg, to find a way out of this predicament. Inez's presence made him feel awkward and foolish. But he had to get out of it. "Pardon, Princess, a thousand pardons, but I cannot accept this role you would have me play. I would serve you in any way I can, but I am too weak a piece for this game you are playing."

"Stupid words from such a handsome man," Inez offered.

"Pilot, do I understand you?" Fairy Peg asked, looking at him carefully. "Do you not wish to be my consort?"

"I told you that before you dragged me in there."

"So you did. I thought your protests were born of humility. I did not realize you had other concerns. However, Pilot, it is too late to change your status. You were named consort, and consort you are. As such you will do what must be done. Send in Commander Alpluakka, Inez."

Gerard sensed a touch of sadness beneath the cold surface of her words. That might be an opening. As soon as Inez left the room, he went to Fairy Peg and offered his hands to her. With a smile she accepted them. "Is there no other way, Fairy Peg?"

"None. I want you, Pilot. I want you by my side. This is the only way I can have what I want with honor." Her eyes and her voice were soft, her tones those of their bed.

As though a great valve had opened and drained off his will to resist, Gerard felt deflated. Logic said he should immediately turn himself over to FedDiploService because of his personal involvement and tell them to replace him. His heart said, "Love. Give. Do what must be done." Drawing Fairy Peg to him, he wrapped her in his arms and held her tenderly. "As the Badh commands," he said softly.

After a quick kiss, she gently pushed him away. Moments later Targ Alpluakka entered the room.

"Princess." The knee-drop bow to Fairy Peg. "Consort." A brief bow to Gerard. "How may I serve?" The question was purely a formal one. Everyone in EllKoep knew what Targ's task would be.

"At midday tomorrow, you will take the consort into your company and train him until such time as he can meet your test and become Fize."

Targ eyed Gerard narrowly, as though evaluating a piece of merchandise he did not approve of. When he spoke, his smile was one of manners rather than emotion. "As the Badh commands, but we suspect it will take a while to train him."

"As long as it takes, but no longer, Commander."

"At midday, as the Badh commands." With another brief bow to Gerard and a knee-dropper to Fairy Peg, he turned and left. No sooner was he gone when Inez returned.

"Many await without, Sister. What will you have them do?"

"I will hold audience tomorrow afternoon. Until then we are not to be disturbed. And Inez," she said as Inez turned to go, "we do thank you for your help."

Inez bowed slightly. "Sister."

Following Fairy Peg into her bechamber, Gerard wondered how he had become such a pawn. Is this what love does?

Have I surrendered my will for the love of this woman? Not wanting to believe that, he kept searching for answers in a corner of his mind, even after Fairy Peg suggested that they undress.

A royal sunburst design in one wall gave the room warmth as well as light. Fairy Peg had stepped into the small dressing hall that adjoined the room, and Gerard felt slightly silly standing naked in the middle of the room. Wondering suddenly what Marradon would think if she could see him, Gerard decided to wait in bed for Fairy Peg.

"I am ready, Pilot," she called from behind him.

He turned and was amazed by the vision that greeted him. Fairy Peg stood in a long robe that was open to the floor, revealing the sinuous curves of her body. On her head a jeweled tiara with the royal sunburst seemed to glow with a light of its own. So did her robe, which cast sensuous shadows over her flesh that beckoned to him with shifting highlights. Without a word he stepped softly to her, hesitantly, not wanting to let the sight of her escape him. She was more beautiful than anything he had ever seen in his life.

Gently, they came into each other's arms, flesh brushing flesh, then pressing firmly, then clamping hard against each other, flattening, spreading, nerves seeking maximum contact with nerves, lips greedily seeking the fire which burned in both of them. Gerard was dimly aware of something pressing hard into his chest, but his passion pushed the discomfort aside. Suddenly there was a clanking sound, and Fairy Peg broke their embrace with a laugh.

"That *chota* never did fit right." With casual grace she picked up the tiara and placed it on the small bedside table. When she turned back to him, Gerard noticed the ring on a chain around her neck. His ring.

Drawing her back into his arms, he asked, "I thought you said you couldn't wear my ring?"

"I cannot wear it on my finger, Pilot, but I shall always wear it close to my heart."

The rest of the day had a sweet harmony for Gerard. They made love with passion, then later with tender patience. He reviewed the first secrets of her body and verified them with gentle, probing repetition. Fairy Peg was wildly passionate, struggling with him to draw out

68

every heated nuance of lust, then she was softly seductive, teasing and coaxing him with fingers and tongue, lips and flesh.

Gerard responded in kind, searching for the smallest signs that he was pleasuring her with each touch and caress. Then he tried again to compose sensuous melodies with their bodies, melodies that would rise slowly into concertos of ecstasy. They came close late that night, and afterward, as they lay heavy in each other's arms, Gerard wondered at the beauty of it all.

"One must face the day, Pilot," Fairy Peg said softly in his ear. He didn't want to open his eyes, afraid that if he did, she would pull her warm softness away from him.

"Pilot, Pilot," she crooned softly, brushing her hard nipples against his chest, "it is time to face the day."

He responded by pulling her firmly against him, covering her neck and shoulders with kisses, and letting his fingers renew their acquaintance with her curves and hollows. Mentally he might have been content with no more than that, but his body was fully aroused and refused to be denied.

Later, as they bathed and dressed together, making each moment surrender its token of communion, there seemed to be nothing more important to either of them than sharing their togetherness.

"It is almost the appointed hour," Fairy Peg said after a long, lingering kiss.

Gerard tried to resist the change of mood, but with little success. In less than an hour Targ would be coming for him, coming to take him to the Ratchets' training barracks. It was unavoidable. "Shall I see you while I'm in training?"

"It is forbidden." The tone of her voice said she wished it was not.

"Then I will do my best to learn quickly, my Fairy Peg."

"That would please me greatly."

"Will you miss me?"

"Am I the Badh?"

They said their formal goodbyes in front of Targ, but it was not that which lingered in Gerard's thoughts as he rode with Targ in the skimmer to the Ratchets' training barracks. Targ warned him that he would not be treated differently from any other trainee, that he would be expected to perform exactly the same tasks and meet the same criteria. He also told him that no one could know his true identity, but all Gerard could concentrate on was a vision of Fairy Peg, a silhouette of sensous shadows against her glowing robe, arms out, beckoning to him.

When they reached the barracks he was given a plain grey jumpsuit, a bag of other clothing which was shoved roughly into his arms, two slightly different pairs of soft brown boots, and some towels and toilet articles. Then Targ took him to the novice barracks and turned him over to Tigigent Neereg.

"Treat him as you would any other novice, Tg Neereg," Targ said with more than a hint of malice. "No special privileges, no leniency because he is not one of us. Understood?"

"Understood, Commander."

It was not until the next morning, after a restless night on a hard pallet, that Gerard fully understood. A hard kick against his legs brought him fully awake. Before he could react, another kick rolled him off the pallet.

"Youse by our nivvy-novice," the tall, burly Tg Neereg said as he towered above him. "On you feet, nivvy!"

Gerard came slowly to his feet, too slowly, and Neereg kicked him again. "Faster, nivvy, faster. Wouldn't want to anger you tigigent, would youse? STRAIGHT! Stand straight, nivvy!" he roared in a voice that made Gerard cringe inwardly. He stood as straight as he knew how. Neereg brought his face to within millimeters of Gerard's, bending down slightly to do so. The smell of his breath was foul and repulsive.

"Lissen, nivvy. Lissen good. My nie-name is Neereg. My first name is Tigigent. Youse can call me Tigigent, sir. Understand, nivvy?"

Gerard bobbed his head slightly in affirmation.

"SPEAK, nivvy! Say, 'yes, Tigigent, sir'"

"Yes, Tigigent, sir," Gerard said flatly, hoping this was all a bad dream, and knowing it wasn't.

"We can't hear youse, nivvy."

"Yes, Tigigent, sir," he said louder.

"Are youse whispering, nivvy? Don't youse want you tigigent to hear youse?"

"Yes, Tigigent, sir!" Gerard shouted directly into the scarred face.

"Oh, poor nivvy," Tg Neereg said with no hint of sympathy, "we can see youse need much training. Much training."

Gerard trembled as Tg Neereg walked slowly around him, expecting to be struck again at any second. It was ridiculous to be in this position, and he was ashamed of his reactions. Why was he submitting to this buffoon's harassment? Fairy Peg.

Tg Neereg stopped several paces in front of him. "Lissen to you tigigent, nivvy. Until youse pass on my word, I be you mother and father, you sister and brother, you whole family. Youse can give you soul to the gods, but you ass is mine. Understand, nivvy?"

"Yes, Tigigent, sir!" Gerard shouted after a moment's hesitation.

"What, nivvy? We didn't hear youse!"

"Yes, Tigigent, sir!" Gerard bellowed as loudly as he could.

"Weak, nivy, weak. Best youse follow me." Tg Neereg led the way out of the barracks and started running down a gravel path between the tall, windowless walls of the stone barracks. Gerard ran after him. The gravel path turned onto a hard-surfaced road, where Tg Neereg picked up the pace, lengthening the distance between them with every step. Gerard struggled to catch up with him, but each breath he sucked into his laboring lungs was more ragged than the previous one. Already his legs ached, and his arms felt heavy and uncontrollable. Tg Neereg circled back and goaded Gerard with a running kick from behind that almost sent him sprawling.

The pattern was set. Gerard ran, fighting each step. Tg Neereg ran beside him, kicking Gerard every time he faltered, kicking him harder when he collapsed in a tumbling heap until Gerard forced himself to his feet again.

Gerard sought escape in his mind, trying to conjure the image of the dark pool of unconsciousness where he had hidden from Markl Holsten, but it wasn't there. Grey mists clouded his vision, pierced only by bright, stabbing pain. His mind and body slowly separated from one another until the only connection between them was a dull, pounding awareness that he was still moving and Tg

Neereg was still shouting at him and kicking him. Then finally, even that awareness disappeared, and Gerard floated above his suffering body with an awful detachment, feeling nothing, thinking nothing, watching from a distance to see what would happen.

When his body collapsed in total exhaustion it created a vaccuum which sucked him back into contact with his senses. Breathing was a series of rapid hacking sounds that grew louder and harsher as he slipped slowly down through the channels of his nerves and sensed the build-up of waste, the heavy fatigue, and the lack of oxygen. Tears rolled uncontrollably from his eyes while his mouth cried for even a drop of water. When he tried to raise his face out of the dirt, he trembled violently as though his soul was vibrating in agony.

He was spent, used up, empty of everything but an overload of pain. All he wanted to do was slip into unconsciousness. But slowly, ever so slowly, his breathing smoothed out, the pain eased to a burning ache, and the pounding of blood in his ears faded. Then he tried again to raise himself. Strong, rough hands helped him to his feet, where he stood unsteadily.

"Very good, nivvy. Now we return." Tg Neereg smiled at him almost gleefully.

Gerard made the return trip at an agonizingly slow pace, constantly goaded, prodded, and encouraged by Tg Neereg to move forward through the shades of his pain. When he awoke the next morning he barely remembered stumbling into the barracks the day before and collapsing.

As he tried to compose his thoughts, he was distracted by a sweet pungent odor coming from his skin. He was lying naked on his pallet, his skin tacky with smelly oil. Why, he wondered? After pulling himself into a sitting position, it occurred to him that his muscles should be stiff and sore. Instead, they only ached mildly. Was the oil responsible for that? And who had rubbed him down with it?

"On your feet, nivvy!" Tg Neereg's roaring command cut short any further reflection. Gerard was too slow to rise for Tg Neereg's satisfaction, and got a kick behind his knees for his slowness. As quickly as he could he jumped up again and stood at attention, feeling embarrassed by his nakedness. This time Tg Neereg hit him in the chest with a small bundle. "Dress, nivvy."

"Yes, Tigigent, sir." Gerard remembered to reply as loudly as he could. He swiftly undid the bundle and climbed into the grey jumpsuit, coarse socks, and soft boots. At Neereg's command, Gerard followed him out of the barracks for a repetition of the previous day's run.

Again Tg Neereg forced him to run until he couldn't be goaded to run any further. Then he let Gerard recover, helped him to his feet, and goaded him back to the barracks. On the third day of this routine, Gerard ate ravenously before collapsing on his pallet. On the seventh day Tg Neereg told him to stop and rest before Gerard had even fallen down once, and actually praised him as a "good nivvy" on their return. On the eleventh day they ran out and back without stopping, Tg Neereg pacing them at alternating speeds so that when they slowed down Gerard actually felt like he was resting.

As they ran, he also felt the nagging return of questions that had been circling dimly in his mind since his survival test aboard *Shivelight*. Why was all this happening? Why did he feel like a pawn in a game he didn't understand? Was he being used? By whom? But the question that dominated all the others was, Why was he so passively accepting all that had happened? He had no answers beyond speculation, but in their place was the beginning of an angry determination to find answers.

"Shower and change, nivvy," Tg Neereg told him when they returned to the barracks that eleventh day. As soon as he was dressed in a clean uniform and boots, Neereg came for him and took Gerard in another building, to a mess hall where fifty or sixty other novice Ratchets were eating in their plain grey jumpsuits. When he entered the mess hall at Tg Neereg's heels, the sound of conversation slowed and stopped as he was appraised by all present. Gerard tried to avoid the stares, especially those of the ridlows, whose wide-set, black eyes seemed to bore through him.

After they filled their trays, Neereg led him to a table occupied by two ridlows and three humanoids, all of whom ignored him once he sat down. "A nivvy-nivvy," Tg Neereg said in a tone that caused all of them to look at him. "You string, Brunnel."

"Yes, Tigigent Neereg, sir," one of the ridlows said casually around a mouth full of food. "Nivvy got a name?"

"String name, Nivvy Fizzle," Neereg said with a grunting laugh and the briefest flicker of a smile. It was the first time Gerard had ever seen any amusement on Neereg's face. Then he understood why. Tg Neereg knew who he was. The name Fizzle was a joke.

"Good to have full string. Be you welcome, Nivvy Fizzle," Brunnel said in a deep monotone. Using one of his hooked lower arms, he pointed to the others at the table. "Knip, Closgemon, Hoose, Woltol." The other ridlow was Woltol. Each nodded to him slightly when his name was mentioned, then they all turned their attention back to the food and ate in silence.

Gerard followed their example, content for the moment to be left alone with his thoughts and his food. Something important had happened to him this day. He had passed the first test the Gabriel Ratchets had put before him. It wasn't much of a test, he reminded himself, proving that one could be conditioned to run forty kilometers without collapsing. But he was proud that he had passed it. Better still, he felt good. There was a tautness in his muscles and a hardness in his belly that had been missing since his days at The Academy. Water and fat had been wrung from his body, making him harder, leaner, better balanced. For the first time in days he allowed himself to think about Fairy Peg, and an unbidden smile crossed his lips when his image of her called to him in naked lust.

"No smiling, Nivvy Fizzle," Brunnel warned.

Gerard looked up to see they had all finished eating and were waiting for him. As quickly as he could he shoveled down his last few bites. Without a word, Brunnel led the way from the table, through the tray-washing line, and out of the mess hall. There they formed a line, and Gerard took his place at the end of it trying to match steps with the string as Brunnel marched them down a series of long corridors to a small open bay with six pallets perfectly aligned down one wall.

"Shut door, Nivvy Fizzle," Brunnel ordered.

Gerard turned and shut the door. While his back was still turned, the rest of the string jumped on him and beat him with rhythmic blows that drove him to the floor.

      *   *   *

Message to: Pelis Foffey Turingay-Gotz
           FedTreatySvc

Situation on Evird is developing far too rapidly. Have instructed our agents to slow it down. Instruct yours to do the same.

As regards Key-One, he is being fitted into our plan very carefully so that he suspects nothing. When the proper time arrives he will be ready to take the first steps to assist us. In the meantime, other resources are being strengthened and expanded. Perhaps now you will see the need for patience.

—Toehold

      *   *   *

7

In the middle of the beating Gerard realized they were pulling their punches just enough so that he wasn't severely injured. It was a strange sensation to be beaten up and know that he wasn't really going to be hurt.

As suddenly as the attack started, it stopped. Brunnel picked Gerard up and carried him gently to a pallet, where he was stripped of his clothes then generously coated with the healing oil and rubbed down by each member of the string, starting with Brunnel. As they massaged the healing liniment into his aching body they chanted softly. At first Gerard didn't realize what they were saying, but as he paid closer attention, he heard a series of vignettes describing the past exploits of the Ratchets in rhymed couplets. At the end of each vignette came the same chorus.

Three full moons mean a terrible night
When the Gabriel Ratchets come to fight.

Somewhere in the middle of one of those choruses, while strong, firm hands rubbed warm oil into his shoulder muscles, the newest member of Brunnel's string fell asleep.

Two voices, distant and low, argued softly. "He will grow out of it. Dependence will fade—"

"Too passive your son is—"

"Not passive, gentle. Understand he has lost much, his mother, his friends. Time will heal him." His father.

"Or ruin him. Trust I ask, to help him—" The woman.

"Help him? It is not clear to me how this will help."

"Trust I ask. Is that too much?"

"Best first we wake Gerard . . . wake up . . . wake up . . ."

"Wake up, nivvy. Our string awaits us." The voice and face were strange. Gerard couldn't remember if it belonged to the one called Knip, or Hoose, or the other humanoid, Something-mon. "Come, Nivvy Fizzle, your training begins."

As he dressed, the man talked to him. "I, Knip, was newest to our string before you. My job it is to help you as is allowed. We are Ratchet now."

Gerard guessed that Knip was very young, less than twenty standard years by the smoothness of his pale yellow skin. Knip's deep-set green eyes and high hooked nose gave him a bird-like look that was enhanced by a warbling kind of pronunciation Knip gave his rounded consonants. There was something innocent about this lanky boy with his short, black hair that Gerard liked, but he also sensed the Knip was not as innocent as he appeared. For all their open green clarity, Knip's eyes were cold, belying the warmth in his voice.

"Your running boots, nivvy," Knip said when Gerard started to put on the wrong ones.

The day started with a run of twenty kilometers, not on the road he and Tg Neereg had run on, but on a path through the hills outside Ell City where they passed other strings of Ratchets, some running in the opposite direction, some in small clearings off the side of the path, doing exercises. Brunnel stopped them twice to exercise, showing Gerard first how each exercise was done, then leading the string through a vigorous series of repetitions. Everything was done to the cadence of various chants or songs, each with a rhythm designed to pace the activity and bring the mind into harmony with the body. Gerard soon realized that the words were meaningless and the rhythm was everything, and he took up the chants with great enthusiasm. It was another way to escape the tedium of what they were doing.

After a hearty breakfast they went to a small arena, where Gerard was introduced to Tine, the swordmaster, a wiry giant two and a half meters tall, whose quin cutlass looked like a toy hanging from his belt.

"A nivvy-nivvy," Tine said with a huge grin as he looked down on Gerard, "come to learn Tine's craft. Here, Nivvy," he said handing Gerard a quin cutlass, "let us see you fight."

The cutlass felt heavy and awkward in Gerard's hand. What was he supposed to do with it, anyway? A moment later Tine stepped aside and Knip took his place, standing before Gerard in a half-crouch, knees flexed, the point of his cutlass aimed straight for Gerard's heart.

"*Kiaree*," Knip shouted at him.

Defend? How? Gerard glanced quickly left and right, and saw that the others were spreading out in a wide circle around them. He looked back at Knip and tried to readjust his grip on the cutlass, searching for a more comfortable way to hold it. Then he tried to match Knip's stance.

Immediately, Knip made a half-thrust which Gerard clumsily banged aside. Someone behind him laughed, but he was too busy backing away from Knip's flailing blade to pay much attention. Stumbling off balance and constantly moving his own blade back and forth in front of him, Gerard managed to keep from being struck until Knip doubled the pace of his strokes. In short order Gerard lost his cutlass to a blow that caught it under the handguard, and stood helpless before Knip's naked blade.

"Point," Knip said triumphantly with a quick thrust that pricked Gerard's chest and brought forth a small spot of blood.

Gerard couldn't believe Knip had done that after disarming him, but as he looked with dismay at Knip's grinning face, his focus was drawn to Knip's frozen green eyes. Then he understood why Knip's innocence seemed flawed. He was a killer. Had it not been a training exercise, Knip would have killed Gerard with relish.

"Much you have to learn from me, nivvy," Tine said interrupting his thoughts. "First is this." He shoved the cutlass back into Gerard's hand and twisted his fingers until he was satisfied with the grip. "Like so. Hold firm. No, no, do not clutch. Hold firm like the wrist of a lover. Good, nivvy, good. Now point up blade like this."

So it went for hours. The other members of the string broke into pairs and practiced man against man, man against ridlow, and ridlow against ridlow. Gerard practiced against Knip, with Tine always towering over him from behind, correcting and adjusting. Finally fatigue took its toll, and Gerard could no longer hold up his cutlass, much less move it properly.

"Ah, now this," Tine said, exchanging a short dagger for Gerard's cutlass. Soon the dagger felt just as heavy as the cutlass had felt. They stopped the training only briefly for a quick meal of dry rations and water, then took up where they had left off. Only when the arena was totally filled with late-afternoon shadows did they finally stop. Gerard sat down, exhausted, exactly where he had been standing. All he wanted to do was lie down and go to sleep.

"No rest, Nivvy Fizzle," Brunnel said, helping him to his feet. "Must run now."

They ran, twenty kilometers that passed like a slow dream for Gerard. They ate, a meal without taste or texture. Then they showered, and as soon as Gerard dried himself, he collapsed on the pallet and went instantly to sleep.

The days passed in an endless series of repetitions of the same type activities. Run. Train with swords, daggers, staff and glove, hand to hand. Learn team maneuvers, methods of attack and defense. Run. Eat. Shower. Sleep.

Gerard began to learn, and slowly he got stronger, finding the runs less exhausting, the drills physically easier. Even better, he began to grow attached to the members of his string, learning that Brunnel was something of a poet and singer as well as a disciplined fighter, and that Knip, except for his bloodthirst, truly was an innocent. He had been in the care of the Gabriel Ratchets since he was five or six years old, and their world was the only one he knew. Hoose and Closegemon were brothers by the same mother and different fathers, who delighted in pulling practical jokes on each other.

Only Woltol kept his distance from Gerard. He was not unfriendly, but neither did he accept or offer any of the normal exchanges of friendship. It didn't take Gerard long to realize that Woltol was a loner, preferring no company so much as his own. But Woltol was also an observer who seemed to always be watching what everyone else was doing.

Six weeks to the day after joining the Ratchets, Gerard was called from the barracks immediately after the evening meal and taken to a small office in the headquarters building. Commander Targ Alpluakka and Fianne Tackona were waiting for him there.

"Novice Fizzle, reporting, sir," Gerard barked with a perfectly executed salute when he saw Targ.

"At ease, Diplomat," Targ said, returning the salute.

"Novice *Fizzle*?" Fianne asked.

"My Ratchet string name, sir," Gerard said formally. Seeing Fianne's dumbfounded look, he broke into a grin. "How am I doing?"

"That is what we have come to talk to you about," Targ said before Fianne could reply. "Your training reports show acceptable progress. Friend Fianne felt it was time you learned the protocol of your new position . . . just in case you need it."

Gerard returned Targ's little sneer with one of his own. "As a contract diplomat, I'd say there was no doubt that I'll need it. As Novice Fizzle, I have my doubts. Not about whether I can pass the tests, but whether I'll be allowed to pass the tests."

"What are you suggesting, nivvy?"

Gerard knew from Targ's tone that he was treading on soft ground. "Nothing of conseck, uh, consequence, sir. But with Fianne Tackona as our witness, I note that certain things have occurred which endanger my chances of success. No more can I say by the bond of the Ratchets."

It was a dangerous tactic to involve Fianne as a witness, but Gerard had been paying close attention to the unwritten rules of Ratchet conduct. By announcing the possibility of foul play, then refusing to point an accusing finger, he hoped to force Targ to take a closer look at his training. By involving Fianne, Targ would be put under a great deal of pressure to explain why if Gerard did not pass the tests. He didn't fool himself into believing that the tests would be rigged in his favor, but he did not discount the possibility that Targ might put subtle pressure on those who tested him.

Gerard felt no sense of shame about trying to get an edge in the tests. He had been pushed unwillingly into this position, and if putting a little extra pressure on Targ would get him out of it faster or easier, so much the better.

"Well," Targ said after a long pause, "we shall certainly see that your tests are fair."

"I should hope so," Fianne said sternly. "It seems to me, friend Targ, that we must not lose sight of the fact that we are dealing with an extraordinary consort, a diplomat, a man must fulfill two roles, a man—"

"Yes, friend Fianne. I understand. Now I leave you two for your protocol."

Gerard gave Targ a smart salute, which he automatically returned. As soon as Targ closed the door, Gerard turned to Fianne. "How fares Princess Peg? Is she well? Have you talked to her?"

"Gently, Diplomat, gently. It is because of our princess that I am here. She inquires almost daily about you, and friend Targ gives her little information. Other than her unseemly concern about you, our princess is in good health and state. How fare you, Diplomat? You appear frightfully thin."

Gerard laughed. "That I am, Fianne, but only because the training here has burned off my excess fat. I haven't been so fit since I was a youth."

"Good. Now what will you tell me about the truth behind your exchange with friend Targ?"

"There's nothing to tell." Gerard paused and looked thoughtfully at Fianne. "What will you do if I don't pass the Ratchets' tests?"

"Why, I shall report this conversation to our princess, of course."

"Exactly. Targ knows that, and consequently, he will do whatever is necessary to insure the tests are fair."

"Mean you just like all the others?"

"Fara, no, Fianne. I mean *fair to me*. The others have spent years, sometimes lifetimes preparing for these tests. Already there are hints from Swordmaster Tine that I will be given my final tests very soon. They must be fair in that context."

"How soon?"

"That I don't know. A month? Six weeks? What does it matter? Now you must teach me protocol, so that whenever the Day of Conclusion comes, I will not embarrass myself."

Hours later, Gerard was sorry he had asked for the protocol lessons to begin. They were dry and boring, consisting mostly of memorizing appropriate forms of address and response in particular situations. Gerard had never been good at that kind of memory work, and finally he sent Fianne away and returned to his string-room. The others had waited up for him.

"What? Do you waste the precious hours of sleep?" he asked lightly.

"Who be you, Nivvy Fizzle?" Brunnel asked. There was no friendliness in his voice.

"I be Nivvy Fizzle, lowest of Brunnel's string. Why ask you?"

"You were visited by the commander," Knip said accusingly.

"So I was, young Knip. So I was."

"And a high servant from EllKoep," Hoose added.

Gerard didn't like the tone of that. "So what is it you want of me, string members? Shall I cower against the door while you beat me again? Shall I bore you with the dull history of my unworthy life? Why do you ask these questions?"

"We would know who you be, Nivvy Fizzle, that the commander hisself should come with a high servant of the Badh to visit you."

Gerard didn't know what to do. If he told him who he really was, he would probably destroy the rapport he had built with them. If he didn't tell them, they wouldn't trust him, and the rapport would be broken anyway. Either way he lost.

Suddenly he had an inspiration. "What I tell you is string-bond and must not be heard by other ears."

Brunnel was first to assent. Woltol was last. Gerard decided to look at Woltol as he spoke. "You know I am not from this galaxy," he said, letting them signal affirmation before he continued. "You also know that I will be tested much sooner than is normal."

"So it is said," Woltol interjected.

"Then listen to me, brother Ratchets. When the lowest member of Brunnel's string is tested first, it will be an important day. If I pass my tests, you will know who I am

81

and why I could not tell you. If I don't pass my tests because of my own weakness, then you won't have to suffer my shame. If I don't pass my tests because they were made impossible for me, then you must not be burdened by the revenge bond against those who used me." Gerard paused, waiting for their reactions. Surprisingly, it was Woltol who spoke again.

"It is said in the barracks that an outsider has been named to high position by the Badh, but that he cannot assume that position until tested by the Gabriel Ratchets."

"I have heard such things," Gerard offered.

The others seemed to be waiting for him to say more. He had thought at first to tell them they would be made principal guard to the Fize if he passed the tests, but he dared not. It wouldn't be fair to them. Worse, it would color their relationship, mar it even more than it already was. He decided to wait them out. They had apparently decided to do the same thing. So they sat there in the chilly barracks, four humanoids and two ridlows, waiting for someone to break the silence.

Knip was the first to give in. "Are you the Prince Consort?" he blurted.

"I am Nivvy Fizzle," Gerard said quietly.

"He *is* Nivvy Fizzle, lowest of my string," Brunnel said finally and firmly, "and that is all. Rest now, all of you."

Gerard went to sleep that night to the sound of his string whispering to each other.

Fianne came weekly after his first visit, drilling Gerard in the form and substance of protocol. Sometimes Targ sat is on the sessions, but more often than not it was just Gerard and Fianne moving through the dry intricacies of protocol for the Consort and Fize, like travelers on a desert track stopping to examine in detail every rock above a certain size. It was dull work compared to his training, but Gerard began to welcome the break in routine the lessons gave him. He also welcomed Fianne's companionship.

After their meeting on the night of Fianne's first visit, his string had kept him at a distance from them. He still worked out with each of them individually, and with the string as a unit, but, if they felt any continuing sense of camaraderie with him, they were holding it back. After trying repeatedly to break through their new reserve,

Gerard had decided to ignore it and treat them as if nothing had happened. That change of tack didn't seem to make any difference to them, but it made him feel better.

One morning, after their run and breakfast, Brunnel announced that they were going to begin training with power weapons. That meant a trip off Kril to the largest of her three moons.

"Why can't we train with them here?" Knip asked sullenly.

"Even training with power weapons is forbidden here, nivvy. Know you not such simple things?"

"Cuz my pack, Brunnel. I know what is forbidden. But we are Ratchets, guardians of the throne. Why is it forbidden for us?"

"It is forbidden for all. Our Badh, herself, is forbidden power weapons on Kril. Such is the law. Now we go to draw equipment." With that flat statement, Brunnel turned and left the room, and the string fell in line behind him.

They made the trip to Hivod, the largest of Kril's moons, wearing their pressure suits, in the first available freighter Transport Authority could send them up on. Except for their sleeping periods, they spent the next twenty days in their suits learning to fire lase rifles, stun-blasters, and various team-fired weapons. Other than the constant awareness of his own odor, Gerard enjoyed the training, and he especially enjoyed the light gravity.

The last day on Hivod included a mock attack through a live-fire obstacle course. All went well until they were a third of the way through the course, working their way single file down a narrow ravine with Woltol in the lead and Gerard immediately behind him. Suddenly there was a soundless explosion of rock and dust, and the wall of the ravine collapsed on them.

Whether he moved by instinct or training, Gerard didn't know, but when he saw the wall collapsing he leapt on Woltol. The force of his tackle threw them both against the base of the rocks. Fragments of stone bombarded them for several seconds, then a heavy slide of pea gravel buried them.

Gerard tried to move and discovered he was only pinned from the waist down. Then he realized the gasping he heard in his suit helmet was Woltol's. Feeling underneath him, he ran his hands around Woltol's helmet until he found the air hose. It was pinched by a rock that Gerard couldn't move.

"Woltol! Woltol! Roll left," Gerard heard himself scream.

"Ummgh!"

"Roll left!"

"Ummgh," Woltol repeated as he tried to roll to his left. More loose gravel sifted into their small space, but Woltol turned enough so that Gerard could get his gloved hand around the air hose. "Stay still," he shouted as he tried to squeeze the hose open.

"More, nivvy," Woltol gasped as he felt the inrush of air.

Gerard squeezed until his whole arm trembled. Every time he tried to relax his grip, the hose started to close again. His arm throbbed with pain, and his own breathing was coming in ragged gasps. Only a sudden lightening of the weight on his legs told him the rest of the string was digging them out and gave him the strength to hang on.

Then they were free, and other hands replaced his to keep Woltol's hose open. It had been close, but they had survived. As he leaned against the side of the ravine and tried to catch his breath, Gerard sent a silent prayer of thanks to Fara.

"Time to move out."

He couldn't believe what Brunnel had said. Looking up, he saw that Woltol's hose had been repaired, and Knip was offering him the lase rifle he had lost in the slide. Wearily, he rose to his feet and followed Woltol around the slide and down the narrow ravine, impressed by the calm reactions of his string.

They finished the course without further trouble, but were assessed ten penalty points for the time it took them to complete the course and only scored eighty-two percent. Still, there was much back-slapping and laughter as they gathered their equipment together and headed for the shuttle that would take them back to Kril.

Nothing was said about the slide incident until after breakfast their first morning back. As Gerard was changing into his training uniform, he suddenly realized that the string had gathered around him in a semicircle.

"You are one of us, Nivvy Fizzle," Brunnel announced. "We know not who you are outside the Ratchets, but you will always be one of us."

The others grunted in assent, but said nothing. Then

Woltol brought one of his hooked lower arms from behind his back and held out a small metallic object to Gerard. "For my life," he said simply.

It took Gerard a second to recognize the short, razor-sharp ridlow dagger. Immediately he knew he was being highly honored. The only way a Ratchet other than a ridlow could carry one of those daggers was if he received it as a gift or killed a ridlow in battle. In the five-thousand-man corps of the Gabriel Ratchets, less than half a dozen humanoids carried ridlow daggers.

"I am honored, Woltol." Gerard wanted to say much more, but he knew it would be out of place. With a long bow, he took the dagger in its dull black sheath and attached it to his belt so that it lay horizontally against his body just left of the buckle, exactly as Brunnel and Woltol wore theirs. As he straightened up, he gave Woltol a crisp salute. Woltol returned it sharply. Then suddenly everyone was attending to their own gear, and the ceremony was over.

That afternoon he purposefully paired himself with Woltol for quin cutlass practice and went at him with a fury which Woltol easily parried. It was Gerard's way of acknowledging he could never defeat a ridlow in battle and was doubly honored by the gigt. Woltol was laughing as they finished the first drill, but his laughter was cut short by a familiar voice.

"Nivvy Fizzle." It was Tigigent Neereg standing in full dress uniform beside Swordmaster Tine. Gerard ran to the proper position in front of them and snapped to attention with a quick salute, wondering all the time what was going on.

"Nivvy Fizzle," Tg Neereg boomed so every member of the five strings in the arena could hear, "by order of Commander Targ Alpluakka, and with the consent of the throne, youse are ordered to report to the Battle Arena tomorrow for you final tests." Neereg paused as though making sure he had everyone's attention. He did.

"It is with great honor I announce that you opponent and master for the tests will be Commander Targ Alpluakka."

Gerard was stunned. To be tested by Targ was the last thing he had expected. He knew he was supposed to make some reply, but he couldn't remember what. "I accept," he said finally.

"Report to me immediately after breakfast tomorrow."

Gerard saluted and walked slowly back to his string. The thought of being tested by Targ Alpluakka did not please him at all.

*　*　*

Message to: Greaves Lingchow
　　　　　　FedDiploSvc

We were greatly disturbed to learn that several of the rioters captured on Evird are suspected of being Federation agents. We do not accuse your service. However, we believe it is mandatory that you do everything within your power to see that any and all remaining Federation agents on Evird be extracted immediately. Failure to do so could ruin the plans we have so carefully constructed.

We demand to know as soon as possible what action you and your service will take on this matter.

—Glyph

*　*　*

8

As Gerard stood with Tg Neereg looking out over the Battle Arena, he realized that it was the fifth anniversary of his arrival in Ribble Galaxy. Or close to it. In five Standard years he had managed to earn the love of the Badh of the Seven Systems and become the center ring attraction for the crowds of Ribble nobility already filing into the arena's plush seats. Other than that he had done very little worth mentioning, yet Fed had expressed no displeasure with him or his actions. Gerard shook off the growingly familiar feeling that he was a pawn in a bigger game, and tried to listen to Tg Neereg's recitation of the schedule of tests.

Most of them were not really tests at all. They were

demonstrations of skill and technique in various formalized drills with sabers, staff and glove, short daggers, and hand-to-hand combat. The only true test was one-on-one combat with quin cutlasses between each novice and his tester. On this day eleven novices were to be tested, and all the formalized tests would take place simultaneously in the arena. Then the quin cutlass tests would take place two at a time for the other ten novices. The last event would be Gerard's test by Targ Alpluakka.

After reviewing the schedule with Gerard, Tg Neereg led him down to the dressing room. The other novices ignored him as they ignored each other and concentrated on getting their uniforms and equipment exactly right. Gerard dressed with a calm sense of detachment. Each lace in his soft fighting boots seemed to pull tension from his as he tightened it. Each button and clasp took away more. As he attached the ridlow dagger to his belt he felt totally relaxed, and stood looking with pride at his image in the mirror. He liked the way he looked in the spare grey uniform, liked the way it hugged his newly taut muscles and bulged slightly over his belt to show the classic lines of his hard gut. He was still admiring himself when the call came for the tests to begin.

Gerard moved through each series of the demonstrations easily, finding the formalized drills far more pleasurable in an arena, where they drew applause, than on the training ground, where they drew blood and criticism. The first time the crowd cheered and applauded, it almost threw him off stride. But after that he anticipated when the applause would come, and enjoyed it when it did. He was almost disappointed when they completed the last series and ran back to the dressing room.

As he changed into a fresh uniform he began to wonder if Fairy Peg had been up in the cheering crowd. During the whole series he had not dared to look up past the banked walls of the arena for fear of losing his rhythm. But surely she had been—

"And I say he must have stolen it," a voice behind him interrupted his thoughts.

"Shut you up, Corfun. You talk too much."

Gerard turned to see the one called Corfun sneering at him.

87

"Tell us, fellow nivvy, where did you steal that fine ridlow dagger? From one of their women's garters?"

With a small shake of his head Gerard turned away. He wasn't about to dignify Corfun's questions with answers.

"See, Kuto? Must have struck a nerve. Our little nivvy must had a ridlow wench on the side. 'Tis said they have a special opening for tiny men."

Gerard pivoted slowly and appraised Corfun's towering form with a small smile. He let his hand play loosely over the hilt of the dagger as he spoke. "My friend Woltol said I should never draw this dagger and then return it to its sheath unblooded. Perhaps you'd like to help me test its sharpness, Nivvy Corfun?"

Corfun looked uncertain, but not afraid. Gerard tightened his fingers on the hilt. A small rush of exhilaration made him suddenly ready to draw the dagger. "Well, Corfun?"

"Kuto! Corfun! First duel," the testmaster bellowed.

The tension of the moment was broken, but, after Corfun left Gerard felt a knot in his stomach. He finished dressing, then waited his turn, hoping that someone was taking a nick out of Corfun.

When Kuto returned alone, looked strangely at Gerard before sitting down on the bench opposite him. "Too slow," Kuto said. "Got hisself cut and carried off."

"Bad?" Gerard asked, feeling a little guilt about his thoughts.

"Bad," Kuto answered as he started unlacing his boots.

The knot in Gerard's stomach drew a little tighter. Tg Neereg hadn't lied when he said the quin cutlass duel was not a demonstration. Both members of the second pair came back from their tests, but one of them had a wide smear of blood across his chest. Gerard only glanced at them, then withdrew into himself, trying to review everything he had been taught by Swordmaster Tine. Step by step, move by move, he tried to remember how each felt and looked. The harder he tried to picture them in his mind, the less sure he was that he had them right. Then he went back to the basics and tried again.

The fact that the third and fourth pairs returned from their tests unbloodied did nothing for the tension that was building inside him. It only meant that in a short while the fifth pair would return, and it would be his turn to walk into the arena to face Targ. He stood up, surprised to find that his muscles had stiffened, and immediately began his limbering exercises, forcing himself to do them slowly and methodically. He had barely completed the whole limbering routine when the fifth pair returned. It was his turn.

Gerard checked his appearance once in the mirror, straightened his collar slightly, and began the long walk down the corridor to the arena. The soft echo of his boots on the plasteel floor was almost drowned out by the sound of his pulse pounding in his ears. Surprisingly, Tg Neereg was waiting for him at the entrance to the arena.

"Ah, Nivvy Fizzle, nothing youse can do but you best. Our commander loves an underhanded swing."

"Thanks, Tigigent, sir," Gerard said weakly. Tg Neereg stepped aside and Gerard walked slowly out into the arena.

Sporadic cheers and applause greeted him. The crowd seemed hesitant. When Targ Alpluakka stepped into the room seconds later, the sound of their applause and cheers rolled like thunder down from the crowd. The champion had arrived.

Gerard matched his pace with Targ's so that they met almost exactly in the center of the arena. Targ signalled "now" with his eyes, and they both saluted at the same time. Then they each took a step backward, drew their cutlasses, and the duel began.

The speed and grace of Targ's first series of attacks told Gerard he was totally outclassed. It was all he could do to back up and keep from getting hit. With each step he took backward, the crowd cheered. Gerard was too busy parrying Targ's blows to pay any attention to the crowd. As he watched Targ's moves for signs that might help him defend himself, he realized he was being toyed with. Targ was greatly amused.

The tension Gerard had felt until that moment was washed away by a wave of anger—anger at Targ for seting him up like this and then toying with him, anger with Fairy Peg for putting him in this situation, and anger with himself for going along so meekly with everything that had happened. For the blink of a second as he backed around the arena, Targ's face became Corfun's.

The anger intensified, and with it came a rush of energy that filled his mind as well as his body. It crashed through his brain like a huge wave. For an instant he was paralyzed by it.

Then he saw the opening. Targ was attacking so casually he was leaving himself open to a whirling attack. Without hesitation Gerard ducked the next slash, spun low and fast on the ball of his left foot, and swung with all his power for Targ's open left side.

The clash of their cutlasses jarred his bones. But it also jarred Targ. In the split second it took them to recover their balance, Gerard stepped forward and spun again. Again he met Targ's cutlass in a jarring blow that made them both stumble. As he recovered his footing and came back on guard, Gerard saw a new light in Targ's eyes. They, too, glowed with anger.

Targ feinted a thrust, did his own spin, and swung from his heels for Gerard's ribs. His cutlass whistled through empty air. Gerard had spun at the same time and desperately tried to put his cutlass into Targ's side. He was too far away and off balance. Instead of striking Targ, he stumbled past him.

Fear ripped through his legs as he righted himself, and without thinking he leapt high in the air. Targ's cutlass whacked the heel off Gerard's right boot and flipped him over. Somehow he managed to bounce up from his knees to face Targ again. Standing unevenly on his ruined boot, and breathing heavily, Gerard was unsure of what to do next.

Then he saw it. Targ was going to come at him with a series of thrusts and try to make him lose his balance. Gerard started his own series of thrusts at the same time Targ did, cutlass metting cutlass in a fury of sparking steel. Neither retreated. Neither advanced. Thrust, parry, slash, thrust, parry, parry, thrust.

It was a nightmare in slow motion. Unable to advance, and unwilling to retreat, Gerard fought off every tactic that Targ tried against him. His prescience was working at full force, but his arm ached, and his anger swelled. He wanted this duel over an done with. Surely he had passed this test. Surely he had proven he could defend himself.

Way in the distance the crowd roared its approval. That made Gerard even angrier. With a screaming roar he doubled his blows and forced Targ backward. First a half-step, then a full step, then two, then three he forced

Targ to move away, his rage pulling him onward into the whirlwind of ringing blades.

But the rage passed. Targ held his ground. Then it was he who was pressing the attack. He forced Gerard out into the center of the arena with a steady rain of blows.

Gerard knew it had to end soon. His strength faded with every thrust he parried, and his prescience faded with his strength. Whatever inner resources had carried him this far were draining like the sweat from his body. It could only be a matter of time until Targ brought him down.

Then, totally without warning, Targ stepped back and sheathed his cutlass. Gerard was stunned. It was over. He had passed the test. With every muscle trembling, he sheathed his own cutlass, brought himself to attention, and saluted. Targ returned his salute, and the crowd roared its approval.

It was over. He didn't believe it. Walking awkwardly on his ruined boot and still gasping for air, he followed Targ out of the arena.

"You surprised me, Diplomat," Targ said as Gerard collapsed on a bench in the dressing room. "I had not expected such fury from you."

"Mad. Angry," Gerard said between deep breaths.

"Whatever the reason, you fought well. Report to my office after the evening meal." Without waiting for acknowledgement, Targ left. Gerard fell back on the bench and let himself tumble down the ragged stairs of exhaustion into sleep.

Tg Neereg woke him. "Come, Ratchet, youse cannot sleep the day away. There is celebrating to do." Wearily, Gerard allowed Neereg to help him undress, then drank the mug of bitter broth Neereg had given him while he stood in the shower. An hour later he was back in the barracks receiving the congratulations of his string.

"Listen to me now," he said when they finally calmed down. "There is something I have to tell you."

"Who you are! Who you are!" Knip chanted as he bounced up and down in front of him.

"Yes, Knip, who I am. I am Gerard Manley, Universal Contract Diplomat, hired agent of the Federation." The silence in the room was deafening. Gerard smiled. "I am also Prince Consort to the throne, and will shortly be installed as Fize of the Gerard Ratchets.

For a moment none of them reacted. Then Woltol said, "You will be our new Fize?"

"Yes, Woltol, and as soon as the rest of you pass your tests, this string will become my personal guard."

They all started asking questions at once, and it took Gerard the better part of an hour to answer them. Brunnel finally announced it was time to eat. As they went off to the mess hall together, Gerard realized that he had once again been separated from his string, but this time by position. They would make a good guard for him.

When he entered the anteroom to Targ's office, two Zks who were waiting there immediately snapped to attention and saluted. Word had traveled fast. As Gerard returned their salute, Targ opened the door to his office and invited him in.

"Sit, Diplomat, sit," he said, offering one of two chairs at a small table. Gerard noted that the offered chair had its back to the door, so he took the other one. Targ laughed. "Good, Diplomat, good. One can never be too cautious." With a quick shift of the table he arranged it so neither of them had their back to the door. "Wine?"

"Yes, Commander, that would be nice." Try as he would, Gerard couldn't read Targ's mood. The man was like a sealed box.

Targ handed him a crystal goblet of wine, then took the other seat. "In two weeks you will become my Fize, and I will be subject to your command. That is an interesting situation, I think."

"Meaning what, Commander?" The wine was delicious.

Targ's smile was cold. "You cost me stature today, Diplomat. You were on the brink of the chasm of death, and I had to sheath my cutlass."

"I had passed my test," Gerard said quietly. "You knew it and so did the crowd."

"True, Diplomat. That is how I lost face. I should have killed you in the beginning."

"Perhaps you toyed with me too long. This is truly excellent wine you serve." Gerard took a slow sip as he waited for the reply.

"Perhaps I did. One could say that saved your life."

"One could."

"A Fize would remember that his commander had saved his life, would he not?"

"I suspect he would," Gerard smiled, "but he wouldn't want to be reminded of it very often."

"No, that is true. Perhaps he need never be reminded of it."

"Let's drink to that, Commander." Gerard wasn't sure what Targ had meant to accomplish by the exchange, but Targ seemed pleased as they drank to the proposal. Before the evening was over, they drank to much else as well. They drank to Princess Peg. They drank to the Gabriel Ratchets. They drank to the future of Ribble Galaxy. They drank to each other. By the time Gerard left he was very, very drunk. When he woke up on his pallet the next morning, he had no idea how he had managed to find his way back to the barracks.

It didn't occur to him until he stood in the shower why the string had left for training without him. He was beyond all that now. As the hot water ran over his throbbing head, he was grateful that he was. He would never have made the twenty-kilometer run with the hangover he had. After dressing he went to the mess hall and ate a hearty breakfast, despite his stomach's initial protests. As he fingered over his third cup of tea, Fianna Tackona sat down across from him.

"Our Badh is angry," Fianne said simply.

"Why?" Gerard couldn't imagine why Fianne would be telling him that Fairy Peg was angry.

"For many reasons, Diplomat. First, I think, she is angry because your test got out of hand yesterday. Second, I think, she is angry because you did not come to EllKoep after the tests. Third, I think, she is angry because she did not send for you. Yes, indeed, our Badh is certainly angry."

"Did she send you to tell me all this?"

"Oh, no, Diplomat. If she knew I was hear, that would probably give her greater cause for anger." Fianne's voice hinted at amusement.

"Well, Fianne, what do you suggest we do about our Badh's anger?"

"Oh, I am in no position to make such suggestions. But if I were, I would advise the Prince Consort to return to EllKoep as soon as possible."

"Thanks, Fianne. The Prince Consort might just do that."

The Ratchets at the door of Fairy Peg's private quarters refused to let him enter unannounced. Apparently they had not received the word yet about his status. Fairy Peg's elderly maid, Winsea, finally let him in, and then left. Moments later Fairy Peg entered the room at a run with her arms outstretched to him. He caught her under the arms and whirled her around while she smothered his face with kisses.

Then she stopped. "Put me down immediately," she demanded.

"No. I love you too much to ever put you down again."

"If you loved me so much, why did you not come to me last night?"

Gerard smiled and set her gently on the floor, letting his hands fall to rest on her waist. "Because, my dear Fairy Peg, no one told me I could go anywhere. And I am such a well trained Ratchet, and such a slow-witted diplomat, that I didn't have sense enough to leave on my own."

"You mean Targ kept you there," she said spitefully.

It occurred to Gerard that she might be right. "No, he didn't keep me there. He just didn't tell me I could leave. Perhaps he assumed I knew that. And perhaps, my love, you did too?"

Fairy Peg turned her eyes away from his. "Perhaps I did. Oh, Pilot, I've missed you so."

It was difficult to reply through her kisses, so he didn't try.

Later, as they lay curled against each other in her bed, sated momentarily by their passionate love-making, Gerard asked, "When is the Day of Conclusion? I mean, when will we have the big ceremony and make all this official?"

"Two weeks from tomorrow," she sighed. "There is much to be done in preparation."

"Mmmm. What do I have to do in the meantime?"

"Make me happy."

"And how would I do that, my sweet Fairy Peg?"

"If you keep moving your fingers like that, I am very sure you will figure it out."

"You mean this is all it takes for a lowly diplomat to make a princess happy?"

"No, more. Please."

"Like this?"

"Mmmm-hmmm."

*   *   *

Message to: Pelis Foffey Turingay-Gotz
                      FedTreatySvc

Key-One's influence has greatly increased in the last half-year. There is a bond between us which he has acknowledged, a small debt for our services to him. At the proper time we will use that to our advantage.

As for the other, I warned you about the situation on Evird. Now you must live with the consequences. If you cannot control your operatives there, the results could be devastating.

—Toehold

*   *   *

9

"The consort will stand here to your left, Badh, until all the members of the Noble Assembly have entered the hall and been seated. And you, Commander, will stand to the Badh's right. Now, you must both remember to keep your shoulders touching the throne."

"Why?" Gerard asked, to break the tedium of Fianne's directions. It was the third time they had gone over all this, and he was beginning to tire of it.

"Because, Consort," Fianne said, his voice echoing in the empty hall, "it is the symbolism of tradition. The Gabriel Ratchets support the throne. By keeping your shoulders against the throne, you symbolize that support."

"We have been over it before," Targ snapped. "Houn Almighty!"

"Commander!" Fairy Peg's look was even sharper than her voice. "I will not have blasphemy in this hall. Nor in this Koep."

Gerard thought he saw a burnt umber blush beneath Targ's dark skin.

Targ dropped quickly to one knee beside the throne. "A thousand pardons, Badh, but I do weary of this. Surely you are too kind a ruler to make us suffer through another recital of the traditions of the Day of Conclusion."

The laugh escaping Fairy Peg's lips turned into a cry of alarm. Hooded figures, each armed with a long sword and a short dagger, were rushing through the side entrance to the dais. With a leap Gerard drew his quin cutlass and positioned himself between them and Fairy Peg. Targ had also drawn and moved several paces to Gerard's left.

The headlong rush of the attackers almost bowled them over. With a vicious defense Targ and Gerard held their ground until the odds sorted themselves out at four to one and the attackers started spreading out.

Gerard glanced quickly at Fairy Peg and saw that she had drawn her short ceremonial sword and stood ready to defend herself. Against the long swords of the attackers, it would be of little use. Where in Fara's name were the Ratchets?

As the hooded figures moved silently to encircle them, Gerard felt a rush of the same kind of anger that had infused him in the duel with Targ. The attackers were cautious, but working as a team. A thrust from Gerard's right was followed almost instantly by a slash from the left.

With a light-headed detachment, Gerard grudgingly gave ground. His anger cooled and hardened with each clash of swords until it became a brilliant crystal distorting his vision.

He shook his head slightly. Then he saw one of the attackers slow his swing. Suddenly Gerard knew what was happening. He saw how the attack was forming. He knew which of the hooded figures would move next, and every movement was sharpened by his prescience. They were his for the taking.

With a roar of triumph and a wide, arcing swing of his cutlass, he leapt at the closest attacker and beheaded him. Using his momentum, he spun to his right in a mist of blood and caught the next one right above the belt, cleaving him almost in two.

The fight moved across the floor in a whirlwind of blades, curses, and blood. Targ fought one-on-two as the other four went after Gerard. Like a man possessed with burning madness, Gerard attacked them. He anticipated their moves and countered them with perfectly executed strokes.

One attacker advanced too far with a thrust and lost his sword and the hand that held it. One of his companions guarded high and found himself on the edge of a cutlass that rested for a moment beneath his sternum. The third attacker lost part of his chin before Gerard's cutlass sank deeply into his collarbone.

As he tried to free cutlass from bone, Gerard was blinded for a moment, unable to see what would happen next. During that moment the long point of a blade stabbed deeply into his left side. Lurching away from the pain, he freed his cutlass with a jerk that sent him sprawling on his back. Clutching his side, he tried to raise himself, and saw the last three attackers being overwhelmed by a group of Gabriel Ratchets. A hesitant smile crept over his lips as he heard Fairy Peg scream, "Pilot!" Then everything faded to an annoying buzz.

Cool water bathed his head. Soft hands caressed his cheeks. He opened his eyes and was surprised to find himself still lying on the floor of the Grand Hall. His head rested in Fairy Peg's lap. As he looked up, he chuckled. The chuckle sent a ripple of pain through his waist.

"Shh, Pilot. Omna-Seay's on his way."

"You look funny upside down."

"Shhhh," she said again, stroking his face. "Shhhhh."

He closed his eyes and let his thoughts drift until he heard Omna-Seay's rich voice. When he opened them, Omna-Seay was kneeling beside him. "Hey, Physm, how'm I doin'?" he asked weakly.

"Fine, Consort. Try to relax."

Something stung his arm. Something else stung his side. Numbness crept over him. He wanted to open his eyes, but they wouldn't move. His tongue stuck to his palate. "Quizen wirt," he said thickly, and a voice said,

"Shunshee." Then another said, "Jimbly magoosee...boo-boocoo," and he decided to quit listening.

The she-grisk stared directly toward his hiding place in the tree. Gerry was sure she could not see him, but her three beady eyes continued to stare out of her massive, scaled head. With a sudden snort she turned away and went back to covering her eggs with sand. Gerry sat motionless and patient, knowing that eventually she would leave the eggs and go to the deep pool where she liked to feed. It would be dangerous to try to steal one of her eggs, even when she was in the pool, but if he could do it, he could sell the egg for a full credit in the market and be the richest boy in The Academy.

After what seemed to Gerry like an endless wait, the mother grisk finally satisfied herself that all was well and lumbered her one-ton body down the beach and into the water. As soon as she slid out of sight, Gerry eased himself out of the tree and crawled over to the pile of sand that covered the eggs.

Just as he shoved one of the heavy eggs into his sack, he heard the mother grisk break water with a moaning cry. He stood up, hefted the heavy sack over his shoulder, and ran for the trees. If he had not started running, she probably never would have seen him. But she did, and with amazing speed she roared out of the water in a huge wave and charged after him.

The egg felt like it weighed as much as he did, but the thought of being trampled by a mad mother grisk spurred Gerry on. Fifty meters into the trees, as the crashing grew closer behind him, Gerry took advantage of a low branch on a bicard tree and swung himself off the ground, pulling the sack after him.

She saw where he went, and rammed the tree with the flat bone of her broad head. Gerry climbed like his life depended on it, which it did. He was grateful he had found such a solid tree.

The mother grisk kept him in the tree all night, leaving occasionally to check her eggs, then returning to ram his tree again and again. Gerry was never sure why she finally left him alone. But a long time later, when she wandered away in the dark and did not come back, he scrambled out of the tree, scraping his side badly as he did so. Then he ran all the way back to town with the grisk egg thumping his back in the canvas bag.

The market was just opening when he arrived, and he sold the egg to an old woman whose stall was near the center of the market. She gave him a full credit and a couple of centimes for the egg, and, as he lay in the infirmary having his scrape attended to and listening to the lecture from the headmaster, Gerry clutched the coins in his pocket. They made the pain in his side very bearable.

The pain stabbed through him again, and Gerard opened his eyes. Fairy Peg was bending over him.

"Oh, Pilot, I am so pleased that you are awake. Omna-Seay said you should have awakened hours ago. Does this hurt?"

He flinched as she rubbed something into his wound. "Mmhm," he said through clenched teeth. "What happened?"

"It was an Evirdian death squad," Fairy Peg said simply. "Hired assassins. They all died. And you were wonderful, Pilot." She punctuated that statement with a kiss. "Now, you must tell me how you fought so quickly."

"I'm not sure. I think it was a flash of prescience again." He sucked in his breath through clenched teeth as she tightened his bandage. "But it came and went so fast that, that, well, I'm just not sure." The memory of what happened sent a shiver through him. How could he ever depend on something that disappeared at a critical moment? Marradon must have overestimated his talent. "What happened to the others? And what took the Ratchets so long to get there?"

"Commander Alpluakka received a slight wound in his shield arm, but mends nicely. Fianne, dear Fianne, was frightened out of his wits, but he too recovered . . . with the help of a flagon of wine. The Ratchets came immediately. You were just too eager to do their work for them, you and your prescience."

Gerard laughed a little, but it hurt deep inside when he did so. "And you, my lovely Badh? You seem to have taken all this quite well."

Fairy Peg's eyes darkened like a flash of black midnight. Her laugh was not one of humor. "No, Pilot, one does not take such an assassination attempt in stride. Never. My mother, the great Tania Houn Draytonmab, was almost killed in just such an attempt on her life. I was only a child, but I remember well the terror of it. How does one cope with such an obscenity? Evird will have to be punished for this."

"Punish a whole planet for the acts of a few? Surely—"

"Surely, you do not understand, Pilot. Evird is a nest of insurrection. The offspring of that nest tried to topple our throne into a pool of blood. They cannot be alowed to remain unchastised.

"Oh, but you look so tired, Pilot. Perhaps you should rest now."

"Perhaps," Gerard answered slowly, "but promise me we'll talk more about Evird before you do anything. Please?" He felt Evird was important for a reason that wasn't yet clear. Perhaps it was only because there had been idle talk in the Ratchet barracks of going to Evird to help put down the insurrection, but he sensed it was deeper than that. "Please?" he asked again when she didn't answer.

"Very well, Pilot. If you be strong enough, we will talk of it again. Rest now." She brushed her soft fingers over his brow in gentle strokes.

He closed his eyes, letting the soothing caress of her fingers wipe the lines of tension from his face. Sleep came easily.

Gerard awoke once in the dark of night with a desperate thirst. In the light of a small lamp on the other side of the room, someone dozed in a chair with a small book in her lap. Hoarsely, he called out to her, and she came quickly to his side. She offered him small sips of water, then bathed his face and gave him a small lozenge to suck on. "Thanks, love," he said weakly.

"Welcome you are, Diplomat."

His eyes were to heavy to open again, but he knew it wasn't Fairy Peg. But who? Who? As he drifted toward sleep, the obvious answer floated gently into his last conscious thought: Inez Nare-Devy.

The following day Gerard was allowed to sit up and drink a small bowl of broth before being visited by Omna-Seay. The physmedicant examined his wound thoroughly and gently, then rendered his verdict. "You will live, Diplomat."

"Was there a question about that?"

"Such questions are always valid when one is wounded as deeply as you were. However, since you had very little internal bleeding, and we found no serious damage to your organs, we were not overly distressed by your condition."

"That's nice to know. How long will I be laid up?"

"Laid up? Oh, mean you . . . ah, I see. You should be almost fully recovered in a month if there are no complications."

"How fares he, Omna-Seay?" Fairy Peg asked from somewhere out of Gerard's line of vision.

"Well enough. Tomorrow make him walk a little distance in the morning. I will check him after his walk."

The complications that set in later were not serious, but they slowed Gerard's recover. Five weeks passed before he could walk without serious discomfort, and seven weeks before he felt strong enough one day to chase Fairy Peg into one of the secluded bowers in the garden and make love to her there amidst the lush perfumes of the flowers. Of course, that was not the first time they had made love since the attack. Fairy Peg had become very adept at straddling his prone body and riding him slowly and carefully into another garden of climactic bliss. And he had learned how truly adaptable the human hand was when he sought to return the pleasure she gave him.

Also during those weeks Fianne Tackona came to see him almost daily, bringing him company when Fairy Peg was attending to her duties. The more Gerard saw of Fianne, the more his appreciation grew for this narrow-faced man with his pessimistic view of the world. Gerard's awareness of the kinship he felt was heightened one afternoon as he and Fianne strolled slowly through the Koep garden.

"Tell me, Fianne. You seem to be aware of all the political tensions in the government. Just how seriously did our Badh weaken her power when she named me Prince Consort?"

"See those flowers," Fianne answered, pointing to a tall blossom whose orange and green sepals rose almost a full meter up the stalk to support a crown of violet petals.

"Those flowers are rare Lartuen *scrophylaria*. Periodically, our botanists peel the bracts from the lower part of the stem. Doing so causes the exposed stem to become tough and woody, and a new crown of flowers to appear at the top. So it is with the throne of Ribble. Those who reach up from below and attempt to steal part of its power for themselves find that their treasure quickly withers and the throne grows stronger.

"No, friend Gerard, our princess was not weakened by her choice of consort. The danger lies elsewhere."

Gerard had admired the tall flowers before without ever knowing anything about them. Fianne's analogy made him wonder how much he really knew about the politics of Ribble. "Some other danger to Princess Peg?" he asked.

"Perhaps." Fianne seemed lost in thought as though debating with himself. Finally he spoke again. "Whatever danger lies ahead for the Badh, I can only speculate upon. The danger to you is plainly visible."

"But what—"

"Let me finish. Your Federation wants very much to resume normal relations with our galaxy. So our Badh wants the same thing. However, there are those in positions of tremendous influence who have much to lose if such normal relations are reestablished. Such people do not appreciate your presence. Certain bits of information I am privy to lead me to believe that the Evirdian death squad had no intentions of harming the Badh. The danger, Diplomat, is to you."

Gerard didn't know what to say. It had never occurred to him that his peace mission to Ribble might threaten his life. Stupid, he thought. Stupid. "Would these influential people you spoke of try to use me to get to Princess Peg?"

"Again you would have me speculate. I cannot. Let this guide you, though. Be aware. Be suspicious. Be careful. You have friends and allies who cannot reveal themselves to you, and enemies who would act as your friends. Trust no one totally."

"Even you."

"Trust no one totally, not me, not our Badh, not even yourself when you make any decision that appears questionable. That is the only help I can give you."

Long after that conversation, Gerard continued to puzzle over Fianne's advice. He had allowed himself the luxury of complacency, fighting only the obvious enemies to his well-being like Markl Holsten, and Targ Alpluakka, and Corpus Privy. But even then he had only fought to hold ground, not to win it. Again and again he asked himself why he allowed himself to be manipulated, why he seemed incapable of taking a more active role in his alien universe? For all his searching, he could find no answer.

The only other person he saw regularly during his recovery period was Inez Nare-Devy. Why she insisted on visiting him, Gerard never understood. Her excuse was that Fairy Peg had asked her to teach him to dance in preparation for the ball on the Day of Conclusion, but he knew that wasn't her real motive. Whenever he was in her company he felt awkward and out of place. Her physical resemblance to Fairy Peg was constantly jarred by her sharp tongue and sarcastic wit.

"Where were you when manners were taught," he asked one day when she walked into his bedchamber unannounced, "hiding in a closet?"

"Learning to tempt the souls of men. Are you not tempted by me, Diplomat?" She threw off her cape to reveal a dress that was daring even by Kril's liberal standards. Except for a few subtly shaded areas, the thin dress was totally transparent. "Or does my sister have you so locked in her power that you cannot see anyone else."

Gerard looked at her steadily, unable to resist appraising all of her. Beautiful, he thought, and treacherous. "Do you always use such clumsy tactics?"

"Only for clumsy men," she replied. "Doubtful it is that you could handle subtlety."

He should have let the remark pass, but he didn't. "Doubtful it is," he said, mocking her tone, "that you know the meaning of subtlety."

The next day she came to visit him in a black, sack-like dress that totally hid her body. She brought with her a small portfolio of drawings she said were done by one of Kril's foremost artists, and asked if Gerard would like to see them. Out of politeness, he reluctantly said he would. They sat at a small table in the anteroom and examined the exquisite drawings slowly and carefully. All were scenes from nature, and each seemed a minor masterpiece to Gerard. Soon he was enthusiastically talking about them.

"The use of line! Like here, and here," he said, pointing

out the places he meant on the landscape that lay before him. "It's almost as though the form she records had a life of its own. There's a certain sinuous character in these pictures which—"

"Which demand your attention," Inez finished for him.

"Exactly. Exactly. Look at how she has taken this low line of hills and used them to draw your eye, not up to the mountain where it would normally go in a picture like this, but down into the valley and the trees nestled at the base of that small hill. It's almost suggestive of—" Gerard stopped. It wasn't almost suggestive, it *was* suggestive.

"Almost suggestive of what, Diplomat?" Inez asked teasingly.

Gerard ignored her and flipped back to the previous drawing. What he had admired minutes before as a beautiful picture of a flower, now showed through as something else. He looked at Inez with a slightly shocked expression on his face, and realized as he did so that he was physically aroused. He blushed.

Inez laughed at him. "Long enough it took you. I was beginning to think you blind."

Gerard bit back his anger at having been tricked. Hidden in the pastoral forms of the drawings were the sensual outlines of female genitals. He didn't have to look back to know they were in all the pictures.

Not wanting to offend Fairy Peg by taking his anger out on her sister, he decided to get away as politely as he could. "A hundred pardons, Chattel-shi Nare Devy," he said, rising slowly and hoping the bulge in his pants wasn't really noticeable. "It is time for my rest. If you will excuse me?"

Inez gave him a phony pout while staring opening at his crotch. "Will you not at least acknowledge that I can be subtle?"

"Acknowledged," he said curtly. "As subtle as slow poison."

With that he turned and left the room, taking care to bolt the bedchamber door behind him. When Fairy Peg returned late that afternoon, he told her about the incident, starting with the business about the dress the day before.

Fairy Peg was amused. "So my sister finds you attractive. You should be flattered, my Pilot."

"I'm not flattered, I'm offended. What right does she have trying to seduce me like that?"

"Pilot, Pilot, do not be so upset. Sisters have been trying to steal men from each other since the first star went nova. It is nothing new, and after tomorrow you will be freed from her unwanted attentions."

"Tomorrow?"

"Did I not tell you, Pilot? Tomorrow is the Day of Conclusion."

* * *

Message to: Greaves Lingchow
            FedDiploSvc
The insurrection on Evird could set back our plans for years. We are not pleased. Furthermore, we maintain a growing suspicion that you are not bargaining in good faith. Were we not already so deeply involved with this process, and had not your emissary already gained the confidence of the throne, we fear all would be lost. Such is still a very real possibility. You must see that your agents on Evird are withdrawn immediately. Otherwise we can only predict a prolonged delay in achieving peace.

—Glyph

* * *

10

The dawn sky was just begining to turn grey as Gerard settled himself in *Windhover*'s pilot couch.

"Don't have much time, Windy. Have to get back to EllKoep in an hour or so to begin dressing for the ceremonies. Let's see what you've saved up for me."

A list of seven mesages popped up on the vidscreen. Two of them were of interest. The rest dealt with regulation changes and required only formal acknowledgement of their receipt. The first of the two messages he read was from his immediate supervisor, Assistant Sub-Secretary Merita.

> Avoid, repeat, avoid involvement with internal divisions in your area of responsibility. No reply necessary. Continue following standard orders.

Merita must be referring to the touble on Evird, Gerard decided as he called up the second message. Dated ten standard days earlier than Merita's message, this one was from Merita's immediate supervisor, Sub-Secretary Nevararms.

> Sound intelligence indicates rival service assuming an interactive role in Ribble Galaxy to the detriment of our goals. Take whatever effective measures you can to restrict their activities and limit the damage.

Just like the damn service, Gerard thought. Send out conflicting instructions, and hang the agent for following the wrong ones.

"Windy, when's the earliest we can punch through a message to the FedRelay on Gossamer? . . . Sorry, give it to me in local days . . . All right, send a standard request for clarification to each of these addresses, and I'll check back with you in ten days or so to see what they say.

"You know what I need, Windy? With all the technical marvels Fed has come up with, why don't I have a pocket transceiver I can take with me to communicate with you? Seems like that ought to be fairly simple—

"What? Well why couldn't you decode here and . . . no, that wouldn't work. Or would it? Suppose it had a scrambler. You think about what it would take. See if we could modify a memocorder with some of the parts we have aboard. Or if that won't do, maybe you can find enough parts in our inventory for us to build one from scratch that will do the trick."

Gerard spent the rest of his hour doing routine maintenance chores, and really didn't want to leave when Windy buzzed him. "Okay, Windy, I'm going. I think the rest of these can wait until I get back in a couple of weeks to check on the replies. Anything else? . . . Yeah, you follow standard safety orders too."

Fairy Peg held the slender, gleaming sword in a two-handed grip high over her crowned head. "On this day," she said in a loud, clear voice that reached to every corner of the packed Great Hall, "you, Gerard Hopkins Manley, conclude the old phase of your life and pass into a new life. As you have sworn your allegiance before these witnesses, I name you Prince Consort to the Throne of Ribble Galaxy, and Fize of the Gabriel Ratchets."

Fairy Peg lowered the sword in a slow, sweeping arc until its fine point rested on the bridge of Gerard's nose. With a deft twist of her wrists she nicked his skin, and a drop of blood welled up and spilled over onto his cheek. "As you give your blood freely now, so shall you offer it always in defense of the throne." She brought the sword up until it crossed between her breasts. "Rise, Prince Consort. Rise, Fize of the Gabriel Ratchets."

Gerard rose slowly and stood facing Fairy Peg. Slowly, she brought the sword to a vertical position and held it out to him. As he took it, his fingers tingled from her touch. Fairy Peg stepped around and behind him as he raised the sword high over his head.

"Let none doubt that they will have to pass through this sword to touch the throne. Let none doubt that I stand before all threats to the Badh. Let none doubt that my first allegiance is to her, or may Houn strike me as I stand." Gerard said the last phrase with some trepidation in his heart. His personal allegiance was to Fairy Peg, but his political allegiance was to Fed. Still, at the moment he pledged his allegiance, he meant exactly what he said. Later he would have to sort out what it meant to his life.

Squo Lyle, in the front row with the rest of Corpus Privy, was the first to rise and lead the applause. As Gerard's gaze swept over the rest of the crowd, he was pleased to see Brunnel's string, his personal bodyguard, standing proudly at attention by the door. Yet he also saw many people standing and applauding with little or no enthusiasm, not looking at him, but past him, through him as though he were invisible.

If he lowered the sword, it would be their signal to stop applauding. After a moment's consideration, he decided to keep it held high, to demand their respect, not for him, but for the Badh who had chosen him. He let the tip of the sword waver slightly, and the applause wavered with it as people reacted prematurely. Then he raised the sword even higher, extending his whole body upward until his heels almost came off the floor. The increase in volume grew slowly until everyone seemed to realize they would have to clap until he was pleased with their performance. When the applause rose to a crescendo, Gerald slowly lowered the sword and the clapping slackened in response. Even then many people, including Squo Lyle and most of Corpus Privy, continued clapping in approval of what he had done.

Finally the applause subsided, and the royal orchestra began playing "The Hymn of the Badh." Gerard carefully sheathed the sword and offered his arm to Fairy Peg. Side by side they led the recessional out of the Great Hall, their personal string of Ratchets falling in before and behind as they reached the door. Never in Gerard's life had he felt so important, so needed, so vitally alive. Or so powerful.

Hours later, after the seemingly endless reception, he was still beaming with pride when they closed the door to their chambers and turned to face each other.

"Kiss me, Pilot," she said softly, holding out her arms to him.

He drew her to him. "As my Badh commands," he said with a smile. The soft fabric of her dress seemed to melt against her skin under his hands. He kissed her slowly, gently, fighting an urge to crush her mouth against his. She sensed the hidden heat of his desire and drew slightly away from him.

"By custom you must wait until after the ball before claiming your rights to me."

"Then I shall wait," he said with a gentle laugh, "but if, when the time comes, my passion overwhelms us, do not be surprised."

"Constantly you surprise me, Pilot, as when you forced our reluctant court to honor us. What moved you so?"

"Anger? Defiance? I don't know exactly. Remember what you kept saying when you insisted on naming me consort? You said, 'Honor will be served, Pilot.' Well, I guess I just thought it was time for the court to serve honor."

"Well you did, my love, and gained respect from it even from those who do not love you as I do."

"In your service, Princess," Gerard said with a twinkle. "However, I will be of little service to you if we don't eat pretty soon."

"That appetite I can satisfy immediately. Shall we have guests? Or would you rather dine alone?"

"Alone, I think. I will have had my fill of people before this day is over."

Standing in the receiving line at the Concluding Ball, exchanging brief pleasantries with the umpteenth member of the Nobel Assembly, his wife, and eldest daughter, Gerard remembered his prediction and had to smile. The assemblyman's wife was flattered by that, as was her daughter, who giggled and chirped the rest of the evening about how the Prince Consort had graced her with a special smile.

When Privy-Admiral Holsten came through the line somewhat later than expected, he whispered conspiratorially to Gerard that he needed to talk to him privately later in the evening. Gerard knew that even the Fize of the Gabriel Ratchets dared not deny such a request from the ranking military leader of all Ribble Galaxy, and quickly assented.

When the line finally disappeared, Gerard was convinced it was only because he and Fairy Peg had to open the ball with the first dance. Thanks to Inez's tutelage, he managed to lead Fairy Peg around the floor, if not gracefully, at least not clumsily. When the music ended, he accepted the polite applause with a brief bow and started to lead Fairy Peg from the dance floor. They were stopped by Privy-Admiral Holsten, who was accompanied by a young woman with impenetrable black eyes and a small, boyish figure.

"Pardon, Badh, Consort, but my grandaughter, Branbinie, was unavoidably delayed in arriving and begged the honor of being introduced."

"Honored I am, noble ones," Branbinie said with a deep curtsey and a girlish voice.

"Graced with your presence," Fairy Peg replied formally.

"And your beauty," Gerard added by rote. He was distracted by the Privy-Admiral's handsigns, which indicated an urgent need to speak to him. "Perhaps, Badh, you would grant a small favor to your consort and allow me a brief moment with our Privy-Admiral? I urgently need to discuss a bit of protocol with him that I seem to have forgotten, and I have no wish to make a fool of myself in front of you and this charming lady." His wink to Fairy Peg told her he was making an excuse.

"Certainly, Consort. Admiral."

They both bowed deeply to her.

"Come, Branbinie, you must tell me why we have not seen you in our halls before now," Fairy Peg said as she led Branbinie away.

Gerard followed Privy-Admiral Holsten in the opposite direction and out of the Grand Hall. Brunnel's string immediately fell in behind them.

"They are not necessary," Holsten said quickly.

"Perhaps not, Admiral, but they are new to the job of protecting me and quite enthusiastic. It would be poor form for their Fize to dismiss them."

Holsten snorted, but said no more. After negotiating a series of long halls and corridors, they came to a small door several floors below the Great Hall.

"Stand," Gerard commanded his string. He gave Brunnel a quick handsign of approval, then followed Holsten into a small, well-appointed room.

"Please, Consort, be seated," Holsten said, offering Gerard a chair which faced the door. "A most delicate problem has arisen which requires your assistance." He poured Gerard a small glass of wine, then sat in the chair beside him.

"I am at your service, Privy-Admiral." Gerard studied the old man's profile and noted his firm jaw was beginning to sag a little and his eye looked like it was sinking into a dark pocket of puffy skin.

"Pardon, Consort, but awkward it is for your Privy-Admiral to seek help from anyone." Holsten emptied his glass, looked at it sadly, the set it down on the wide arm of the chair before turning to Gerard. "Little more than an hour and a half ago some of your Ratchets caught another Evirdian death squad."

Gerard was shocked. "Where?"

"Coming up through an ancient passageway through the cellars of EllKoep. Two died in the fight. The other four lay down their weapons and collapsed, dead from some self-inflicted cause. Commander Alpluakka was examining their bodies when I left him."

There was a sadness in Holsten's voice that Gerard couldn't account for. "What has this to do with you, sir?"

Holsten looked steadily at Gerard. In their dark sockets his tan eyes looked cold and distant, as though reflecting some frigid desert of empty sand.

"A serving girl was caught with the death squad. She claims to have discovered them only moments before the Ratchets arrived. Commander Alpluakka believes she was leading them through the Koep." Holsten hesitated only for a second. "Her name is Imitatas, and as head of her family, I must claim responsibility for her."

Gerard wasn't sure what that meant. "Pardon, Admiral, but exactly who is this girl to you?"

With a sigh of resignation, Holsten rose, poured himself another glass of wine, refilled Gerard's glass, and sat heavily back down. "Perhaps I should explain," he said with a surprising firmness in his voice. "When my niece, Latisha, was very young and impetuous, she had an unfortunate involvement with one of her first cousins. Because she managed to conceal her condition until abortion was out of the question, she bore an incestuous daughter, the girl, Imitatas. By the grace of the Badh, the girl was brought here and raised by a serving woman. Now she has brought new shame to my family. But still I must ask you to spare her life if there is no real evidence against her."

An illegitimate Holsten leading an Evirdian death squad? No wonder the admiral was so troubled. "Where is she now, sir?"

"In the adjoining room under Ratchet guard. She refuses to talk, claiming she has told all she knows."

"I would see her."

Privy-Admiral Holsten spoke quietly into the communicator beside his chair, and moments later the girl was brought before them by two Ratchets. She was slender and wiry, with dark skin and matching eyes that burned with defiance. Targ followed them into the room.

"Privy-Admiral. Fize," he said formally. "This is the traitorous wench. She was sent to the cellars on an errand, but not to the part of the cellars where she was found. She says she got lost. My Ratchets say she was leading the assassins. Request permission for full interrogation."

Gerard winced at the memory of his own interrogation, but the evidence plus the girl's attitude hardened him quickly. He wanted to see no more death squads. He looked quickly at Privy-Admiral Holsten for some sign of his reaction, but the old man's face was blank.

"Very well, Commander," Gerard said carefully, "but if you cannot prove without a doubt that she is guilty, she must be allowed to live." Gerard felt slightly sickened by the thought of what his words would mean for her. "Take her away."

After they were gone, Gerard rose to leave. Privy-Admiral Holsten looked at him oddly. "Please, Consort, there is one more thing we must discuss."

"I'm sorry about the girl, Admiral, but—"

"No, Consort, you did what had to be done. Now you must do one more thing. Tomorrow I will recommend to the Badh and Corpus Privy that a full-scale military force be sent to Evird to quell the rebellion there. There will be much arguing, but they will consent. As Prince Consort and Fize of the Gabriel Ratchets, it will be your duty to accompany that force."

"But sir, what use could I be on such an expedition?"

Holsten sighed. "Believe me, Consort, you will be of much use. Your presence represents the throne. It might help avert great bloodshed."

Gerard had just sent a young girl to be tortured, and now Holsten was telling him that his presence in a distant corner of Ribble Galaxy might help avoid bloodshed. His emotions were too confused to cope with either situation properly. "Very well, Admiral. I will consult with the Badh. Will you return with me to the ball?"

Holsten's eyes flicked toward the door where Targ had taken Imitatas. "Perhaps in a short while, Consort. There are a few small duties I must perform first."

As Gerard walked with his string back to the Great Hall, he was deeply troubled by what had happened. More assassins. A girl, perhaps an innocent girl, sent to be tortured. A punitive expedition to Evird with his presence requested. Little remained of the pride and elation he had felt earlier in the day. He needed to talk to Fairy Peg and to think about all this, but his duty required reappearance at the ball with no hint of the dark mood he had fallen into.

He fulfilled his duty, but only by constantly forcing himself to appear carefree and happy. He might have convinced others with his performance, but when at last he left the ball with Fairy Peg and returned with her to their quarters it was obvious he hadn't fooled her.

"What troubles my Pilot?" she asked as he helped her undo the tiny hooks down the back of her gown.

After hesitating a moment, he told her everything that had happened when he left the ball with Privy-Admiral Holsten. "I didn't want to burden you with this earlier, but now I must have your counsel."

Fairy Peg stepped into the dressing room and out of sight, but talked to him through the open door. "In the case of the girl, you did what had to be done. Also in the line of duty, you must attend the fleet to Evird as my personal representative. Be hopeful that your presence will indeed benefit a peaceful solution. I shall miss you, but when you return, I shall have a great gift for you."

"I don't want any gifts," he said wearily. He had stripped down to his briefs and was slouched in one of the overstuffed chairs, nursing a glass of cold water. "If I must go to Evird, I just want to go, and come back to you, and be done with it."

"Ah, but Pilot, this will be a very special gift, one that only I can give you. Look at me, Pilot."

As Gerard looked up at her an involuntary shiver of excitement passed through him. Fairy Peg stood in front of the dressing room door wearing the glowing sunburst robe which so sensually flattered the contours of her body. His eyes drank her in from her finely tapered ankles, to the secret folds of her loins, to her full, rounded breasts, to her radiant face topped by the loose swirls of her dark hair and sparkling tiara. A fine golidium chain suspended his signet ring in the warm valley between her breasts. He started to rise and go to her.

"No, Pilot. Now yet. Just sit you there and look at me. Do you see anything different about me?"

It was a strange question, but he looked at her carefully. "Yes," he said finally, "you've grown more radiantly beautiful."

113

"That is the gift, Pilot. What you see is the beginning, for I carry in my womb the growing gift of our child."

"I . . . do you . . . do you mean . . ." Gerard shut his stammering mouth and rose slowly from the chair, looking at her again as though for the first time. Perhaps there was a new fullness in her beauty, a stronger radiance about her, a swelling of pride that had come too slowly for him to notice.

"Come to me, my consort," she said, holding out her arms to him. "Come possess the mother of your child."

"Oh, Fairy Peg," he said as he wrapped her in his arms, "what have I done to be so fortunate?"

"You seduced me, of course," she said between nibbling kisses on his neck.

"I think it was the other way around. I was the one who was seduced."

"No," she whispered as she flicked her tongue in his ear, "the Badh would never stoop to seduction."

"Oh, hush." Smothering her mouth with an open kiss, he let his tongue slide along her lips with rapid little touches. She pressed harder against him with a deep moan as she sucked the air from his lungs and his tongue into her mouth.

That night, like dancers after months of practice, they found the perfect rhythm for their bodies and moved united through a faultless ballet of their senses. Each movement brought them to new heights of rapture until they peaked together in one grand harmonic climax of flesh, spirit, and ethereal music.

*   *   *

Message to: Pelis Foffey Turingay-Gotz
      FedTreatySvc

Will try to salvage what we can out of this debacle you have created. Count on nothing. If Key-One follows our lead, we might still obtain the desired results. However, a backlash could just as easily occur. Then neither you nor we would gain anything but bitter defeat, and all this effort will have been wasted.

What will you do if there are no spoils to be divided?
                    —Toehold

*   *   *

11

Gerard stood at the viewport and stared at the growing pink ball that was Evird. In less than an hour *Avenger's Heel* would pick up the shuttle carrying Governor Shoso Cessaid-Malee, and his mettle as a diplomat would be tested. Cessaid-Malee wanted the fleet to bombard the rebel strongholds with neutronic missiles. She had argued in a lengthy message to Gerard and Privy-Admiral Holsten that the populace in those areas must be sacrificed so that the government could reclaim the valuable agricultural land in time to get in a crop before winter set in. Otherwise, she claimed, half the loyalists on Evird would starve to death within a local year.

Unknown to Cessaid-Malee, *Avenger's Heel* had also received a message from the rebels requesting negotiations with Privy-Admiral Holsten. Gerard had read his copy of the message several times, disturbed by its wording. Then he had suddenly realized why the message bothered him so. Hidden in the simple text there was a second message, one which so angered him that he could not control his emotions. With a loud curse, he had left the control center and gone straight to his cabin, telling Hoose and Woltol to allow no one to disturb him.

The hidden message was contained in the final paragraph of the rebel communique, which read:

> We call our brothers to find a diplomatic solution and are awaiting your negotiator. Our service to the true orders of peace demands trust between all of us.

The key words were *brothers* and *diplomatic*. Finding them in the same sentence, each the fourth member of a series of four words, gave him the rest of it. *Brothers diplomatic awaiting service orders/trust us*. Some FedService officer had worded the rebel message.

Gerard's anger was provoked from several directions at once. He had been assured that the only FedService officers who would be in Ribble Galaxy would be deep cover intelligence officers. No d.c.i.o. would have sent such a message. That left a host of other possibilities, but the series-four code and the use of the key term *brothers diplomatic* narrowed them quickly to either FedDiploService or FedTreatyService. Either possibility only increased his anger. Compounding that was the frustration of not being able to tell anyone what he knew.

"Kravor in Krick!" he cursed aloud. Sub-Secretary Nevararms had been dead on the credits when his sources indicated other services might be taking an active role in Ribble. Well, if FedTreatyService was foolish enough to actually send in their own agents, they would have to live, or die, with the consequences of their actions. And he would have to make his decisions without regard to his privileged information.

Governor Cessaid-Malee greeted Gerard with the barest minimal courtesy, then turned warmly to Privy-Admiral Holsten.

"How well you look, Deton. What a shame you had to come to see us under such strained circumstances." Her voice had a musical quality that Gerard found appealing in spite of her attitude toward him.

"You seem more vibrant than ever," Holsten said, leading her to one of the many comfortable chairs in the Admiral's Lounge. With a flick of his eyes he signalled Gerard to join them. "I too wish the circumstances were different. Will you have some wine while you tell us the latest situation?"

Cessaid-Malee glanced at Gerard with a look of appraisal. He acknowledged it with the barest of nods. "Perhaps, Privy-Admiral, we should first tell Her Excellency that we have received a request for negotiations from the rebel forces."

Her reaction was as strong as he had hoped it would be. "Lies," she spat. "Those vipers negotiate with no one. Surely, Deton, you and the consort do not plan to engage in such negotiations?"

"We have planned nothing, Shoso, but the consort believes we should consider the idea, and I quite agree with that."

As Cessaid-Malee took a slow, deep drink of her wine, Gerard could see her flush with anger even through her heavy makeup. "Certainly there can be no harm in considering that option, Governor, unless, of course, you have reason to—"

"Of course I have reasons! Did I pack my old bones into that shuttle and come up here for a social visit? Those *rebel forces*, as you so civilly called them, are nothing but bands of thieves and murderers set on destroying Evird any way they can. And you," she said, pointing a dark finger at Gerard, "you and your Federation are supporting them."

"That's a serious charge, Shoso."

"But a true one," Gerard said flatly. "At least it is true that there are Federation agents on Evird with the rebel forces." They both stared at him in amazement. "There was a hidden message in their request for negotiations, Privy-Admiral—"

"So that is why—"

"Yes, that's why I was so angry when I left the control center. I had been assured that no service of the Federation would be allowed to interfere in Ribble's affairs. I was obviously lied to."

"But since they are your friends, down there, you want to negotiate with them," Shoso said with heavy sarcasm.

"No, Excellency. *If* we decide to negotiate, one of our demands will be that those agents be turned over to the Corpus Privy for trial. Then they could be used as pawns in any future dealings with the Federation." Already Gerard saw Fed's mistake as something to be used later.

"I quite underestimated you, Consort," Cessaid-Malee said finally. "You seem to take your allegiance to our Badh very seriously."

"Of course I do."

117

Holsten looked at him thoughtfully. "The idea has merit. What say you, Shoso, shall we give it consideration?"

"Well..."

Hoping to swing her decision, Gerard said, "I will leave the decision to the two of you." With a nod to both of them he left the table and moved to the other side of the lounge, where he sat with his back to them and prayed they would choose the non-violent way of trying to settle the problem.

Minutes later Holsten put his hand on Gerard's shoulder. "I see now why you are a diplomat, Consort. We will try negotiating with these people."

It took a week of back-and-forth communications with the rebel forces before a meeting could be arranged. Both sides agreed that Privy-Admiral Holsten would be the negotiator for the government, and that any decisions he and the rebels agreed upon would be binding on both parties. Then he, Cessaid-Malee, and Gerard worked for almost ten hours outlining what terms they would ask for and what they would settle for. Finally Holsten boarded *Graveclaw*, the smallest landing ship in the *Avenger's Heel* bays, and departed with a crew of three and ten fleet marines for the negotiating site. Gerard went immediately to his cabin to get some much-needed rest, but was awakened after only an hour's sleep with the news that they had lost communications with *Graveclaw*, and the pilot's last words were "out of control."

He rushed to the control center and was greeted by a furious Cessaid-Malee. "I warned you those vipers could not be trusted. Now they have shot down one of the bravest, truest patriots this galaxy has ever known. Why, oh, why did I listen to your vile suggestion? Why did I ever agree to—"

"Shut up, Governor," Gerard bellowed in the voice Tg Neereg had taught him to use. Not only did Cessaid-Malee stop babbling, the whole control center quieted.

Seemingly out of nowhere Privy-Vice-Admiral Gannack stepped in front of him with a smart salute. Gerard deeply appreciated her acknowledgement of his position and returned the salute crisply.

"Sir," she said formally, "I will fill you in on the latest status reports."

"No-o-o-o-ooo!" Cessaid-Malee screamed in a wavering voice as she jumped on Gerard and clawed at his back. Almost as quickly as she moved, Knip and Brunnel pulled her off and pinned her between them.

"Take her to sick bay," Gannack ordered. With a signal of approval from Gerard, they disappeared with Cessaid-Malee in tow, wailing at the top of her voice.

"*Graveclaw* is down, sir," Gannack said as though nothing had happened. "The only signals we are receiving are the automatic distress signals. We have located her position about forty kilometers south of the intended landing site and are readying the *Deathpoint* for a rescue mission. We should be able to launch in an hour."

"That long?"

"Yes, sir. And one more thing. The rebels are claiming they had nothing to do with the crash."

"What do you think, Admiral?"

"Well, sir, the pilot reported violent turbulence and an explosion immediately prior to going out of control. From the evidence, I would be led to believe *Graveclaw* was shot down."

"Besides sending down the *Deathpoint*, what do you recommend, Admiral?" As Gerard said that he realized that he and Gannack were playing a very formal, very serious game. She deferred to him because of his position as consort, but she was the one who had the true command of the fleet, and the final military decision would be hers.

Privy-Vice-Admiral Gannack looked at him carefully, as though sensing his realization. "The fleet is zeroed in on all the known rebel strongholds. If it becomes necessary, we will use all reasonable force to eliminate them. Those were Admiral Holsten's orders to me before he left."

Gerard swallowed. The thought of raining down neutronic missiles on half-a-hundred communities full of men, women, and children made his stomach do a slow, queasy roll. If Gannack decided that was to be their course of action, Gerard would have to endorse it and in some way take responsibility for it. Thus, if he wanted to keep the blood off his own hands, he would have to do something himself to prevent the fleet's actions.

"Admiral," he said slowly, "I want to command *Deathpoint* when it goes on the rescue mission."

The surprise on her face came through in her voice. "But sir, that would be highly irregular and very dangerous."

"And it also might save a lot of lives. If the rebels know that I'm on *Deathpoint*, they are much less likely to attack it."

"Or much more likely to, sir."

"Surely they can't be that stupid. If they attack *Deathpoint*, they would be risking the wrath of the fleet."

"However, sir, if they managed to capture you, they could hold off the fleet indefinitely."

"I still think it's worth the risk," Gerard said, thinking of towns and villages strewn with bodies. "If they capture me, you have my permission to fire at will."

"I cannot do that, sir."

"Then I will enter it as an order in the ship's log."

"Sir," Gannack said with a steely tone in her voice, "I formally request that you set aside this plan."

Staring straight into her cold blue eyes he said, "I can't do that, Admiral. Privy-Admiral Holsten told me my presence on this trip might help save some lives. I have to find out if that's really true...and going down with the *Deathpoint* is the only way I can do that right now."

Deathpoint fought the buffeting top winds, then slid easily through the fluorescent pink clouds of Evird's atmosphere and began homing in a great tightening spiral on *Graveclaw*'s distress beacon. Gerard rode beside the pilot, Zk Lichian, wondering if he'd made the right decision, yet at the same time feeling pleased with himself. It was obvious, however, that Zk Lichian wasn't at all pleased by Gerard's presence, and his answers to Gerard's questions were brief and abrupt. It was also obvious that Zk Lichian was an excellent pilot. He brought *Deathpoint* to within two hundred meters of *Graveclaw* before setting the ship down gently on a small grassy knoll.

As Zk Lichian put the ship on standby, Gerard scanned the area with the view cameras. They sat between a rolling plain on one side and a low range of rocky hills on the other. *Graveclaw* lay on its side between them and the hills, its whole tail section blown away. From the lack of debris, it was obvious that the explosion had not occurred on landing. Other than the wreck of *Graveclaw*, there were no signs of human occupation or activity anywhere near them.

Satisfied that they had arrived before the rebels, Gerard ordered Zk Lichian to remain with *Deathpoint*, ready for immediate launch, and went to prepare for the rescue. His string, along with a volunteer string of Ratchets, was already waiting for him in full battle gear when he reached the portal deck.

"Ready, Fize," Brunnel said with a crisp salute.

Closgeman helped Gerard into his power rig, and Knip handed him a lase rifle. They were ready to go.

"Who has the cutting equipment?" Gerard asked. One of the volunteers raised his hand. "Good. String leader?"

"Ibit, sir."

"Ibit, detail three of your string to guard the ship. Then we will advance in a chopped wedge with you on point." Gerard hoped that by giving Ibit the honor of the point position, he would take away the sting of security guard duty. Ibit's quick shift of expression from disappointment to pride told Gerard it had worked.

They disembarked one at a time, using the slide chute rather than the ladder, and formed a perfect perimeter around the ship. Gerard checked with Zk Lichian on his communicator.

"Still no sign of anyone, sir, and still no response from *Graveclaw*."

"Very well. We're moving out." The chopped wedge was formed like a small inverted V followed by a larger one. In the center of the wedge were Gerard and the Ratchet with the cutting equipment.

As they advanced through the thick clumps of grass, Gerard tried to analyze the cool smell of the air and the strange stillness around them. Evird was known for its great variety of birds, and on this continent there were several large species which regularly attacked men in the open. Yet he saw no birds and heard none. Gerard didn't like that.

Just before they reached *Graveclaw* a deep, narrow ravine blocked their path. It was too wide to jump. The strew of ragged boulders down its sides would make it very difficult to climb down and back up. And as far as they could see it stretched away in both directions just as impassible.

"A twin span?" Ibit asked.

Gerard nodded. He hated twin spans, a kind of horizontal rope ladder, but he was glad the Ratchets had taught him to use one. It only took Ibit and Knip two minutes to fire the anchors across, pull the lines, and set the tension. Ibit led the way. Then, one by one, they followed him across the slender bridge. Gerard took his turn in the middle, got down on all fours, tried to blank his mind to what lay below him, and went quickly through the crab-like motions that had been drilled into him. He was across the span and a meter into the grass before he realized it. Brunnel smiled at him approvingly.

Graveclaw was only thirty meters up the slight slope from them, but they fanned out carefully around it before Gerard and Brunnel actually approached it. As soon as they did, they heard a banging noise coming from inside.

"They be alive, sir," Brunnel said with amazing restraint.

They were indeed alive, but all their systems were dead, and they were slowly suffocating to death. Using the universal tapping code, one of the inside crewmen led them to the spot where the hull was thinnest, and they started cutting with the lase torch. The work went quickly, but to Gerard it seemed like an eternity. He kept checking with Zk Lichian for signs of rebel activity, and responding to Lichian's negative reports by ordering his Ratchets to double their vigilance.

Less than thirty minutes after arriving at *Graveclaw*'s side, a blackened piece of her hull plate fell away, and eleven gasping men crawled from the wreck. Privy-Admiral Holsten was not one of them.

"Where is he?" Gerard demanded. "Where is the admiral?"

"Escape pod, sir," one of the crewmen gasped.

Gerard immediately called Zk Lichian. "Patch me through to *Avenger's Heel*." After a brief flurry of static Gerard heard Privy-Vice-Admiral Gannack's muffled voice. "Admiral, this is the consort. The crew here says Admiral Holsten ejected in the escape pod. Are you picking up any signals?"

"Negative, negative. High gain receivers . . . that frequency since . . . no signals."

"We have a storm front moving in, sir," Zk Lichian broke in. "It is disrupting communications."

"All right, Lichian. Tell Admiral Gannack to keep monitoring for signals from the pod. As soon as these men catch their breath, we're heading back. I want to lift as soon as we're aboard."

"Affirmative, sir. Should I plan to retrace *Graveclaw*'s course?"

"That's right. Consort out."

"What about the bodies, sir?" the leader of the fleet marines asked.

"Get them out of there, on the double." Only the pilot and one of the fleet marines had died in the crash, but Gerard had no idea how they would get their bodies across the ravine. "Lichian," he called into his communicator.

"Sir?"

"After we lift, can you destroy this wreck?"

"Affirmative, sir."

"Good. Plan to do so."

As soon as the bodies were out of the ship and wrapped securely in space blankets, Ibit led the group down the slope to the twin span bridge. The unarmed fleet marines looked very uneasy, but with good discipline kept themselves from bunching up.

Ibit's point went across the bridge first. Then the fleet marines followed. When the firing started the marine in the middle of the bridge looked as though he had been kicked in the side. As he fell from the bridge, his scream almost hid the distant crack of a rifle.

"Down," Brunnel screamed at the crewmen. The Ratchets and marines were already hugging the dirt. Gerard brushed debris off of his communicator, then saw a dark spot appear on its dull grey surface. For an instant he thought it was blood. It was sweat. Below, the dying marine groaned feebly on the rocks.

"Lichian, we're taking fire from the hills. Can you see anything up there?"

"Negative, sir. Wait. Infrared has something. Hard to tell, sir. Too many heat patterns coming off those rocks."

"Dammit, Lichian, one of the marines just got shot." As he said that, Knip slid past him and lowered himself hand over hand down the ravine. A rock exploded to Knip's left, and Gerard started counting. One thousand one. One thousand two. One thousand—the crack of the rifle stopped him. "Concentrate on an area five to six hundred meters above our position," he shouted into the communicator. It was a rough calculation, but the best they had.

"Dead, sir," Knip called up to him. "Throw me another rope."

As the marines lay on their backs and hauled their dead companion out of the ravine, a series of explosions rang from the hills.

"I think I got them, sir," Lichian's voice squaked from the communicator.

"Keep watching."

"Affirmative, sir."

After the rest of the marines made it safely across the bridge, Brunnel clutched one of the bodies against him with his lower arms, and, using his upper arms and feet, hauled the corpse across the span. As soon as he was across, Woltol followed with the second body. For as long as each was on the bridge, Gerard held his breath, waiting for a shot that didn't come.

They both returned quickly, then Brunnel took the body of the fleet marine across. "All right," Gerard said to the crewmen, "you two next."

The first one hesitated in the middle of the bridge and almost fell off. But he managed to keep his grip, and Brunnel grabbed him as soon as he was in range. The second crewman went slower and had less trouble.

"You next, Woltol."

Woltol looked at him carefully. "I cannot cross until you have, Fize."

Gerard knew there was no sense arguing about the order, and he sensed that Woltol had a reason for his decision. "Very well, Knip, you go next. I'll follow you. Then Closgemon, Hoose, and Woltol. Go."

They moved across the span in good order and were soon on their way to *Deathpoint*. Zk Lichian lowered the lift for them as they arrived. Gerard held his string until last, and allowed himself a small sigh of relief when they were finally aboard. As he climbed quickly up to the flight deck, he heard strange pinging sounds.

"We're taking fire, sir," Lichian said calmly.

"Then let's get out of here."

Deathpoint lifted slowly and gracefully to an altitude of one thousand meters before Lichian leveled her out and blasted *Graveclaw* to dust. Then they retraced *Graveclaw*'s flight path at the slowest safe speed. The only thing they picked up on the escape pod's frequency was static.

"Take us back up, Zk Lichian," Gerard said after they had covered the flight path twice.

Lichian's jaw tensed. "Pardon, sir, but should we not continue the search?"

"No. Take us up."

"Sir—"

"Now! Zk Lichian." Gerard heard the anger in his voice and knew why it was there. When they returned to *Avenger's Heel* he would have to approve the orders to destroy the rebels in their strongholds. The negotiations ploy had been a trick of the worst order. Now the rebels would have to pay with their lives. And with them agents from FedTreatyService would also die.

As Lichian maneuvered *Deathpoint* into the docking bay, Admiral Gannack's voice broke the silence of the flight deck. "Consort, we are receiving a signal on the pod frequency."

"What?"

"Yessir, a signal on the pod frequency. It is the universal distress signal."

"Location?" Gerard asked.

"Two hundred kilometers north-north-west of the crash site."

"That sounds impossible. As soon as we dock I want to see what you've got."

At Gerard's order, Zk Lichian accompanied him to the control center. Gannack's face was set in a hard, grim expression when she greeted them. "The signal is still coming in, and so are conflicting messages from the rebels. They seem to be split. One group is disclaiming any involvement with the crash, and another is taking credit for it."

"Do you think it's really the escape pod's signal?" Gerard asked.

"No, sir, I do not, but can we take a chance? If—"

"No!"

Zk Lichian's interruption startled them both. "I know I am out of place, Admiral, but I request permission to check out the signal site. *Deathpoint*'s engines are still warm."

Gerard didn't like the idea at all. "I'm not sure that's a wise move."

Gannack looked at him coldly. "If Admiral Holsten is

alive down there, we must make every attempt to rescue him."

"And if he's not, if this is another trick, we stand the chance of losing another ship and its crew," Gerard retorted.

"True, Consort." Gannack paused, then straightened her shoulders slightly. "It is my formal recommendation that we send *Deathpoint* to recon this new signal site."

Gerard knew he was being tested, that she was measuring his authority. If he agreed with her recommendation, he would lose stature. But if he didn't, Holsten's life might be lost, assuming he was still alive. There was only one choice. "I approve, Admiral."

Zk Lichian gave them a running report as he spiraled in on the signal site with two squads of fleet marines. The site lay in a desolate area just on the fringe of rebel-controlled territory. The last thing they heard from him was, "Great Houn! They have missiles!" Moments later *Deathpoint*'s distress signal started chattering. Then it, too, stopped. There was silence in the control center.

Gerard wanted to grab something and smash it. "Admiral," he snapped, the fury in his voice drawing all eyes toward him, "what are your standing orders?"

"To destroy the rebels with neutronic missiles when all else fails," she replied sharply.

"Follow your orders, Admiral."

Gerard forced himself to remain in the control center as the orders went out to the fleet. He tried to imagine the horrors that must be happening as the first of the neutronic missiles exploded high above cities and towns and struck down men, women, children, and animals with their deadly radiation. He wanted to understand the full impact of his decision, to know that he was responsible for hundreds of thousands of deaths. But deep inside his brain, a cold, hard center refused to accept the pain.

That coldness frightened him, made him try even harder to visualize the agony he had ordered. He couldn't do it. Instead, a great sense of sadness enveloped him, not for the loss of life on Evird, but for the loss of part of himself.

During the five months the fleet spent over Evird, sending down decontamination teams, mercy teams, agricultural teams, and political action teams, Gerard was unable to shake the sadness.

Even Governor Cessaid-Malee noticed his depression and tried in a clumsy way to cheer him. Nothing did any good. He remained detached and remote, even from himself, until the fleet began making preparations to return to Kril. Then and only then did he think about seeing Fairy Peg and the child who would have been born to them. And for the first time since he had given the order to bomb Evird, Gerard felt sick to his stomach and torn in his heart. Then he wept.

*　　*　　*

Message to: Greaves Lingchow
　　　　　　FedDiploSvc
　　The horror on Evird will have repercussions throughout our galaxy for a long time. Your government must accept a great part of the responsibility for that obscenity. Even a formal apology and reparation payments may not save what we worked so hard for.

—Glyph

*　　*　　*

12

　　Orees Gerard On'Kril looked up into his father's face, squinched his eyes shut, turned bright red, and bawled at the top of his tiny lungs.
　　Gerard looked helplessly at Fairy Peg with a silly grin on his face, but she only laughed.
　　"Do not squeeze him so hard," Inez offered.
　　"I might drop him."
　　Orees suddenly went silent. Gerard looked down at his son, totally perplexed, but Orees was only catching his breath. The brief silence was broken by another piercing wail. Finally Winsea held out her arms and took Orees to

her ancient bosom. He stopped crying almost immediately as she cooed and cuddled him.

"There's a strange lesson somewhere in all this," Gerard said as much to himself as to Fairy Peg and Inez.

"The lesson, my dear Pilot, is that you must introduce yourself to our son very slowly and very quietly. Your voice is strange and frightening to him."

"Well, his wail is strange and frightening to me. I guess we both have some adjusting to do."

That night, as Fairy Peg lay curled softly in his arms, she said, "There will be trouble because of Evird."

"I know. I've been thinking about that since we landed this morning, watching the faces, trying to guess what people are thinking about me."

She laid a finger across his lips. "You did what you had to do. I should have waited to mention it. Forgive me, Pilot?"

"No need. You only confirmed what I already knew. There's something you should know, too. Fed had agents on Evird."

"Yes."

"That's all? Just, yes?"

"We have known that for some time, Pilot."

Gerard shifted away from her and propped himself on one elbow. "And you didn't tell me? Why?"

"Listen, my love. Listen carefully. Against strong advice, I have trusted you. When it was learned that the Federation's agents were on Evird, I was not surprised. Neither did I believe that you knew. I maintained my trust. So you must trust me. I cannot explain why you were not told, and you must not ask again. Is trust too much to ask?"

It didn't make any sense. Gerard felt like a child being told he wasn't old enough to know the family secrets. But if that was the way the game had to be played, well . . . "As my Badh, my seductive Badh commands," he whispered, pulling her to him.

"I know, Windy, I know. You have a ton of messages for me and a dozen chores you want done. Well, I'm planning to be here most of the day, so we might as well start with the messages."

FedDiploService had been working overtime amending its rules and regulations. There were thirty-seven updates to be posted, but Gerard set them aside. Assistant Sub-Secretary Merita had also been working overtime. There were sixteen messages from him, but there were also two messages from Sub-Secretary Nevararms and one from Vice-Secretary Graczyk.

He decoded Graczyk's message first. Its contents angered him at first, then saddened him. Graczyk's message told him there was no validity to any rumors that Federation agents were working coercively on Evird or any other planet in Ribble Galaxy.

"Shows how much they trust me, Windy. Let's see what Nevararms has to say."

Nevararm's message parroted Garczyk's: no Fed agents in Ribble.

"You know, Windy, with bosses like these two, I'm beginning to wonder where my allegiances really should come to rest? How can I work for these people if they continue to lie to me? It's been almost six years, no, wait a minute—according to your clock it's been over six years since they sent me out here with the vague instructions to lay the groundwork for a resumption of normal relations. They told me to keep communications to a minimum, not to pressure the Ribble power blocs, and gain the trust of those in authority. I did all those things, and what does it get me? Lies!

"Don't blink your damn lights at me. You decode Merita's stupid messages and buzz me when you're finished. I'm going down to the galley."

After digging around in his supplies, Gerard found a small canister of Brandusian coffee. Of all the bean-brewed drinks he had tasted, Brandusian coffee was his favorite, if for no other reason than it helped elevate his moods. Deciding that he needed a great deal of elevation, he brewed three cups and put it in a small vacuum server. Then he returned to the flight deck just in time for Windy's buzz.

"Roll them on the vidscreen, Windy," he said as he sipped his first cup of the rich, aromatic coffee, anticipating the little charges it inevitably gave his system.

Windy rolled the messages at exactly his reading speed and in the sequence in which they were received. After seven messages, Merita's litany of complaints had become redundant.

Not your place to question directives . . . more frequent communications . . . do not question . . . more frequent communications . . . etcetera . . . etcetera . . . etcetera.

Gerard was frustrated. After all this time Merita suddenly wanted him to become a line-toeing, communicating fool. What in Fara's name was going on?

By the time Windy rolled the last message, Gerard was hardly reading them. Then a word caught his eye. "Start this one over, Windy."

The first two-thirds of the message resembled all the others. But the last third startled him severely.

> Furthermore, you will take all necessary actions to insure that the leaders of Ribble Galaxy do not seek to rush into negotiations with the Federation. Unforeseen circumstances demand that any move toward reconciliation be slowed immediately.
>
> Should you be unable to slow their interest in reconciliation by any other means, you are to suggest to them that a delay would allow the current political situation here to shift in their favor. You are authorized to fabricate whatever reasonable-sounding explanations are necessary and sufficient to accomplish these ends so long as this office is given detailed descriptions of those fabrications.
>
> NO COPIES MADE. ERASE AFTER READING.

Gerard couldn't believe it. Fed was telling him to lie to Ribble Galaxy in order to stall any movement toward a resumption of normal relations. It broke with everything he had been taught in DiploSchool. It was a request, no, an order for him to break his oath as a Universal Contract Diplomat.

"Take a message, Windy. To Assistant Sub-Secretary Anello Merita, FedDiploSvc, Landburg, Proctor, X113-T224-A996. Sir: May Binkley of Baun and her twelve, blind, illegitimate offspring chase you so far into the dust of damnation that Fara herself cannot find you with a microbeam. Signed: Gerard Hopkins Manley, Universal Contract Diplomat."

Windy rolled his message on the screen for him. "You take good dictation, girl. Code and send. I'll bet old Conehead bursts a vessel when he reads that. Think we ought to give Golifa a by-line? No, that would only confuse him. Besides, Golifa said it was an ancient curse."

Gerard spent the next five hours updating the directives and doing the shipkeeping chores that Windy had listed for him. But as he worked, he kept mulling over Merita's instructions. He even went back and reread them just to make sure he hadn't misunderstood. He hadn't. Then, instead of erasing the message, he put it in Windy's log under his personal code. If Fed ever discovered he had done that, they could cancel his contract and throw him into prison, but he decided it was worth that remote risk. Having a copy of that message just might prove useful in the future.

After he finished the chores, he did not want to leave. The last cup of Brandusian coffee was still warm, so he sat nursing it in his pilot's chair and tried to puzzle his way through his emotions. When he finally sorted out all the complications his cup was empty and the basic list in his mind was very short.

He felt betrayed by Fed and angry with them. He loved Fairy Peg, was delighted by their son, felt a growing allegiance to Ribble Galaxy, and was fairly pleased with himself, especially with his increasing willingness to be active instead of passive. Suddenly he was in a much better mood than he had been in months. With a quick goodbye to Windy, he left the starport and told Hoose and Closgemon to get him to EllKoep as fast as the skimmer would go. Fairy Peg was waiting for him in their chambers.

"So there you are, Pilot. I have some urgent news for you."

Gerard rushed to her, picked her up, and whirled her around the room. "I love you, you know that?"

"I do, Pilot, I do. Now put me down."

"No. I think I'll hold you forever."

"Pilot, I am serious.

"So am I. Give me a kiss." As Gerard tried to kiss her, she turned her head. She really was serious. "Very well,

131

Badh," he said, setting her gently on the floor. "What's so serious that you can't even kiss me?"

"The Nobel Assembly has called for an inquiry concerning the loss of Privy-Admiral Holsten, and Corpus Privy has consented. It starts tomorrow and, and—"

"And what?"

"There are rumors that you and Privy-Vice-Admiral Gannack will be charged with dereliction of duty."

Gerard's good mood fled like a mirkaloy from an open field. "Maybe you'd better tell me just how serious this is," he said, leading her to the couch, "and how in Fara's name they can charge me with dereliction of duty."

Fairy Peg looked at him sadly. "Actually, the only charge to which *you* are subject is one of failing to properly represent the throne. Such a charge can be couched in many ways, depending upon the degree of failure the ducas wish to imply."

"Wait a minute. You mean I can be charged for failing to properly represent you?"

"Not me, Pilot, the throne. Only Corpus Privy can decide whether or not you properly represented the throne. You must always remember that I am not the throne."

Slumping down in the couch Gerard said, "I remember you telling me that, but, well, it doesn't matter. What can they do to me if they decide I've failed?" He was beginning to feel the strings of the unknown puppeteer again.

"Oh, Pilot, that question cannot be answered. A special case you are . . . for them and for me." Fairy Peg traced her fingers along the back of his neck as though trying to ease the tension there.

"Well, Princess, seems like I'm a special case for the Federation, too." Gerard paused, wondering if he should tell her. Then he decided that he had to. "Windy had a whole tape full of messages waiting for me, and a couple of them were very interesting. One absolutely denied that there were any coercive Federation agents on Evird or anywhere else in Ribble. And the other, the other was a real pile of grisk dung. It told me to slow down any movement in Ribble toward reestablishing normal relations with Fed, *and*, if necessary, to *lie* to you."

Fairy Peg looked at him as though expecting more.

"Don't you understand? I took an oath as a Universal Contract Diplomat that strictly prohibits lying to any of the parties being served. I'm not surprised, I guess, that Fed would lie to me . . . but to ask me to break my oath, that's, that's just unthinkable."

Gerard doubled over until his head, his clenched fists, and his knees were pressed into a block of solid flesh. "Don't you understand?" he asked through clenched teeth. "I've been asked to dishonor what I was trained to uphold."

Wrapping herself around his taut form, Fairy Peg whispered, "Honor will be served, my wonderful Pilot. You have proven that time and again. Let not this falseness tear at your soul. Please? Please?"

Like a heatherfly slowly uncoiling from its chrysalid heart, Gerard unwound into Fairy Peg's arms. Neither spoke until Gerard let out a long, quiet sigh. "Perhaps it's time to dissolve my contract."

"Do not think such things, my love."

"But how can I—"

"Shhhhh. Think with me. Now is the time to clasp the trust you have earned firmly to your soul, and do that which you came here to do. Can you not see the gift your Federation has given you?"

"Hmmph. Some gift."

"It is a great gift, perhaps the greatest of all a government can give. They have given you freedom, Pilot, the freedom to act as you think best. By offering you dishonor, they have surrendered their control over you."

Fairy Peg's radical thought split the darkness of Gerard's depression like a laser beam through a practice target. It took him more than a moment to realize the truth in what she said, but when he did, the force of it was stunning.

"Do you know why I was so happy when I came back from Windy today?" he asked without waiting for an answer. "Because I had sent my supervisor a curse in response to his wretched directive. And, because after that I took stock of myself and decided that I really was rather pleased, especially pleased with you and Orees."

"As you should be," Fairy Peg said with a quick kiss.

"Of course, all this fancy talk about freedom doesn't do anything to solve the problem of the inquiry, but somehow that doesn't seem as important as it did a while ago."

"It has lost no importance, but perhaps you have put it into a new perspective."

"You're damn right I have. Admiral Gannack and I did

the best we could under the circumstances, following the standing orders Admiral Holsten had left. If Corpus Privy can't cope with that, that means they can't cope with the whole chain of command. What will the Fleet do if Corpus Privy acts against Admiral Gannack?"

"The Fleet has many top officers who chafe daily under Corpus Privy's heavy reins. It would bode no good for our galaxy. Perhaps you should talk to Fianne about this."

Gerard laughed, and it felt good. "Just what is Fianne, anyway?"

"Pardon, Pilot?"

"Just what *is* Fianne to you?"

"Friend Fianne is a Junior Archivist, and, of course, my trusted advisor."

"And your agent, and spy, and Fara only knows what else." Gerard gave her a hug with his grin. "Very well, I'll talk to him. The Badh wouldn't know where he was, would she?"

It was Fairy Peg's turn to laugh. "He is waiting for you in your office."

"Good. When shall I return to eat?"

"Better you dine with Fianne. There are things I must accomplish before tomorrow."

With a wink Gerard asked, "Meet me in bed?"

She answered his wink with a passionate kiss. "Most certainly, Pilot. Most certainly."

"Ah, Diplomat, that is a very complex question. However, it is also a very premature one. This rumor of charges was told to me three times within an hour by two of our most respected admirals and a member of the Noble Assembly who is a strong supporter of the Fleet. Even if it is true that Duca Echi intends to level these groundless charges, there is already tremendous pressure being brought to bear to have the inquiry itself dismissed." Fianne paced the long carpet in front of Gerard's desk as he lectured, formulating his thoughts aloud.

"Furthermore, there is another element at work which may be greatly to our advantage. The preliminary report from the Recovery Section suggests that evidence found in the rebel territories may point to involvement by people high in our government, perhaps even to members of the Noble Assembly and Corpus Privy itself.

"That report is being circulated now to Corpus Privy and the leaders of the Noble Assembly. If some of them were involved in supporting the rebellion in any way, they should be very reluctant to have a full-fledged inquiry laying out suggestive evidence, however tenuous that evidence might be."

"So we could have friends and enemies both on our side?" Gerard asked.

"Exactly."

"Or they could get desperate and go for a full power play."

"Unfortunately, that too is possible. Ah, but here is our meal."

How Fianne guessed that the knocking on the door was the food they had ordered, Gerard didn't know. Nor did he care. He was suddenly ravenous, and interrupted his eating only to comment on the excellence of the food. Fianne barely grunted in response, apparently distracted by both the food and his thoughts about the inquiry.

After he finished the last crumbs of an exquisite toasted pie, Gerard poured himself another glass of wine and settled back in his chair. Fianne had stopped eating several minutes before, leaving half his food untouched.

"I have neglected to tell you something, friend Fianne, something you should find most interesting." Gerard waited until he was sure he had Fianne's complete attention. "I suggested to Princess Peg that it might be time for me to dissolve my diplomatic contract with the Federation."

"But Diplomat, why?"

The shock in Fianne's voice and on his face was far stronger than Gerard had expected. "It seems that Fed insists upon lying to me," he said flatly, "and worse, they want me to dishonor my oath by lying to Ribble Galaxy."

"Please, Diplomat, I fear I still do not understand. Be as precise as you can."

Gerard shook his head. Was he the only one appalled by the orders telling him to lie? "Very well. An assistant secretary in the Diplomatic Service, my supervisor's supervisor's supervisor, sent me a message here while I was with the Fleet at Evird. That message denies outright that there were any coercive Fed agents on Evird or anywhere else in Ribble Galaxy."

"That should not surprise you."

"But it does, and it angers me too. Then my supervisor sent me a directive telling me to slow any movement here toward negotiations with Fed, and ordering me to lie if necessary to accomplish that end."

Fianne put his palms together, hooked his thumbs under his chin, and furrowed his brow. "So, you are quite right, Diplomat. I find that most interesting indeed. Yes, yes I do. But tell me, why should that make you want to dissolve your contract? And why would you tell me all this?"

"The second question first. It's blatantly obvious to me that you are the Badh's most trusted advisor. I suspect you are much more than that, but I don't expect either of you to say what. Anyway, if I hadn't told you now, she would have told you later, so I thought you might as well get the information directly from me.

"As to why I thought about dissolving my contract, that too is simple, but less simple than it was when I suggested it. On the surface it is because they asked me, no, ordered me to dishonor myself by breaking my oath." Gerard paused, trying to think of how to formulate the next part.

"And underneath, Diplomat, you have discovered that your love for our Badh, combined with the presence of your son and your sense of honor, have caused you to question your allegiances." Fianne smiled at Gerard's open-mouthed expression. "That was not difficult to deduce, Diplomat. Do not look so shocked."

"Am I that transparent, Fianne?"

"No, not you, not you at all. But the circumstances over the last year have been pointing in this direction. It was only a matter of time until you faced the questions yourself."

"So what took me so long? I feel rather stupid now."

"You are a complex man, Diplomat, filled as all of us are with many basic assumptions you do not even know you have. To recognize that some of those assumptions may not be valid, and force yourself to question them, takes intelligence, not stupidity. You do yourself injustice when you say such foolish things."

"I appreciate your thoughts, but I still feel stupid. You'd better brief me on what's going to happen tomorrow so I don't act stupid at the inquiry."

Hours later, Gerard tiptoed into the nursery and stood over the peaceful form of his sleeping son. He felt a bond with Orees that went beyond flesh and blood. For both of them their worlds had changed, and they were entering new phases of their lives. Gerard stroked the fine, dark hair on Orees's head and adjusted his blanket. The feeling he had at that moment grew into a warm, indescribable sense of belonging that comforted him as he lay in bed waiting for Fairy Peg.

* * *

Message to: Avarignon Cloznitchnikoff
         FedTreatySvc
  The departure of your predecessor is a burden we will have to accept with mixed sentiments. Since your first communications have indicated both a general understanding of the problems, and a more reasonable attitude than Turingay-Gotz, we can only hope for a continued improvement in our mutual efforts.

  Events here will soon determine whether Key-One will be useful to us in the future. We must plan for all possible contingencies. If we cannot use the tool for its primary purpose, perhaps some other task can be found for it.

—Toehold

* * *

13

Ducas shouted at assemblymen. Assemblymen shouted at each other. Squo Lyle gaveled futilely for order. In the midst of the bedlam Fairy Peg sat calmly on the throne, looking for all the universe as though she were enjoying herself. Seated at an angle to her left and slightly below her, Gerard did his best to look as calm as she did. Seated symmetrically to Fairy Peg's right, Targ kept flashing him little signs of assurance.

The inquiry had opened two hours earlier, and thus far had produced nothing but arguments about rules and procedures. A very combative group of fifteen or twenty Noble Assemblymen rose on points of order almost every time Squo Lyle completed a sentence. When others became frustrated by those actions and tried to shout them down, support for their position seemed to spring up from all over the hall.

Finally Squo Lyle managed to restore order, and announced a recess of the chair. That was greeted with scattered shouts and boos, but also by a flood of people running for the doors. Gerard followed Fairy Peg to a small room behind the dais and as soon as Targ shut the door behind them, he asked, "What in the galaxy is going on out there?"

Targ and Fairy Peg both laughed. It was Targ who answered first. "Our Badh decided to create some excitement for the opening session so that you could see our efficient form of democratic debate in action."

"Our commander jests, of course, Pilot. We merely suggested to certain assemblymen that the inquiry should be conducted according to the strictest rules of procedure. Unfortunately, some of those who demanded the inquiry are not totally familiar with those rules."

Gerard chuckled. Now he had some idea of what Fairy Peg had been doing half the night. "So how long will this go on?"

"For some time, Pilot. Let us eat while I explain what will happen."

They ate a leisurely meal while Fairy Peg and Targ explained that motions of dismissal would be made from the floor, countermotions would be made by several ducas, points of order would continue to be called, and, in about a week, someone would demand a full reading of the rules. That would take at least a day.

"And we have to sit through all that?" Gerard asked.

"Certainly not, Fize."

"Commander Alpluakka is correct. We will appear each morning for the opening session. Squo Lyle will then announce that our presence is not required for the debate, and we will leave."

"Why are you doing all this?"

Fairy Peg smiled. "The more delay and disagreement we cause, the better are our chances that the inquiry will never actually accomplish anything. Furthermore, the longer the inquiry goes on, the more it will disrupt the routine business of the Noble Assembly and Corpus Privy, which will put them under pressure from other directions to bring it to an end."

"Sounds simple enough to me. Stall them till they give up. What do we do with our days while we're waiting?"

"You may do as you wish," Fairy Peg said with a look of annoyance. "I shall be attending some of the debates, and conducting as many of the normal duties of my office as I can."

"In that case, I think I'm going to spend some time getting to know Orees. But I'd also like to set up a workout schedule with my Ratchets, Commander."

The days quickly settled into a pattern. Breakfast with Fairy Peg each morning was followed by a brief visit to the Council Hall. After being relieved of that duty, Gerard and his string would go to the Ratchet barracks, change into training uniforms, and work out until early afternoon. The workouts were much more exhausting than Gerard had expected them to be, but he was glad for the opportunity to get himself back into shape. Following a light lunch with his string, Gerard would return to his chambers and spend the rest of the afternoon with Orees.

The first day, Orees wanted no part of Gerard's presence, much to the amusement of old Winsea. Gradually, however, he seemed to accept this new presence in his life, and on the fifth afternoon actually stopped crying when Gerard picked him up and cooed to him. For Gerard that was an important moment, and that signal of acceptance from Orees marked a new phase of their relationship.

Fairy Peg was gone most of the time, but when she returned in the evenings Gerard tried to tell her everything he and Orees had done together. At first she seemed surprised and slightly put off by his enthusiastic descriptions of their son's activities, but finally one evening, after he had described at length a simple game he and Orees had played with a rattle, she reached out and squeezed his hand.

"Our son is truly a part of you, Pilot. I am glad."

"Now that's a strange statement if I ever heard one. Of course he's part of me. He's a part of both of us."

Fairy Peg laughed. "Sometimes, Pilot, we neither say what we mean, nor hear what we say to each other.

Certainly Orees is part of both of us. However, it is unexpected to have you feel so strongly for him."

"But why? He's my son. And I love him almost as much as I love you." Gerard's tone was slightly defensive.

"You do not understand, my dear, sweet Pilot. In our society it is uncommon for a father of rank to take such an interest in his son until the child is much older. Infants are considered the province of mothers, and nurses, and female relatives until they have been trained to talk and control their bowels. Only then do fathers usually enter their lives."

"Sounds stupid to me. Any father who does that is missing a lot of fun."

Fairy Peg moved to Gerard's lap, clasping her hands behind his neck and leaning back to look at him. "Had I not witnessed your enthusiasm myself, I would not have understood such a statement from a man in your position. You are a wonder for me, Pilot. Do you know that?"

"I'm a wonder? You're a wonder! Kiss me, you silly wench."

On the twenty-second day of the inquiry Squo Lyle announced, to no one's surprise, that the formal testimony would begin with *Graveclaw*'s two surviving crewmen. By the end of the day the basic incidents of *Graveclaw* being fired upon, Admiral Holsten entering the escape pod, the direct hit blowing away *Graveclaw*'s engines, the crash, and Gerard's rescue mission had been recounted by the crewmen and substantiated as much as possible by the surviving fleet marines.

As Gerard and Fairy Peg ate a cold supper that night with Orees contentedly asleep in the crook of Gerard's arm, he asked, "What happens next?"

"Privy-Vice-Admiral Gannack will begin her testimony in the morning. Then either tomorrow or the next day the log entries from *Avenger's Heel* will be read into the record, including the false escape pod signal, and the last communications from *Deathpoint*. That will take at least another day or two. Then Squo Lyle will move for consideration, and we will wait for their judgment."

"Hold it. Hold it. When do I get to testify?" Orees reacted to Gerard's raised voice with a little series of whimpers.

"It is not required for you to testify, Pilot."

"I don't care if it's required or not. Since your stalling tactic didn't work, I want to tell my side of the story. After all, I'm the one who's on trial." Orees woke up with a cry, and Gerard rocked him gently against his chest until he quieted.

Looking slightly annoyed, Fairy Peg answered slowly and deliberately. "This is no trial, Pilot. I worked many days convincing people that you should not be asked to testify, that it was not required, and would be an insult to the throne."

"So?"

"Do not be foolish. You must remain above this inquiry."

"I can't, Fairy Peg. I have to tell my side of the story, to clear those stupid accusations against me and Admiral Gannack. If you'd asked me, I would have told you that. I just assumed I'd be allowed to defend myself."

"Pilot, Pilot, listen to me. We are not conducting a defense, we are providing facts for an inquiry. If you insist on testifying, you will indeed have to defend yourself, and that is what we sought to avoid."

Gerard didn't know what to say. He felt compelled to testify, to add his point of view to the record. However, he had to admit that Fairy Peg understood far better than he ever could just how the system of inquiry worked, and how best to take advantage of it. "Let me put Orees to bed," he said. "Then I would like to talk about this some more."

They talked half the night, until sleep fuzzed their thoughts and they rolled, mumbling, into each other's arms.

When Privy-Vice-Admiral Gannack entered the hall the next morning, Gerard left the dais and went to talk to her. As he returned to his seat after a long, hushed conversation with the admiral, Fairy Peg frowned at him, but he gave her a cheery smile in return. Shortly thereafter Squo Lyle gavelled the inquiry into session.

After swearing in Admiral Gannack, he asked, "Do you have an opening statement to make before we begin the questioning?"

Gannack looked at Squo Lyle, then glanced over toward Gerard. "Yes sir, I do. When the events which are the subject of this inquiry took place, I was working first

141

under the verbal orders, and then under the standing orders of Privy-Admiral Holsten. Only the standing orders can be verified by the record in the ship's log. After Admiral Holsten's disappearance, I assumed acting command under Standing Fleet Directive Forty-Two with the verbal approval of my civilian superior, the consort to the throne." Several gasps from the audience were followed by murmured conversations. "At the direction of the consort," Gannack continued, "I must refuse to testify before this inquiry until such time as I am guaranteed the consort will be allowed to confirm my testimony."

The last part of Gannack's statement was almost drowned out by the ensuing bedlam.

"Point of order!" "Against the rules!" "Cashier her!" Those were but a few of the cries from the floor that Gerard could understand. He allowed himself only a swift sideways glance at Fairy Peg, then turned his full attention to the arguments and shouting matches that were going on in front of him. Fairy Peg was furious. Gerard was delighted.

Without Gannack's testimony, the inquiry could not proceed. A key portion of the testimony would be missing. If they requested him to testify, Fairy Peg would fight it, with a great deal of support from the assemblymen and several of the ducas. If they allowed him to testify, then he could give them a full account, including the fact that he knew there were FedAgents on Evird when he authorized the attack on the rebel strongholds. And he could also pull in the reports from the Recovery Section indicating that powerful members of the government were involved with the rebellion.

Gerard glowed with a sense of power. Squo Lyle hopelessly gaveled for order over the chaos Gerard had caused. Admiral Gannack smiled at him and sat straighter in her chair. She had already known about the Recovery Section report when he talked to her, so it hadn't taken much persuasion to get her to refuse to testify.

"Pilot," Fairy Peg said harshly, "you had better be able to explain yourself."

He turned to her with a smile. No matter how hard he tried, he couldn't keep it off his face. "I can, my Badh, and I will."

Fairy Peg looked at him in disbelief. Then she rose from the throne and held her hands over her head, palms facing

142

the audience. Her anger gave her a dark rose coloring that Gerard found very attractive. Slowly the noise in the hall subsided, like a wave receding from a beach, as assemblymen saw or were forced to see her regal presence on the dais.

"The Badh requests a recess until tomorrow," she said sternly.

"So be it, so be it, so be it," Squo Lyle shouted.

The hall again broke into shouts and arguments as Fairy Peg led Gerard and Targ out the small royal door and down the long hall to her official office. Her anger was so obvious that Gerard had no trouble keeping quiet until she waved him to a chair in front of her massive desk. Then he fought off a smile as he said, "A thousand thanks, most gracious Badh."

"What in the name of Houn," she exploded, "caused you to do such an insane thing?"

"Self-preservation," Gerard answered.

"Self-destruction, you mean!"

Targ smiled when she said that, and Gerard thought he saw a flash of malice in Targ's eyes. "No, Princess, self-preservation. Please, let me try to explain."

"You had better explain."

"I'm not sure I can, totally. It was only when Admiral Gannack entered the hall that the pieces of this puzzle fell into place for me and I knew what I had to do. When I left the dais, the first thing I asked her was whether or not the Recovery Section's preliminary report on the Evird insurrection had been released. She said that it had been, but only to Corpus Privy and concerned committee chairmen in the Nobel Assembly. That's when I told her to refuse to testify unless I did also."

"We still await your explanation, Consort." Fairy Peg's voice was calmer, but the anger had not faded from her eyes.

"Don't you see, Princess? If Admiral Gannack doesn't testify, the inquiry begins to fall apart at the seams. By having her refuse to testify unless I do, she's telling Corpus Privy that my testimony is also essential. And if I testify," Gerard paused with pleasure as he saw a look of understanding pass over Fairy Peg's face. "And if I testify," he continued, I will be sure to mention the Recovery

Section's report, and might even read it into the record of the inquiry."

"Thereby causing great distress to certain members of Corpus Privy and the Noble Assembly," Fairy Peg finished for him.

"Exactly."

"The inquiry can still proceed with neither you nor Admiral Gannack giving statements," Targ offered.

"I know. Fianne told me that. But what would it prove? Only that they were capable of carrying on an inquiry and establishing the already-known facts. Am I right, Princess?"

"Yes, perhaps you are. Our strategy was to weaken the proceedings by insulating you from them. It never occurred to us to insulate Admiral Gannack also."

"Which brings us to another question. What can they do to Admiral Gannack if she refuses to testify?"

"Fianne would know more specifically than I. Would you find him, please, and bring him to us, Commander?"

"With pleasure, Badh. Fize." With a bow, Targ left the room.

"It was a dangerous thing you did, Pilot."

"Probably. But I was angry. No," he added, seeing the expression on her face, "not at you. At myself and the situation. Ever since I arrived in this galaxy I've felt like a heatherfly caught in the wind. No matter what I did, I seemed to be blown hither and thither, with no control over the direction. But then some of the things that happened to me made me change my tactics."

"The Concepcycline Cloud?"

"That was probably the start of it, but Markl Holsten's cruel hospitality was the thing that really set me in motion."

"Tell me about what Markl did to you, Pilot." Her voice was soft and concerned.

"No. I can't. It's not important now. Don't you see, Fairy Peg? None of that matters except for what it did to my way of thinking. And my way of life. In a way I owe Markl a debt. He woke me up." Gerard thought about the dark pool in his mind where he had escaped Markl's torture, but decided the paradox made sense. "Then you pulled me into your life with our walks and talks, and finally the trip to see Marradon, and I changed. I began to make certain decisions based on what was good for me, not on which way the wind was blowing."

"Back to your heatherflies again."

"Yes. When I pledged my allegiance to you as consort, I meant every word of it. I didn't know at the time how much I meant it, because at the time I still felt that my peace mission from Fed took first priority. It doesn't. It didn't then and it doesn't now. Merita's orders for me to lie to you finally made that clear to me. That's why I suggested that I dissolve my contract. My allegiance is here, in Ribble Galaxy, to you, not to the Federation."

"I know that, Pilot."

"Ha," Gerard said with a half-laugh, "you and Fianne seem to know lots of things about me before I do."

A quick knock on the door was followed by Fianne's entrance.

"I was just talking about you, friend Fianne. Did your ears burn?"

Fianne looked at him strangely as he crossed the room and took the chair beside Gerard.

"Never mind. That's just an old star witches' saying that if someone is talking about you behind your back, your ears will burn."

"Nonsense for children." Turning to Fairy Peg he said, "Commander Alpluakka sends his apologies, Princess, but a duty called him away. How may I serve you?"

"The consort asked what Corpus Privy could do to Admiral Gannack if she continued to refuse to testify. You may answer that question for him."

"Ah," Fianne said as he leaned back in his chair, "the range of possibilities is rather extensive. However, we need not concern ourselves with all of them. Furthermore, any actions taken by Corpus Privy in this matter can be overruled by our Badh, although to do so would involve a certain risk of creating ill will against the throne."

"Seems like there's already some 'ill will' in Corpus Privy."

"True, Diplomat, true," Fianne said with a smile. "If Corpus Privy chose to punish Admiral Gannack, they would create even more ill will. But their options range from a written reprimand, through demotion of one rank, to recommendation for cashiering."

"Cashiering?"

"In the vernacular, Diplomat, to boot her out of the service. That, however, is not to be expected, since the Badh can veto any such action. In fact," Fianne said with an expectant tone, "you, Princess, can further stymie Corpus Privy's actions by recommending her for promotion to Privy-Admiral."

"And Omega Commander," Fairy Peg added.

"Oh, no, Princess, not Omega Commander. Even your allies would not stand for that. But surely Admiral Gannack has proven herself worthy of being Privy-Admiral."

"What's Omega Commander?" Gerard asked.

"The highest rank in our military, Diplomat, usually reserved for times of war. The title is often carried out of a war, but very seldom into one."

As Fianne and Fairy Peg discussed all the ramifications of promoting Admiral Gannack, and the people they could depend on to support such a recommendation, Gerard let his thoughts wander. His initial feelings of elation at having stymied the inquiry had passed and left behind a muted sense of accomplishment. He wanted to share that with someone, but it was obvious that Fairy Peg and Fianne were going to be busy for quite a while organizing their new plan to bring the inquiry to a halt.

Finally, after letting several opportunities pass, he broke into their conversation. "Pardon, both of you, but, unless you need me further, I think I'll go visit Orees."

"Go, Consort," Fairy Peg said with a wink, "and kiss our son for me. You have contributed enough for one day."

Knip and Hoose accompanied him as he walked back to his quarters humming to himself. "Our Fize is pleased," Knip said.

"Oh, very pleased," Gerard replied absently.

* * *

Message to: Greaves Lingchow
FedDiploSvc

We are most disappointed with your current attitude, especially in light of recent developments here which will soon greatly increase your agent's usefulness. He has proven himself more than worthy of his mission, and any suggestion that he be replaced must be totally abandoned by your superiors. It is literally quite fair to say that you could not have a more effective agent in place.

As for the delays you suggest, we are most agreeable and wish you good fortune in solving your internal problems.

—Glyph

* * *

14

First days, then weeks, then several months passed swiftly for Gerard. The inquiry was postponed repeatedly while various factions struggled in the Nobel Assembly and within Corpus Privy for position and consensus. The top echelon of Ribble Fleet's officer corps let it be known that they supported Admiral Gannack's position and would support her in *any* way they could. Fianne told Gerard several times that the inquiry would probably be dismissed in the long run because the divisiveness was causing too many problems in the normal business of government.

For Gerard the inquiry faded from concern in direct proportion to his involvement with Orees. Father and son, with their ever-present complement of Ratchets, became a regular sight in EllKoep, Orees carried in Gerard's arms, or perched somewhat precariously on his shoulders as they strolled the corridors, or watched the changing of the guard on the walls, or walked in the gardens.

They often spent their afternoons in the gardens, playing in the grass, splashing in the small ponds and creeks, or napping in the pavilions, Orees sprawled contentedly on his father's chest. Sometimes they were joined by Fairy Peg when her duties allowed her the time, and sometimes they were accompanied by Inez Nare-Devy.

Gerard was at a loss to explain why Inez bothered to spend her time with them. He found her far less interesting than Orees, and often spoke no more than two or three sentences to her in the course of an afternoon. But Inez seemed totally unperturbed by his absorption in Orees, and perfectly contented to provide a silent feminine shadow to their sunlit play. One afternoon, as they sat in the cool shade of a small pavilion with Orees sleeping quietly in Gerard's arms, he asked Inez why she spent so much time with them.

"For peace, Consort," she answered with a slight smile.

"Peace? A hundred pardons, Inez, but that is hardly an answer."

"Ah, Consort, but that is the whole answer. Would you deny an aunt the tranquil pleasure of her nephew's company?"

"Certainly not, but—"

"And is there any time I could spend with Orees when you are not in attendance?"

Gerard blushed. "Very little," he said. Inez was an enigma, a disturbing enigma because she caused him to react in unexpected ways. "But that still doesn't answer my question."

"The consort is dense. I will leave you now. However, you will welcome my company someday without question."

Gerard watched her walk away with a sense of annoyance. He supposed he had been rude to her, but he couldn't quite determine how. That evening he told Fairy Peg about the incident.

"Inez is jealous, Pilot. She envys your closeness to Orees and would be part of it if she only knew how. When she asked my permission to join you—"

"She asked permission?"

"Of course, and I gave it quite willingly. Her request seemed harmless when she made it, as it does now. Why does her presence disturb you so?"

It was a question Gerard couldn't answer for himself, much less for Fairy Peg. "I don't know. Maybe it's because she looks so much like you, but reacts so differently. It's as though when I look at her, part of me sees you and expects something that isn't there. Is that silly?"

"Neither silly nor unusual. Inslowhe once expressed a very similar sentiment."

Fairy Peg mentioned Inslowhe's name in the same flat tones she always used when speaking of her previous consort, but this time Gerard thought he detected a hint of anger, and wondered what Inslowhe's relationship with Inez had been like. He wanted to ask Fairy Peg more about that, but the faintly distant look in her eyes made him hesitate.

"If Inez truly bothers you, Pilot, I will instruct her to restrict her visits. Would that please you?"

Gerard sighed and took Fairy Peg into his arms. "It's really of no consequence, and I wouldn't want to hurt her feelings just because I feel awkward around her. The fault is probably mine."

Fairy Peg nestled softly against him. "There is another fault that is yours also. It grows in my womb."

"What? Are you pregnant again?" Gerard tried to pull back so he could look at her, but she clung to him fiercely.

"Yes, you wicked seducer of the Badh, I will bear you another child to romp in the garden with."

"Fairy Peg! That's wonderful . . . but you don't seem very happy about it." Again she refused to let him pull back and look at her.

"I am not unhappy, Pilot. For now that must suffice. As my time approaches, happiness will come, and most happy will I be when I deliver. The journey between our conception and birth ill suits me," she said pulling away from him after a sharp hug. "But look not sad for me, Pilot. My spirits will rise."

"I love you, you know that?" It was a ritual question he asked whenever he thought she needed to hear it.

"Oh, I know," she said, releasing him and patting her abdomen with a little laugh. "The evidence swells inside me."

"I didn't mean that."

"Of course you did. That and everything else. But come, let us eat and talk. There is a duty you must perform with me soon that I have failed to prepare you for."

Two weeks later Gerard stood alone with Fairy Peg in a circular stone room in the deepest cellars of EllKoep. As he stared up at the high domed ceiling a jagged shiver twitched through his shoulders.

"Tomorrow," she said, "I will stand on that small platform, with you one step down and to my left. When the accused is brought through that door you must not take your eyes off of him until he is standing on the star in the center of the chamber. Then you must not take your eyes off *me* until the ceremony is concluded. No matter what happens, do not be frightened."

"Why can't you tell me what will happen?"

"It is forbidden. So it is forbidden for you to tell anyone else what you see here. The Covenant Chamber is sacred

149

ground, Pilot, for here and only here has Houn ever shown His holy face."

"You mean you've seen Houn?"

"Just once."

"But you can't tell me what it was like."

"No. You must trust me, Pilot. And trust in Houn. If the accused has truly broken covenant and taken the life of his children's mother, judgment will be rendered by Houn Himself, and you will see all that you want to see."

"And if Houn doesn't appear, does that mean he's innocent?"

"No. It means only that covenant has not been broken."

Gerard was incredulous. "And you believe all this?"

She seemed unperturbed by the hint of sarcasm in his voice. "As you will if we are graced by Houn's presence," she answered calmly. "Do you not believe in your Fara?"

"Certainly, but I don't know anyone who's ever claimed to actually have seen her."

"Ah, Pilot, is that not a shame to have such a distant goddess?"

"No. Not at all. How many people can actually claim to have seen Houn?"

Fairy Peg's eyes brightened. "Many, my love. Houn comes to many people in various guises."

"Mystic visions."

"Visitations, Gerard, undeniable visitations by a benevolent god. Only here can Houn's true face be seen and some live to remember it."

"Hmmph. And I have to be present for this?"

Fairy Peg looked at him sternly. "Do not take this lightly, Pilot. The accused is a priest to your Gabriel Ratchets. That is why your presence is mandatory. So also is an open heart. But go now. Spend your pleasant hours with Orees and dispel the doubts from your mind. I will stay here and pray." With a gesture she dismissed him to find his way back to their son.

When he returned with her the following morning he tried to dismiss the feeling he had that he was participating in some kind of superstitious circus. But only when the accused murderer was led into the chamber by two hooded figures did he really begin to sense the oppressive weight of the proceedings. As he watched the short, fair-skinned priest being led to the white stone star inlaid in the floor of

150

the chamber, Gerard felt as though the room was suddenly beginning to close in on him. When the priest finally stood in place, head bowed and hands clasped before him, Gerard had to force himself to look at Fairy Peg.

She was radiant, as though lit by a glowing ether which touched only her. When she spoke, her voice echoed in the chamber. "Cossin Wonisht stands accused of breaking the convenant. Will he speak?"

Gerard didn't need to remind himself to keep his eyes on Fairy Peg. His attention was riveted on her as he waited for the priest to reply.

"Cossin Wonisht is accused of murder. Will he speak?"

Only silence followed the last echo of her voice. But the silence grew almost imperceptibly into a buzz, and the buzz into a deep bass hum which rose through the stone floor.

"Cossin Wonisht stands accused and silent before the judgment of Houn," Fairy Peg said in a voice that no longer echoed. "Will Houn speak?"

Wild, dissonant music grew out of the hum. The iridescent gold sunburst on the front of Fairy Peg's dazzling white robe flashed in concert with the harsh sounds. As the music rose to a grinding crescendo, Fairy Peg lifted one arm high above her head, holding in her clenched fist a short black rod that formed a line of pure darkness through a brilliant column of light that surrounded her.

The impenetrable black line rose to the ceiling, and when it touched the dome of rock the music shrieked in wild cacophony and stopped.

Gerard watched unbelievingly as the ceiling peeled soundlessly back in huge ragged tears to reveal a shimmering face distorted by rage and anger. It was the most frightening thing Gerard had ever seen, ugly and vicious, a twisting parody of humanoid deformities with eyes as empty and black as the deepest voids of space.

Then a growling voice boomed inside his skull. "Breakers of the Covenant must Die!"

Terror filled his heart. The room seemed suddenly upside down and he saw himself falling, falling into the darkness of those eyes.

The room was dim. Privy-Admiral Holsten said someone was coming. A swirling mob of hooded figures rushed toward him. Gerard tried to draw his sword. It stuck. He couldn't pull any harder. His legs refused to move. The flat blade of a black sword whirled around his head. Pain shot from behind his ear. Blackness.

"Pilot? Pilot?"
Fairy Peg's voice was insistent. "It has ended, Pilot. You must help me."
Gerard opened his eyes. He was lying on the floor of the Covenant Chamber. The ceiling was back to normal. His aching head was resting in Fairy Peg's lap. "What—"
"Shhh. Try to stand."
Leaning heavily on Fairy Peg, he climbed to his feet, then almost toppled them both as a wave of dizziness swept over him. With a grunt of determination she held him steady, then slowly led him across the chamber and out the door. Quickly, other hands took hold of him and he saw Woltol's grim face before he passed out again.

Orees was crying. Gerard opened his eyes and started to rise, but a hand pulled him gently back into the soft pillows.
"I am sorry, Pilot," Fairy Peg said as she sat up beside him. "I did not mean for you to—"
"What happened?"
"You collapsed in the middle of Houn's appearance."
"In the middle? But what about—"
Fairy Peg's eyes held a strange light. "The accused died. He was consumed by the wrath of Houn."
"And I failed you." Gerard felt a numb pressure in the back of his head.
"No, Pilot, you did not fail me. The appearance of Houn overwhelmed you."
"Houn? That was Houn?"
"Yes," she said simply, "that was Houn."
"Terrible." He shivered. "Terrible."
"Yes," she agreed. "Here, drink this." She nursed him through a small cup of sweet-smelling liquid which burned slightly as he swallowed it. "Good. Rest now."
He heard Orees cry again, but he was too far from consciousness to do anything about it.

Omna-Seay ran his fingers lightly over the bump on Gerard's head. "You will mend, Consort. It is not serious."

Omna-Seay pulled his hands back into his lap and appeared ready to say something else, but he didn't.

"Are you sure?" Gerard asked. "You certainly look like it's serious."

"Oh, no, Consort. There is something I would tell you, but it must not be known to the Badh." Omna-Seay looked tired, the worry lines on his face deepening into a grim set.

"Tell me."

"The Badh would have me dismissed if she knew about this. You must promise not to—"

"I promise. What is it?"

"Her pregnancy goes badly. Wait," he said with a raised hand, "allow me to finish. She carries twins, but will not let me test them. They must be tested, Consort. Their echoes are not natural."

"What do you mean, *not natural?*"

"Please, Consort, that is what we must discover. I am sure something is wrong with the foetuses she carries. However, I am helpless in the face of her refusal to be tested. Somehow, without letting her know I talked to you about it, you must persuade her to submit to the tests."

"And if she won't?" Gerard only half heard his own question. His mind was trying to cope with the idea that something might be wrong with the baby. *Babies*, he corrected himself.

"If she continues to refuse, there is little I can do but pray. Her winderwomen and old Winsea scoff at my fears, and the Badh listens to them, not me."

"What proof do you have that something's wrong?"

Omna-Seay stood up angrily. "Do you not listen. Consort? I have no proof. The Badh will not allow me to gather it. If I could only—"

"If you could only what, Omna-Seay?" Fairy Peg asked from the doorway.

"I, I," Omna-Seay stuttered. Then he straightened his shoulders. "A thousand pardons, Badh, and my resignation if you wish it. I spoke to the Consort about—"

"You may leave," she said harshly. "Now."

Omna-Seay did a quick bow, and left with his chin tucked into his chest. Fairy Peg ignored him and came immediately to Gerard's side. "He's worse than an old winderwoman sometimes," she said as she sat on the edge of the bed, "with all his senseless speculations. What did he tell you, Pilot?"

Gerard looked at her carefully. "He said he wanted to test the babies," he said evenly. "That can't be a bad idea, can it?"

"Did he also tell you his *tests* could kill them? No, your face denies it."

"But why, how . . ."

"Listen, Pilot. Listen to me now. Her voice was quiet, but carried a hard edge of determination. "Omna-Seay means well. I know that. I also know there is a possibility, just a possibility, as there always is, that he has grounds to be worried. However, I will not risk the lives of your children by submitting to his tests. If there is something wrong with them, it is Houn's will."

He couldn't quite believe what he was hearing. "But Fairy Peg, what harm could the tests do?"

"Total harm, my beloved," she whispered sadly. "He would inject me with certain chemicals. If the . . . if our babies are normal, nothing would happen. But if they are not . . . if they are not, they could react violently, and I would have to abort." A single tear ran down each cheek. "He wanted to check Orees the same way, Pilot."

Gerard gathered her into his arms and rocked her gently as she cried. He couldn't imagine Orees dead, or how he would have felt if he had returned from Evird to discover he had lost a son he never knew. "Isn't there some safer way to test?"

"None," she sobbed. "The differences in our bloods . . ."

As Fairy Peg cried, so did he, quiet, simple tears that demanded a greater release than he could allow them. Omna-Seay would not run his deadly tests. But surely there was another way, some more sophisticated physmedical approach that could be used. On one of the Fed planets, maybe, but in Ribble Galaxy? Gerard didn't know. He just didn't know.

The next day Fianne met his questions about the tests with a grim look of sadness. "I searched, Diplomat. Half the archivists searched with me. For all the marvelous techniques that have been developed by the physmedicants in our galaxy, we could find nothing that would solve this dilemma."

Gerard had a suggestion that he was afraid to make. "Suppose we asked Fed for help?"

"Impossible. Even if they would give it, which they probably would, neither the Badh nor Omna-Seay would consent to it."

"You don't know that."

Fianne sighed. "Unfortunately, I do. I made the same suggestion three weeks ago."

"You?"

"Yes, Diplomat. I suggested that to our Badh. She would not hear of it."

"But why?"

"Think, Diplomat. Consider our Badh's situation. She is the royal leader of all Ribble Galaxy. For her love of you she has risked much, much you can never know or understand. For her love of Ribble she will risk much more, because her goal is the same as yours: peace. As her consort, she can depend on you, seek your counsel and advice, but as the Federation's representative, she must keep you at a distance, as she must keep the Federation itself at a distance.

"When I made my suggestion to her, I was thinking only of her welfare and the welfare of the children she carries. She, as she must, was thinking of something far greater. We must respect her for that."

"But they're my children too."

"Indeed they are, which is why she refuses Omna-Seay's test. She protects them for you, Diplomat."

Gerard opened his mouth. Then he closed it. There was nothing to say. By not seeking assistance from Fed, Fairy Peg was performing her duty as Badh, her duty to Ribble. By refusing Omna-Seay's test she was performing a duty of love, a personal duty to him. Gerard felt humbled by her decision and quickly left Fianne to seek her out. He had to let her know in some way how proud and unworthy he felt.

On the anniversary of his seventh standard year in Ribble Galaxy, Fairy Peg gave a small party in Gerard's honor. Targ, Inez, Fianne, and Admiral Gannack joined them for a quiet dinner and an evening of congenial conversation. Fairy Peg was huge in her fecundity, but radiant in a low-cut gown that emphasized her swollen breasts and the golden amber flush of her skin. As they sat enjoying after-dinner drinks, Fairy Peg made a sudden announcement.

"Squo Lyle reported to me today that Corpus Privy will officially dismiss the inquiry." She beamed as she said it and took Gerard's hand. "Thanks to my consort for that, and, of course, Admiral Gannack."

"And Fianne and Targ," Gerard added with a smile.

"Yes, and Inez also. Furthermore, it will be my privilege to inform the Noble Assembly that Admiral Gannack will be our new Privy-Admiral."

Admiral Gannack looked totally surprised. "I am unworthy, Badh," she said finally.

"Nonsense," Targ said quickly.

"A toast," Gerard said rising to his feet. "To our new Privy-Admiral. May she serve long and well."

The chorus of approval was led by Inez. Fianne refilled everyone's glasses, and since Fairy Peg remained standing they all did.

"The Badh would also propose a toast," Fairy Peg said with a slight trill in her voice. "To Gerard Manley, the Prince Consort of Kril."

"To the consort," Admiral Gannack said quickly.

"To the consort," they all echoed.

Fairy Peg went into labor late that night. Omna-Seay and the winderwomen were called, and with them they brought a large wooden box that was placed across the room from Fairy Peg's bed.

"For the father," Omna-Seay said curtly.

Fairy Peg had told Gerard about the watching box, but Gerard entered it with great reluctance. As soon as he sat on the hard wooden bench inside, Omna-Seay closed the door. There was no handle on the inside, and the holes in the grating were too small for Gerard to get his hands through. His job was to sit and watch the birthing.

What followed was a living nightmare. For seventeen hours Fairy Peg struggled in labor, and, despite the anesthetics Omna-Seay gave her, she often cried out in pain. Gerard cried out too, demanding to be released from the watching box, but everyone ignored him. His body ached from sitting in the box, and his heart ached to see Fairy Peg in distress.

When the twins were finally born, Omna-Seay held them up almost with pride for Gerard to see, as though they vindicated his concern. The infants were horribly deformed, joined at the forehead, and quite dead.

Anger overcame Gerard's exhaustion. He braced his back and with a loud scream burst open the door to the box. Hard hands grabbed him and restrained him.

"No. You must not touch her." It was Targ.

"Let me go!" Gerard screamed, twisting to free himself.

"No, Fize."

"*Chon!*" The command came from Fairy Peg. She was propped weakly on one elbow pointing her other hand at them. "*Chon,*" she repeated. Obey.

Reluctantly, Gerard allowed himself to be taken from the room. He felt sick in the same way he had when Evird was bombed. In a daze he let Targ lead him through the corridors, little knowing nor caring where they were going. When Targ finally sat him in a chair, Gerard was numb with pain and nausea, but realized he was in his own office.

Targ poured him a huge goblet of liquor. "Drink this," he commanded.

Gerard downed the goblet, choking violently on the last few swallows. Then he held it out to Targ to be refilled. His eyes watered from the burning liquor, but it was only early in the morning, when he was thoroughly drunk, that he broke down and cried for Fairy Peg and the horror he had brought upon her. He was vaguely aware of Targ's arm around his shoulders as he sobbed, and knew then, in some dim way, that he was crying mostly for himself.

*   *   *

Message to: Avarignon Cloznitchnikoff
            FedTreatySvc

You must prevail upon your superiors to release the information to us. Key-One can only be used to the greatest possible advantage if we know the controls that have been implanted. Your claim of ignorance is insufficient and unacceptable.

—Toehold

*   *   *

15

Gerard awoke on the couch in his office with a splitting headache. Brunnel sat next to him in a chair.

"Youse slept long, Fize. Would youse eat?"

Gerard groaned in response. "No. I want to go back to my chambers."

"A hundred pardons, Fize. Five hundred pardons, but youse cannot go there. Our Badh has entered the cleansing."

"The what?" Gerard asked as he sat up. The pounding in his head increased.

"The cleansing, Fize. Is custom for youse to remain away until it is over."

"Get me some water. As soon as I can stop this ringing in my head, I'm going to see the Badh."

Brunnel left the room, but it was Fianne who came in with a pitcher of water and a glass of murky brown liquid.

"Ah, Fianne. What's this nonsense about a cleansing?"

"Drink this, Diplomat. It will ease your head. The cleansing is not nonsense. It is a custom that must be observed."

"But Fair—the Badh, I need to see her." Gerard sipped the brown liquid and recognized its bitter, salty taste.

"In four days you can see her. No sooner."

"Now. I want to see her now."

"It is forbidden," Fianne said simply. "You cannot see her until the cleansing is complete. Drink the worash."

Gerard drank it as quickly as he could, desperate for anything to relieve the throbbing in his head. He had to see Fairy Peg. "Who will stop me if I go to her now? You?"

"Yes, Diplomat. And if I fail, the Badh's Ratchets will stop you. And if they fail, the winderwomen will."

Through his pain, Gerard sensed that Fianne was deadly serious. "How?"

"With words. With force if necessary."

"And if I fight force with force?"

"They will try not to kill you."

Fianne said it so flatly that Gerard almost didn't believe that he'd heard it. "Try not to kill me?"

"Yes, Diplomat, they will try."

Slowly it sank in just how serious the cleansing was, and, how little power he really had. They probably would kill him if they had to, to keep him from violating their custom. It was stupid. It was insane. It was cruel. He needed to be with Fairy Peg, to share his grief with her, to comfort her if he could. And be comforted. He needed Fairy Peg, and he was sure she needed him. But maybe she needed the cleansing more.

"What will I do, Fianne?"

"You will wait, as all fathers must wait."

Four days loomed like an eternity to Gerard. Every instinct in him told him to damn their custom and rush to Fairy Peg's side. It was the only right thing to do, the only natural thing. He looked hard at Fianne and saw grief in his friend's eyes. "Is there no way?" he asked desperately.

"None."

"Then I'm going to the barracks. I can't sit around here for four days. I'll go crazy. What about Orees?"

"You may have him brought to you whenever you wish. You may also send one message to the Badh."

One message. What could he say in one message? Gerard held his head, hoping to ease the pain and clear his thoughts. He seethed inside with pain and frustration and anger and sorrow. But overriding all that was the feeling that he was again a pawn in a larger game, a piece without power on a board where power was all-important. He tried to tell himself that what he felt was only self-pity, but deep inside he knew that wasn't true.

The irony was that honoring the cleansing custom was the right thing to do, regardless of how it affected him. But he knew he could no longer drift with the political currents and wait for a fair wind. It was time to take his own tack.

"I've changed my mind, Fianne. I will stay here at EllKoep.

And if you would be so kind as to have a light breakfast sent to me, I will compose my message to the Badh."

Fianne looked at him approvingly. "Very well, Diplomat. Shall I have fresh clothes brought to you here?"

"Please. And a small bed." After Fianne left, Gerard looked around his office. The stone and wood walls with their dark tapestries were not exactly what he would have chosen for a temporary home, but in his new mood they didn't bother him. He had more important things to think about.

He wrote seven drafts of his letter to Fairy Peg, interrupted by the appearance of his breakfast, which Knip told him was actually dinner, and Woltol with a small trunk of clothes. He nibbled on his food as he wrote, not caring what it was, so long as it filled him. The seventh draft still wasn't perfect, but he decided it would do.

> My dearest Fairy Peg,
>
> Love is a complex mixture of bright and dark emotions which complement and counterpoint each other. We have just passed through one of the darkest, but I pray that means we will be moving toward a brighter, happier time.
>
> I love you, Fairy Peg, love you as I have never loved anyone else in my whole life. Yet I have few tangible ways of demonstrating my love. I cannot shower you with gifts or build you a home. I can only direct my actions in ways that offer constant signs of my affections.
>
> Therefore, I believe the time has come for me to take a more active role in bringing Ribble Galaxy and the Federation back to a lastingly peaceful relationship. With your permission I will begin goading Fed out of its plodding approach to this problem and demand that it present Ribble with positive, comprehensive proposals for lasting peace.
>
> There is much more that I want to say, but it can wait until I see you again. I love you. I love Orees. I love us.
>
> Gerard

As he copied the letter over, Gerard almost added something. He wanted to tell her that if they were successful in their negotiations with Fed, he would renounce his Fed citizenship and ask for Ribble citizenship so he could be with her always. He decided against it. What if they failed? What if Fed refused to compromise on key issues, or stalled and stalemated? What would he do then? Could he ask for Ribble citizenship as a failure? Or at least as a failed diplomat? He didn't know.

Following the custom, Fairy Peg sent no response to his letter, but Gerard decided to begin his new campaign with Fianne the next day. They met in the Archives, and Gerard got straight to the point.

"You're the Badh's closest advisor, Fianne. How do you think she will react to a proposal that we begin pushing Fed toward active negotiations?"

Fianne's expression was unreadable. "Ah, Diplomat, that is a difficult question. Have you not wondered why the Badh has not made such a suggestion herself?"

"As crazy as it may sound, no, I haven't. When I was sent here, I was told that I might spend my full ten-year contract in Ribble, and that neither government was in any hurry to reestablish normal relations. My supervisors said both sides wanted a cooling-off period."

"Perhaps they still do."

There was more in Fianne's eyes than in his words, but Gerard didn't know what. "Why?"

"Ah, that is part of the same difficult question."

"You mean you won't tell me," Gerard said flatly.

"I mean exactly what I said, Diplomat. If is a very difficult question."

"The same thing. I guess I'll have to ask the Badh."

"I would recommend that you do so." Fianne's tone was almost imperative.

"Fianne, I trust and respect you a great deal, but unless you can give me some solid reasons and reasoning, I am going to ask the Badh."

"Mmmmm. Perhaps if you could explain to me why you have made this decision, I could answer your questions in a way that would satisfy you."

"Don't talk down to me, Fianne. I made this decision because I'm tired of being treated like a pawn."

"But you are a pawn. All diplomats are pawns. They are moved in certain ways to present a strategic front to the opposition. Sometimes they advance, and sometimes they

161

merely hold a fixed position. Always they are valuable, and often one pawn can be used by both sides. But they are always pawns."

Gerard hated the metaphor, and hated even more to admit there was truth in it. "It doesn't have to be that way."

"It *is* that way. Please, Diplomat, I mean no offense by what I tell you, but neither will I try to hide from you the truth. You are a tool to be used as effectively as possible by both sides. If you insist on action when both sides are content to let you rest, you destroy your potential effectiveness."

As unwilling as he was to concede, Gerard didn't know where to take the argument. Then he thought of Kurmody Duff. "I'll tell you a story, Fianne. Then I'll let this matter drop for the time being.

"The first man to become a contract diplomat was forced into the role in order to save his family and his system. He was manipulated and ill-used, but he accomplished his mission and saved the ones he loved by taking an initiative that neither side expected or wanted him to take. There's an expression named after him: Kurmody's Luck. It has a lot of implications, but at the heart of them all is the knowledge that Kurmody Duff took matters into his own hands and helped make his own luck."

"As you and Admiral Gannack did with the inquiry."

"Exactly."

"Then perhaps you should speak to the Badh about this. However, for her sake, let her regain some of her strength first."

Fairy Peg was slow to regain her strength. After the cleansing period was over, Gerard went to see her and was received with open arms and kisses. Somehow, though, he sensed a change in her that created a distance between them he didn't know how to bridge. It was as if she had pulled part of herself back from him and was holding it in reserve.

Gerard moved back into their chambers, but at her request, because she was sleeping fitfully and restlessly, she said, he slept in a small room off the nursery. There *he* slept fitfully and restlessly. On the sixth afternoon of his return he decided to confront her with his unhappiness about the arrangement.

"Neither of us sleeps well alone. Isn't that obvious?"

"Nothing is obvious, Pilot."

"But why can't we at least try it?"

She took his hands in hers and looked at him tenderly. "What would happen then if it did not cure this problem? Then I would ask you to go back to the attendant's room, and you would be more unhappy than you are now. Is that not so?"

"Maybe. But I'm willing to take that chance."

"I am not. Please, Pilot. When the time is right, I will know it . . . and so will you," she added suggestively.

Every day Gerard spent as much time with her as possible, as though trying to compensate for her missing presence at night. They took brief walks in the gardens, sometimes with Orees, and sometimes alone when Gerard almost felt sure that the distance between them was closing. But every evening, as he waited for a sign that did not come, his impatience grew. He knew it was too soon for them to make love again, but he needed her presence by his side. Her continued denial was extremely frustrating.

So was her refusal to talk about their stillborn offspring. He had tried several times to bring the subject up, only to be told coldly and bluntly that it was not to be mentioned again. He thought they needed to talk about it, that it was part of what was holding them apart. Fairy Peg adamantly thought otherwise.

One evening, when it was obvious that he was going to sleep alone again, he said, "It's the babies, isn't it? That's why—"

"Silence!" She hurled the royal command at him like a dagger.

"No! We have to talk about it. We have to talk about it *now!*"

Fairy Peg rose and stared at him as though he were a stranger. Then without a word she left the room.

Gerard roared in anger. He wanted to kick something or someone, to vent his frustration in violence. As he stalked from the chamber he said to Hoose, "Take me to the barracks. We're going to run."

He took his whole string with him, and together they ran thirty kilometers in the cold night air. Gerard was exhausted when they finished, but still angry. As soon as they cleaned up and changed into fresh uniforms, he ordered the Officer of the Night to open the Ratchet Club and proceeded to get himself rip-roaring drunk.

He woke up in the morning on a pallet in the barracks. When he got back to EllKoep there was a note from Fairy Peg saying she had some duties to attend to and would meet him for dinner. Gerard spent the whole day with Orees, hoping that his demand the night before had finally made an impression on Fairy Peg. He was sorely disappointed. When Fairy Peg entered the room, she announced that she wanted no repetition of the previous night's conversation. Gerard tried subtly to lead her in that direction anyway, but she changed the subject every time with steely determination.

That night he got drunk with Fianne.

The following night he got drunk with Targ.

The night after that he got drunk with Fianne, Targ, and Inez.

The pattern was set. He spent his mornings recovering from the night before, his afternoons with Orees, his evenings being frustrated by Fairy Peg, and his nights drinking himself into a stupor. Back in the corner of his mind he knew he was not solving anything and was probably just creating new problems, but that knowledge wasn't strong enough to stop him.

Targ and Fianne tried to slow his drinking, but he refused to let them. In the alcohol he had found a warm, comfortable home for his self-pity, and he was not about to let himself be dragged away from it. Only Inez seemed to understand that, and while she never encouraged him, she always had a laugh for Fianne or Targ when they suggested that he had had enough.

Late one night when he was well on his way to oblivion, Gerard got sick to his stomach. After a great deal of vomiting, he allowed Fianne to help him back to his tiny, empty bedroom. When Fianne left, Gerard turned out the lights so he wouldn't have to look at the room. He undressed in the dark and threw his clothes at the corners as though trying to dispel the ghosts of his loneliness. Finally he collapsed naked on the bed and quickly fell asleep.

Kisses woke him, soft, teasing kisses on the inside of his thighs. He couldn't believe it, couldn't believe that Fairy

Peg had finally come to him like this. He was afraid to move for fear of really waking up and discovering it was all an alcoholic dream. But the kisses persisted and were combined with hands that stroked him tenderly and intimately.

Then in a sudden sliding movement of flesh against flesh she was on top of him, devouring his mouth with hungry lips, moaning softly as he pulled hard against her. With brief twists of thighs and jerks of hips they worked themselves together in a frenzy of passion that ended all too soon in their sharp cries of joy.

Moments later as they lay side by side, the misty fog of alcohol in Gerard's brain parted for a message from his fingers as he caressed her breasts. She was not Fairy Peg.

He jerked back from her. "Who . . . who are you?"

She laughed as she stepped quickly from the bed into the darkness. But her laugh was cut short as the room suddenly blazed with light to reveal Fairy Peg standing in the doorway and Inez naked in the center of the room.

Time slowed for Gerard as Inez stooped to pick up a long, loose robe and put it on. Then she laughed again and swept slowly out of the room past her sister.

In a slow whirl of motion Fairy Peg moved across the room, screaming at him. "I trusted you! I trusted you!" She struck him repeatedly with clenched fists as he lay on the bed.

"Stop it! Fairy Peg! Stop it!" he shouted as he tried to protect himself from her blows.

"I trusted you! I gave you my body when you were cold, and a son who loves you!"

"Stop it. Listen to me! I didn't—"

"How could you do this to me?"

Her blows slackened and Gerard managed to grab her wrists. "Listen to me. I thought it was you."

"Liar!" she screamed, trying to break free from him. "Let me go. I will not be held by a cheating liar."

"I swear. I swear. I thought it was you." He released his grip, and she immediately pulled back from the bed.

Tears ran down her face and she shook visibly as she spoke. "I cannot believe you any more. Go! Go! Go back to your animal Ratchets." The anger in her voice was laced with venom.

Gerard got quickly out of bed and held his arms to her.

"Please, Fairy Peg, listen to me." When she stepped away from him, he dropped to one knee as a sudden sob ripped its way out of his throat. "Oh, Fara, Fara. Can't you see? I was drunk. She climbed into bed with me. I thought it was you."

"Lies," she spat at him.

Three long, racking sobs escaped him as he let himself fall to the floor and cry.

"Cry hard, Gerard Manley," she said through clenched teeth. "This filthy night of lust will cost you dearly." With that, she left him.

Gerard was admitted to Fairy Peg's office late the next afternoon. After the quick knee-touching bow he said, "Diplomat Gerard Manley requests permission to say good-bye to the Badh and her son."

The stern anger which had been on her face when he entered the room shifted slightly toward surprise. "What mean you, Diplomat?" she asked formally. There was even surprise in her voice.

"May I speak in front of Fianne Tackona?" he asked, looking straight into her eyes.

Fairy Peg looked quickly at Fianne. With a brief bow he turned and left them alone in the room. "Speak, Diplomat."

He cast his eyes down at the floor and then looked back up at her. "I have failed you, most noble Badh, as a diplomat, as a friend...and as your consort. I have come to resign my positions and—"

"Unthinkable!"

"To resign my positions and return to the closest FedBase where I can dissolve my contract." Gerard fought to control his voice. If she accepted his statements at face value, he would lose all that he loved in the universe.

Fairy Peg looked at him with a softer expression. "You are serious, Diplomat?"

Dropping to one knee, Gerard looked down at the carpet and asked, "Do I have a choice, Badh?"

"You speak too softly, Pilot. What did you say?"

Gerard looked up at her as steadily as he could. Even his eyes were trembling. "I asked...if I had any other choice, Badh?"

"Did you seduce my sister?"

"No, Badh."

"Did she seduce you?"

"No, Badh. She climbed into my bed and I thought it was you."

"Why should I believe that?" Fairy Peg's question had a hard edge to it.

"Because, Badh, it is the only truth I have to offer."

"Inez says you seduced her."

Gerard sighed shakily and knew there were tears in the corners of his eyes that he dare not wipe away. "You are the Badh," he said finally, trying to blink the tears out of his eyes.

"Yes. But I am also my sister's sister, and the mother of your child. I offer you a choice, Pilot. You may resign your position and leave us, if that is what you truly wish to do. Or you may serve the throne in your roles of consort and diplomat, and begin preparing for negotiations with your Federation."

"I will serve the throne," was all that Gerard could say. The relief he felt caused as many tears as the fear of losing Fairy Peg and Orees.

"You may rise, Pilot. Fianne will brief you."

* * *

Message to: Greaves Lingchow
             FedDiploSvc

The stage has been set. Now you must play your part and play it well. He is not as malleable as you led us to believe, but he will complete this task to the best of his ability. However, if you do not convince him, I suspect we will both have much to answer for.

—Glyph

* * *

16

As *Windhover* entered its braking orbit around Tyboren, Gerard felt a growing sense of unease. It was the first time he had left Ribble Galaxy in over seven years, and despite the facts on the surface, his allegiances were no longer clear. The voice of Tyboren Control really brought that home to him. She had given him instructions in Standard, and it had taken him more than several seconds to understand her. He was so accustomed to the soft, guttural inflections of Kulitti that the sibilant slurs of Standard sounded grossly alien to him.

"You know what I did, Windy? I translated Control's instructions into Kulitti. Shows how strangely the mind works sometimes. At least my mind, anyway. I don't have that trouble when I'm talking to you. Makes me wonder how long it will take me to think normally in Standard again.

"You know what part of the problem is, don't you? Translation is at best inaccurate. Control said, 'Maintain present attitude,' but the only effective Kulitti translation would translate back into Standard as, 'Preserve current relationships.' See what I mean?

"You don't, do you? Okay, run Control's message through the translator, and let's see how it comes out in Kulitti. Then we can run the Kulitti through and see how it translated back into Standard."

The Baird Z-Rangel translator performed its functions very well, but by the time it had translated the phrase "maintain present attitude" from Standard to Kulitti and back to Standard, the result was "hold onto immediate beloveds." Gerard was glad he understood both languages well enough to gain some insight into the translation problem, and spent the better part of three days in braking orbit trying to think through a program for the Baird that would help solve some of them. It was only as he prepared to land at Vardezee Starport that he realized he had used the translation puzzle to avoid what he should have been doing—planning for the pending negotiations.

"So, you are Gerard Manley," the tall, white-haired man said as he rose from his desk. "I am Greaves Lingchow."

As they shook hands, Gerard noted that Lingchow looked much younger up close than he had first appeared. Then he realized that the white hair was a genetic trait. "Pleased to meet you, sir."

"Sit down, Manley, sit down," Lingchow said as he

resumed his seat behind the desk. "We have much to discuss."

Indeed we do, sir, and I'm not quite sure where we begin."

"Well, you can start by not calling me *sir*. In many ways you and I are peers."

Gerard didn't believe that for a minute. "I doubt that. Uh, what will I call you? Mister Secretary?"

Lingchow laughed easily. "All right. You may call me sir, or Diplomat, or even Greaves if you're more comfortable with informality. The title of Secretary, however, is inappropriate."

There was something about Lingchow that Gerard liked, but behind that congenial front he sensed a certain detachment, a cold harshness that often developed in men who fought their way toward power. "Thank you, sir, but perhaps we should stick with formalities for the present."

"As you will. So tell me, how does it feel to be back on Federation soil?"

"I have to admit that it feels slightly awkward." Gerard knew the question was loaded with another implication, so he added, "But the hardest part is forcing myself to think continuously in Standard. After seven, almost eight years in Ribble Galaxy, I think in Kulitti without realizing it, if you know what I mean."

"You haven't gone, ah, how shall I put this? Do you feel like you *belong* in Ribble?"

Another loaded question. "In a way I do, sir." Gerard had to be careful. If Fed knew how intimately he was linked to Fairy Peg, it could cause all Krick to break loose. "The Badh, Princess Peg, and her staff have been more than kind to me."

"So I understand. You've been holding back on us, Manley. That worries me."

"In what way, sir?"

"You know what way I mean. Shouldn't you have kept us better informed?"

Was Lingchow fishing for information, or did he actually know something? Gerard couldn't be sure. "With all due respect, sir, I believe I did a better job of keeping the service informed than it did for me."

Lingchow frowned. "You are referring, I suppose, to the presence of certain other agents in Ribble Galaxy?"

"Exactly, sir. And the denial that those agents were there. And—" Gerard cut himself off. He had almost added the unsupported directive for him to lie to Ribble in order to delay the negotiations, but he wasn't sure if Lingchow was in a position to know about that.

"And what? Come now, Manley, what else is bothering you?"

"I'd better not answer that until you can prove you have a *need to know . . .* sir."

"What proof do you want? And what would you accept? A message from Service Secretary Wattersshaw? I could provide you with that, but how would you validate it? You see, Manley, you have no choice but to trust me."

"Houn's ass," Gerard said flatly in Kulitti.

"Ratchet crap," Lingchow responded in the same tongue.

That told Gerard a great deal. Not only did Lingchow speak Kulitti, but he was conversant in the prejudicial slang of the nobility. He would have to tread even more carefully with this man. "You want to know my complaints, sir? You want to know what bothers me about this whole mission? Too bad. There are lots of things *I* want to know, things the service refuses to tell me.

"You want me to sit on Kril like a good little diplomat and make nice to the Ribble hierarchy? I can do that. Fara knows I haven't been doing much else since I got there, so I've had a lot of practice. You want me to come here and begin the negotiation process? I can do that too, but not nearly so well. In a way, Mister Secretary, I know much more about Ribble's position and attitudes than I do about Fed's." The more he talked, the angrier he got.

"That's why you are so valuable to us."

"What?"

"That's why you have been given so little information. We didn't want your attitudes about Ribble to be prejudiced by the Federation's plans and goals."

Gerard stood up and looked steadily at Lingchow. "Why don't you take a flying leap into the void?"

"With Binkley of Baun?" Lingchow smiled as he said that, but it was a cold, hard smile.

Gerard wanted to storm out of the office. But where would he go? The waves of his anger were battering futilely against a seawall of reason. Slowly he sat back down, and after a moment he laughed. "So, I guess that answers that question."

"I'm not sure I follow you."

"It doesn't matter, sir. I'm not sure I could explain it." But he could. Fianne had been right in the worst possible way. Not only was he a pawn in the game between Ribble and Fed, he was a helpless pawn. At least that's what they thought. Well, they had some things to learn about pawns. "When do we start discussing specifics, *sir*?" The sarcastic inflection was stronger than he meant it to be, but Gerard didn't care. It was about time for him to let Fed in on a little more of his anger. If Lingchow was to be the conduit for that, so much the better.

"I think tomorrow will be soon enough. You probably want to rest up from your trip."

And you probably want to get off a preliminary report, Gerard thought. "Fine. I'll stay aboard my ship."

"But it's such a bothersome trip from here to the starport. Why not stay here?"

"I will. Tomorrow. There are some shipkeeping chores I'd like to get done before I settle in here." Gerard almost said 'sir' again, but thought better of it.

"Yes, yes, of course. Well then, shall we meet here then at nine hundred local time?"

As soon as he was back aboard *Windhover*, Gerard went straight to the galley and fixed himself a large pot of Brandusian coffee. It almost exhausted his supply, but for the moment, he didn't care. Later, if he couldn't buy any more in Vardezee, he would be unhappy with himself, but he didn't care about that either. His anger had settled into a stagnant pool and he needed to flush it out of his mind.

Underneath that anger he knew there lay a hard deposit of defiance, an accretion which had been building for over seven years until it had reached a size where it could no longer be ignored. Gerard wanted that defiance. It was a rock he could build upon to change the shape of the game and show Fed, and Fianne, and Fairy Peg too, that pawns do not always follow the plans laid down by others.

But first he knew he would have to get everything he could out of Lingchow. He needed as much information as possible, so that when the time came for him to act he would be as prepared as possible. Lingchow had said he was valuable to them, valuable because his ignorance of their plans gave him an unbiased assessment of Ribble's situation and attitudes. That would be his lever. For everything he told Lingchow about Ribble, he would demand something for himself... in advance. What Lingchow didn't know was how little Gerard actually had to offer him. But Fed had given him license to lie. If necessary, he would lie to Lingchow, give him half-truths and interpretations as fact. Let *him* sort it out.

"Ah, but you know what, Windy? Lingchow has other sources of information in Ribble besides me. That means I'll have to be very, very careful if I have to lie to him. Should I give him big lies? Lies so huge that he'll have to accept them? Or just small ones? Little shadings of the truth that will pass unnoticed through his ears until he thinks about them much later? What do you think, girl? A mixture of both? How about big lies of no consequence and little lies of deep significance? Maybe that's the answer."

Gerard actually did do some shipkeeping chores, but all the while he kept reviewing his information in the light of his new approach. Fianne had told him Corpus Privy and Fairy Peg wanted negotiations to begin, but not too quickly or energetically. That matched closely enough with his directives from Merita to annoy him. Suppose he implied to Lingchow that if the basic negotiations didn't start immediately, Ribble would be very displeased? And suppose he insisted on a timetable for top-level negotiations, a summit meeting between Fairy Peg and Chairman Valunzuella?

If Lingchow refused the idea, he could offer to dissolve his contract, claiming that he could be of no further use to them. Then he'd find out just how valuable they really thought he was. Or maybe... the stream of ideas flowed endlessly, and late that night Gerard had to move from his cabin to the autodoc and turn on the soother in order to get to sleep.

"Get all your chores completed?" Lingchow asked by way of greeting.

"The ones that needed it most. And you?"

"My chores are never done." Lingchow paused and picked up a small memocorder. "If you are ready to begin,

I'd like to ask you some questions in order to better understand how we can best proceed." After giving Gerard the opportunity to respond, he continued. "What is the Ribble leadership's current attitude toward the Federation, in general, I mean?"

"That's a very broad question, sir. Could you be more specific?"

"Very well. What is Corpus Privy's attitude toward the Federation?"

"In what respect, sir?"

"Overall."

"Wary. Cautious. Suspicious."

"We need more information than that, Manley, if we are going to make any headway."

"What kind of information, sir?"

Lingchow stared at him for a minute, then turned off the memocorder and laid it back down on the desk. "Look, Manley, it took me almost a year to set up this meeting, and I didn't come here to play games with you."

"Certainly not, sir."

"Then stop stalling and answer my questions." Lingchow's tone was surprisingly flat.

"I can't, sir, at least not until you are more specific. Remember, sir, we're in this together, on the same team and all that."

"Don't get sarcastic with me, Manley. I'll get your contract dissolved and have you shipped to the other side of the universe."

"Fine, sir, if you think that will bring Ribble to the negotiating table," Gerard said as evenly as possible while fighting a twitch of a smile in the corners of his mouth.

"Dammit, Manley, what do you want from me?"

"The same thing you want from me: answers."

Lingchow laughed. "All right, let's start over. I want information about the political situation in Ribble Galaxy and the attitudes of the leaders. You want information about our negotiating position. Am I correct?"

"Only partially, sir. I also want to know what TreatyService agents were doing on Evird aiding the rebels, and," Gerard paused for effect, "who your other sources of information are in Ribble, and specifically on Kril."

"I'm afraid that's out of the question."

"Perhaps out of the question, sir, but not impossible.

173

Let me help you. I was told by the highest authorities in the Ribble government to return with a specific schedule of negotiations leading to a summit meeting between the Badh and Chairman Valunzuella."

"Incredible. And totally preposterous."

"Which? The schedule, or the summit?"

Lingchow folded his arms and looked at Gerard as though trying to measure him. "Do you play trychess?"

"I used to. Why?"

"Are you familiar with the Silverbond Convention?"

Gerard hated questions like that. He knew the general principles of the convention and also that Lingchow would try to make a point with it whether he knew the convention or not. "I know the basic principles."

"Good. Then you know that the theory behind the convention is that a defense to block the middle board will allow the player to divide and conquer his opponent."

"So?"

"One sets up the middle board defense with a dangerous and unorthodox attack from the top. I believe you are trying to do the same kind of thing."

The analogy wasn't clear to Gerard, so he kept his mouth shut and let Lingchow talk.

"Let me explain something to you, Manley. Despite some critical messages you've received, the Service is very pleased with what you've done in Ribble Galaxy. You've befriended and impressed members of the hierarchy, gained a certain measure of their confidence and trust, and done about as well as we could expect of someone with your experience and training.

"As I told you yesterday, you have become valuable to us. But it is obvious that you have also become valuable to Ribble Galaxy. However, you must not let your value in either case confuse you. You work for us. We pay you to do a job as a citizen of the Federation. Now we want you to help us complete that job, and you seem reluctant to do so."

Lingchow paused to clear his throat and Gerard took advantage of it. "Not at all. I want to finish this mission as much as you want me to," so I can go back to Fairy Peg and my son, Gerard thought, and if you knew about that,

174

you'd scream. "But I've reached a point where I have to have more information if I am to do it properly."

"I understand that, but—"

"Please, let me finish."

"Very well."

"I don't know who you are, Mister Greaves Lingchow. You won't tell me your rank, nor how you fit into these negotiations. You ask me vague, general questions, then get upset when I ask you to be more specific. When I told you what Ribble Galaxy wanted, you said it was preposterous and took me off into a trychess analogy. Dammit, sir, either play straight with me, or dissolve my contract, take my ship, give me my pay, and let me go." Gerard sat back with a sigh. That wasn't exactly the speech he'd intended to make, but maybe it would do.

Like an echo, Lingchow sighed also. "My superiors foresaw this possibility, Manley, and authorized me to give you certain highly classified information. But before I do, let me ask you something. If I told you that what you are involved in was of great importance to the future security of Ribble Galaxy and the Federation, and has been proceeding with the approval of the highest levels of both governments, would that be enough for you?"

"No. That's only so much shadow-talk."

"If I told you that your knowledge of these plans could directly endanger your life and the plans themselves, would that satisfy you?"

"No more than the other." Gerard was curious to see if Lingchow was really leading up to something or just spraying space dust.

"I was afraid not." Lingchow reached into his desk and took out a small microcard, a stamp pad, and a pen. "Sign this," he said, pushing the card across the desk.

Gerard let it lay. "What is it?"

"A security agreement. There's a viewer in the arm of your chair. Read it. Then sign it and put your thumbprint in the box."

It was a security agreement under which Gerard swore his life and honor never to reveal the contents of certain numbered documents. He signed the card, thumb-printed it, and handed it back to Lingchow, who dropped it into a processing slot in the wall behind him. When a blue light above the slot came on, he turned back to Gerard.

"Ten years ago, six years after the temporary truce was signed between Ribble Galaxy and the Federation, we began receiving certain messages indicating that the leadership of Ribble Galaxy was interested in negotiating a permanent peace. There has been a regular exchange of messages ever since.

"Shortly after you were sent to Ribble Galaxy, our chief correspondent there reported that Ribble's leadership might be interested in discussing confederation."

"I don't believe it," Gerard said flatly. It was too incredible to be true.

"You don't have to. It's true whether you believe it or not. At any rate, to explore such an idea is very complicated and takes a great deal of time. There are a myriad of details still to be worked out, but the basic tenets of an agreement have been tentatively approved by both sides. Unfortunately, politics in both places have complicated the matter even further, and the appropriate time for bringing the negotiations into the open has been delayed. That is why you were told to publicly stall and lie if necessary."

Gerard laughed. "Now you're the one making preposterous statements. However, just for the sake of the joke, why wasn't I told?"

"The fewer people who knew, the fewer there were to leak the information. Don't look so amused. Even the chairman didn't know about this until a year ago. Besides, I meant what I said before. If you had known this, you might have viewed what you learned in Ribble Galaxy in a totally different light. This way we had the luxury of your unbiased opinion. Now can you see what our problem was?"

Gerard shook his head in disbelief. The whole idea of Ribble Galaxy, with its history of fierce independence, joining the Federation was almost incomprehensible. "Only partially. First, I don't understand why Ribble would want to join the Federation, or how anyone could expect them to give up their independence. Second, if what you say is true, why were TreatyService agents working with the rebels on Evird? And third, I don't see how either you or the leaders you are supposedly in contact with in Ribble expect to convince the power structures in either place to accept this idea. It's all too preposterous. Your word still fits."

"Imaginative, yes. Difficult, yes. Preposterous, no. Listen, Manley, you and I are going to spend a lot of time talking about this for however long it takes to convince you. You know the secret now, so you have to go back to Ribble convinced, believing with all your heart that not only is this true, but that it will work. Then one day, hopefully not more than a couple of years from now, you and I will sit in on that summit you mentioned and take pride in the roles we played bringing two great powers together."

Three months later, as Gerard prepared for the first warp that would take him back to Ribble Galaxy, he still wasn't convinced. Lingchow thought he was, because in the end Gerard had done everything he could to make Lingchow believe that. But somewhere, way back in the corner of his nose, Gerard smelled grisk dung, mountains of it rotting in the heat of Lingchow's persuasion. Lingchow had refused to reveal anything about his contact in Ribble except to say that it was close to the throne. Somehow, without breaking his secrecy oath, Gerard would have to get the truth out of Fairy Peg when he got back to Kril. If he could not get her to volunteer some validation of the confederation plan, he would have to choose between Fed and Ribble. And he knew already which he would choose. He had always hated the stench of grisk dung.

* * *

Message to: Avarignon Cloznitchnikoff
     FedTreatySvc
Indications are that you have inadvertently been granted more time. However, we still must have the control information as soon as you can appropriate it from your rival service. Without the control our task will be much more difficult, and your superiors will have to provide much more visible support than will make them comfortable.

Things go badly for us now, but we can use the ill winds to our ultimate advantage if we have the control. Suggest you do your utmost to expedite your efforts.

—Toehold

* * *

17

Gerard strode through the halls of EllKoep, Ratchets by his side, feeling dirty and tired. But Fairy Peg's instructions had been very clear. Come at once. Brunnel had been waiting at the port with a skimmer, and ten minutes after *Windhover* landed Gerard had been on his way. It felt good to be back. It would feel even better when they let him see Orees.

Fairy Peg and Fianne were waiting for him in her office. "Welcome, Pilot. You have been missed."

Hearing the warmth in her voice, he almost responded informally, but caught himself in time. With a knee-dipping bow he said, "You are most gracious, Badh. I am pleased to return."

"Be seated, Pilot," she said with a twinkle in her eye and a wave toward a small couch.

He waited for her to sit first, and to his surprise she sat on the couch and patted the cushion beside her. His heart skipped a beat with the joy he felt, but he tried to keep his face straight. If she had forgiven him, he would know it soon enough. As gracefully as he could, he sat beside her without touching her. He had to restrain himself from reaching for her hand.

With a laugh she took his hand and kissed it. "Look not so somber, Pilot. We know that Inez tricked you. She has been exiled to Sun's March."

His heart skipped another beat. Then he started racing. "You . . . you," he stammered, "you mean I am forgiven?"

"There is nothing to forgive."

"But, I . . . oh Krick. I'm so happy I can't talk." Even as

178

he said it, Gerard felt himself holding back a little, wary in a small way of her warmth. Still, he was relieved that one problem, at least, seemed to have been taken care of.

"Then do not talk, Pilot. Listen. Fianne has much to tell you."

Fianne looked somehow older than when Gerard had last seen him, but his voice was strong and clear. "Certainly our Badh speaks the truth. Much has happened in the two hundred days since you left. Admiral Gannack was confirmed as Privy-Admiral, and brought charges of aiding the rebellion against seventeen officers. Duca Nocen of Evird and Duca Iskkyyoo of Leewh resigned from Corpus Privy in the face of allegations that they were also involved in supporting the rebels."

Only half of Gerard's attention was on Fianne's words. The other half was acutely aware of Fairy Peg's presence, the light scent of her hair, the softness of her hand in his.

"And the Noble Assembly passed a resolution proposing a three-year timetable for negotiations with the Federation."

That got Gerard's total attention. "What prompted that?"

Fianne smiled. "Our Badh suggested to them that it would be better to be involved in active negotiations with the Federation than to have it trying to subvert planets behind our backs. Do you not approve, Diplomat?"

Looking at Fairy Peg he said, "Certainly. Most certainly. It just catches me by surprise, that's all."

Fairy Peg squeezed his hand with a smile, then a sad look crossed her face. "Tell him about, about the *treachery*," she said haltingly.

"Perhaps that should wait, Princess."

"No," she said sternly, her jaw setting into a hard line. "He needs to know."

"Very well." Still Fianne hesitated, looking with great concern at Fairy Peg.

Gerard's curiosity got the better of his patience. "What treachery? What is the princess talking about, Fianne?"

"A thousand pardons for what I must tell you, Consort," Fianne said slowly. It was the first time he had ever called Gerard *Consort*. "While you were gone we learned that our Badh's food had been drugged during her pregnancy."

"Is that why—"

"Yes."

Gerard looked at Fairy Peg, who tried to smile at him and failed. Then she looked down into her lap and squeezed his hand.

"Did you find out who—"

"Yes, but we could not prove it."

"Who?"

"Admiral Holsten's daughter, Latisha, and the serving girl, Imitatas. They have been sent to Hinson Keep."

Gerard looked quickly from Fianne to Fairy Peg and back to Fianne. "But the Holsten family controls Hinson Keep?"

"And will be harsher on one of their own for having dishonored the family," Fianne answered quickly.

Gerard shook his head slightly as though trying to make that idea settle into place. "Why?" he asked. "Why?" He looked at Fairy Peg and was surprised to see no tears in her eyes.

"Revenge," she said quietly in a cold, clear tone. "Latisha holds you responsible for her father's death."

"And the serving girl?"

"We believe she acted under Latisha's instructions."

"What was her name again?"

"Imitatas. Do you not remember her? She was the one caught with the Evirdian death squad on the Day of Conclusion. She is Latisha's nay-daughter."

"I don't understand. After this, why was she allowed to live?"

"Because as Fianne said, there was no proof."

What was wrong with these people, Gerard wondered? He dropped Fairy Peg's hand and rose from the couch, staring at them. "So? Since when did anyone around here require proof? I was sent to Hinson Keep and tortured without any *proof*." Anger and sarcasm punctuated his words. "Now you tell me that Latisha Holsten and her already suspicious daughter poisoned and killed our children *in the womb*, but they live under their family's protection because you have no *proof*! I don't understand this at all! Get the proof. Let Markl Holsten use his magic pain machines to get it from both of them. Then bring them both here and I'll kill them myself. Damn it to Krick! What's going on around here?"

"Please, Pilot," Fairy Peg implored, "you must understand. Under the circumstances we did all that we could do."

"You? The Badh? That was all you could do to the *murderers* of our children?" His voice rose to an hysterical pitch which he immediately stifled. "Why?" he asked with controlled bitterness. "Why was that all you could do?"

Fairy Peg looked away from his angry stare as she answered. "Because we need the support of the Holsten family," she said flatly.

"*What?*" Gerard didn't believe what he'd just heard. "You mean this was a *political* decision?"

Looking back at him with a hardness in her eyes that Gerard found chilling she said, "Yes. That is exactly what it was. I have a galaxy to run, Pilot, and I need Holsten support to run it. Do you think it was easy for me to make such a decision? Do you think I liked what I had to do? Or do you care?"

"You're damn right I care! What do you think I'm so angry about?"

"I do not know. I did what I had to do with great pain, and in return I receive your abuse and selfishness. What happened to your tenderness and understanding while you were gone?"

Gerard didn't know what to say because he didn't know if he was right or wrong. There was a great emptiness where his thoughts should have been, and an ache under his heart that sent him dull, throbbing messages of pain. With a heavy sigh he sank into one of the chairs against the wall, putting as much distance between himself and Fairy Peg as he could. He had to block this new information from his mind and give it time to settle before he could cope with it. "Fed wants to negotiate," he said finally.

Fianne cleared his throat and Fairy Peg looked at him with surprise. "That is not news," she said evenly, her eyebrows arched slightly in question.

"No, it isn't, but there may be more to it than that." Gerard knew it was a weak response, but hoped that it might head Fairy Peg in the right direction. If she and Fianne did the talking, he could push the pain further away from him. "The Fedrep I talked to implied that . . ." Gerard let his voice trail away. He wasn't thinking too clearly and didn't want to say the wrong thing.

"Implied what, Diplomat?"

"I don't know. Look, maybe we should talk about this later. I'm not thinking very well right now and—"

"Yes, perhaps that would be best. We will talk with you tomorrow, Fianne." There was a hint of softness in Fairy Peg's voice, but it was mixed with something cold and calculating.

Gerard acknowledged Fianne's departure with a slight wave of his hand, and was surprised when Fairy Peg came and knelt beside his chair after Fianne left.

"I am sorry, Pilot," she said looking up into his eyes, "but you must see that I had no choice. My duties as Badh must always come first."

He reached for her face and let his fingers linger on her cheek in a light caress. "I know. I know. I'll be all right. It'll just take me a little while to accept the idea, that's all. Perhaps if you had broken it—"

"More gently?"

"Or something. Fairy Peg, I love you. But sometimes I feel like I don't know you at all. Shhh. Don't look at me like that. It's true. I love Fairy Peg, but that's not the same thing as loving the Badh. It's easy to love Fairy Peg. I do it without thinking about it. I have to work at loving the Badh. Am I making any sense?"

"Yes," she said sadly as she laid her head on his arm, "you make great sense."

As he stroked her hair Gerard knew he was holding back from her, but didn't want to let go of himself. This reserve was a buffer to protect him from whatever shocks the Badh had in store for him. He felt far too vulnerable to let his guard down, even to her.

That night they slept together for the first time in over eight months. Long after they had made love tentatively and awkwardly, and long after Fairy Peg had fallen asleep in his arms, Gerard lay awake staring at the ceiling. A confusing parade of thoughts and emotions demanded that he sort them out before they would let him rest.

First came his allegiance to Fairy Peg and Orees, for they were part of him and he of them. Then came his allegiance to the Federation, with which he had formed a pact of honor. Finally came his allegiance to the Badh, and because of her, to Ribble Galaxy. He wasn't sure what that delineation of allegiances was going to mean, or how he was going to make it work, but the act of clarifying his relationships finally brought an end to the parade and let him sleep.

"I can't tell you that, Fianne. All I can say is that the man I talked to refused to discuss anything but the most general outlines of a schedule, and suggested that if all went well we should be able to reach and sign a permanent agreement in about two standard years."

"And he gave you specific terms to negotiate?"

"Of course."

"And he empowered you to make certain compromises?"

"Of course he did. What are you getting to?"

Fianny leaned back in the chair across from Gerard's desk and crossed his fingers over his stomach, letting his thumbs beat a nervous rhythm on his solar plexus. "I am not sure, Diplomat. Why is the Federation making this offer now? Why is it willing to let you do all the initial negotiations? No offense, Diplomat, but it seems to me that such discussions would be far more complex and detailed than one person could or should handle. Perhaps if you outlined the terms for me, I would better make sense of this arrangement."

"I'd rather wait for the Badh."

"Surely you do not think—"

"Please, Fianne. I want her to hear the terms first from me. In this instance the Fedrep was adamant, and I agree with him. It is her right as Badh to hear them first." And my right to watch her reaction, Gerard added to himself.

"As you will, Diplomat." Fianne's tone carried none of the acceptance that his words did. "But suppose our Badh requests that you tell me first?"

"Then I would decline."

"You would refuse the Badh?"

"I have no choice."

"Yes, I believe you would." Fianne seemed mildly surprised. "Suppose she asked you to tell her in the presence of Corpus Privy?"

"I would decline that also. She must be the first to hear, Fianne. You can be present. Squo Lyle can be present. And one or two leaders from the Noble Assembly. But no more."

"Not even Privy-Admiral Gannack?"

Gerard hesitated. He had already given more ground than he wanted to. "Well, I suppose the military would have to be represented. Okay, add Privy-Admiral Gannack. But that's it. And if all those people are present, I have to add another condition: No interruptions until I outline all the terms. In fact, I will insist on that condition no matter who is present."

With a frown Fianne said, "I cannot guarantee that."

"The Badh can."

As Gerard sat down at the opposite end of the table from Fairy Peg, he felt suddenly nervous. He would much rather have outlined the negotiating terms in private to her first so that he could have gauged her reactions up close. At this table, with everyone else present, it would be much more difficult. Still, he told himself, it might also be more revealing. If there really were a secret movement toward confederation within Ribble's leadership, maybe he would find some signs of it here.

Besides himself and Fairy Peg, the group included Squo Lyle, Privy Admiral Gannack, Fianne, the Co-Serits of the Noble Assembly—iskin and Premgraff—and surprisingly, Targ Alpluakka. Gerard had not objected to Targ's presence, but he had certainly been surprised when Fairy Peg had told him Targ would be attending. He had not asked why, and Fairy Peg had offered no explanation, but once the surprise wore off, Gerard began to wonder if Targ could be Lingchow's contact. As Commander of the Gabriel Ratchets, Targ was certainly close enough to the throne, yet he was removed from the main political lines. Targ's reactions would bear watching also.

Fairy Peg tapped a small gavel on a metallic disk in front of her and opened the meeting. "We welcome you all. For reasons you already know, what you hear today must remain absolutely secret until such time as we can determine a mutually acceptable course of action. Furthermore, I request each of you to listen to Diplomat Manley without interruption and reserve your comments and questions until after he has finished his presentation. Diplomat?"

"A thousand thanks, Badh," Gerard answered formally. He looked around the table at the expectant faces and took a deep breath. "Five days ago I returned from a lengthy series of meetings with a representative of the Federation

184

on Tyboren in the Bestoff system. The result of those meetings was a basic proposal for negotiations leading to the ultimate signing of a permanent peace pact between Ribble Galaxy and the Federation. The substance of that proposal is included in the folder in front of each of you, as is an annotated list of terms and agreements the Federation would like to discuss and resolve."

Gerard paused to take a sip of water, and used the moment to glance over the top of his glass at Fairy Peg. She made no move toward the folder lying untouched in front of her, and the others were following her lead.

"First," he continued, "the Federation proposes that both sides agree to work toward a pact that will remain in effect in perpetuity." Serit Pemgraff, Targ, and Squo Lyle reacted with looks of surprise, and Squo Lyle opened his mouth as though to speak, but shut it quickly after looking at Fairy Peg. Her face remained fixed in an unsmiling attitude of attention.

"Second, the Federation proposes that the borderspace between itself and Ribble be patrolled by a combined force under a joint command, the makeup and organization of which shall be mutually agreed upon by both parties." Admiral Gannack grunted briefly in disapproval, and her reaction was supported by frowns around the table.

Gerard plunged on. "Third, the Federation proposes open resumption of trading and a mutually acceptable set of limitations on import and export duties and tarifs, and a joint commission to establish and maintain them." Only Serit Iskin seemed moved by that proposal and his reaction was barely noticeable. Gerard tried to relax a little, and crossed his mental fingers that the rest of the proposals would go as smoothly.

"Fourth, the Federation proposes a permanent reestablishment of diplomatic relations including, but not limited to, trade consulates, planetary ambassadors, system ambassadors, and governmental ambassadors at the highest levels."

"Why that's—" Squo Lyle blurted before he caught himself. "A thousand pardons, Badh."

"Certainly, Squo Lyle. You may continue, Diplomat."

Gerard took a breath to relieve his own tension. If Squo Lyle had guessed that the proposals were only one step away from confederation, the others wouldn't be far behind his thought.

"Fifth, the Federation proposes the establishment of a joint economic commission to set standards and rules for the exchange of currency, its valuation, plus all such matters of mutual economic interest as are assigned to it by both governments.

"Sixth," Gerard continued without a pause, "the Federation proposes that commissions be established for the purpose of fostering the exchange of cultural groups, sport teams, students, and organized tourist groups; furthermore, that such commissions be empowered to—"

"No!" Squo Lyle's exclamation with its vehemence, including Gerard. "A thousand pardons, Badh, but this is outrageous. These proposals are totally out of order. Totally out of order."

"So are you, Squo Lyle," Fairy Peg said firmly. "We agreed to listen and reserve our comments."

Squo Lyle bowed his head. "Again, a thousand pardons, Badh. I will refrain from further comment."

With a nod from Fairy Peg, Gerard continued. "Let's see, uh, ah, yes. Students and organized tourist groups; *furthermore*, that such commissions be empowered to make recommendations to both governments for broadening these exchanges.

"Seventh, the Federation proposes that the two parties begin discussions about the possibilities of joint exploration of the vast, uncharted regions of the universe."

Gerard read the remaining thirty-eight proposals without interruption, but it became more and more evident from the expressions around the table that everyone was going to have strong comments and questions—everyone, that is, except Fairy Peg and Fianne, who seemed to take all the proposals with perfect equanimity.

"And lastly," Gerard said with more than a little sigh of relief, "the Federation proposes that negotiations on the above begin as soon as is mutually agreeable."

"Thank you, Diplomat," Fairy Peg said. "I believe we should take a short recess for refreshments before we open the discussion."

There were reluctant murmurs of approval from around the table as everyone stood and followed Fairy Peg into an adjoining room where a table of finger food awaited them. Fianne stayed behind with Gerard. "You did well, Diplomat."

"Thanks, Fianne. You weren't surprised by any of that, were you?"

Fianne laughed. "Should I have been?"

"I don't know. Squo Lyle certainly was."

"Ah, but has Squo Lyle been thinking about what might be contained in such proposals? Probably not."

"And you have, of course?"

"Certainly, Diplomat, certainly. It is part of my job."

"Like corresponding with Fedreps?"

"Certainly. Does that surprise you, Diplomat?"

Gerard looked at him carefully. "Not the correspondence, no, but your casual admission of it does. Did you set up that meeting on Tyboren?"

Fianne laughed. "Ah, Diplomat, you read far more into my simple answer than was there. The tone of your questions makes me wonder if you think... but now, tell me what you think. Or better yet, tell me what you *suspect*."

Sometimes trying to read Fianne was like trying to read a blank stone wall. The patterns, like Fianne's laughter, were regular but meaningless. "I don't know what or *who* to suspect, Fianne, but you're certainly on my list."

"Of possible what? Spies for the Federation? Agents of provocation? Come, tell me what you think I have done."

Fianne's voice was light, carried by a tone that said he wasn't taking Gerard's suspicions seriously. "I was told that FedDiploService has a regular correspondent high in the government close to the throne."

"And you think I might be that correspondent?"

"Didn't you admit as much?"

"Ah, I see. Because I have had occasion to transmit and receive certain messages between the Badh and your Federation, you think I might be this mysterious correspondent you were told about. I regret disappointing you, Diplomat, but you must continue your search. If you don't believe me, we can continue this discussion later. Now I suggest that we join the others and get something to eat. The rest of this session may be difficult to endure on an empty stomach."

"Later, then," Gerard said, motioning Fianne ahead of him into the other room. He didn't know whether to believe Fianne or not, but that decision could wait. It was enough to know that Fianne had been in contact with Fed, and that neither he nor Fairy Peg were surprised by Fed's proposals.

Despite some minor modifications and the deletion of a few key terms, the heart of the proposals he had read to the group was taken from the Standard Proposal of Confederation. He had had to argue long and loudly with Lingchow to get him to agree to use the S.P.C. language, but finally Gerard had convinced him that it would be better to begin with language already acceptable to Fed. Now he knew that the language and terms were already familiar to Fairy Peg and Fianne. At least he thought he knew that, because he could think of no other reason why their reaction was so mild.

In fact, it seemed that everyone in the group had reacted mildly except Squo Lyle, and the more he thought about Squo Lyle, the more Gerard questioned his reaction. Somehow it had been too perfect, too neat to be real. Gerard wasn't sure why he felt that, but he did. As certainly as if he had paid admission to see a show on one of Fed's RecWorlds, he knew Squo Lyle had just given him a performance; a small one, perhaps, but one of beautiful proportions. That realization startled Gerard for a moment, and in that moment made him question its validity. Maybe he was just imagining things.

Fairy Peg's ad hoc committee questioned him for the better part of five hours, wanting specific interpretations for every generality in the proposals. Gerard did his best to answer the questions with examples of how similar arrangements with other systems worked within the Federation. He hoped that by taking that tack eventually one of them would mention the key word: confederation. It did not work. Even Squo Lyle, who asked the most pointed questions, seemed unwilling to approach the idea of confederation even as a negative to be railed against. When Fairy Peg finally called an end to the discussions for the day, Gerard felt more than a little frustrated.

"You look tired, Pilot," Fairy Peg said softly as they returned to their chambers. "You must not look tired at the ball tomorrow."

He gave her a tight smile. "Ah, yes, I had forgotten the ball. I suppose we must attend."

"Of course we must. The ball is being held in your honor."

"The return of the prodigal consort."

"Pardon?"

Gerard sighed and took her into his arms. "Never mind, love. I'm just a little weary, and it's showing. You didn't say much in the meeting. How come?"

Fairy Peg nestled her head against his neck. "There was no need, Pilot. The questions were asked for me, and you gave the appropriate answers."

"Mmmm," he said as he stroked her hair, "but there was one question that wasn't asked *or* answered."

"And what question was that?"

"The biggest one of all."

"Ah," she sighed with a hint of amusement, "you mean no one asked what these negotiations could ultimately lead to? Surely they did not need to ask that question."

Gerard leaned away from her slightly so he could see her face "Why?"

"Because, my dear Pilot, everyone there knew. If we accept your Federation's basic proposals, one day we will join it."

"But—"

"Do not look so startled, my love. Confederation is neither a new idea nor an alien one."

"But I don't—I mean, what about Ribble's independence?" Fairy Peg's admission was so startling in its openness that he had difficulty organizing his words. Had Lingchow told him the truth after all?

Fairy Peg pulled him down onto the couch and covered his mouth with a long kiss. "There," she said softly as she finally let him catch his breath. "We are confederates of a sort, are we not? Yet we are also independent."

"That's hardly a very good analogy."

"Ah, but it may be the best analogy." She ran her fingers inside the open front of his tunic. If you and I can bring our disparate selves into confederation, why should it seem so farfetched for Ribble and the Federation to do the same?"

Her hand moved in little sensuous circles over his skin. His passion stirred. The subject of confederation could wait. He leaned back and let his fingers trace the outline of her breast under her tight bodice. With a

189

smile he said, "Nothing is farfetched when I'm with you, Fairy Peg."

∗   ∗   ∗

Message to: Greaves Lingchow
         FedDiploSvc

Your last message was deeply disturbing to us. The sacrifice that would have to be made and the blood that would be spilled are totally out of keeping with our previous agreements. We fail to see how this act will serve to seal our bargain. Consequently, we must decline.

Any political difficulties you have with your chairman must be resolved by your actions, not ours. If you cannot give us assurances that you will abandon this foolhardy plan, then further negotiations must be postponed indefinitely, and any move toward a summit meeting will be destroyed.

We repeat, you must abandon this plan.

—Glyph

∗   ∗   ∗

18

"Come on, Orees, you can do it. That's a good boy." Gerard smiled proudly as Orees tottered across the room on the little skimmer seat and set it down at Gerard's feet.

"Dee it good, Daddy?"

Gerard picked him up with a laugh and gave him a big hug. "You did it good, son. You made Daddy very proud."

"Printhess good?" Orees asked with a twinkle in his bright green eyes.

Fairy Peg joined them in the hug. "Yes, you little gurgler, princess good. Now it is time for you to go to bed."

Screwing his face into an exaggerated pout, Orees said, "No."

Gerard laughed again and gave Orees a loud, smacking kiss on the neck. "Want me to tell you a story first?"

"No. Pay with simmer."

"Tomorrow. Now give us a kiss goodnight."

"No. No kiss-kiss," Orees whined.

With a wink, Gerard said, "then I'll have to tickle your belly."

Orees made a sound that was half laugh and half gurgle, and pulled his tunic up to reveal his smooth, round stomach. "No tickle, Daddy. No tickle."

Gerard buried his face in Orees's belly and blew with a hard, buzzing sound. Orees laughed in high-pitched glee. "Now do we get a kiss?" Gerard asked.

"No tickle," Orees answered breathlessly, pulling his tunic even higher.

They did not get their goodnight kiss, but Orees was still laughing when Winsea carried him off to bed. "We'd better start getting dressed," Gerard said as he gave Fairy Peg a big hug. "Wouldn't want to be late for our party."

After standing in the reception line for over an hour, Gerard was more than ready to exercise his legs in a dance. When the orchestra started on a quick-step tune, he grinned with pleasure at Fairy Peg as he took her into his arms. "Sounds like they picked something I know how to do. Your choice?"

"Of course, Pilot. I would not want you uncomfortable."

They danced the first half of the piece with flourish, and when the midpause came they were joined by other dancers, who whirled about them in shifting patterns of color and motion. Dresses, uniforms, and skins of all hues formed a happy kaleidoscope around them which swirled to a slow stop as the first piece ended, only to start moving again when the orchestra immediately struck up a new song. Gerard quickly twirled Fairy Peg off again in a series of one-two-three steps, laughing all the time.

"Why are you so happy, Pilot?"

"I don't know. I just feel good. That's what I'm supposed to do, isn't it?"

"Of course, but—"

"But nothing. Hold on, Princess. We're going to do a triple spin." They did two triple spins in quick succession, then, after a shifty bit of navigating through the crowded

191

dancers, did another. When the dance finally ended, they were both close to being breathless. As they turned to leave the dance floor, they were confronted by a rather plain-faced young woman in an unadorned, dark green dress.

"A thousand pardons, Badh," the woman said with a deep curtsy, "But I beg the privilege of the consort's first free dance."

Gerard looked to Fairy Peg, then to the woman, then back to Fairy Peg with his eyebrows raised in question.

"Consort," she said with a strained look in her eyes, "this is Branbinie Holsten. You met her on the Day of Conclusion."

"Lady," Gerard said formally. "a pleasure to see you again." He had no memory of meeting her.

"The pleasure is all mine, Consort," the young woman said with another curtsy. "My grandfather spoke highly of you."

"Your grandfather?" Gerard asked.

"Privy-Admiral Holsten," Fairy Peg answered before the young woman could speak.

Gerard looked carefully at this Branbinie Holsten as she rose from her curtsy, remembered her finally, but wondered why she was appealing to him for a dance. An attempt to show that the Holstens were not all his enemies? Perhaps, but, despite her smile, Gerard detected no warmth in her and hoped he could politely refuse her request.

"My consort is yours," Fairy Peg said, taking her arm from Gerard's, "but for one dance only."

"A thousand thanks," Branbinie said with another curtsy.

Fairy Peg flashed Gerard a strange look he could not interpret, then turned to a group of officers who had realized she would be free for a dance and were already crowding up to make their offers.

"Miss Holsten," Gerard said formally, holding out his arms.

She stepped into her proper position, and just as she did so the orchestra started playing again. It was another quick-step dance, much to Gerard's regret, and before they had gone halfway around the floor his feet got tangled in a turn and he fell. Fortunately, he did not take Branbinie with him. As he looked up from his rather stunned position on the floor, he thought he saw genuine amusement in her eyes. But before he could be sure several people reached down and helped him to his feet.

"My apologies," he said when she stepped back into position. "I seem to have lost my footing." Her only response was a smile.

They picked up the beat and started off again around the floor. Two turns later Gerard fell again; only this time he realized that Branbinie had tripped him. He was immediately angry and confused. He pushed away the helping hands and jumped to his feet. "I beg your pardon, Miss Holsten," he said, trying to keep the anger out of his voice, "but perhaps we had better sit this dance out."

"Oh," she said mockingly. "I had not realized the dance was too difficult for you."

"Nor had we realized that manners were too difficult for you," Fairy Peg said from behind him.

As Gerard turned to Fairy Peg he heard Branbinie laugh, and realized that all the dancers around them had stopped and were paying close attention to the confrontation.

"Perhaps you would be happier on Concepcydus, Branbinie," Fairy Peg said coldly as she took Gerard's arm. A gasp rose from those within hearing distance, but she ignored it. "I understand they have a fine school of manners there."

Branbinie's face had lost all traces of amusement. "Is the Badh ordering me to exile?" she asked in a low, incredulous voice.

"Not ordering, Branbinie, offering. Of course, there are places I could order you to go if you fail to appreciate the advantages of Concepcydus."

The corners of Branbinie's mouth twitched, and her eyes blazed with anger. Finally she made a bare curtsy with her head bowed and said in a hard voice, "How could I refuse such an offer from our Badh?"

Gerard was fascinated by what was happening, his anger supplanted by this encounter. Surely Fairy Peg was not going to banish this girl just because of her immature behavior on the dance floor? Yet that was exactly what seemed to be happening, and both of them seemed to accept the way things were turning out. He started to speak, but a look from Fairy Peg made him shut his mouth.

As Branbinie recovered from her curtsy, Fairy Peg said,

"Perhaps you should make preparations for your journey. And please give my regards to your family."

"Of course, Badh," Branbinie said flatly, backing away several steps. Then she turned, and the circle of observers parted to let her pass, almost shying away from her physically as they did so.

As he watched her walk across the floor, Gerard realized that the music had stopped. Just as he was about to turn back to Fairy Peg, he saw Targ step out of a group by the door and offer Branbinie his arm. Moments later they diappeared together.

"What was that all about?" he asked quietly.

"Later, Pilot." Fairy Peg signalled to the orchestra to begin playing, and put herself in the dance position, forcing him to dance.

As they moved around the floor, Gerard was vaguely aware that they were being watched by faces that were not totally friendly, but his thoughts concentrated on questions about what had just happened. Why had Branbinie Holsten made such a fool of herself? Why had she tripped him? It was a meaningless gesture that would not benefit her or her family. And why had Fairy Peg's reaction been so harsh? That question he thought he knew the answer to. Branbinie Holsten was being punished for the insult, not the act.

Gerard and Fairy Peg spent another hour at the ball, then withdrew to their quarters. During the whole hour, Fairy Peg was the perfect, smiling, gracious hostess, but as soon as they were alone together she burst into a string of curses that startled Gerard. When she finally relented in her verbal frenzy he asked, "Now, would you mind telling me what that was all about?"

Her eyes softened as she looked at him. "Politics, my dear Pilot. The Holstens wanted to test my reactions, and I foolishly overreacted. Now I will have to do something for them to make up for it..."

"Why?"

"Because those are the rules we play by. Just as one day I will have to do something for you, so now I—"

"What does that mean?"

Fairy Peg shook her head slightly as though trying to clear her thoughts. When she looked at him again there was a different light in her eyes. "It means you should make love to me immediately so I can purge this from my mind."

"But—"

"Now," she demanded, ripping the front of her dress away to expose her breasts. "Now."

Gerard obeyed.

Later, as he lay exhausted against Fairy Peg's back, he puzzled over the cold fury with which she had used his body.

The array of ships was like a lace curtain of light that Gerard moved toward the center of. Suddenly there were brilliant blue sparks and starburst flashes. Ships exploded briefly, silently, and a battle between starships blossomed around him.

He was paralyzed, unable to move or speak, knowing that he had been the cause of all this destruction. A Ribble ship exploded. Then a Fedship. Then two Ribble ships. And from deep in his heart there rose a roaring scream of anguish that exploded from his throat like a death cry. He was buffeted and twisted about, but still he screamed until he heard a voice calling to him from the shattering lights of space.

"Gerard! Gerard! Wake up!"

As he opened his eye he realized that Fairy Peg was shaking him violently. "What? What?"

"Wake up, Pilot! You were screaming in your sleep."

"A nightmare. Space battle. Death. My fault. My fault." Ghostly pinpoints of exploding lights still flickered behind his eyes. "My fault. My fault. Don't you see? It was my fault."

"What are you talking about, Pilot? It was just a dream."

Gerard looked at her and knew for an instant that she was crazy. It wasn't a dream. It was real. Or was it—was it something else? "Yes," he said finally, "a dream. A bad dream. I'm sorry."

"Just rest, Pilot. Rest." She cradled him stiffly in her arms as he drifted slowly back to sleep.

During the next few weeks Gerard forgot about the mightmare. The days were filled with meetings, sometimes with the advisory council which had first heard the

Federation's proposals, and sometimes just with Fairy Peg and Fianne. There were endless questions and details to be dealt with, and when he was not in the meetings, he was aboard Windy, sending messages to Diplo-Service asking for clarification, or outlining revised proposals from the council.

When he could, he stole time to be with Orees, but it was never as much as he wanted. Too often he could only tiptoe into the nursery late at night and stare at his son in wonder. And too often it would be hours later before Fairy Peg joined him.

Then the nightmare occurred again. Gerard woke up screaming and alone. He didn't tell Fairy Peg about the recurrence, but she was with him the next time. And the next time. And the next. Always it was the same battle between Fed and Ripple ships, blowing each other to space dust.

Omna-Seay gave Gerard some medication to help him sleep, but still the nightmare kept repeating itself, as though playing on an endless tapeloop in his mind. He stopped sleeping at night and tried to get enough rest with little naps during the day. Fairy Peg was solicitous, but he could tell his dreams put a separation between them. They both grew irritable and short-tempered, until finally one morning she announced there would be no meetings for the next week.

"But we have so much to do," Gerard protested. "Squo Lyle insists that we have to draft a final set of proposals to present to Corpus Privy and the Noble Assembly, and Privy-Admiral Gannack wants even more explicit clarification in the border patrol section."

"That can all wait, Pilot. The tentative date for the summit is still well over a standard year away. Besides, we have a visitor."

"Who?"

Before Fairy Peg could answer, Marradon walked through the private entrance into the office. It had been more than five years since they had been to see her on Filif-cy-Nere, but Marradon looked as though she had aged a century. Gerard could almost hear her withered body straining as she walked into the room. Only her eyes looked alive.

"Marradon," he said, rising to take her outstretched hands, "what a surprise to see you." He glanced quickly to

Fairy Peg then back to Marradon. "What have we done to bring the honor of this visit?"

Marradon took his hands without a word and stared straight into his eyes. "Your dreams," she said in her low, creaking voice. "Your dreams have brought me here."

Her eyes bored into the center of his brain, but Gerard could not look away from her. "Because of my dreams?"

"Yes, seer, because of your dreams. Now let me sit, and bring me something to drink."

Gerard helped her into his chair and went to the sideboard to get wine and glasses. He felt her eyes upon him the whole time. When he turned back to her with the tray, he was surprised to see that Fairy Peg was gone. "Where—"

"Do not worry about her, Gerard Manley. She will return when she is needed. Tell me about your dreams."

After handing her a glass of wine, Gerard sat in the chair facing her. "Only one dream," he said quietly, "the same dream repeated over and over again, a battle between ships of Ribble and the Federation. But the important part of the dream is that I know I'm responsible for the battle." As he spoke he realized how totally he accepted her presence.

"Your talent," Marradon said simply.

"I thought of that, but if it is the prescience, this is the first time it's manifested itself in this way, so I'm not sure that's what it is at all."

"Will you try something for me?"

"I'll try anything to get rid of this nightmare."

"Be careful, Gerard Manley, and listen before you agree. I want to give you a drug which will open your mind. Then I will use the Truth Bell to search out a reason for this disturbance. It will be dangerous for you and exhausting, but it may also be a *gitzabedera*, an open door to your talent." The creaking rhythms of her voice had a hypnotic effect on him.

"You will hear voices and talk to the dead. You will smell the feces of your infancy and taste the sour portions of your soul. But if you reach the *gitzabedera*, it will always be open to you."

197

Gerard looked at her carefully. "This has a lot more to do with me than just my dreams, doesn't it?"

"Of course. Does that frighten you?"

"I don't know."

"It should."

"I've been frightened before. Let's try it."

"Very well. Move one of the chairs beside the couch for me, and then lie down."

He took the small handful of dark, seed-like grains she gave him, and washed them down with a few swallows of amber liquid she produced in a small vial. For a moment he felt nothing. Then he sensed each seed nestling into the folds of his stomach lining, each seeking a separate place to dissolve. One by one, they exploded in little pin-pricks of pain. He looked at Marradon questioningly, but felt no desire to speak. In fact he felt nothing, not the couch pressing against him, not the awareness in his stomach, not the light in the room. There was no light in the room.

"Anger creates and anger destroys..."

"By the shape of a wave you can visually deduce its source..."

"Who is the sign..."

"Ask the others..."

"Where were you born?"

The voices began to overlap. Faces shifted in and out of focus, going faster and faster until he felt dizzy and nauseous. He fell face-down into the grisk dung and vomited. Anger boiled through him like steaming foam. Hot fingers touched him and he arched his back in orgasm. Laughter swept away the cacophony of voices. She pulled the sheet off him and covered her three luscious breasts with it. A cool wind chilled his sweaty loins.

A bell rang.

"Where have you been, Gerard?"

He recognized the voice, but he didn't know whose it was. "Visiting," he said thickly.

"Have you looked at the dream of death?"

"No."

"Do you want to?"

"No."

"Why?"

"Because it is not a dream, it is truth."

"Good. Do you see a door?" The voice was old and insistent.

"Yes, I see a door, a small door with a heavy latch. My hand is on it, touching the latch. It is very cold and sad."

The door fell away, and a warm, perfumed breeze swept over him. He stepped through the opening into a long, narrow hallway lined as far as he could see with doors and windows and archways. Without hesitation, he started down the hall.

Death stepped in front of him. He walked through her.

Fear tackled his legs. He stepped over it.

Shame spat in his face. He ignored him.

He was shoved into a room where his mother was dying. When he tried to approach her, she dissolved into a putrid jelly. The stench sent him spinning through another door where someone stabbed a long needle into his neck. He tore himself away and fell back into the hallway.

Facing him was Gerard Manley holding a small black key. His grinning self swallowed the key and dove through an archway. Gerard tried to follow, but the blackness beyond was a wall that threw him back to the hard floor.

"Enter there," a voice commanded.

Panic seized him. He stood up and looked desperately for the way out. The hallway stretched endlessly in either direction.

"The old novice knows the way," a new voice said.

He ran blindly down the hall, pursued by echoes of laughter and screams of pain. Suddenly the hall branched, and as he tried to decide which way to go he froze in mid-stride. A wave of noise threw him to the floor.

"You will obey. When you hear the command, you will obey."

"No, no, no," he screamed. "No," he cried. "No," he whimpered. "No. No. No."

"You will obey. It is necessary. You will obey."

"Spinnertel commands."

Gerard pulled himself up from the floor. Something shoved him from behind, and he fell into a dark, cold pool. Claws tore at his legs, pulled him down, and down, and down. Then they softened and soothed him as he drifted into the darkness.

*   *   *

Marradon was speaking quietly. "He carries a darkness in his mind that is blocked off from him. He almost broke through, but it is very, very strong."

"What can it mean?"

"I do not know. I cannot be sure. But once I dealt with a ridlow who had been implanted with a mind-control suggestion. His reaction was much the same as Gerard's. It appears..."

Gerard tried to concentrate on her words, but they refused to stay in focus.

"Mind control, mind control," a voice whispered to him.

"No," he answered as he drifted back into the darkness. "No."

*　　*　　*

Message to: Avarignon Cloznitchnikoff
　　　　　　　FedTreaty Svc

The division of power is not subject to negotiation. That subject was settled long before you entered the discussion, and cannot be changed. We agreed to give up those border systems in exchange for your assistance, but nothing more. Any further demands by you and your superiors can only further jeopardize what you have already weakened with your blundering efforts on Evird.

Furthermore, if you cannot obtain the control information, we will have to use our alternate plan and risk the resulting chaos. It occurs to us that either you are no more competent than your predecessor, or you are withholding the information. Your actions now must speak in your defense. Time sifts away.

　　　　　　　　　　　　　　　　　　　　—Toehold

*　　*　　*

19

"What is this garbage, Windy? Fed must really be having problems with their relay stations. Either that, or there's some kind of interference garbling the messages. Sort them by real time, and let's see if they make any sense."

Gerard was in no hurry. It had been ten days since his mind-search with Marradon, and ever since he had felt nothing but melancholy, a lassitude of pain. Marradon was dying. Her trip back to Filif-cy-Nere would be the last she would ever make. The day before, when he said his farewell to her, he had felt a tremendous sadness because she had given him so much that he could not return to her.

The knowledge that he would never see her again, and the sadness of her departure only added to the dark mood he had carried with him out of the mind-search. If Fed had indeed implanted him with a mind-control suggestion, as Marradon suspected, he was angry. But more than that, he was defiant, and the defiance brought with it a burden of unshakable sorrow.

He knew that, however he had to do it, he would work to resist the mind control and act on his own. He also knew that such actions would exact a heavy toll on his mind and on his life. Whether that was true knowledge arising from his prescience or the speculation of deep-seated apprehension he did not know. But he feared that resisting the mind control could also cost him Fairy Peg and Orees. That thought nurtured his melancholy as it sank its dark roots deep into his soul.

"Finished already, Windy? All right, let's look at them one by one in real-time sequence."

(7033-6.6)

... and suggest you act accordingly as ou... cannot be guaranteed to...y the estimate of probable damage...e time frame will be of the utmost...

(7033-6.24)

...hen we divide, your area of control must not exce...and in all border systems above, the assuran...rstand your concer...

(7033-7.11)

...lyph...indications are correct...feder...will provide...

(7033.712)

...ghting than necessary...provide that system of identification...ot offer any insurance against acci...ver, and you must be prepared to accept that risk...

(7033 7.18)

...hat ultimately the union will be of much greater benefit than any of us can anticipate... forward to the...gchow...

"You know what, Windy?" Gerard said as he finished reviewing the fragments. "I have a feeling that we have been accidentally receiving messages intended for someone else. But what I don't understand is that they don't seem to fit together. I mean, part of them look like they refer to confederation and union, while the rest talk about risk and damage, and division of control.

"Give me the code sections you used.

"Hmm, if that's not confirmation of my suspicions, I don't know what would be. They've never sent anything to us in the subteam codes. In fact—give me the code directory.

"That's what I thought. These subteam codes are restricted for headquarters use only. And, let's see, sixteen of the twenty subdivisions are restricted to communications with non-members of the Federation.

"What does that tell you, Windy? Tells *me* that Fed's been very active talking to people around here. At cross purposes, too, it looks like. There's something very wrong about all this, Windy. If someone in Fed is planning for trouble around here, they were damned careless.

"Or were they? Maybe these fragments were never more than that, and were designed for us to intercept. Does that sound crazy? I'll have to think about it."

Gerard pushed the fragments to the back of his mind while he sorted through the latest batch of messages from DiploService. Most of the messages were from Merita and Graczyk and urged him to obtain a definite date for a summit meeting and to push for a firm set of accepted proposals. He had been a little surprised by the first message like that after he returned from his meeting with Lingchow. Now he was just annoyed that they were pressing so hard. It was so unnecessary.

Finally he drafted answers to Graczyk and Merita that told them in effect to be patient. He had Windy send them, and began getting ready to return to EllKoep. The entry lock buzzer startled him. When he opened the intercom, he was even more surprised to hear Targ Alpluakka's voice.

"Permission to come aboard, Fize."

"Granted." Gerard cycled the port lock and scrambled down to meet Targ. "Well, Commander," he said as he landed lightly on the entry deck, "I certainly didn't expect to see you here."

"Nor I to be here, Fize," Targ said with a quick salute. "However, I wanted to take advantage of the opportunity to see you alone."

"Let's go up to the galley," Gerard said, leading the way. "I picked up some Brandusian coffee on my trip, and I think you might enjoy it."

Targ looked uncomfortable as he sat at the small galley table, as though he wanted to say something, but did not know how to begin. "The coffee will take a couple of minutes," Gerard said as he leaned back against the bulkhead and crossed his arms over his chest, "but it's well worth the wait. So tell me, Commander, what brings you to see me this way?"

"Several matters," Targ said almost reluctantly. "One is personal, and the other concerns some intelligence information I have gathered that indicates a possible threat to the throne."

Personal? Gerard couldn't believe that Targ would come to him with a personal matter. It was too out of character. He waited for Targ to continue.

After a moment's hesitation, Targ said, "I must ask your forbearance, Fize, for no matter which problem I discuss with you first, you may find questions and provocation about the other."

"Your request is unnecessary, Commander," Gerard said evenly, wondering as he spoke what in the universe Targ was going to tell him. "However, for the sake of your concern, I grant you forbearance."

Targ looked surprisingly relieved. "Five hundred thanks, Fize. Let me begin, then, with the personal matter. Our Badh, as was her right and privilege, set no specific term on the banishment of Branbinie Holsten to Concepcydus. I would appeal to you to ask her to do so."

"May I ask why, Commander?"

"Such is your privilege," Targ answered, looking away from Gerard for the first time, "but my reason must be a bound secret between Ratchets."

From the tone of Targ's voice, Gerard had already leapt to a conclusion about Targ's reason. "Agreed, on my honor as a Ratchet." As he spoke, Gerard didn't know whether to feel proud or used that Targ had bound him to secrecy with their Ratchet kinship.

"Branbinie Holsten carries my child," Targ said simply.

Gerard felt a sudden compassion for Targ, but he tried to keep it from showing. Targ was the last person he knew who would appreciate overt sympathy. Still, after the companionship Targ had shown him during his estrangement from Fairy Peg, he had to reveal his sympathy in some way. "I will speak to the Badh, and urge her to limit the banishment to a brief time. Neither your name, nor any reference to Branbinie's condition will enter into my efforts on your behalf."

"Fize, I cannot thank—"

"No need, Commander. No need. Look, our coffee's ready." He used that excuse to break the awkwardness of the moment and allow Targ to recover his normal demeanor. With his back to Targ as he poured the coffee, Gerard said, "I should have warned you that this is a stimulant stronger than most of its kind. However, I don't think you will find it excessive." He set the mugs down on the table and seated himself opposite Targ. "Let it sit for a minute before tasting it. It's better when it has cooled slightly." Targ's smile seemed awkward and forced. "Now, what have you learned about some possible threat to the throne?"

Targ's smile vanished, and his eyes narrowed before he looked down at his cup. When he spoke, his voice was low and hesitant. "I have many unique sources of information, Fize, most of which have always proven highly reliable. Thus, when this information was passed to me by one of those sources, I could not ignore it. Neither could I believe it to be true. When a second, independent source passed on the same information, I knew I had to consult with you."

Gerard wondered why Targ was hedging. "These preliminaries are unnecessary, Commander. Exactly what was this information?"

Targ looked directly at him and seemed to make a decision before he spoke. "My sources indicate that any proposed summit meeting with the Federation will actually be a trap to eliminate the leadership of Ribble Galaxy."

The undertone in Targ's voice upset Gerard as much as his statement did. The slightest hint of accusation had crept through, mingled with something Gerard couldn't identify. "This sounds like a matter for the advisory council, not just for me," he said as evenly as he could.

Targ looked at him steadily. "A hundred pardons, Fize," he said with quiet sincerity, "but my sources indicate that you are aware of this information already."

"Are you *accusing* me?" Gerard exploded.

Targ did not flinch. "Not yet, Fize, but it may come to that."

Gerard was stunned. Targ had the audacity to ask him for a personal favor, then accuse him of setting up a death trap. It was incredible. "That's the stupidest thing I ever heard, Commander, and I demand to know what your supposedly reliable sources are."

"Please, Fize, you granted me forbearance. Listen to what else I must tell you."

Gerard's anger was subsiding almost as quickly as it had come, because he knew the accusation would fall flat on its face if it was brought before the advisory council. He had been questioned by the Truth Bell. "Proceed, Commander," he said with a hard calmness in his voice. The reaction on Targ's face told him the sudden change of tone was an effective surprise.

"My sources are not infallible. One of the aspects of this information I had to consider was that it might have been leaked to them intentionally by someone in your Federation, in an attempt to discredit you and your efforts. This morning I received a message which appears to confirm that idea. I believe someone in the Federation is working against you, Fize."

Gerard felt more relieved than surprised by Targ's statement. It was obvious from the whole situation surrounding the uprising on Evird that TreatyService was playing their own game in Ribble. Targ's information only added to the growing body of evidence. "So where does that leave us, Targ?" he asked finally, hoping the switch to his first name would help ease the tension. He took a long sip of his coffee and discovered it had cooled too much.

"In a difficult situation. It is my duty to report any threat to the throne that I have reason to believe is valid. However, I do not know how to measure the validity of my information. If I report the possible threat to our Badh and Corpus Privy, there will be many questions that cannot be answered. Worse, such a report could jeopardize the peace negotiations. But then—"

"Then what? If you don't report, you will be derelict in your duty? Only if you believe the information is valid." Gerard was still angry, but something else was pushing past his anger, a faint mixture of curiosity and suspicion. Targ was a man of action. All this pondering of decision wasn't like him.

"Yes," Targ said slowly.

"And you want me to help you with the decision?"

"You are my Fize, and you are involved. Honor and duty demanded that I discuss it with you."

It didn't ring true. Targ's motives, whatever they were, had nothing to do with honor and duty. Gerard weighed his response carefully. "Are you asking for my advice, or are you just letting me know ahead of time that the problem is going to be discussed formally?"

Targ hesitated. "I suppose I am asking for your advice."

"Tell the Badh and Corpus Privy."

"But Fize—"

"Tell them. Tell them exactly what you told me. After all, it's *our* job to report any possible threat to the throne. It's their job to act on the information we give them. Tell them, Targ. Let them decide what to do."

Targ gave him a thin smile. "And if they decide the threat is valid?"

"Then they will act accordingly. Now, if you'll excuse me, I have some things I need to do here before our meeting this afternoon with the advisory council."

"Certainly, Fize."

They exchanged brief salutes at the port lock, then Targ was gone. Gerard went back to the galley and reheated the rest of the Brandusian coffee. He felt sure he had missed something during Targ's strange visit, but he could not figure out what it was. Despite that, he had a growing feeling that the real purpose of Targ's visit had never been revealed—and that whatever it was, neither honor, nor duty, nor any supposed threat to the throne was at the heart of it.

For the first time he wished there was a way he could call on his prescience and look into the future and see where all this was leading. He had considered that idea before and rejected it as being somehow unnatural. But now, now he didn't care how unnatural it was. He wanted to know what was going to happen.

The forcefulness of his desire to look forward startled him. Had Targ's visit really disturbed him that deeply, or was something else at work in him? Gerard didn't know. Wasn't that the whole story? He didn't know. He lived in the midst of his own ignorance and never truly coped with it.

Feeling himself slide down a path of thought that led nowhere, Gerard pushed those ideas out of his mind and reviewed everything he could remember about Targ's visit and conversation, looking for some clue that would help him understand why he felt so strongly suspicious. Then he reviewed it several more times, but in the end had to chalk up his reaction to a gut feeling that something was not right.

When he walked into the meeting of the advisory council five hours later, that gut feeling was still with him. As soon as everyone was seated Gerard requested permission to speak, and announced that Commander Alpluakka had discovered a possible threat to the throne which had a direct bearing on their discussions.

"That is a matter for Corpus Privy and the Badh," Squo Lyle said immediately.

"Under normal circumstances I would agree, Squo, but in this case I think an exception needs to be made—with the Badh's permission, of course."

Fairy Peg gave Gerard a questioning look then turned to Targ. "Perhaps the consort is right, Commander. What have you to report?"

Targ looked very uncomfortable, but under Gerard's watchful eye he related the two reports that suggested a summit meeting could be a trap which Gerard had knowledge of, and the third report, which suggested that the first two might have been planted to discredit Gerard.

As soon as Targ was finished, Fairy Peg turned to Gerard. "Do you have anything to add to that, Consort?"

Gerard was dumbfounded. None of them had reacted the way he had expected them to. They all seemed to take Targ's statements totally in stride. "Don't you understand what Targ just told you?" Gerard demanded.

"Of course we do, Pilot," Fairy Peg said calmly. "Such reports are to be expected. There are many who would like nothing more than to discredit you and stop all interaction between Ribble and your Federation."

"But if what he said was true—"

"Is it?"

"Of course not."

"And you have nothing to add to it?"

Gerard looked around the table, but could read nothing out of the ordinary on any of the faces. Even Targ looked relaxed. He shook his head. "No, Badh, I have nothing to add to Commander Alpluakka's report."

"Then I believe the first item on the agenda is Admiral Gannack's proposal concerning the patrolling of border-space."

As soon as the meeting was over, Gerard went back to their living quarters and Fairy Peg went off to attend to other business, promising to meet him for a late supper. He had time to play with Orees for several hours, help Winsea put him to bed, and skim through several of the Ribble history books Fianne had loaned him. When Fairy Peg returned, he sent Knip to get their supper, then listened to her talk about some of the administrative problems she was currently coping with, until their meal arrived.

As soon as they were settled at the table and Knip had left the room, Gerard said, "Tell me again why you and the advisory council weren't upset by Targ's report."

Fairy Peg looked surprised. "The answer remains the same, Pilot. Such things are to be expected. Furthermore, when you insisted that Targ make his report, any credibility such information might have had was dismissed."

"I could have insisted for that very reason."

"Did you?"

"No, but I—"

"Ah, Pilot, sometimes you are a wonder to me. So strong, so honest, yet so naive. Perhaps that is why I treasure you so."

"Grisk dung! Suppose Marradon was right, and that Fed messed with my head and implanted some kind of mind control? Then Targ could be right and I wouldn't know it, and neither would you. What about that?"

With a sigh Fairy Peg leaned back in her chair. "Pilot, Marradon only suspected this mind control problem—as one of several possibilities—and she told you there was an excellent possibility that even if it did exist, that you could and would be able to fight it." She smiled strangely when she said that. "Marradon was quite intrigued by what she termed a growing sense of independence in you. I have too many realities to cope with to worry about idle speculation and third hand reports and rumors."

Gerard started to respond, but she held up her hand. "I have not finished. I am going to eat one more small piece of meat and another slice of that excellent white cheese. If you must talk while I am eating, you will restrict your comments to ones concerning my beauty and charm. Then you may help me undress, and perform the duties of consort as tenderly and lovingly as you know how. Can you do that for me?"

The weariness in her voice woke Gerard to the realization of how tired she looked. Suddenly any discussion about Targ and his report was easily put aside. Gerard gave her a slow, suggestive wink. "I'll do my best," he promised.

After they had made love she snuggled up against him, talking softly in little fragments that didn't quite fit together. But just before she fell asleep, she said something which pushed Gerard back toward wakefulness. "My regret, Pilot . . . is not to hold you forever . . . and because I shall miss you."

The words of a sleeper, Gerard told himself, even as he puzzled over them. Finally he allowed himself a little chuckle. The day had started with fragments he didn't understand. Why shouldn't it end the same way? As though she had read his mind, Fairy Peg pulled herself closer to him and mumbled, "It's unavoidable."

* * *

Message to: Greaves Lingchow
             FedDiploSvc
Your message 118422 does much to clarify your request and the rationale behind it. If you can substantiate your claims with supporting evidence, it will be in our mutual interest to destroy the opposing forces.

However, it must be recognized that such actions carry very serious risk factors, and neither this new plan nor any other can be guaranteed to produce the proper results. That, combined with the sacrifice you ask, makes substantiation an absolute necessity. This demand comes from the highest level.

Since time is now a very real factor, we will have to test the control. We pray it is truly as foolproof as you would have us believe.

—Glyph

* * *

20

Orees spoke in complete sentences without slurring his words, and demanded to dress himself. Woltol bluntly told Gerard he was getting fat, so he went back to a regular training schedule and managed to lose almost six kilograms. Branbinie Holsten was notified by Targ that she could return to Kril when their child was six months old. Fairy Peg tired easily, or was tired all the time—it was difficult for Gerard to tell—and her weariness produced a growing distance between them. Messages and meetings turned into months, and suddenly everyone had agreed to a specific date and place for the summit meeting.

In just a little less than six standard months Princess Peg On'Ell, Badh of the Seven Systems of Ribble Galaxy, and Borjhya Valunzuella-Bai, Supreme Chairman of the Federation of Sentient Worlds, would meet in the neutral void of Dinsey space and sign a permanent peace agreement that would one day lead to Ribble Galaxy becoming a member of the Federation. At least, that is what it looked like to Gerard.

Fianne and Fairy Peg might be too busy and tired to talk to him except at meetings, but everyone else seemed very interested in his point of view and opinions. And the word *confederation* had leapt out of hiding, and was being used by everyone who talked about the long-term future.

There was even a joke making the rounds of the Noble Assembly that if the summit meeting worked out well, Corpus Privy would vote to remain in Dinsey space to negotiate the terms of confederation and thereby save the cost of future negotiations and another massive movement of people to attend. Gerard didn't know anyone except himself who thought the joke unamusing. Even Squo Lyle had smiled broadly when Serit Iskin told him the joke.

"Maybe I'm just too ignorant about Ribble politics to understand it," Gerard said when he got a huge laugh after repeating the story to Fianne.

"No, Diplomat, no. That is not it at all. The humor, I fear, lies deeper than that. At least for me it does. If you had grown up knowing the personalities of Corpus Privy, you too would find great humor in the story.

"However, I did not come to share jokes with you. In all the rush of the past week I forgot to ask if you had received an agreement on the protocol proposals for the summit?"

"Yesterday," Gerard said, handing Fianne a printout from the stack on his desk. He was beginning to feel more like a bureaucrat than a diplomat. "As you will see when you compare it to the original, they made a few minor changes, but nothing that looks like it will cause any difficulty. The transmittal note with their reponse indicated that they were impressed with the idea of forming the two fleets to encompass a spherical space. They congratulated me for the suggestion. I pass the congratulations on to you since the concept was originally yours."

"A small thing," Fianne said with a wave of his hand as he studied the printout. "Hmm, this schedule calls for you to proceed to the *Casserine* only six standard hours before the Badh. Did we not ask for twelve? Will six hours be enough time?"

"Yes, and no. In my acknowledgement I told them about twelve hours would be the minimum. I'll be busting my boosters to get everything done in twelve hours. I already have a seven-page check list, and now the chairman wants to be personally briefed *by me* before the Badh arrives. I damn near asked them for twenty-five hours instead of twelve."

Fianne cocked an eyebrow. "We can do that if you think it is necessary. I'm sure they will understand."

Gerard laughed. "No, I can get it done in twelve. Have you heard yourself lately, Fianne? You're using contractions in your speech."

"A vulgar habit I acquired from a diplomat I know," Fianne said with a smile. "I try to avoid it, but sometimes they just slip out."

"You should be more careful about whom you associate with. You could pick up all kinds of bad habits."

Fianne's smile twitched. "I know. Perhaps I should retreat to my archives again and lead a civilized life."

"Only when you're old and grey and the Badh will no longer put up with you. Then you can tell tall tales to the royal brats who come sneaking into those musty halls." A picture of an old, wrinkled Fianne doing just that flashed through Gerard's mind, and he smiled.

With a grunt Fianne looked up from the printout. "I see nothing else here that surprises me. Of course, I'll—I will have to compare it to the original, point by point."

"I've already made you a list of the changes," Gerard said, handing him another page, "complete with page numbers and references."

After a quick glance at the page, Fianne said, "Had I known you were so efficient, Diplomat, I would have made you my clerk years ago."

"And I would have declined the offer. You work too hard. And so does our Princess. Can't you get her to slow down?"

Fianne frowned. "Can you? This summit is a huge enterprise which eats her time like a ravenous ridlow."

The thought of Woltol and Brunnel eating hungrily gave Gerard an instant image.

"Yet still," Fianne continued, "she must attend to the daily affairs of running Ribble."

"Can't she delegate some of that?"

"She has delegated as much as she dares, but she never forgets that she is the Badh, and the Badh cannot shirk her responsibilities."

Gerard sighed. "I know. It's just that I miss her. So does Orees. I guess the two of us will just have to make do."

Fianne looked at him strangely. "That reminds me," he said suddenly, "there is one other matter I want to discuss with you, and, since I have some time, maybe we should do it now. Will you be free for the next hour or so?"

"Certainly. Admiral Gannack hasn't come up with another list of nit-picking complaints, has she?"

"No, Diplomat, nothing like that. In fact this is something quite unconnected with the summit. One of the senior archivists brought me a text I thought might interest you. It's called *Dangure in Maytar, High on the Barcley Star.*"

Gerard wanted to correct him. He knew the text. It was *Barcley on Maytar Beside the Dangure Star*, a geographical primer he had carried with him as a physical memento of his birth planet. He wanted to tell Fianne that the title was all backwards. Then he just wanted to be able to speak, or move, anything to give Fianne some signal. He felt as though he were having some terrible kind of seizure in which time had frozen him in place.

Fianne looked at him with a curious expression, not of surprise or concern, but of triumph. "Do not panic, Gerard. You are not ill. You are quite well. In fact, you feel very good. You feel better than you have felt in a long, long time. Tell me how you feel."

"I feel fine," Gerard heard himself answer from a distance. He did feel fine.

"Good. Now I want you to listen carefully to me. We are going to try a little experiment. I am going to count slowly backward from five to one. When I do, you will not remember a thing that has happened. When I get to one, you will be totally normal and we will continue our conversation as before. Do you understand that?"

Gerard did, but he didn't know why. "I understand," he heard himself say thickly.

"Good. Now, before I start counting, I want you to remember a very important word for me. The word is *norrace*. Can you say that? Say it for me."

"Norrace."

"Very good, Gerard. Whenever I say *norrace* three times in a row like this, *norrace-norrace-norrace*, you will return to the state you are in now and quickly touch your right forefinger to your nose. Do you understand?"

"Yes." Gerard was sure the voice he heard was his own, but he really didn't understand any of what was happening.

"All right, Gerard, I'm going to start counting. When I get to one, you will forget everything that has happened, but in the hidden corners of your mind you will not forget what I have told you. Five. The word *norrace* is slipping to the back of your mind, and you are beginning to forget everything else that has happened. Four. That word is sliding into a corner where only I can call it forth, and you are forgetting everything else that has happened. Three.

You are beginning to feel perfectly normal. You have forgotten everything that happened. Two. You feel almost normal. One. You are fine."

Gerard blinked and felt like he'd missed something Fianne had said. "I'm sorry. My mind drifted there for a second. If the problem's not with Admiral Gannack, what is it?"

Fianne smiled. "Actually, Diplomat, it doesn't have anything to do with the summit meeting. See, I used another contraction. You are a bad influence on me. Anyway, the matter I want to talk to you about is quite unrelated to anything else we have been discussing. It seems one of the senior archivists, maybe you met him once, old *norrace-norrace-norrace . . .*"

Much to Gerard's surprise, his right forefinger came up and briefly touched his nose. Then he felt frozen in time, and confronted another surprise. The feeling was familiar. He had felt this same way before, but he couldn't remember when. It wasn't a bad feeling, just odd, different. He started to ask Fianne if he was acting strangely, but he couldn't form the words. The thought was there. The will was there. But the words just would not come.

"Very good, Gerard," Fianne said calmly. "Do not try to talk. You are fine, just fine. From now on when I say that word three times, you will do exactly what you did just now. What is the word? Tell me."

"*Norrace.*"

"Fine. That's going to be the most important word ever hidden in your mind, Gerard. You just never forget it, do you understand?"

"I understand." Gerard was sure he was repeating himself.

"Excellent, Gerard, excellent. Now I am going to count backwards again from five to one, and you will do the same thing you did before. You will slowly forget everything we have done since I said *norrace-norrace-norrace*. But you will slide that command into a back corner of your mind where only you and I can find it. Are you ready?"

Gerard nodded without knowing why.

"Five. You are feeling better and better as you forget what just happened. Four. You are beginning to feel normal. You have hidden that word in a safe place. Three. You feel more and more normal as you forget everything else that happened. Two. You feel almost totally normal. One. You are fine."

With a shake of his head Gerard looked at Fianne. "Maybe I'm the one who's tired. Can this wait, Fianne? I think I need to go wrestle with Orees or something to get my blood flowing."

"It is of no urgency," Fianne said in a pleased tone. "Perhaps some other day."

After Fianne left with a quick bow and a smile, Gerard felt as though something had passed between them that he had missed. When he thought about what they had discussed, however, it all made good sense. He would rather have gone to wrestle Fairy Peg than Orees, but he knew his chances were very poor. She was supposed to be in some meeting with representatives from the Prindleswitch system. Since that meant Evird was on the agenda, the meeting could go on all afternoon and half the night. Maybe what he needed was a good forty-kilometer run with his string.

The ancient notion that running would actually relieve sexual tension made him smile. "Brunnel!" he shouted. His string leader was in the door almost before Gerard's vocal cords quit vibrating. "A voluntary run, Brunnel. Forty kilometers. You want to come?"

The ridlow gave Gerard his best approximation of a grin. "Dumb question, Fize," he answered.

"You're right. Let's go."

When Gerard got back to the living quarters early that evening, he was surprised to find Fairy Peg waiting for him. "What happened to the Prindleswitch delegation?" he asked after he had given her a huge hug and a smothering kiss.

"They were left to argue among themselves."

"Their loss is my gain," he said with a grin. "Can I take you someplace quiet for supper?"

"I am sorry," she said with a lack of any kind of sincerity that Gerard could accept. "I have already eaten and will have to return to the meeting shortly. But I could share a glass of wine with you while you eat."

Even though he tried to keep the disappointment off his face, Gerard knew she saw it. For whatever reason, she chose to ignore it, and that bothered him more than the fact that she had to go back to the meeting. "Red, white, or green?" he asked as he moved toward the cooler.

"I believe there is a bottle of Piercegold," she said. "Bring that."

"Thought we were saving that for some special occasion," he said as he pulled the slim black flask out of the rack.

"This is a special occasion, Pilot. It is the anniversary of your arrival in Ribble Galaxy."

Gerard did some quick mental arithematic. It had been nine and a half Standard years. That mean . . . "Thirteen years?"

Fairy Peg laughed. "Fourteen, Pilot, fourteen. I know you have never fully adjusted to our dating system, but surely you could have figured that out. If you just take—"

"No lectures, please." Gerard grinned as he held up his hand. "No matter how hard I try, I still can't work the year conversions in my head."

They drank the Piercegold very quickly. Then, much to Gerard's surprise, Fairy Peg insisted that they make love before she returned to the meeting. It was a hurried, agressive lovemaking, full of unspoken tensions and unsatisfied desires. Still, Gerard thought as he lay alone in bed later with a fresh bottle of wine open beside him, it was better than no lovemaking at all.

For a moment he thought about Inez and wondered what her life was like in exile on Sun's March. Then he dismissed her from his mind. She was a forbidden subject, and he had no reason to want her otherwise. But in the midst of a strange stillness as he paused on the edge of sleep, Gerard remembered Inez standing naked in the center of his room, laughing at him.

The laughter rumbled like distant thunder or the roar of a chemically fueled shuttle. Then a hissing voice whispered in his ear and sent spastic shivers through his body. *"Norsiss says must serve . . . srffrr . . . norass says . . . norsays . . . serve . . . norsays."*

A giant light flared then dimmed against a black curtain alive with moving stars.

"Serve norsezzz . . . serve."

A face screamed, then laughed, then grinned at him like an old friend.

"Sezz serve, norriss face . . ."

217

Gerard sat up and heard the voice beside him. In the few seconds it took him to come fully awake, the dream hissed at him like a chunk of ice from the heat of a blazing fire. Then it was gone. With a shiver Gerard laid back down and pulled the blankets tight around him. He tried to dismiss the dream as a meaningless aberration, but it was a long time before he again drifted off to sleep.

Fairy Peg smiled at him across the meeting table. Only Targ and Fianne had remained with them after the meeting ended. "Do you not feel a certain sense of elation, Pilot, that your efforts in our galaxy are so close to producing such positive results?"

"Perhaps I will later, Princess, when I see you and the chairman signing the treaty. We've worked so hard on this that it doesn't seem quite real sometimes."

"Do you have doubts?" Targ asked unexpectedly.

Gerard leaned back in his chair and stretched. "No, not doubts, Commander, just fatigue. And I've probably done less than any of you."

"You are too modest, Diplomat," Fianne said flatly.

"Indeed," Fairy Peg added. "However, we did not ask you to remain with us to flatter you. Commander Alpluakka has some concerns he asked to share with both of you. Commander."

"My thanks, Badh." Targ flashed Gerard a quick smile before continuing. "Admiral Gannack and I have discussed the procedures that will take place when we rendezvous with the representatives from the Federation. She has assured me that our Badh will be totally safe should anything happen of an aggressive nature against our fleet . . . Pardon, Fize, but it is my duty to consider these things."

"Please continue, Commander," Gerard said easily. He had come to the conclusion that this meeting of great powers was really too big for Targ to comprehend. That seemed to be the only rational explanation for Targ's incessant worrying about threats and plots and traps.

"As a guarantee of good faith, I would like to propose that the chairman and a high-ranking delegation come first to meet the Badh before she returns with them to their conference ship, ah—"

"The *Casserine*," Fianne offered. "Yes, the *Casserine*.

And that the chairman and the Badh proceed to the *Casserine* in one of our ships to be designated at the last possible minute."

Gerard shook his head. "I don't think it will sell."

"What do you mean, Pilot?"

"I mean we only have four Standard months until the summit, two until we actually leave here, and it's a little late to start making changes like the one Commander Alpluakka proposes. I appreciate his concern, but I'm afraid Fed won't. They'll see it as a sign of mistrust, and rightfully so. I don't see where we have much to gain by it."

Targ looked like he was holding back a sneer. "You do not see our Badh's safety as something to be concerned about?"

"Of course I do," Gerard snapped.

"Please," Fairy Peg said calmly. "I understand both of your positions, but I am not sure I agree with either. So, Commander, you arrange the details with Admiral Gannack as a contingency plan to offer to the Federation in case they suggest some changes of their own. Pilot, you notify your supervisor that there may have to be some adjustments made in the arrangements for the first meeting. Suggest that we are considering an invitation to the chairman for an informal conversation before the official ceremonies begin." She rose and signalled an end to the discussion.

Targ gave her a quick bow and left. Surprisingly, so did Fianne. "Let's go to my office, Pilot," she said with a smile. As they walked down the long corridor with their Ratchets fore and aft, Fairy Peg chatted about Orees and his latest activities. As soon as they settled in her office with Fairy Peg on one side of her desk and Gerard on the other, her mood shifted immediately.

"Something troubles you, Pilot. What is it?"

Gerard heard concern in her voice, but also an undertone that warned him she was not offering sympathy. "Why do you think something's troubling me?"

"I am not speculating, Pilot. Be you aware that almost every night you thrash in your sleep and cry out? I thought the death dreams left you after Marradon's visit?"

"They did. But I've had other bad dreams before."

"Do not try to humor me, Pilot. I know you feel I have

219

neglected you and Orees these past months. Is that the source of your discontent?"

"Probably part of it."

"And the remainder?"

Gerard looked at her quizzically, trying to understand why she was expressing this sudden concern in such a formal way. If she really cared about what he was going through, would she have put a desk between them?

"What is the matter with you, Pilot? Do you not want my help and advice? Does my concern annoy you? Why will you not talk about this?"

"I will," he answered quickly. Then after a pause he added, "When I think you're ready for it. Now you're too wrapped up in other, more important duties."

"Your words sting me, Pilot, yet I am not wounded by them. It puzzles me that after all these years you still do not recognize that my first duty must always be to Ribble and—"

"Oh, I reocgnize it all right."

"But you do not accept it."

"I accept it as best I can. That doesn't mean I have to like it."

"Quite true," she said coldly, "but neither do you have to abuse me for fulfilling my responsibilities."

"Abuse you? How have I abused you?"

"Is this not abuse? Are you not treating me rudely and coldly for causes beyond my control?" Her voice rose with each question. "Is it not abuse to share my bed, then refuse to tell me what troubles your sleep? Is it not abuse to take what little time we have alone and use it to build barriers between us? Is that not abuse?"

Whatever truth was implied by her questions was overshadowed by the near-hysterical pitch of her voice. It was something he had never heard from her before, even when she caught Inez naked in his room. Apparently the strain she was under was truly taking a toll on her. He looked straight into her deep brown eyes before answering. "We have both been under a great deal of pressure. If there has been abuse, my love, it was not intended."

"Then you admit it," she said quickly, refusing to respond to his soft tone with one of her own. "Is there method in this, Pilot? Is this your way of putting distance between us, so that once the summit is concluded you can return more easily to your beloved Federation?"

"But I . . ." Gerard said before shutting his mouth. He wasn't thinking about returning to the Federation. As soon as the negotiations were completed and the summit successfully concluded, he planned to dissolve his contract and remain in Ribble.

"Are you crazy?" he asked finally. "Or blind? Or what? If you can't see that I love you and Orees and want to stay with you the rest of my life, then you're blind as Krick. How in Fara's name can you run a galaxy when you can't even see how your family feels about you?"

"Enough!" Her command was filled with the absolute demand of the royal imperative. "The Badh need not suffer such foul treatment, especially from her consort. Leave me at once."

Late that night, when the hissing voices returned to haunt his dreams, Fairy Peg gathered him to the warmth of her breast and stroked him mechanically until he went back to sleep. When he awoke the next morning alone in the bed, he wasn't sure if she had actually been there or not. The lingering hint of her perfume on her pillow suggested that she had slept with him, but the evidence was too weak to be trusted. So was his memory of the dream.

Gerard shrugged and decided to get up. The dream would return. He knew that with dreaded certainty. But so would Fairy Peg, to comfort him as she must have that night. No matter what the tensions were between them, their basic strength lay in their love for each other. As long as they continued to share that love, they would survive.

* * *

Message to: Avarignon Cloznitchnikoff
             FedTreatySvc
Your information reassures us of your intentions. We will test the control before our arrival.

—Toehold

* * *

221

21

The pastry came out of the oven golden brown around the edges, with high swirled peaks that had just begun to turn a rich umber color. "Perfect," Gerard said to the skeptical cook, "just perfect." He slid the *trudle* carefully onto a golidium serving tray and covered it with a fine mist of sweet glaze. Then he fitted to the crystal dome onto the tray and with a hurried thanks to the cook headed for Fairy Peg's office.

The *trudle* was a peace offering of sorts, a way to tell Fairy Peg that in spite of the problems they had been having, he loved her greatly. The recipe was one his father had taught him, but he had had to practice it several times with the head cook before he had found the proper Krilian ingredients to substitute and achieved the appropriate thin layers of pastry with the melting flavor of ambrospice.

As quickly as he could, Gerard hurried through the back passages to Fairy Peg's office. It occurred to him momentarily that she might not be pleased with a surprise visit, but that was a chance he was prepared to take. He was bearing a love offering, and once Fairy Peg realized that he had made something special just for her, whatever displeasure he might cause by his interruption of her work would surely be overruled by that.

Fairy Peg's Ratchets passed him on to the private entrance to her office with formal salutes. They were too well-trained to ask what he carried, but he could see the look of curiosity in their eyes, and that pleased him.

He unlatched the inner door slowly and silently, planning to step into the office with a loud "Surprise!" However, as he started to ease the door open he heard Fianne speaking in a loud, frustrated voice and paused for a moment to listen.

"...have convinced me that we have no other choice, Princess. If we are to save you and our galaxy, he must be sacrificed."

"You confuse yourself, Fianne," Fairy Peg answered. "I accepted that sacrifice when we set this course, but I object to the wholesale slaughter and the risk of war that will follow it."

"Unavoidable," Fianne said with sudden tiredness in his voice. "It is a risk we must take. It is too late to withdraw."

"We will think on it. I am still unconvinced."

When she paused, Gerard lifted his hand to knock loudly on the door and enter with his surprise, but he held back. He wanted to know more about what they were talking about.

"Be you assured he will do as instructed?" Fairy Peg asked.

"The control worked as I told you, Princess. We must assume that it will continue to do so."

Gerard regretted waiting. He didn't understand what they were talking about, and he didn't want to. It was ugly. Suddenly the tray was very heavy in his hands. He wanted to retreat, to avoid hearing any more. Then he decided to interrupt them and see what happened.

With a loud knock on the door he yelled, "Surprise!" and stepped into the office with a big smile, holding the tray well out in front of him. The expressions on their faces were of total shock.

"I made you a gift," Gerard announced proudly, trying to avoid looking directly at them. He set the tray on Fairy Peg's desk and lifted the crystal dome with a flourish. "Da-dah! The most delicious confection in the universe, made by my own crude hands for the Badh of the Seven Systems... and the mother of my child," he added as lightly as he could.

"What is this, Pilot?" Fairy Peg still hadn't fully regained her composure, but she leaned over slightly to stare at the *trudle*. The warm, sweet scent of it filled the room.

"It looks delicious," Fianne said stiffly with a glance toward the door and then back to Gerard.

"Fresh out of the oven, Fianne. But don't just look at it.

Break off a piece and try it. This is the ultimate finger food."

Fairy Peg broke off a small piece and put it first to her nose and then into her mouth. Almost instantly her face broke into a smile. "It is wonderful," she exclaimed. "What is it? Did you truly make it yourself? Why?" She stopped her questions to break off a larger piece and stick it into her mouth.

"Yes I made it. It's called a *trudle*. And I did it because I love you and wanted to give you a surprise."

"Mmm," Fianne said thoughtfully as he licked his fingers, "you certainly surprised us. But what a pleasant surprise."

"Thought you'd like it."

Fairy Peg broke off a small piece and held it out to Gerard. He stepped close and took it in his mouth, letting his tongue flick over her fingertips as he did so. He shut his eyes to savor the taste, but also to avoid looking at Fairy Peg. He had done well. The *trudle* was delicious. But his pleasure would have been infinitely greater if he had not overheard the conversation. As he swallowed the last bit, he opened his eyes and saw Fairy Peg smile around a mouth full of *trudle*. "Good, hunh?" he said with a grin.

The three of them ate the whole *trudle*, Gerard and Fairy Peg doing most of the damage, then washed it down with a light ale from her cooler. As soon as he finished his ale, Gerard put down the goblet and picked up the tray. "Break's over," he said with a smile. "Time for you two to get back to work."

With a deft step to his side, Fairy Peg gave him a quick kiss on the cheek. "Our thanks, Pilot. It was a wonderful gesture."

"My pleasure," he said with a bow. Then he left quickly and headed back to the kitchen with the tray. The words from the conversation he had eavesdropped on kept running through his mind.

"He must be sacrificed . . . wholesale slaughter . . . unavoidable . . . control worked . . ."

No matter how he tried to sort it out, Gerard neither understood nor liked it. Whatever Fianne and Fairy Peg had been talking about, it was nasty business, and he would rather not know what. Maybe there was another uprising on Evird. Or maybe some political fac getting out of hand somewhere else. If he was lucky, wouldn't have to get involved in it.

After thanking the cook who had assisted him, Gerard decided that a workout with his Ratchets might help clear his mind. With Gerard setting as fast a pace as he could, he and his string ran twenty kilometers in a pouring rain that chilled him to the bone. Even after he had taken a hot shower and changed into warm clothes, he still felt cold. To break the chill he took his string to the Ratchet club for a drink.

Gerard took small sips of the Vierwayne brandy, but his string drank with enthusiasm. Gerard watched them with affectionate amusement as they drank their way toward the bottom of a second flagon and chatted happily among themselves. It reminded him of their days together before he was Fize, and he allowed himself to slip into a relaxed enjoyment of their camaraderie.

When a voice said, "Greetings, Fize," from behind him, it took Gerard a moment to pull himself back to the present. When he did, Targ was standing beside him.

"I have some better brandy in my office, Fize," Targ offered politely.

Something in Targ's tone told Gerard he wanted more than to share brandy and conversation. Gerard hated to surrender the feeling his string had brought to him, but the mood was already broken. "Lead the way, Commander," he said. But before he left the table he gave Brunnel a credit chit for another flagon and told him they need not worry about him for a while.

Targ poured the brandy with great ceremony, then raised his glass. "My thanks, Fize, for what you did for Branbinie. We now have a daughter."

Gerard had almost forgotten. "Well, congratulations, Targ. It's a shame you can't make a public announcement." As soon as he said that, Gerard regretted it, but Targ didn't seem to mind.

"Thank you, Fize. I received the news several days ago, but had no opportunity to tell you. I also received some other good news. Dangure in Maytar, high on the Barcley star."

A slow coldness spread through Gerard. He had heard

before, but he couldn't remember when, or why they were significant. He started to ask a question. Nothing happened. He tried again. Still nothing.

"Relax, Gerard," Targ said with a deadly smile. "You will only cause yourself discomfort if you try to fight it."

A face oozed into his memory, Fianne's face. Fianne had said those words. Gerard wanted to scream, but talons of pain siezed his throat. Involuntarily he relaxed.

"That is much better. Can you understand me?"

Reluctantly, Gerard said, "Yes."

Targ smiled. "I was worried about that. Oh, I am quite familiar with various forms of control, but this is the first time I have ever used one so foreign to our techniques. Raise your left hand as high over your head as you can."

Gerard felt his hand go up and up until it threatened to pull him out of the chair.

"Put it down."

The hand fell with a lifeless slap into his lap. Gerard knew what was happening to him, but he was powerless to stop it. He wanted to jump from the chair and strangle Targ. Instead, he sat motionless and expressionless, and waited.

"I see anger in your eyes, Gerard, but when I end this meeting, you will not be angry. You will not remember any of it except an order I will give you. That you will remember in a dark recess of your mind, and when the time comes, you will act on that order. Let me explain it to you."

Something snapped in Gerard's mind. He heard Targ's instructions and was powerless to ignore them. But part of his mind had broken away and was watching and listening with great detachment. Yet that small part seemed to embody all of *him*, all that was the essence of Gerard.

"Two. You are feeling better and better. One. You are fine."

"What was I saying?" Gerard asked. Somehow he had lost track of the conversation. "Oh, yes, I just want you to know that I hope you and Branbinie enjoy your daughter as much as I enjoy Orees."

Gerard felt a little disconnected, even from his own words, but Targ was smiling at him in such a friendly way, and the brandy was so relaxing that he continued. "The most amazing part, I think, is to watch all the changes children go through in such a hurry. One day they burble gibberish at you, and a week later they are speaking in complete sentences."

Targ poured him some more brandy. *"Norrace-norrace-norrace,"* he said quietly.

Gerard froze. He wanted to touch his finger to his nose, but that didn't seem right. The center of his mind stopped working. Only the separate self continued to compute, to watch, to listen, as though it couldn't escape the fascination of watching him. But below the fascination, anger frothed like sea foam on the beach under a quarter moon, a mad efflorescence that marked a shifting boundary in his mind.

"... return and ram the *Glospogh*," Targ was saying. "Do you understand?"

"Yes," a voice answered from Gerard's mouth.

"You will do it?"

"Yes," the voice answered again.

Targ droned on, full of rationalizations that seemed perfectly reasonable. They satisfied every argument Gerard's weakened brain tried to raise against what he had agreed to do. In the distance, his Self screamed in defiance.

When Gerard returned to the living quarters late that evening he was well on his way to being drunk, and not quite sure of what he had done all day. Surprisingly, Fairy Peg was there to meet him.

"You are feeling no pain, Pilot," she said when he flopped naked into bed beside her.

"Very true. I was talking about children."

"I loved your surprise this morning," she said, giving him an affectionate kiss on the cheek. "How long were you hiding behind the door waiting to spring it on us?"

"Didn't wait at all," he lied. He wasn't that drunk.

"Come here, you silly diplomat." One of her hands was suddenly between his legs manipulating him, and he came to her as quickly as he could.

"Norriss-iss—iss—iss—iss——iss————ss————sss," the voice hissed at him from a dark corner of his brain. His Self screamed. His arms tried to crush Fairy Peg against his chest. Anger jerked him like a puppet on a string.

He didn't understand when he awoke why Fairy Peg had decided to sleep on the couch, but he was too groggy to complain.

"*Iss–iss–iss–sssss*," faded the voice through his dreams. He fled. Refuge was an island full of bright, unspeaking forms, all of which looked like his father hovering above him in the early morning light of Maytar.

"Maytar," the silence said.

"Home," a voice answered.

"Barcley," the silence responded.

"Home," the voice cried.

And the night went on in a series of uncontrollable dreams.

Gerard flew *Windhover* up into orbit, and, with the help of *Glospogh's* technicians, made sure Windy was nestled securely in the huge ship's belly. The great fleet had been gathering for a month, and, even though the ships orbited Kril at fifty-kilometer intervals, Gerard had easily seen the massiveness of the assembly when he flew Windy into position. Then, as the shuttle returned him to Kril and EllKoep, he was even more impressed by the size of the fleet and the event they were gathering for.

And this is not all of it, he reminded himself. Only half the ships involved would be leaving from Kril. The rest would rendezvous with them along the way. Some of those had already begun their journeys, as the Badh's fleet would in just ten local days. Gerard wished the departure was a year away, and said as much to Fianne when he walked into his office.

"I don't know what's the matter, Fianne. If I knew the answers, I wouldn't be seeking your help. All I know is that I've been having terrible nightmares, and that I'm beginning to question my sanity. Omna-Seay give me sleeping drugs from his seemingly endless pharmacopoeia, but they only make the dreams worse. Princess Peg refuses to sleep with me because I thrash around so much she can't sleep herself. I don't know what the Krick's the matter."

"How may I help, Diplomat? I know nothing about sleeping problems."

Gerard sighed. "I wish I knew the answer to that. But I don't even know why I'm telling you this. It's just that you're the only person I feel I can open up to besides our princess. And, like I said, she's not feeling very sympathetic right now. But I guess you really can't help me either, can you?"

He had never felt quite so alone before. He needed a friend with whom he could share his problem, but Fianne, like Fairy Peg, seemed unwilling to draw close enough. In this instance, however, Gerard was sure Fianne could help if he wanted to. He didn't know why he was so sure of that, but he was. "How am I going to function at the summit if I'm robbed of sleep every night by these dreams? Answer me that, Fianne."

Fianne looked at him and seemed genuinely troubled, but when he spoke, it was not compassion Gerard heard in his voice. "If I try to help you, you must do exactly as I say," Fianne said with quiet coldness.

"Like what?"

"Like whatever I say. Do you understand that, Diplomat? Before I seek assistance for you, you must agree to obey me and do exactly as I command—"

Into the back corner of your mind, a voice echoed deep inside him in tones that sounded just like Fianne's. Gerard felt almost frozen in place, paralyzed by Fianne's cold tones.

"Are you ready to do that, Diplomat? Are you ready—"

To slide that word, the voice whispered. The shadow of Self snatched the word away from him, and Gerard felt suddenly afraid. Fianne was staring at him impatiently and Gerard knew something was wrong.

"No," he said hesitantly. "No, I can't do that. Perhaps they'll just go away. I'm sorry to have troubled you." He looked away from Fianne, not wanting to see the hard, unyielding eyes in his friend's face. "I thank you for your offer, though. I know how busy you are." Gerard stood up, hoping Fianne would take the signal and leave.

"The offer stands, Diplomat. Perhaps..." Fianne hesitated, but when Gerard looked directly at him, he looked away as though he had made a decision he did not want Gerard to see. "Perhaps later I can be of assistance. Now I must attend to my duties. Diplomat," he said with a slight nod of his head. Then he wheeled and left the office.

Gerard slumped back into his chair, unsure of what had just happened. It all seemed so familiar, yet, he felt as though he had been watching it from a distance. He rubbed his temples, trying to ease the tension there, and wondered if he was losing his mind. Maybe the strain had been too great. Maybe he wasn't cut out to be a diplomat after all. Maybe, as soon as this summit was completed—

Something fell to the floor of his brain with a loud clatter, something jagged and hard that he wasn't supposed to know about. The tension in his temples built to a pain, but Gerard pushed it aside as he tried to focus his thoughts. "In the back corner of your mind," the voice had said. What voice? Fianne's voice.

But Fianne had been talking about something else. What was Fianne's voice doing as an echo in his skull? When had he heard those other words?

The pain grew toward an unbearable level. Gerard fended it off again with all the strength he could divert to defend against it. There was an answer right in front of him if he could only reach out and pull it close enough to see. The pain grew like a great black wave and threatened to smother him. Anger gave him strength and determination.

Gerard stretched his internal senses as far as they would go toward the dark key to his suffering. Then, as the wave of pain rushed toward him with a deadly, curling crest, he heard Fianne say in a clear, calm voice, *"Two. You feel almost normal. One. You are fine."*

He sat in a daze. Time, thoughts, light, all seemed to float around him in a little fragments. Some were bright and fascinated him for a moment before they drifted out of sight. Others were dark, ugly things that gave him relief when they passed.

Gradually, he became aware of a tingling sensation. His legs had fallen asleep. With tremendous effort he looked down at them as though he couldn't believe those leaden stumps which held him to the chair actually belonged to him. He touched them and could barely feel his own touch. Slowly he rubbed his legs and moved them against the burning tingle to bring their feeling back.

First he remembered the pain in his head and was surprised that it had left so quickly. Then he remembered Fianne's words. *"One. You are fine."*

Gerard was sure he had been alone in the room. The words had come from his memory—or his imagination.

They had swept away the pain, but they had also swept away whatever it was he had been trying to focus on.

Even as he walked gingerly around his office to bring the final circulation to his legs, he knew he was going crazy. First the nightmares, then ghost voices in his head, and now, hallucinations. Somewhere, somehow, part of his mind had broken away from the rational center and was running rampant.

He remembered a mirkaloy once which for no apparent reason had rushed from the south woods near Posiman Township and trampled a huge field of grain. The mirkaloy had finally been shot by an irate farmer, but no one could ever explain why a normally shy, solitary beast had suddenly gone berserk.

There has to be a reason, Gerard said to himself. I'm not a mirkaloy. I'm a man. And some*one* or some*thing* is making this happen to me. And if I find out who it is, I'll drive them into the chasm of death.

* * *

Message to: Greaves Lingchow
      FedDiploSvc

The original schedule we agreed upon must be adhered to. The control has caused him great difficulty which may lead to a breakdown of its effectiveness. We cannot afford that.

For great rewards there are often great dangers. Pray that all goes as we planned so that we receive only the great rewards.

—Glyph

* * *

22

The meeting of the two fleets was too large to be seen with the naked eye, yet Gerard couldn't tear himself away from *Glospogh*'s largest viewport. Each fleet was arranged in points like equal halves of a giant geodesic sphere that encompassed an empty hollow of Dinsey space eighty kilometers in diameter.

Every ship was sending visual signals as well as regular navsignals, and by the time they all eased into their proper positions, all the space he could see through the port was crowded with the lights of an artificial constellation.

Directly across the sphere from *Glospogh* was the *Casserine*, distinguishable only as a tiny circle of flashing blue strobes with a pale orange center. That it was distinguishable at all told Gerard how huge it actually was.

Standing almost mesmerized by the sight of hundreds of ships arranging themselves in space, Gerard was startled when Fairy Peg spoke from close over his shoulder. "Beautiful, is it not, Pilot?"

He half-turned to her and saw she was staring past him. "Indeed, Princess, in more ways than one. How soon before we reach our final position?"

"Admiral Gannack said it would probably take an hour for everyone to be perfectly aligned." She slipped her arm through his and pulled him close to her side. "Then you will be going, will you not?"

She asked the question with a sadness in her voice that surprised him. "That's the plan. I'll take Windy over to the *Casserine*, and if all goes well, you'll see her move in about twelve hours to the center of this sphere we've created. That will be your signal to bring Corpus Privy and the Noble Assembly to the *Casserine*, and the first of the ceremonies will begin. Aren't you excited?"

Staring out the viewport as though looking beyond the assemblage of ships, she answered without looking at him. "No, I am not excited. Concerned, yes. A bit nervous, perhaps. There is much to be gained from this meeting if all goes well, and much to be lost if it fails." When she turned to him he thought he saw the beginnings of tears in the corners of her eyes. "And some things will be lost if we succeed," she added quietly.

Gerard hadn't expected her to be so emotional. "True," he said with a sigh. "Ribble will lose part of her treasured independence, and part of her identity, too, I suppose, but the—"

"No," she said in a fierce whisper. "We will always be Ribble Galaxy. No treaty, no peace pact, no articles of confederation will ever take that away from us."

Again her emotional reaction surprised him. "There's something I want to discuss with you before I go across to the *Casserine*, something I have to tell you before all this begins."

"Not here," she said suddenly, "for there is something I must tell you also."

Without a word, Fairy Peg led the way to their suite. "What must you tell me, Pilot?" she asked after carefully closing the door behind them.

He poured them both small glasses of wine and sat facing her, perched on the edge of his chair. "I've reached a decision," he said as calmly as he could. He didn't want to let his voice shake under the swell of emotions he felt. "As soon as this summit is safely concluded, I want your permission to resign what little remains of my contract and apply to Ribble for citizenship. Now wait. Let me finish. I know there will be some difficulties involved. I mean, first of all Fed's going to want to debrief me, and Fara only knows how long that will take. I also know that one of the ways you got Corpus Privy to accept me as consort was because they believed it would be a temporary arrangement. But I'm willing to cope with them."

"Pilot, I—"

"Please," he said softly, "there's something else I have to say, then I'll listen to your reply." Gerard sighed deeply, trying to steady himself. "I know that our relationship hasn't been ideal for you, especially for the past half-year or so. But I also know that I love you, and Orees, and I don't want us to be separated. That may be too romantic for the Ribble view of family, but that's the way I feel.

"There. I've said it. I love you. I want to stay with you. Now I'll shut up and listen." Gerard leaned back in his chair, still feeling the tremble of emotion, but pleased that he had put his declaration to her so simply. And effectively, he thought, as he watched her wipe a tear from each eye.

"I am touched, Pilot, as you have touched me many times before. Now there is something I must tell you. Dangure in Maytar, high on the Barcley star. *Norrace, norrace, norrace.*"

A silent curse echoed through Gerard's mind as he heard those words. His right forefinger twitched, and even before he felt himself freeze in place he knew what they meant. A question followed the curse, drifting lazily through his thoughts. Why? Why was she doing this?

"I am sorry, Pilot." Her voice sounded distant and strange. "There might have been another way to handle this, but it is too late now to change our plans. Can you hear me, Pilot?"

"Yes," his mouth said for him. He felt an empty calmness, knowing he had been in this static place before. Then he realized that part of his Self had separated from the paralyzed Gerard and was listening and watching with cool detachment.

"Then listen to me, Pilot. Your Chairman Valunzuella arranged this summit so that he could destroy Ribble's leadership, including me. Then he plans to launch Federation fleets into the heart of Ribble and destroy what he cannot subjugate. He cannot cope with the idea of confederation with a power as strong as Ribble. With our leadership gone there will be chaos in the systems, and he will destroy them one by one. Do you understand that? Answer me!"

The intensity of her voice pushed her even further away from him. "Yes," he said thickly, "I understand."

"Be you aware of my love for you, Pilot?"

There was a long hesitation before his voice said, "Yes."

"I have loved you as much as I can, as much as any Badh may love an individual. You must believe that, Pilot. You must."

"Ratchet crap," a voice said from behind him, the voice from before, the voice of Fianne Tackona. "Be honest with him, Princess. You don't love anyone, even your own son. You use him as you use all of us who serve and love you."

"Silence!"

Fianne moved into Gerard's line of vision before he spoke. "No, Princess, not this time. You are sending him off to be killed. The least you can do is be honest with him. Tell him to do this thing for Orees. Or tell him to revenge himself against his mighty Federation for putting him in this position. But don't tell him you love him. Don't send him to his death with that lie drugging his brain."

Gerard's anger rose and fell, battering against some dark force that kept him from exploding. He couldn't believe what Fianne was saying, but he questioned the reality of everything that was happening. His separate Self pulled into a smaller, tighter ball, and moved closer to the center of his paralysis, whispering, *patience, patience*.

Fairy Peg looked angry, but when she spoke, her voice was cold and flat. "Do you deny me the right to love, Fianne? Or do you deny me the ability?"

"Neither, Princess. I believe you loved Gerard in the beginning, and might still love him if your sister, Inez, had not—"

"Her name is forbidden in my presence!"

"Had not despoiled him for you," Fianne continued with a determined look on his face. "Once she used him, his value to you was greatly diminished, and you could use him also. Admit it to yourself. Then tell him."

"Why do you care so, Fianne? What has he done to cause this great passion for truth?"

His anger had subsided, and somehow Gerard found it almost relaxing to sit and listen to their argument, as though it no longer concerned him, but rather someone he had known long ago.

"He offered me friendship," Fianne said, looking at Gerard, "friendship that I could not openly and honestly return. This is the only way I can repay him."

"By hurting him?"

"By telling him the truth. He deserves the truth from me, and even more from *you*."

"Do you think he will be better motivated to ram the *Casserine* out of hate for me than out of love?"

"That does not matter, Princess. You can always tell him to forget it before you bring him out from under the control. You can tell him to think of nothing but doing this because of your love. But at least you will have been honest with him. Then, in that brief instant before the bomb in *Windhover's* hold blows him to space dust, maybe he will know the true reason he is dying."

Fairy Peg laughed without humor. "He knows that already, Fianne. Look at his eyes. He knows. He knows. Do you know, Pilot? Do you know that I am about to use you in an attempt to save Ribble?"

"Yes." The word popped out of his mouth.

"Do you know that after you seduced *her* I could never love you again? Do you know that?"

"Yes." He didn't want to believe it, didn't want to know that this woman he adored, this mother of his son no longer loved him, but he knew it. He knew it as surely as, as surely . . . *Patience*, Self whispered.

"Then listen, Gerard," Fianne said. "The Federation planted this control in you, a control designed to guarantee that you would be a useful tool to them and to us. Now your chairman wants to use you to bring about the destruction of Ribble and all you have worked for. If you kill him, if you go berserk and destroy the *Casserine*, then you will get the blame, not us. But you will also get revenge on them. Revenge, Gerard, revenge." Fianne's voice was down to a whisper. "Do you understand that?"

"Revenge," Gerard repeated mechanically.

"That is right, revenge. When you get to within five kilometers of the *Casserine*, you will alter *Windhover's* course for the center of her and apply full power. The bomb we have planted in *Windhover* will destroy the *Casserine*, and you will have your revenge. Do you understand what you must do?"

"Yes."

"Do you understand why you must do it?"

"Yes."

"Good, Gerard. Now I am going to bring you back to normal like I did before. As I count backward from five to one, you will block all this from your conscious memory—"

No, Self whispered.

"—but you will ram the *Casserine* exactly as I told you to. What are you going to do, Gerard?"

"Ram the *Casserine*."

"Good, Gerard. Now I am going to start counting. Five. You are letting this conversation slip from your mind. Four. The words..."

Self whispered noisily to him, hissing with determination, screening Fianne's words with sibilant static.

"Two. You are feeling..."

Revenge. Yesss, the voice cried as it faded from hearing.

"One. You are fine."

Gerard shook his head. "Oh, I didn't hear you come in, Fianne." A faint band of tension pulled at his neck.

"That's quite all right, Diplomat. Are you ready to make the final arrangements?"

"Yes. Of course." How had he missed Fianne coming in, he wondered? And why hadn't Fairy Peg responded? Didn't she want him to join her? Didn't she want them to be together? He felt a little disconnected, as though she had already told him how she felt and he had missed it.

"Good. We will see you to *Windhover*." Fairy Peg walked with him arm in arm through the corridors and down to *Glospogh*'s docking bays. She seemed intent on reassuring him that all would be well, but her tone told him her mind was filled with other things.

Targ was waiting for them when they arrived. "Greetings, Badh, Fize, friend Fianne," he said with a broad smile. "It appears the time has come. I will be your escort ship."

The band of tension in Gerard's neck tightened. There was also a tension in the air. "Yes, it has. I didn't expect such a royal sendoff."

"Ah, my strange darling," Fairy Peg said with a trembling laugh. "Just remember that the people of Kril and all of Ribble are depending on you."

"And when we get back, your Ratchets are going to throw you one giant party. Fare well and prosper, Fize."

"Good speed, Pilot," Fairy Peg said with a quick kiss on his cheek, "and be careful."

Fianne was the only one not cheerful. "You have served us well, Diplomat. Accept our thanks."

Suddenly Gerard felt uncomfortable. "Well, I'd better get going." He gave Targ a quick response to his salute, kissed Fairy Peg's hand, nodded to Fianne, then stepped quickly through Windy's entry port and closed it behind him.

As he stood there for a second staring at the closed port, Gerard felt totally alone and depressed. The tension in his neck had settled into his shoulders and was slowly drawing them together. As he went forward to the flight deck he kept rotating his shoulders, trying to work out the kinks, but they only grew worse.

"Tension, Windy," he said as he settled himself in his couch. "Better than having heatherflies in my stomach, I guess. You ready, girl?"

It only took him ten minutes to check Windy's systems and receive permission for departure. As soon as the docking boom released them, Gerard eased Windy a safe kilometer away from *Glospogh* and pointed them toward the *Casserine*.

As they began their slow acceleration across the sphere of space, a sudden voice on the vidcom startled him. "Fize," we have an emergency. Do you read me?"

"I read you, Commander. What's this—"

"*Norrace-norrace-norrace!* Return to *Glospogh*."

As though moving in a trance, Gerard reached for the controls. Pain shot up his neck to the center of his brain.

"Ram the *Glospogh!*"

"Ram the *Casserine!*"

Voices screamed at him. Angry red tears opened in his mind like deadly blossoming flowers. Pain tore at the back of his eyes. Slowly his hands crept toward the controls as he sought release from the agony. *No. No. No,* Self shouted at him.

It was too late. He knew what he had to do. He knew there was only one way to escape the pain.

Slowly his fingers slid through his agony to the directional controls until he had one smooth knob in each hand.

Self said, *yessss*.

With all the strength he could muster, Gerard wrenched the controls as the black fist of pain slammed him back into his couch.

...ontrol not worki...must be stoppe...andon...ehold ...fenses prepar...ll not suffer this lig...your responsibil ...isaster...yph...

23

Slowly, ever so slowly, the pain subsided into a terrible ache in the back of his head, and Gerard allowed himself a weak grin. He was winning.

Windy was circling an imaginary point in the center of the sphere in an orbit only thirty kilome s in diameter. Her readout said she was moving at a kilometer per second. Gerard grinned again. Too fast for anyone to board them.

Almost reluctantly he turned up the volume on the vidcom. Angry voices kept breaking in on each other. Voices that never had a chance to complete their sentences shouted threats at other voices with the same problem. Even through all the confusion it didn't take very long for Gerard to realize that the Ribble fleet was warning the Fed fleet to stay away from him, and vice versa. Each side was afraid of what the other would do next.

Then he realized that he didn't know what to do next. He had saved himself from death. The deep Self of his resistance and some primal refusal to be used by anyone had pulled him back from the chasm of death. He had beaten the control that Fed had planted in his brain, but the instinct that had saved him had also placed him on the horns of a dilemma. He couldn't keep doing this whirligig orbit and expect either fleet to sit patiently and watch the show.

Gerard rubbed his neck, trying to milk the fading pain out of his head. Had he blacked out? For how long? How much time did he have before someone decided to act? They were questions he had no answers for. But he knew he had to start doing something fast or he would be surrendering his fate to others again.

With a wicked flick of his wrist, he opened his transmitter. "This is Gerard Hopkins Manley, Universal Contract Diplomat, Fize of the Gabriel Rachets, and Consort to the Throne of Ribble. I demand an open channel." The calm sternness in his voice surprised him. "Now!" he said firmly in his best imitation of Tg Neereg's command tones. The crackling protests on the com subsided.

Gerard grinned bitterly. He still didn't know what he was going to do. "I want to speak to Greaves Lingchow and Fianne Tackona," he said finally. "And I want those patrol ships to move away from my orbit. Now!"

It was a full minute before Fianne answered the com, and another minute before Lingchow came on. Gerard put them on a split screen so he could see them both. "I'm sorry for this confusion, gentlemen, but I seem to have had a problem with my life support systems. However, *Windhover* has corrected the fluctuations, and everything is fine now." Lingchow's face remained impassive. Fianne looked nervous.

Before either of them had a chance to respond, he continued. "Fianne, I just want you and the Badh to know that everything is all right and will proceed according to the agenda. Oh, and please tell Commander Alpluakka the same thing."

Fianne did not appear to be reassured, but he said, "Thank you," and signed off.

"Secretary Lingchow, meet me at the docking bay aboard the *Casserine*. Choose the bay closest to the command center, because that is where I expect to meet with the chairman when I come aboard. Is that clear?"

Lingchow opened his mouth as though starting to protest, but quickly shut it again. "I understand, Manley."

"Good. I'll be very unhappy if you fail me. Manley out."

As soon as the vidscreen went blank, Gerard switched over to the Ribble command channel. "Get me Privy-Admiral Gannack," he said in his harshest Kulitti tones. She was on the screen almost before he finished speaking. "Greetings, Admiral, and listen carefully," he said all in one breath. "We're being monitored. Be prepared for—"

A rash of static turned the screen to buzzing lines. "Trouble," he finished to himself.

"The fastest safe course to the *Casserine*, Windy!"

They came out of their orbit, and braked all the way to within three kilometers of the *Casserine*. A flashing amber light marked the docking bay Lingchow had chosen for them. As Gerard made the last few manual adjustments that would bring them into the bay, he realized his hands were sweating. At any moment he expected Fianne or one of his henchmen to detonate the bomb in Windy's hold and blow them all to space dust.

As soon as the docking cradle locked onto Windy's nose, Gerard unbuckled and headed for the port. He paused at the arms locker to take out a vaporizer, making sure it was fully charged, then grabbed a cape and fastened it quickly over his shoulders.

Windy settled with a gentle thump into her final position, and Gerard felt *Casserine*'s artificial gravity take hold of him. When the ready lights came on over the port, he cycled it immediately. Moments later it opened to reveal a very winded Greaves Lingchow.

"Had to run...all the way...why so brusque?" he gasped.

Gerard smiled. "Mister Secretary, we're going to the command center without another word. Under my cape I have a vaporizer, and if the chairman isn't there when we arrive, I'm going to turn you into a random dispersion of atoms. Do I make myself clear?"

Lingchow studied the bulge under Gerard's cape, then nodded heavily, his breathing still shallow and ragged. Slowly, he turned around and led the way up the tunnel with Gerard at his side. To anyone watching it might have appeared as though Gerard were supporting him, but the support was actually the flared nozzle of the vaporizer pressed hard in the small of Lingchow's back.

When they got to a riser a Fedmarine started to join them. Gerard twisted the vaporizer. "As you were," Lingchow said with a wave of his hand. The marine eyed them suspiciously, but stepped back into his position beside the door.

As the riser gate closed, Gerard allowed himself a small sigh of relief. "Not bad, Lingchow," he said flatly. Then he remembered the bomb and tensed again. Maybe Fianne can't activate it at a distance, he thought. Or maybe we're shielded in the *Casserine*. He prayed that was true.

The riser stopped silently and Lingchow started to step

forward. Gerard put his left hand on Lingchow's arm and nuzzled the vaporizer against him. "Nice and easy," he said quietly. "Otherwise you might find yourself missing a midsection." Lingchow was still sweating heavily, and said nothing as he let Gerard pull close to him.

They walked almost casually down a short corridor and through another door guarded by Fedmarines. As they stepped into the command center, Gerard gasped slightly at the size of it. Only his Ratchet training kept Lingchow from stepping away from him. They were on a wide balcony overlooking most of the command center, and Gerard didn't see anyone who looked like Chairman Valunzuella. Lingchow was looking frantically around. No one in the command center was paying any attention to them.

Suddenly three people stepped out of an alcove ten meters down the balcony from them on the left. Gerard immediately shifted himself so that Lingchow was between him and the trio and made sure his back was to a blank wall.

"So," the tall, dark man leading the group said in one of the deepest voices Gerard had ever heard. "So this is Gerard Manley, our contract diplomat. Welcome, Diplomat."

The men behind the speaker had stopped, and appeared to be unarmed. From their postures Gerard decided they weren't trained fighters. "Who are you? And where is Chairman Valunzuella?" Gerard demanded.

"Please," the man said, "there is no need to be so defensive. I am Acting Chairman Cloznitchnikoff." The man moved to within a meter and a half of them.

"That's close enough," Gerard said coldly. He was scrambling for ideas and feeling a growing sense of desperation. His original plan, what little there was of it, had been to confront Chairman Valunzuella with the evidence of treachery and play it from there. He was surrounded by treachery and had no place to turn, but he figured that if Valunzuella had given him the wrong answers, he would have at least made a good hostage. Now he was confronted by this Cloznitchnikoff. "Where's Chairman Valunzuella?" he demanded again.

Cloznitchnikoff gave him a diplomatic smile. "Dead. Quite dead. Had a seizure in his sleep and died instantly.

A fine man to have died so fully at the height of his power. Are you holding a weapon on Secretary Lingchow?"

Gerard ignored the question. With a swiftly raised knee he sent Lingchow sprawling to the railing and leveled the vaporizer openly at Cloznitchnikoff. Lingchow moaned as he clutched a bloody elbow, but was otherwise well enough to curse Gerard.

"Now, Mister Acting Chairman, suppose you tell me what in Fara's name is going on? And tell me as quickly as you can, because I've been dying for a chance to practice with this vaporizer and haven't really had the target I wanted. Until now."

Cloznitchnikoff looked from Gerard's eyes to the vaporizer and back to Gerard's eyes. "You really would kill me, wouldn't you?" he asked in an even lower voice.

"Why not? I've got nothing to lose. Fed was willing to see me dead today. So was Ribble. I figure I'm as good as dead now. Why not take you with me?"

"Let me show you why," Cloznitchnikoff said with a smile. "I am going to signal one of the officers over there, and then you will see that I am truly on your side. It was Chairman Valunzuella who wanted you dead, not me. May I raise my arm?"

"Slowly," Gerard answered.

"Slowly indeed." Cloznitchnikoff raised his left arm and held it high so that six of his seven fingers were spread like a fan above him. Seventy-five meters away, on the floor of the command center, someone waved back. Seconds later a giant vidscreen flicked to life overhead and showed the FedFleet opening fire on the Ribble fleet.

In a frozen instant Gerard saw his nightmare coming true. But he also saw Cloznitchnikoff leap for him. "NO!" he screamed as he thumbed the vaporizer on full force and swept it across Cloznitchnikoff. "Noooo!"

Lingchow rose toward him, but a well-placed boot sent him over the rail. Gerard rushed to where Lingchow had disappeared. Screaming, "Nooo," at the top of his voice, he aimed the vaporizer at the officer who had started the battle.

It took him a full second to realize that the short range of the vaporizer was doing no more than heating up the air. He roared his frustration as he flung the worthless vaporizer in a high arc across the command center. It landed short and caused instant panic as it started burning a smoking hole in a multiple console.

Gerard spun around in search of another weapon. He saw the halves of Cloznitchnikoff's body lying peacefully on the blood stained floor. He drew Woltol's ridlow dagger almost by instinct, but seconds later he was buried under a swarm of Fedmarines and committed his soul to Fara.

24

"You have caused us much trouble, Manley, more than you are probably worth."

The voice was familiar, but Gerard couldn't focus on the blob of a face that hovered above him. Half the face was covered with medplast, and the other half was swollen under a dark bruise. The voice belonged to Greaves Lingchow. Gerard started to sit up, and bindings from his head to his feet tightened automatically. As he relaxed into the softness underneath him, the bindings relaxed also.

"What happened? Where am I?" His voice rasped against an aching throat.

The battered face above him seemed to smile. "You killed Cloznitchnikoff. Couldn't have done it better myself."

"The battle," Gerard said hoarsely. The last thing he remembered seeing was the battle raging on the giant overhead vidscreen, the nightmare come true.

"Wasn't much of a battle, really. More like a skirmish. Neither side lost more than a dozen ships or so."

There was a distraction in Lingchow's voice, almost a lightness that infuriated Gerard. The bindings tightened on him again. "A dozen ships," he said through his pain. "You call that a skirmish?"

"Ah, but there will be no war, Manley, thanks to you."

"Me? How?"

Lingchow laughed grotesquely out of the good side of his mouth. "A little luck, a little fury, a little fate, who knows? Apparently you hurled your vaporizer right into the middle of the communications console. Either the officer in charge of that console or someone scrambling to get out of the way of your vaporizer sent the automatic 'desist and retreat' order. It was all over in a matter of minutes."

Gerard didn't believe it. "No. The Ribble fleet would have followed you."

"I would have thought so too, Manley, indeed I would have. But they started retreating as soon as the first shots were fired. Now what do you make of that?"

"Lies. You're lying to a dead man. Why?"

"I'm going to crank you into a sitting position, Manley, because this bending over hurts my head. Don't resist it, or the bonds will tighten. There. Now I can see you from a normal angle." Lingchow sat on a high stool at the foot of the bed.

"Before you kill me, I want to know everything," Gerard said softly, trying to protect his voice.

Another grotesque laugh escaped Lingchow's parody of a face. "Kill you, Manley? How ridiculous. That would be a waste of a good diplomat, and very poor strategy and tactics."

Strategy and tactics? What was he talking about, Gerard wondered?

"Besides, in a perverse kind of way, I owe you my life. Cloznitchnikoff would have gotten rid of me as soon as he was ratified as chairman, if not before. I knew too much. I knew he was dealing with Targ Alpluakka to divide Ribble Galaxy. No proof, of course, but I knew it."

Gerard closed his eyes and tried to shut out Lingchow's voice. Targ a traitor. Fairy Peg and Fianne sending him to his death. Dozens of ships destroyed. It was all too much to think about. But Lingchow's voice persisted.

"Then Valunzuella got wind of Cloznitchnikoff's plan and was very angry. And stupid. He thought I was on his side and told me about his plan to use the summit as a means of destroying Ribble's leadership. That's when he decided to get rid of Cloznitchnikoff."

The room felt like it was spinning. Gerard opened his eyes and tried to steady it. What Lingchow said matched what he knew already, but, "How do you fit into all this? Who were you planning to divide Ribble with?" Each word scrapped his throat like a file.

Lingchow looked at him intently. "No one," he said finally. "I was doing just the opposite. I was working with Fianne Tackona to protect Ribble's interests and work for a true confederation."

"But—" Gerard couldn't finish his sentence. He didn't understand what pieces were missing.

"But what? I was the one who arranged for most of Valunzuella's supporters to be aboard *Casserine*. I was the one who convinced Fianne that you had to destroy them. Then I sent him the bomb to do it with." Lingchow leaned forward on his stool.

"Don't you see, Manley? If you had been the one who had destroyed this ship, if you had done what you were supposed to do, what we programmed you to do, we could have written you off as a berserker, a crazy man. Then we might have saved the chances for confederation."

"And killed hundreds, maybe thousands of innocent people on this ship. I don't believe you. You'd have died too. Then who—"

"That's where you're wrong. Oh, a thousand innocent people would have died all right. But when you demanded my presence here, I had to shuttle over from another ship, and arrived only minutes before you did."

Gerard frowned. It was too big and didn't make sense. "Then what about the bomb?" he asked hoarsely. "It could have gone off and blown us all to Krick and back."

With a sigh, Lingchow stood up and rubbed the unbandaged side of his head. "Maybe I'm too old for these things anymore. I'm certainly too sore and tired to argue with you. I deactivated the bomb as soon as you went into your crazy loop-de-loop out there. I knew something was wrong, but I didn't know what. Then—oh, why am I bothering with all this?"

"Because you want to rationalize all of it before you kill me," Gerard said bitterly. It was the only answer that made sense to his numbed brain.

"I told you you're not going to die," Lingchow snapped. "We're going to mindwipe you."

"Mindwipe?" The thought of being mindwiped sent a

tremor through him that caused his bindings to pull him deep into the bed. "I'd rather be dead."

"Oh, shut up and listen," Lingchow said with a bitter smile distorting his patchwork face. "With everything you know, you are a security risk we can't afford. But you're also a damned good diplomat with potential future value to us...and to Ribble. We're going to selectively block portions of your memory, then send you back to work."

"As a vegetable?"

"As a contract diplomat!" Lingchow exploded.

"Kill me," Gerard said bitterly. He meant it. He wanted no part of the Federation ever again. They had done everything else they could to him, and now they were going to rob him of his memories of Fairy Peg and Orees. They were going to steal part of his life. They were going to—he sighed suddenly and let his body sag. "What difference does it make?" he rasped. "I'll be worthless to you. Why not just let me die?"

Moving down the side of the bed with anger darkening the bruise on his half-face, Lingchow looked like he was ready to hit Gerard. Instead he twisted Gerard's head painfully against the abrasive bindings and stared at him from under the swollen lid of his uncovered eye. "Let you die? Throw away a perfectly good tool when we can clean it up and use it someplace else? No way, Manley. No way."

Lingchow's hot, sickly breath puffed around his face like dirty steam. Suddenly Gerard wanted to live, to fight back, to beat them at their own game. Without thinking, he spat as hard as he could in Lingchow's face. Lingchow jerked back. Then, as one hand reached up to wipe his face, the other struck Gerard hard on the side of the head with the flat of his palm.

Pain rang through Gerard's ear and stabbed his brain. He tried to work up enough saliva to spit again, but Lingchow was backing away from him.

"That's it, Manley. You fight it. You fight to live. That will get you through the mindwipe in better condition. Stay angry. Stay very angry. Then the mindwipers will have an open field to work with." With that Lingchow turned and limped out of the room.

"These security cases are always the most difficult," a voice said. "I am sure you will find this procedure most instructive."

247

There was no way for Gerard to struggle, no way for him to escape the fat tube which fed him gas, or the binding clamps which held his head. But maybe, just maybe, there was a way he could save part of himself. He did his best to push away the voices of the technicians and ignore the sensations of being poked and jabbed.

The anesthesia began to take hold, freeing his mind from his body. He used it to brush away the clutter of thoughts that clamored for his attention, and to calm the swells of anger moving through him. Gerard forced himself to be calm, forced himself to search almost casually for that place in his mind where he knew he would be safe.

His attention drifted. A haze formed. Then a voice whispered, *seeeee*. Through the haze he saw the place, the black pool, the placid refuge where he had hidden before. Numbness pursued him. The haze thickened.

Fingers tugged him away.

Dragging himself back, Gerard focused on the pool. A narrow flash of pain was reflected from its smooth surface. Then another. And another. He stumbled to the edge of darkness, paused for a second, then launched the remains of his sanity toward the sheltering depths.

As he plunged into the darkness, the voice of Self whispered, *yessss, yessss*. Cool, black stillness engulfed him. Gentle fingers pulled him down. Diplomat, Consort, and Fize dissolved in a silent florescence of bubbles. In his last instant of consciousness he thought of Orees, with a face so much like Fairy Peg's.